WATER INC.

WATER INC.

Varda Burstyn

VERSO

London • New York

First published by Verso 2005
© Varda Burstyn 2005
All rights reserved

1 3 5 7 9 10 8 6 4 2

Verso
UK: 6 Meard Street, London W1F OEG
USA: 180 Varick Street, New York, NY 10014–4606
www.versobooks.com

Verso is the imprint of New Left Books

ISBN 1–85984–596–7

British Library Cataloguing in Publication Data
Burstyn, Varda
 Water Inc.
 1. Water-supply – Environmental aspects – Fiction 2. Water-supply –
 Government policy – Fiction 3. Environmentalists – Fiction
 4. Ecoterrorism – Fiction 5. Canada – Relations – Canada – Fiction
 6. United States – Fiction 7. Quebec (Province) – Fiction 8. Suspense
 fiction I. Title
 813.6[F]

ISBN 1859845967

Library of Congress Cataloging-in-Publication Data
Burstyn, Varda.
 Water Inc. / Varda Burstyn.
  p. cm.
 ISBN 1–85984–596–7 (alk. paper)
 1. Water supply – Environmental aspects – Fiction. 2. Canada –
 Relations – United States – Fiction. 3. United States – Relations –
 Canada – Fiction. 4. Water supply – Governmnent policy – Fiction.
 5. Quâebec (Province) – Fiction. 6. Environmentalists – Fiction.
 7. Ecoterrorism – Fiction. I. Title: Water Inc. II. Title.

PR9199.4.B88W37 2003
813'.6–dc22

2003027098

Typeset in Fournier
Printed in the UK by The Bath Press

For David

PROLOGUE

THE intensive care ward at Century City Hospital smelled of antiseptic, overcooked food and fear. In one small room, a dark-haired woman sat on a chair close to a patient, bent over in anguish. The patient's right leg and torso were bandaged and carefully arranged in a traction apparatus.

At the door, the detective hesitated. Through the glass he saw the visitor reaching along the white cotton toward the motionless body mummified in plaster and gauze, to take hold of one of its pale hands. He put his briefcase under his arm, transferred his take-out coffee to his left hand and cracked open the door.

"Oh God," he distinctly heard, "don't die." He heard the visitor sob, then whisper, "I'm so sorry."

His ears were burning. He had been assigned to investigate, and nothing would have been sweeter than to let her words pour forth while he played the fly on the wall. But the visitor was very likely to give him the gears about matters of competence and integrity in any case. At the nursing station he'd been told who she was. She didn't look too fierce at the moment. He closed the door behind him and cleared his throat.

The woman pulled sharply away from the bed and turned to face him. She brushed some tears from her face and regarded him warily.

"Good morning," he said. "You're the friend who called in her 911?"

"That's right." She was exhausted, he could see it in the way her body sagged despite the effort she was making to be strong. She had a striking, intelligent face. She gave off … grief, certainly, in spades, but something else too. Anger? Fear? Her mouth was tight, her jaw clenched. Observant by long habit, he took in her khaki slacks, black T-shirt and sandals. The clothes looked like they'd been slept in, and in uncomfortable places.

"She was lucky to have you," he observed sincerely. The visitor didn't smile or loosen up. He put his briefcase and coffee down on the window ledge. "I'm with the Los Angeles Police Department," he said, unfurling his identification. "I'm glad to have a chance to meet you."

Still no relaxation, no relief. She watched him defiantly, refusing to move. Her eyes were red from crying, full of alarm and disapproval. But he found them remarkable, penetrating and luminous. Jesus, he thought suddenly, that expression. It reminded him so much of his daughter's determined regard.

"So you called in her 911," he repeated, "all the way from DC?"

"Uh-huh," she said acidly. "Isn't that something?"

What she saw was a tall man, somewhat stooped, with a face full of lines and folds all pointing downward. She took his world-weary expression for lack of feeling and braced herself, standing and holding the chair between them.

He sighed. "I'm not your enemy, ma'am," he said, not unkindly. "Or hers, despite what happened."

"So how was she shot with half the night shift on site?" Her tone was venomous. He had no good answer, so he shrugged, an eloquent, frustrated shrug that involved his whole body. She saw that he was losing his hair, wore a rumpled polyester suit, and a navy-and-red striped tie with a sizeable stain – ketchup? – right in the middle. Okay, she said to herself, he's not exactly a storm-trooper. Then she pinched herself mentally. Stay vigilant! Don't fall for the friendly appearances.

The detective's eyes took a careful inventory of the damage the patient had sustained – the body cast, especially thick around the pelvis and abdomen, the bent right leg with a shapely foot hanging limply in the air, the total stillness of the body. Then his eyes reached her face. It was exquisite, angelic even. Despite his disavowed Catholic upbringing he wouldn't have been surprised to find large wings sprouting from her back, right through the plaster. The bandages held the golden hair in a circle of light around her head like a halo; the effect utterly transfixed him. The doctor had informed him that she wasn't expected to survive the day, or even to wake up again. He turned to her friend.

"Believe me, I'm very sorry. Early this morning I got called, special appointment by the Commissioner to investigate, and I'd really appreciate your help here, ma'am. No one else seems to know a thing. And she's not giving us any leads. To say the least." He got a stony silence. "Do *you* know who shot her?"

PART ONE

1

EIGHT months earlier ...

Swiftly, the jet made its way through towering pewter and purple clouds, overflying the boreal forest of the Laurentian massif. Below, millions of hectares of snow-laden black spruce stretched to every horizon, slashed by clear-cut swathes and last summer's forest fires, traversed here and there by the marching legs of huge power pylons carrying electricity from Manicouagan and Churchill Falls to the cities farther south.

Where deep and swift-flowing water would glint below in the spring, now, in January, soft, mysterious white shapes delineated the lakes, and white snakes described the paths of rivers. On the great Saguenay River fjord, hulking masses of white and gray ice were piled up along the shores. Gigantic ice crusts, pale blue like the winter sky and yellow like old ivory, rimed cliffs where frozen waterfalls formed baby glaciers. At the very apex of winter, the lands of the Charlevoix and Chicoutimi displayed their awesome power. William Ericsson Greele found himself breathless with excitement as he gazed down upon them.

They landed at Chicoutimi in a soft snowfall. Flakes plump as goose feathers clung to Greele's black cashmere overcoat. Judging by the banks of snow piled high next to the small terminal building, plenty had already fallen. Inside the tiny terminal, Greele looked around, grimacing at the fug

3

of cigarettes, stale coffee and fuel that permeated the warm humid air indoors. Gabor Mezulis's ginger hair and bristling mustache identified him though he was wrapped like a sausage in his bulky down coat. Mezulis was chief executive of Seattle-based DM Engineering and Greele's hydrologist and chief engineer on the huge project they were planning.

"How are you, Gabe? Good to see you," he said, shaking Mezulis's hand.

"I'm good," Mezulis replied. "Welcome to Chicoutimi."

Mezulis had left the engine of his burnt-orange Grand Cherokee running, and it was warm and dry inside. They drove through the snowbound suburbs of modest clapboard houses, snowmobile trails criss-crossing streets and yards alike. On Boulevard St Paul they passed a hideous strip of hotels and malls. Christ, this is ugly, Greele thought sourly, frowning out the salt-spattered window. But then the Jeep skirted a massive hilltop hospital and looked down onto a tall, spired cathedral. The clouds broke apart, and huge shafts of sunlight illuminated the town below.

"That's better," Greele said, sitting back with satisfaction, as though God had personally arranged the improvement for him.

"All these old Quebec towns are like this," Mezulis lectured, maneuvering the jeep skillfully down the steep hill. "The big church, the big hospital. The Catholic hierarchy here took care of health and education till the 1950s, if you can believe it."

"Uh-huh." Greele wasn't interested. "Do you think we can get down to brass tacks, Gabe? I've been waiting for this conversation for –"

"Hold on, Bill," Mezulis interjected gently. "Just hold on. Let me lay it all out for you properly when we get back to the house." Greele sighed impatiently, but deferred. Mezulis would have his reasons.

The old town was built along the western bank of the Saguenay. A graceful bridge rose from snowy buttresses and spanned the frozen water. Houses climbed prettily up the opposite bank, spreading north and south, all glowing pearly gold and pink in the late afternoon sun. Greele's spirits lifted. The narrow streets were charming, originally designed for horses and carriages, flat-roofed houses made quaint by wrought-iron staircases and balconies. Here and there, the historic homes of old notables, with turrets and wide, rounded verandahs, took up small city blocks. People popped in and out of diminutive shops, well-bundled against the cold, their coats and hats and scarves splashes of brilliant color against the head-high banks of snow piled everywhere.

Mezulis was going on like a tour guide. It was obvious to Greele how much he had taken to the place in the two months he'd been scouting the region, with his furry mucklucks and chapped lips and wind-burned cheeks.

The sunset streaked the sky gold and mauve. They crossed the bridge, drove up the hill, traveled along the ridge until the houses thinned and they turned into a private drive off Terrasse du Fjord. The clouds gathered again and the north wind blew snow devils in front of a hulking, aggressively modern house, all glass and concrete and timber, as darkness fell. Lights blazed from its tall windows. If all went well, the place would do duty for the next ten years.

Mezulis lifted Greele's light suitcase and they went in. He hung Greele's coat next to a huge down-filled parka in the hall closet. Enormous snow boots stood beneath. "Those're for you, Bill. You're gonna need 'em." He directed Greele up the stairs to a large room at the end of the hall. In his bathroom, Greele threw cold water on his face, dried it with a soft towel and came immediately back downstairs. He wasn't willing to wait another minute.

He found Mezulis in the dining room at a colossal table of polished teak laden with charts, maps and books. Mezulis was in front of his laptop, checking e-mail. A meal of savory pastries, coq au vin, salad and profiteroles had been laid out on the buffet. Greele realized he was famished.

"Hey," Mezulis said, looking up briefly, "why don't you try the *Maudite* tonight. Exceptional beer."

Greele's French was filed away with a lot of other stuff he hadn't used in the forty years he'd been out of college, but not entirely forgotten. "The cursed? The damned? What kind of a name is that for a beer?"

Mezulis smiled appreciatively. "Ironic, I guess. Best damn beer I've ever had."

"Scotch will do," Greele said coldly, helping himself to food. "Can we get on with it?" He moved into the living room and took the largest, most comfortable chair next to the blazing hearth. He put his feet on the ottoman.

"I've read every one of your e-mails and faxes, Gabe," he said between mouthfuls, "avidly, as you know. You've been pro-ing and con-ing me to death for the last month. So do me a favor. Back-fill after, okay? Is it, or isn't it, doable?"

"Well," Mezulis replied from the other room, drawing out the word. "From a *technical* point of view, I believe it is."

Greele's expression hardened. He saw the housekeeper emerge from the kitchen and take her coat from the closet. He waited while she quietly opened the massive front doors and stepped out into the night. The sound of a small car starting up and driving away reached them through the moaning wind. Then Greele snarled, "What the hell does that mean? Yes in theory, no in practice? I didn't come all this way to hear that!"

Holding a beer for himself, Mezulis handed Greele a thick tumbler of Laphroaig and took his place on a mushroom-colored sofa. It irritated him the way that the tall, well-knit body occupied his customary chair. Greele was one of the wealthiest men on earth, somewhere in the top twenty, Mezulis guessed. Mezulis was rich, but Greele's fortune dwarfed his own. Greele could finance projects on the mammoth scale that Mezulis loved to work on. And he could be an arrogant pain in the ass.

"Let me remind you," Mezulis said, "that 'technically feasible' was in very serious question from the beginning."

"Not for me, it wasn't," Greele said curtly.

Mezulis bristled. "Bill, I've been telling you all along that this isn't the paradise of eternal waters you think it is, despite appearances from afar."

"But it *can* be done."

"If we go farther northeast than we thought originally, yes. But don't count on any consensus on that score here, because levels are down, to historic lows, as a matter of fact. I think it'll be a very tough sell to the government. Who'll be comparing levels now to what they used to be here, not to the drought in the Mid- or Southwest —"

"Okay. So what's the *real* problem?"

"Politics," Mezulis answered, sitting back. "'The stability of the investment environment.' To be precise."

"Ah," Greele replied, regarding the engineer. Deep lines radiated from Mezulis's pale blue eyes. His attitude, Greele noted, showed respect but not an ounce of deference. That was just fine. Greele needed a very strong man to pull this project off, one who could assume the mantle of acting regent. He'd chosen Mezulis because he was a weathered veteran of the wild and wooly wars that always exploded and entangled and potentially suffocated such projects wherever they were mounted. "Elaborate," he demanded.

"I will," Mezulis said. "Most people think all that crazy separatism is finished in Quebec. The *Wall Street Journal* buried the Parti Québécois six years ago. The only reason they're back in power is because the Liberal Premier went down in flames over a huge corruption scandal. They lost their referendums on independence in the nineties and don't have another

6

planned. Everyone under forty in Montreal wants to speak English so they can work in computers and aerospace and pharmaceuticals, blah, blah, blah." He paused to formulate his words carefully.

"But I don't buy it," Mezulis said. "I've been here the better part of two months, I've looked around –"

"We agreed you'd keep a low profile!" Greele said sharply.

"– Which I damn well have!" Mezulis's pale blue eyes flashed as he shot up off the couch. "Jesus Christ, Bill," he yelled, "what kind of a fool do you take me for?" *Fuck you, you and the chair you're sitting in,* he thought.

"Take it easy, Gabe," Greele said. "Go on."

Mezulis took a deep breath. "Listen. It's my job as your senior expert to advise you. *And* as a major future investor, you can bet your ass I'm gonna protect myself too. I read the papers – well, the English ones – I listen to the radio, I watch the news, I keep my ears open, I pump the guy we've hired here and *I know this business.* Remember? So listen and listen good: the nationalist sentiment in Quebec isn't dead. A politician won't cut a ribbon for a new hockey rink without genuflecting to it. It's the elephant in the damn living room, only the people outside can't see it!"

A small smile played around the corners of Greele's mouth. "You're in Chicoutimi, Gabe," he said. "You're in the cradle of Quebec nationalism. It beats like a war drum here. And you're absolutely right: it's far from dead. I'm glad to hear your perceptions check out with mine." The smugness came through his words. His little experiment had worked.

What the hell? Mezulis thought. "Thanks," he said sarcastically.

"You're welcome, Gabe. I have nothing but admiration for your work, and you know it. But I think you've misunderstood the situation."

"Misunderstood?" Mezulis was incredulous. *Oh, the arrogance of the man.*

"Quebec nationalism isn't our main danger." Greele leaned back into the big chair's embrace, a predator's smile on his face. "It's our most potent lever. And we're going to pull it for all it's worth."

William Greele was up at seven, relishing the housekeeper's thick-cut bacon and French toast and several cups of her strong coffee. By eight o'clock, despite the pearl-gray snow clouds, he and Gabe were in the Jeep with a drawing-case bursting with charts and maps, heading up through Jonquière, then to points north and east. They didn't make it back until ten o'clock that night, ate a late supper and fell into bed exhausted.

7

The second day the sun shone and the temperatures dropped. Through the blinding white snowscape, they drove down to Tadoussac, where the grand Saguenay empties into the even mightier St Lawrence. The Jeep's tires left snakeskin patterns on the road and sheer ice lay beneath the snow. In the crystalline air, smoke rose from the chimneys on the south shore. Their eyes ached as the sun bounced off the multicolored houses and the red roofs of the turn-of-the-century hotel. Handcrafted signs creaking in the wind pointed to places where tourists could rent boats in the summer, to watch the four species of whale that came to play in the conflicting currents of the two rivers.

Early in the morning on the third day, they were borne much farther northeast in a Cessna, past the Pipmuacan Reservoir system. They flew due west for a couple of hours until they crossed the watershed, and surveyed the lands that drained into Hudson's Bay.

Greele was optimistic and ready to move forward as he flew home to Cincinnati.

Back at the teak table in Chicoutimi, Mezulis studied his maps and drew red circles around nine sites they had selected together. He began to finalize the report Greele would draw on when he called his new consortium together.

2

ON a late February afternoon, three Learjets, four Gulfstreams and one Citation landed in quick succession on the two private parallel landing strips of Lunken Airfield on the east side of Cincinnati. Shortly after, two helicopters took off toward the northeast. A young couple, drinking from a bottle of water at the end of a long walk through Mt Ault Park, watched from under the withered wisteria vines of the pergola on the bluff. "Looks like they're heading for Indian Hill," the woman observed, as the aircraft disappeared over the horizon.

Despite street names like Tecumseh Trail and Shawnee Way, Indian Hill has nothing to do with Native Americans. On the contrary. Proctor &

8

Gamble and Chiquita Banana, among other major corporations head-quartered in Cincinnati, bivouac their senior executives there, where they are serviced and provisioned by an elite corps of professionals and merchants. The helicopters headed for a wooded estate on a commanding plateau off Muchmore Road, and touched down on a concrete pad on the edge of gardens temporarily sere under crusts of sleet. The white stuccoed walls and black lacquered shutters of a three-story plantation-style mansion gleamed through the mist. William Greele shook hands with his guests as they disembarked, shouting his greetings over the whipping of the helicopter blades.

Three major companies made up Greele Life Industries: AgrichemCorp, the chemical giant; Techniplant Inc., the seed and gene giant; and the animal-human biotechnology leader GenSysCo, dominant in transgenic therapeutics, life extension and selective gene therapies. All three were headquartered in Minneapolis, where they had had been founded, respectively, by Greele's grandfather, his father and himself. He also held significant shares in a baker's dozen of top Fortune 500 transnationals. Some were in related sectors: petrochemicals, pharmaceuticals, agricultural and resource engineering, chemical disposal, industrial construction, media. Others provided healthy diversification: arms, aeronautics, financial services.

For personal reasons, Greele loathed Minneapolis and had long minimized his time there. For over twenty years now, his favorite residence had been this house in Indian Hill, hovering on the northern edge of the South, with its blossoming trees and lush flowers and gracious living. It gave him two mild winter months instead of six brutal ones. Neville Poindexter, Greele's chief operating officer in Minneapolis, had run the GLI companies smoothly on Greele's remote command for over ten years. And Greele could easily head from Indian Hill to oversee GLI operations in Singapore, Hong Kong, Hyderabad, Cape Town, Marseilles and Essen, as well as attend the many meetings demanded by his other holdings.

In the main hall of the house, Sarah Huntingdon Greele, tall, blonde, beautifully dressed, smiled and made inquiries about wives and children and polo games. The butler and housekeeper divested the men of their overclothes. "Gentlemen, some refreshment!" Greele called hospitably, gesturing toward the wide dining room doors.

Food was laid out on a rosewood sideboard next to an enormous fireplace. The men helped themselves to fragrant apple pie and tangy Amish cheddar, and made themselves comfortable in capacious chairs. None was in Greele's league, but they were only one or two steps behind. Like him, they were hands-on, owner CEOs who knew their companies intimately and guided them personally. They had done a lot of business together, in various alliances and combinations, over the years. Their wives shopped and went to spas together and supported the same charities. They shared a rare knowledge of the compensations of fabulous wealth, and a determination to guard and extend their fortunes in turbulent times. Greele exchanged pleasantries, but insisted that the business be reserved until the meeting began.

Presently, Greele judged it was time. "Gentlemen," he said, raising his voice over the buzz of conversation. "Shall we head downstairs and begin?" The men dropped their plates and made for the large boardroom like a pack of hungry dogs called to dinner.

"We've had seven summers of drought in the near Midwest. In the High Plains, with a break of a couple of years, we've had almost twelve years of drought. And it's nothing – I mean *nothing* – compared to what's coming." William Greele was well launched into his opening pitch. Six foot one, in camel slacks and argyle sweater, he radiated good health, his skin remarkably unwrinkled for a man in his late sixties. His eyes, exceptionally sharp, paused evenly on each of his colleagues. His forehead gleamed a golden tan, and where it finally met the receding hairline it encountered a thick corona of silver hair.

A multicolored map of North America glowed on a plasma screen behind him. "No notes, please, gentlemen," Greele had said. "Not until we've got agreement." Then he had added, "To a plan that will assure each of you personal and corporate viability for the rest of your lives." Known one and all for their egotistical drive, the men were hanging on Greele's every word.

All was not well in the huge companies they captained. Everyone had felt the effects of the trillion-dollar losses the stock market had sustained. At first, the dot com meltdown had shaken most of them only lightly, like a tremor from a faraway earthquake. A. A. Stiller, the no-longer-boy but still very much genius of Seattle-based Cyberonics Enterprises, had been the main exception. He had taken a huge hit. But losing up to a third of his fortune still left him high in the Top Fifty in the US. Stiller's apparel – custom-made sweat clothes and running shoes – his long, sandy hair, and his fluid body posture radically separated him from the others at the table.

So did his bland, childish face whose blank expression seemed to suggest that his mind was elsewhere.

The second tremor had arrived on September 11, 2001. It had shaken the markets till their teeth rattled. Then, nine months later, the Enron, World-Com and Arthur Anderson scandals had stomped on the stock exchanges with hobnail boots. Just when everyone thought it was safe to go back in the water, the US had gone to war in Iraq and everything went nuts.

The military sector had grown like a bloated hog, along with a few big oil and construction companies, while most other sectors had shrunk. Of the men at the table, the contractor, Vittorio Massaro, and the oil man, Houston-based Wilbur Hayes, had benefited but slightly from the vast outpourings of government largesse abroad. Colonel Nicholas Kamenev, of Skypoint Aeronautics, had certainly made money in the military arm, a great deal by the standards of mere mortals, but even he felt he wasn't getting his fair share. And so on around the table, despite the fact that these were committed, loyal Republicans who had all put a lot of cash into the President's campaign coffers.

All were of the opinion that the President had thrown them only crumbs because they weren't evangelical Christians. But they had to bide their time in the shifting sands of Washington.

William Greele's dire talk of drought and climate catastrophe exacerbated their anxieties, as he intended.

"You're familiar with a number of impending realities, gentlemen," Greele leaned forward confidentially. "So I won't mince words. Our friends in the insurance business – absent from this meeting, you'll notice – have been telling us for some time that our planet is in trouble. I know, I know," he said, raising a large hand, "many of us pay a lot of money to Hill and Knowlton, Burson Marstellar, whoever, to debunk this idea and discredit its purveyors. The President himself claims publicly it's the fantasy of bureaucrats. But let's talk honestly now, among ourselves.

"We've had more weather disasters in the last twelve years than in the preceding half-century. We've got a toxic cloud thousands of square miles large hanging over Asia that's going to compromise health and agriculture, putting even more pressure on North American food production. We've got melting polar ice caps. We've got winters in the temperate zones that veer between hot and appallingly cold. The weather changes we're looking at in the next ten years on this continent are going to be – in a word – *catastrophic*." The listeners exchanged glances. Some looked upset.

"Just a goddamned minute, Bill!" The words were querulous, the accent thick Texan. "What kind of a doomsday scenario is that you're paintin'?" Wilbur Hayes, the oil, gas, and shipping magnate, head of Houston-based Petroco, was a huge, paunchy man with a bald scalp covered with yellow freckles. Above his tight collar and bolo tie he was already sweating.

He was a hard-assed fossil fuel champion who invested nothing in alternatives and lobbied for emission control standards that many experts considered murderous. Hayes hated the management at BP with all their talk of green this and that. He also happened to be Bill Greele's longest-standing business associate. Petroco had provided raw materials for Greele's pesticide production for decades, and shipped his chemicals, seeds and supplies all over the world. "Whose side are you on, anyway?"

"Keep your shirt on, Wilbur," Greele said equably. He did not brook disagreement easily, but he had determined to keep his temper and present his plan in the calm voice of reason. "You and your fossil fuels happen to be a big part of the problem. So why don't you hold on to your hat for a few minutes, and let me finish." Hayes closed his mouth, but his eyes bulged with the effort.

"Gentlemen, what does this state of affairs mean for us?" Greele continued smoothly, smacking the shaft of a long pointer against the palm of his hand. "In the mid-nineties, the experts were telling us to expect a temperature increase of one or two degrees in the next fifty years. Recent UN reports tell us it's going to be more like five or six. The extreme weather we've been having is going to get worse. *Everything* will become more unstable – farming, fishing, resource extraction, manufacturing, energy generation, even electronic communications. And it's only a matter of time till the insurance companies put their premiums up so high we won't be able to do business. Not as usual, anyway."

"What, you predictin' the apocalypse?" Hayes asked belligerently. "No wonder the President don't like you!"

Greele's eyes narrowed. "Just listen, Wilbur. Please." It was a command. "The Greens put a stop to further diversions of the Colorado River to California in 2003. Los Angeles, the Central Valley, Nevada – Las Vegas, gentlemen, *Las Vegas*! – Arizona, all depend on rivers that don't deliver any more." He used the pointer to indicate each state and city. "Already, many towns in the Southwest are bone dry. They're shipping all their water in, and all their young people out. There are whole counties in your home state, Wilbur, as you know, where factory farms have polluted every watercourse, where drought has sucked up every drop of water, above *and* below ground. And the High Plains, gentlemen." Here his tone turned funereal. "The heartland. Well. The Ogallala aquifer is being drawn down to extinction, could be dry by 2015, maybe earlier in Texas, New Mexico, Oklahoma. And when it's gone … Well. Take what we've seen the last seven summers, and *intensify* it."

Greele let them imagine a new dust bowl to scorch the very heart from the amber fields of grain on which his own great empire had been based. "With polar melting, the coasts will flood. The Gulf stream will be disrupted and Europe will freeze. Wisconsin, by contrast, is going to burn."

As several men shifted in their chairs and cleared their throats, Vittorio Massaro spoke up. "Excuse *me*, Bill, but the coasts aren't gonna flood." Disbelief was evident in his voice. "Come on. I mean, maybe an island or two. But not New York! Not Boston! That's just anti-business bullshit!" Considering what United Construction had dumped off the East Coast for more than fifty years, he felt a deep proprietorial connection to it.

"Don't kid yourself, Vittorio," Greele said, regarding the dark, handsome man with his steel-blue five o'clock shadow, glossy hairs on the backs of his hands, and impeccable Armani originals. "Lots of insurance companies are already denying coverage to coastal properties around the world and they've got no ax to grind." Greele took a deep breath.

"The Northeast and the eastern seaboard are in pretty bad shape water-wise, too. Virginia and Maryland are at each other's throats, the Carolinas are starting to panic, Tennessee's getting antsy because the other states are eyeing its water — we're talking serious and increasing shortages." Wilbur Hayes muttered something inaudible. Greele ignored him.

"The people who are going to make money in the coming period, gentlemen, are the ones who are prepared to look this reality in the face and jump out ahead of it." He left room for protest, but none came.

"Clearly, water will be *absolutely central* to our continued survival and profitability, and to the ability of our country to play its leading role world-wide. Wise appropriation and use of this resource may well be the only way to really ease the pain of inevitable losses. Most of you are surely aware that already, globally speaking, the profits of the water industry amount to fifty per cent of those of the oil industry? Suez, Vivendi, Thames Water — they're expanding at unbelievable rates right here in the US. It's not right. Americans should be providing water solutions for Americans." He looked around the table. All eyes were wide with anticipation.

"I've got no argument with your analysis, Bill." Bunting Hurst, a short, pudgy banker with a triple chin, thinning wisps of curly hair, rosebud mouth and rimless glasses, weighed in from the end of the table. "So what's the deal?"

"A consortium, Bunting," Greele responded, "to buy up water, in Canada, where it's still relatively cheap for the having. Starting right there!" His pointer landed with a resounding thwack on a small, blue blob in the heart of the great northern province of Quebec.

"We're going to build a pipeline, gentlemen," he leaned over the table and his voice was as smooth as butter. A collective sigh spread around the table.

The meeting went on long into the night. Soft lamps and wall sconces lit the conference room. Greele fielded an inevitable barrage of questions and objections ranging from the ignorant to the well informed.

Richard Bettison Franklin prided himself on his knowledge of world affairs. Top dog in the InfoMedia Group – an integrated empire of studios, broadcasters, newspapers, publishing houses, sports teams and theme parks – his Hollywood good looks were reminiscent of the anchormen his networks employed. "As I understand it," he said in his languid Roanoke drawl, "big water extraction projects, especially when they involve a lot of diversion and physical disruption – which I take it, will be on the agenda here? –"

Greele nodded. "Medium-sized construction," he conceded.

"– are no longer in fashion. UNEP and the World Bank won't fund them, for example."

This project was going to require the most inspired of communications strategies.

"Not a problem, Rich," Greele reassured him. He clicked his remote and a new graphic appeared, a map of the world. The oceans were blue and the continents flesh-toned. Running like veins and arteries through each one, all the pipelines in various stages of hoping, planning and building were figured in vermilion. "Check this out, gentlemen," Greele said.

"All that idealism about megaprojects," Greele said dismissively, "it's a thing of the past, a bygone luxury. Take a look. Spain's going to build a pipeline from the Pyrenees to Madrid. China wants to drain the Yangtze into the Yellow River and bring another pipeline down from Lake Baikal. Israel wants a pipeline from Turkey or Iraq or both. India's got so many planned it's going to make China look conservationist. And a lot of

American companies have their eyes on Western Canada." His pointer traced the red lines snaking down from Alaska and British Columbia and Alberta through Washington and Oregon, then spreading south and east. "We're going to be part of a whole new epoch of hydrological reengineering, the great pioneers of the twenty-first century. And we're going to get there first."

Murmurs of surprise rippled around the table. A. A. Stiller whistled.

"Even more to the point, Rich," Greele purred, "it never occurred to me to go to those places for funding. That's why we're here. This'll be a profit-making enterprise with highly restricted membership."

"It'll only turn a profit if it gets built, Bill," Bunting Hurst said, clasping his chubby fingers and squirming farther down into his seat. He was irritated that his participation was being assumed before he'd agreed to it. "What makes you think you won't have a shit-storm of protest from local environmentalists, even if you can get the Quebec government to go along? That water is the province's life blood, and I still don't see it being sold for bulk export."

"Personally, I think it's a brilliant idea." Andrew Albert Stiller, despite his I'm-not-really-here expression, had been absorbing everything and now he waded in. "Abso-fucking-lutely brilliant. Assuming, of course, the Quebeckers agree to play."

This is no game, you juvenile twit, Greele thought darkly, though he held his tongue because he needed the support. "Thank you, A. A.," he managed. Then he demanded of the one man who hadn't spoken yet but whose support was essential, "Well, Bernie? What about you?"

"I think it's really very good, Bill."

Took you long enough, Greele thought furiously. He'd grown more and more tense as Berendt Vogel, the second richest man in the room, had remained silent. Vogel carried himself like a Hapsburg princeling. With his slender frame, prominent nose, protruding blue eyes, straw-colored hair and receding chin Vogel certainly looked the part. In fact, he was a middle-class microbiologist turned audacious CEO of Bonafabrica, the largest pharmaceutical company in the world. "It is an excellent idea," he gave his blessing now, "providing it is technically feasible, of course."

"Oh, it's technically feasible, Bernie," Greele told him feelingly. "I'm sure you'll find Gabor Mezulis's assurances more than credible."

Vogel took no offence at the way Greele had described the environmental and economic outlook. He was a scientist, a brilliant businessman and nobody's fool. "My companies have had excellent treatment in Quebec," he said in his crisp accent, looking around the room. "For decades in fact. The government – regardless of the party in power, I might add – has been generous with subsidies and tax breaks." He turned to face the banker directly. "I don't believe there is any need to be afraid of the political environment there, Bunting. No, not at all." Hurst nodded, though a little frown of doubt remained.

Greele drummed his fingers on the polished surface of the table. The collective gaze shifted back to him. "I have a plan, Bunting," he told the banker, "a plan that takes protest into account. A plan that relies on one hard reality – the total political isolation of Quebec." He explained why this was important and sensed, finally, like tumblers in a lock, the support of each man fall into place. By midnight they were panting for it.

3

FILTHY, gritty sleet caused William Greele's limousine to fishtail like a hot rod in old Quebec City, which was still, in late March, lashed by winter. The snow-covered, cobblestoned, old-world streets, piercing church spires and the fluted towers of the Chateau Frontenac rising like a fairy castle over all, evoked emotions – wretched emotions – Greele hadn't felt in so long that at first he couldn't even name them. Then he realized that the place somehow reminded him of how he'd pictured the home of the Snow Queen when he was a boy.

At Christmas-time, when the nights were interminable and the north wind howled down from Manitoba, sending freezing fingers of cold air through their old mansion, his maternal grandmother would always come in from St Cloud. While other children were cuddled up reading *'Twas the Night Before Christmas*, his grandmother was telling him about a cruel sorceress with a frozen heart who lived in a land of eternal winter. The Snow Queen's greatest pleasure was to send sharp shards of ice south on the north wind, to penetrate and freeze the hearts of little boys, cutting them off from their families, their villages, and their sweethearts. He knew she was alluding to his own father, whom she loathed for his aloofness and his hateful indifference toward her daughter and grandson. But the story only made things worse, gave him terrifying nightmares. He would see the pipes and refining towers of his father's chemical factory turned into towers of ice, see his own heart pierced with a sliver of glass.

His paternal grandparents were long gone, dead in an airplane accident, the result of his grandfather's boundless confidence that he could do anything, including flying, without learning much about it. During the Christmas holidays his father, only happy at work watching his millions multiply, drank every day, becoming ever more caustic and verbally abusive, so that it would be the work of another year for his mother to rebuild even the appearance of normality.

Greele looked out on the old city. Perhaps the Snow Queen's revenge had been the Great Ice Storm of 1998. That year, the first of his long watch over Quebec, warm El Niño winds brought melting rains instead of blanketing snows. Then, as though in furious response, a harsh, frozen blast blew in from the north and encased every building, tree and bush in a glistening carapace of ice. It destroyed millions of trees and devastated the power grids. Ten million people had been left for a month without heat or electricity in sub-zero temperatures. Then another brief, drastic thaw released tons of water into swollen streams, tearing out bridges and ripping houses from their foundations. Then the freezing temperatures had returned again.

For the last two winters there had been no thaws. The temperatures had stayed so low that large chunks of native flora didn't come back in the spring. Now Quebec City, enveloped in a blizzard, looked as though it would be frozen forever.

The hell with that, Greele thought, shaking off his deep melancholy. I'm going to make it work for *me*. And he permitted himself a seigneurial pleasure in the old streets, in the gaily lit, elegant cafés along the Grande Allée, leading to the provincial parliament buildings. The large townhouse on Rue des Braves in front of which he halted, with its ornate wrought iron, its lamps lit against the impending twilight, pleased him too.

"*Bonsoir, monsieur,*" said the young maid in a knee-length black dress and white apron. "Please to come dis way. Monsieur Lalonde say 'e is desolate to be in retard and 'e is on his way 'ere. But Monsieur Me –, Me –"

"Mezulis."

"– Mezulis, 'e is 'ere now." She led Greele past a set of traditional reception rooms warm with red, blue and gold fabrics, toward the back of the house. In a large study, decorated, by contrast, in stark beige and white, Gabor Mezulis was sitting on a sofa, studying a map on the coffee table. He stood up and gave Greele a tense smile.

"Hi, Bill," he said, shaking Greele's hand. "This is it, I guess."

"Hello, Gabe," Greele returned. "You all set?" They were both aware that they had to snag Serge Lalonde, Deputy Minister of Industry, Trade and Technology, first time out. Otherwise their proposal might end up the hottest item on the Quebec City grapevine, not the resource extraction project of the century.

"I'm ready," Mezulis said.

"Good." Greele went to the French doors and looked out on the snow-covered garden.

"*Merci, Jocelyne.*" A strong voice approached from down the hall and Serge Lalonde entered, breathless and adjusting his cuffs from the rush of fleeing his previous meeting. He called back, "*Du café tout de suite, s'il te plaît, Jocelyne,*" then turned to grasp William Greele's hand. "My apologies, Monsieur Greele," he said, then, shaking hands with the engineer, "and to you too, Monsieur Mezulis, my sincerest apologies for being late. My colleagues would not stop, and with the snow, *ouf!*" Lalonde gave a Gallic shrug and a good-natured smile. Greele caught faint whiffs of tobacco and lemony cologne as he took in the excellent European tailoring, the short, fit body, the high energy, exuberant confidence and palpable drive that Serge Lalonde radiated. Berendt Vogel had informed Greele that Lalonde was the most dynamic and highly favored senior civil servant in the Quebec government.

"Good to meet you, Serge," Greele said. "We've been looking forward to this."

Greele and Mezulis accepted the pâté, sauterne, salmon pie, and endive salad that Lalonde offered. Greele took a tumbler of scotch, and Mezulis amused Lalonde by asking for a bottle of *Maudite*. They exchanged remarks on the weather and the beauty of Quebec City. Then they sat down on the facing sofas divided by the map-laden coffee table and Greele said, "Well now, Serge. I understand you folks have a lot of water up north you're not doing anything with. I believe Bernie Vogel told you that we'd like to put it to use, to our mutual advantage of course."

"He did," Lalonde replied. His expression conveyed enthusiasm and wariness in equal measure. He'd done business with Vogel for years. When Vogel had called to set up the meeting, Lalonde had told him that water was a hot issue and many Canadians were dead set against bulk export.

"Quebec isn't exactly Canada, Serge," Vogel had come back quickly, "especially not to you and the party. I think you'll find that Bill Greele's proposal will assist Quebec to achieve a number of its independent objectives." Lalonde now eyed the sleek, powerful industrialist and the wiry, rough-hewn engineer. *Alors*, he thought, let's see what they've got to offer.

"Just before we get into our proposal, Serge," Greele said smoothly. "I must tell you that Nick Kamenev of Skypoint, one of our group, wanted you to know that if we come to terms, he won't be bidding against Bombardier to build that group of short-flight jets for Brazil."

"Really?" Serge responded, eyes popping. *Incroyable!* With Bombardier the largest heavy industrial employer in Quebec, this would achieve support from key business and political sectors. But support for what, exactly? And why did the pot have to be sweetened even before its contents were revealed?

"You're aware of the water shortages we've been experiencing in the US," Greele said.

"I am no expert in this matter," Lalonde replied. He had done some fast reading in the last week, just enough to learn how little he really did know. "I know that many parts of your Midwest and Southwest have suffered droughts for years. So have the Canadian Prairie Provinces. Even the Northeast has had several winters with insufficient precipitation. I know that the US consumes more water per capita than any country in the world, even more than Canada." He smiled thinly. Greele didn't. "All this I know. But water export is highly controversial. So whatever your proposals tonight," he spoke deliberately, "I will absolutely have to take expert advice before agreeing to take them forward to Cabinet."

"Of course, Serge, of course." Greele had fallen automatically into first name usage, and failed to see the disapproval this elicited from Lalonde. "The fact of the matter is that the problems are much worse than most people know, or care to know. We're running out of water. Fast. We need another source."

"We are speaking primarily of drinking water?" Lalonde asked.

"We are speaking of water good enough to drink, yes. But that's just part of it. We're really speaking of water to keep our agriculture and industry alive."

"I see," Lalonde said and shifted uneasily on the sofa. That's one huge, thirsty agricultural sector, he thought. And American industry? *Merde*.

"What quantities did you have in mind?"

"Well, Gabe here has been working on the detailed plans for some time, so we could explore a real proposal, not just a general idea."

"Indeed," Lalonde replied. "So you can be precise about the quantities?"

"We can," Greele said and turned to Mezulis.

"Okay," Mezulis said, putting down his glass of beer and sitting forward. "Our overall objective is to export a minimum of two and a half billion acre-feet of water from the region north of Chicoutimi over the next ten years. Figure one to two years for infrastructure construction, so export itself takes place over eight years. Five years into the project, we assess your water levels and US needs, and see if we can maybe boost extraction or carry on after our first decade."

"Two and a half billion acre-feet of water?" Lalonde said, puzzled.

"That's right," Mezulis said. "Three hundred and twenty-six thousand gallons per acre-foot."

Lalonde punched some numbers into his calculator. His expression changed to shock. Mezulis quickly added, "But don't think in gallons, Mr Lalonde. It's misleading."

Lalonde felt a weird, sickening sensation in the pit of his stomach: *trillions* of gallons.

"It's there," Mezulis said simply. "We can do it." He told the Deputy Minister that the amounts of water used by US agriculture and industry yearly dwarfed the figure proposed. This was meant to reassure Lalonde. Instead, it jacked his anxiety up into the red zone. He took a few deep breaths, turned to the Americans.

"I know nothing about hydrology, gentlemen," Lalonde said. "But these quantities, will they not completely destroy the regions you're speaking of?"

"Not a bit," Mezulis said. "If we do it right and over time. Which is exactly what we're proposing to do."

"I think it's safe to say, Serge," Greele interjected smoothly, "without exaggeration, that Gabe here is the world's leading expert on water extraction, diversion and management. He knows what he's talking about."

Lalonde looked at Greele. His attitude was friendly, businesslike, courteous, but there was also a nauseating triumphalism that simply assumed compliance. Even as Lalonde's skepticism, fear and anger urged him to throw the bastards out, he knew he had to listen. For — and this was the terrifying part — if these were the first Americans to come after Quebec's water, they would certainly not be the last.

"Take me through it, then," Lalonde said, swallowing. "Let's see what you've got."

Purposefully, Mezulis began tracing things out on the huge map, handing Lalonde various memoranda with specifications for the main work sites. Though the beautiful names of Quebec sounded like gravel in his mouth, Lalonde admitted to himself that the engineer spoke of the towns, lakes and rivers with respectable knowledge. Nevertheless, when he'd finished, Lalonde was struggling for breath.

"That will cost a pretty penny," he said in a strangled voice.

"That'll give you lots of high-paid construction jobs," Greele retorted amiably, confidently.

Lalonde thought, *mon Dieu*, they're going to bleed us dry! He was dizzy and overwhelmed. "Have you calculated how much land you'll have to purchase?" he asked. Mezulis told him. It was an impressive amount, but less than Lalonde had expected. He said so.

"We've calculated very carefully," Mezulis responded, "so we can purchase just what we need for installations and pipeline – no extra. More than ninety-five per cent of the land is publicly owned. So if your people agree to this, we're in business."

Serge Lalonde stared at the two Americans.

"Well, Serge," Greele said heartily, "what do you say?"

Though shellshocked, Lalonde hadn't entirely lost his wits. While Mezulis had spoken the names of each town and region, Lalonde had conducted a check-off on a chart in his mind: constituency, sitting member, Cabinet/backbencher, contractors, job creation. He didn't have enough information yet. "I need to review each site with you, and discuss the numbers of jobs its construction will provide, the source of the raw materials for that work, the financing you're proposing, the involvement of Quebec companies. It won't work unless there is something significant for us in each of those categories."

"Of course, Serge," Greele said, soothing, soothing.

Mezulis, who had been through similar negotiations a hundred times, understood what Lalonde was considering and the pressures he would come under. He and Lalonde went through the exercise. When they were done and Lalonde sat musing, Greele said, "Serge, we do want Quebec partners at the high end. We envisage up to one third of our financing coming from your folks – if you can find us some good people – and I see almost all of the construction led by a Quebec company."

Lalonde was listening to Greele, but he was also thinking of the meta-picture – the meaning of this proposition, what it said about the driving thirst the giant to the south had for water. He felt the need – the desperate need – for some expert advice and some private reflection.

"What about timing?" he asked.

"We'd like to be shipping in not more than two years from now – preferably a year and a half," Mezulis replied.

"That is more or less at the speed of light," Lalonde retorted.

"If we bring the right amount of resources to bear, we can do it. With your government's cooperation."

"There's another aspect to timing that's important," Greele cleared his throat. He reviewed for Lalonde the three deals other companies had attempted with other provinces and why they had died ignominious deaths. He chose his words precisely. "I think, if you people are with us on this, that you'll find it's important to ... how shall I put it? ... work with us discreetly to prepare the deal, have it more or less a fait accompli, before we go public."

Lalonde regarded Greele with an ill-disguised dislike he knew would be bad for business. He couldn't help himself. He knew what Greele was getting at. If they went public too soon, the environmental opposition would have a long time to organize, maybe win. He thought carefully.

"Let me be frank, *messieurs*," Lalonde said at last. "Economically speaking only, this looks like a worthy proposal. At first glance – and that is all this is – it could answer a number of pressing issues for us. But I have no idea about environmental impacts –"

"The installations will conform to the very highest of standards, Mr Lalonde," Mezulis interjected haughtily.

"You'll forgive me, Monsieur Mezulis," Lalonde responded dryly, "if I don't accept your assurances without our own verification. You would not in my place. My job is to begin the process of technical assessment of this plan, and speak with one or two key Cabinet ministers about the other considerations. If I get a green light from them, and from some key finance and construction interests, then and only then will the ministers take it to Cabinet to see if – how do you say – to see if it will fly?"

"Fine," said Mezulis shortly. He wasn't looking forward to a big fight about environmental impacts and Greele had his lips sealed tight.

As the Americans were whisked off to the airport, Serge walked back to his study, where, for another hour, sipping his third Armagnac and pacing steadily in front of the garden doors, he agonized. He had done his best to appear calm, interested and in command. Except for the moment when they announced how much water they wanted and he'd gone as white as a bed-sheet, it had been an excellent performance. But now he grappled with turbulent feelings.

Lalonde, born and raised in Outremont, the traditional Montreal breeding ground of well-to-do Québécois, had received his schooling in a private college run by nationalist Jesuits. Then he went to Paris, took his bachelor's degree at the Sorbonne, and became involved in political activities in the radical aftermath of 1968, before completing a master's degree at the Institut de Science Politique. With that indispensable ticket, he found an apprenticeship in the technocratic civil service that had been President François Mitterand's pride and joy, and spent fourteen happy years working there. He returned to Quebec on the promise of a position as Assistant Deputy Minister in the early nineties, his French credentials shining like stars in the Quebec firmament. He rapidly reached the top position in the Ministry of Industry, Trade and Technology, fighting, always, for Quebec's growth and well-being.

As he reviewed what he'd heard from the two Americans, he was not convinced about the promises of environmental integrity. But even if they were right – that this could be done without serious damage to the central Quebec ecosystem – it rubbed him the wrong way. *Hostie*. He had no desire to sell off Quebec's patrimony to private corporate interests. He also knew that this attitude wouldn't work in the first decade of the twenty-first century in North America.

The former Prime Minister, that *imbécile*, had more or less dismantled the Department of the Environment in Ottawa, so there would be no protection there if the PQ wanted to go for this, even if he were to oppose it. And that moron in the American White House believed that "environ-ment" was a synonym for "exploitation opportunity". This is here and now, Serge thought bleakly, and here and now the markets rule absolutely.

Clearly, after the terrorist attacks of September 11, the US administration would use *force majeure* to secure Canadian water if it became necessary. But of course, he thought, they'll never have to. NAFTA, the World Trade Organization, the World Bank and that floating crapshoot of global rounds and summits, they'll just use the trade rules they've crafted to take it away. Under cover of extending democracy of course. Worse, *much worse*, if we don't seize the opportunity, Ottawa will pre-empt us. A chance we simply cannot take if we're serious about sovereignty. No, he concluded. There's no way I could have refused those men. It would have been madness.

On the other hand – and now he began to face the inevitable and talk himself into what he knew he had to do – if we can get a jump on the process, the prospects are fantastic. We can ensure an orderly process of diversion of water. We can provide jobs in the hinterland, secure our electoral base, feed our construction and finance enterprises. Think of the inflow to the treasury. Think of the next referendum!

With these thoughts, he went upstairs and prepared for bed. Nicole, his wife, was away on business. She would undoubtedly have a fit when she heard. He would have to decide when and how to tell her. He didn't want another huge blowup.

4

"LISTEN, Doug, I gotta bump up our nine fifteen to right now!" Colonel Nicholas Kamenev barked into his cellphone, cruising up the drive, candy-floss pink with blooming cherry trees, of Skypoint Aeronautics' main office tower in suburban Tacoma. "Unexpected thing. Can't help it." Emerging from the swirling morning mist, his 1957 silver Corvette looked distinctly like a bullet on wheels. Kamenev, with steel-gray hair cut short to emphasize his high cheekbones, dark blue eyes and square jaw, looked every inch the kind of guy to drive it. "Meet me in my office in two minutes," he commanded.

He turned into the five-stall garage. Nick Kamenev loved driving and flying machines the way most men loved women. The burgundy Mercedes E55 AMG Sport Sedan, the silver stretch Cadillac and the hornet-yellow Lamborghini LM002 – 6800 pounds of lightly armored, off-road beast that could accelerate from zero to sixty in seven point seven seconds, made the humvee look like a sardine can and made the Arabs drool – he loved them all, but he still loved his Corvette the most.

He headed briskly to the seventh floor, nodding rather brusquely at

Cora, his secretary. One wall of his vast corner office was plastered with military decorations and framed photos of him sitting in the cockpits of Skypoint's many aircraft. Another held floor-to-ceiling shelving devoted to commemorative model airplanes, military and civilian, for every machine Skypoint had produced. A third provided a double doorway to the Colonel's cloakroom and executive bathroom. And the fourth was plate glass. The room had been cantilevered out to give him a panoptic view of all the traffic that passed in and out of the complex. The Colonel ignored it. Got to check the figures Bill sent right quick, he fumed to himself as he pulled a slim laptop computer from the top of the filing cabinet and booted it up. He fished out a piece of paper from his briefcase, punched in his password, then began a heroic struggle with a long list of unfamiliar sequences.

"For fuck's sake!" he exclaimed.

"Do you need help?" Cora called.

"No I don't!" he yelled back. But she came and leaned against the doorjamb anyway, a *café-au-lait* complexion, the features of an African queen, an hourglass figure on long legs, lacquered nails beating a rhythm on her hip.

"*Goddamn cocksucking* ...! How the hell – ?"

"Let me help you," Cora said.

"No!" he said sharply. Then more calmly, "I don't need help."

"Okay," Cora said dubiously.

"Is Boyle here yet?" Kamenev was still punching keys.

Cora turned to look back into her office. "Uh-huh."

"Just tell him to wait a minute. Then call Macpherson and tell him to get down here on the double!"

"Yes, sir!" Cora said with a smart turn, a roll of her eyes, and sarcasm enough to give Kamenev a concussion had he not been completely oblivious.

"Yes!" Kamenev crowed. The computer's screen said, "Welcome, Colonel Kamenev," and displayed its small directory. He called up one of its few files. Finally, text came up. He sat down and read it. Then he powered down and looked up to see Douglas Boyle standing, balanced on the tips of his toes, filling the doorway. Boyle, twenty years his junior, had also retired from the United States Air Force, but as a major; he had been at his desk crunching numbers since oh-dark-thirty this morning, preparing, and he was ready.

"Hey, Doug." Kamenev closed his computer.

"Colonel Kamenev," Boyle replied respectfully.

What a behemoth, Kamenev thought. Though only five foot eleven in his stockinged feet, Skypoint's security chief gave the impression of being much bigger due to the ten hours a week, minimum, of bodybuilding and powerlifting that he put in religiously, year in year out since he was sixteen. He had started back in San Diego when his surfing buddies had made fun of his skinny body and bad acne. No one had ever made fun of him again. Today he showed off his muscles to good effect in a bulging white polo shirt with the Skypoint logo swelling over a huge pectoral. The Colonel was struck again by his curious face. Boyle's tawny eyes under pale, almost invisible brows and a jutting nose gave him a somewhat lupine look.

"You're looking fit as usual," Kamenev said. Boyle held a half-inch report binder very close to his chest.

"Thank you, sir."

"Yeah. Well, get in here. We got three minutes to do this."

"Yes, sir." Boyle sat facing the Colonel's desk. Wow! Three whole minutes, he thought. But he didn't say it. He liked his job. He didn't mind hierarchies as long as he was somewhere near the top.

"So did you manage to solve our little problem in Indonesia?"

"Yes, sir. The Mostyns just got back and –"

"Details later." Kamenev cut him off, started to organize his desk. "I'm in a helluva hurry."

"All right, sir. You tell me whatever you –"

"You're sure there's no trail? No *possible way* they could come back to us?"

"*No-possible-way-sir!*" Crisply Boyle barked each word. Boyle didn't question the Colonel's prerogative to command him as he did, but he was surprised at the unusually short shrift he was receiving. Something big was clearly on the Colonel's mind.

"Good. I'll find you later. Dismissed."

Boyle rose, turned sharply and left. In the doorway he encountered Malcolm Macpherson, a retired USAF lieutenant colonel with a double portfolio. He was vice president for weapons control innovation. But he was also Kamenev's personal assistant in negotiations and industrial strategizing, a choice Boyle had never understood or approved. Kamenev recruited all his key men from the Air Force. He figured they spoke the same language and prized the same things – something Boyle doubted of

Macpherson. For years, Macpherson had been trying to get the Colonel to offload his Defense contracts and build up the civilian wing of the company. Since 9/11 and Iraq, it was a strategy doomed to failure. This cheered Boyle greatly.

"Hey, Doug," Macpherson offered to Boyle's retreating back. Boyle grunted and kept on going. Macpherson, by comparison with the younger security chief, had a decidedly relaxed demeanor. His brown hair, gone halfway to silver, was worn longer than anyone else's in Skypoint's management, and his slender figure was a little uncomfortable in his formal navy suit.

"You'll have to make the final decision with the Saudis alone, Mal." The Colonel was already talking at him as he sorted piles of papers on his desk. "And do the preliminary stuff with the Italians at twelve if I'm not back. I've got an unexpected meeting this morning."

"Excuse me?" Macpherson was astonished. Kamenev was a control freak when it came to big contracts.

"The paper's here on the Saudis," Kamenev nodded to his desk. "Dickering time's over. Are we gonna make them some new fighters or are we gonna refurbish their F-16s? Time to fish or cut bait. You know their air force better than I do, so you won't miss me. Which way you wanna go?"

"I think we should sell them a refurbishing package – the new, multi-mission avionics with the synthetic aperture radar for ground attack, some low-light TV and IR sensors with laser designators – I've got it all right here." He waved some papers. "Our military craft production is backed up out the door right now. Plus we're trying to keep capacity for our new civilian initia –"

"If you say we can't build 'em anyway," Kamenev interrupted, closing his briefcase, "it's okay with me. What about the Italians?"

"I haven't seen your final figures yet. You were going to brief *me* this morning, remember?"

"Sorry. You can download my notes." The Colonel gestured to his dormant computer. Macpherson was familiar with Kamenev's computers because his boss didn't trust the company's IT personnel (too much industrial espionage going around) and assigned Macpherson to maintain them. "We can make them five of the big mamus," Kamenev stampeded on, "some mid-sized liners. Say twelve in all." Macpherson's head was spinning at the rapid handover. "I may not be back till mid-afternoon. Christ, I'm late. Gotta run."

The Colonel dashed out, leaving Macpherson missing one vital piece of information. He followed, saw Kamenev leaning over Cora's beautiful shoulder and heard him say, "Call Bill Greele at the Westin, and tell him I'm on my way." Kamenev pretended not to see Macpherson and stalked out.

"Hey, Nick!" Macpherson, really annoyed, called down the corridor. "What's our bottom line with their highnesses? On the packages?"

"Ten mil per air frame, with five-year service contracts," the Colonel shouted back. "And remind me to tell you about the Varig contract. We're withdrawing from the bidding."

"*What?*" Macpherson came to a halt like a man who'd been shot. But Kamenev had stepped into the elevator and vanished.

Macpherson stood in the corridor, breathless at the casual betrayal.

Just before he'd retired, while teaching a course in pioneering flight and energy technologies, Macpherson had learned about a couple of brainy Oklahoma guys who'd designed an aircraft based on the Coanda effect. Intrigued, he'd gone to visit them. Their company – IWA Technologies, named for the unique, almost circular "internal wing" of their amazing craft – had produced a remote-flying model which they demonstrated for him, and he had fallen in love with it. In a full-sized craft, it would be a breathtaking, streamlined bird with many times the lifting capacity of conventional aircraft. The design was remarkably flexible, with potential fuel economies twenty to forty times better than anything currently in the air. The design promised an almost vertical takeoff and landing, which would open up more than twenty thousand small airports in the US alone to commercial travel. It was a brilliant, environmentally friendly design that had been fought over by several big aeronautics firms – but, in two cases, with the purpose of shelving, not producing, it, and, in the third, of using it for military purposes.

So he'd come to Skypoint with a plan. Macpherson had spent several years befriending the eccentric inventors, who'd been burned so many times. It took even longer to persuade Kamenev that Coanda had the potential to help Skypoint take over, first the global short-haul market, then the entire civilian craft market, and that the investment in new production facilities would pay off. Twelve months earlier, when word came that Varig was going out for bid on a fleet of short-haul jets, the Colonel declared that the moment had arrived. Now, with a cavalier wave of his hand, all of it was history. Jesus, Macpherson thought, choking on his rage, he just can't do that. He pulled himself together and turned back.

"That was some bum's rush," he said to Cora. He stopped in front of her desk. "Bill Greele – would that be William Ericsson Greele?"

Cora was working at her computer. "I don't know, sugar," she said, lifting her eyes from the screen and shrugging. "Guy on the board? Could be."

"Let me know when the Colonel gets back, please, Cora. I have to talk to him."

Macpherson met with the Saudi delegation. He reminisced with the two princes about Riyadh where he had been stationed, carefully dancing around the topic of how much support there was in the vast royal family for Al Qaeda. Finally they clinched the deal, and the Saudis left, pleased. He went on to lunch with the Alitalia team, greeted them with a "*buongiorno, como state*", and hammered out the lines of a working proposal. They talked about a couple of Italian Air Force officers of mutual acquaintance, his colleagues when he had headed up a radar operations inspection team from a NATO base in Vicenza. Then he went back to his department until Cora called, telling him Kamenev was back and wanting a report.

"Put him on. I've got a thing or two to say myself."

"Hey, Mal," the Colonel came on the line. "Everything go okay?"

"We're signed, sealed and delivered with the Saudis, and we've got a letter of intent with Alitalia."

"Great."

"Yeah." Macpherson paused, trying to get his temper under control. "Nick, what's this about Varig?"

"Sorry, Mal. We've got too much on our hands right now."

"But Nick, we've got everything ready, we've been planning for years, we've been saving capacity –"

"Like I said, Mal, it's off. End of discussion. We'll look at the plane again some other time." And, in his characteristic way, Kamenev hung up.

At seven o'clock, Malcolm Macpherson ordered a double vodka on ice in Jaime's Bar on Broadway. His usual drink was a dark beer, but he needed something much stronger tonight. He had arrived in time to slip into his favorite booth at the back, so he could sit alone and catch the news on the big TV over the bar. It was better than what was going on in his head. The bar was quiet, and the announcer's voice came through over the sound of conversation and clinking glasses. He had a headache from hell.

"Good evening," said a generically handsome anchorman as the waiter placed the drink in front of Macpherson. "... story this hour is from London, where, it seems, many Brits are angry with the American president. Our reporter, Dorcas Alonzo, has the story." A dark-eyed, curly-headed reporter in black jacket, miniskirt and stiletto heels fought to keep her balance in a vast sea of people in Trafalgar Square.

"Yes, Brick, there are tens and tens of thousands of them here to show their support for GO KYOTO –" The reporter's voice and body suddenly disappeared as a throng of young people with placards thrust themselves between her and the camera. "Dorcas, what's going on?" the anchorman asked. "Well, Brick," she shouted, having somehow managed to push herself through the thicket of placards, "GO KYOTO is the global campaign to make the Kyoto Accord on greenhouse gases binding for all countries. The European Union, Japan, a small number of other nations, a huge number of NGOs – that's the non-governmental sector – and a number of businesspeople have launched this campaign. It's really gathering momentum, Brick." Someone shoved her to camera left but she kept talking. "It's moving through fifteen or so major cities before it ends in Washington, DC, sometime this fall. The US, as most Americans know, has refused to sign." More jostling. "Global warming is a major threat –"

"Thanks, Dorcas," the anchorman cut the reporter off, "but we've got to go to our next story."

Let her finish, you jerk, Macpherson thought angrily. Let her explain what it's about. But her image faded.

"In other news today, in the nation's capital, the Secretary of Defense admonished Americans to tighten their vigilance against terrorism at home. He said that in the last week, another dozen pipe bombs have been found in mailboxes in Nebraska and Iowa ..." Macpherson turned away.

Aw, shit, he thought in disgust, draining his glass. Face it. The dollars for the military stuff will never dry up and Skypoint will never, ever, go civilian. Kiss Coanda goodbye, buddy. Your life has turned to crap.

When he retired from the Air Force, he'd wanted to complete his Ph.D. dissertation in physical geography, which he'd put on hold for fifteen years. But he had two kids in college and serious alimony to pay. It had been the hope, then the prospect of building the Coanda plane that kept him going, year after year. Now the collapse of the dream – for it was the complete collapse – left him reeling. The vodka helped dull the pain, but he could taste bile in his throat. He took a handful of peanuts, ordered another drink.

His two beloved children, for whom he'd endured an otherwise unendurable marriage for more than twenty years, were much too far away, in Los Angeles and San Francisco, and he didn't get to see them often enough to keep a father's blues away. Molly was doing post-doctoral work in paleoanthropology and she had a good man. She seemed tired all the time, but basically she was all right, or so he hoped. Michael was doing a Ph.D. in supercomputers in Los Angeles. He seemed okay too, now, but he'd gone through a period of black depression when he first went to college – the aftermath, Macpherson believed, of the poisonous atmosphere his parents had created – and he'd been caught speeding in the desert with a beautiful Chicana twice his age and an ounce of pot in the front seat. It got him put on probation for five years. Now he was consumed with rage every time he had to report in, and once a month Macpherson waited on tenterhooks to hear that the visit had gone without incident. In retrospect, he thought for the nth time, staying with Lucille had given the kids one miserable home, instead of, maybe, two happy ones. Good intentions, road to hell, shit. Despair came over him like a hangman's hood. He knocked back the vodka and stood up to pay when his cellphone rang.

"Hi, handsome," said a sunny voice. "Wanna go to a lecture tomorrow night?"

Geraldine Morrow was a young, all-American beauty. She had red-gold hair and soft brown freckles all over her long, creamy arms and legs. She loved nature and the great outdoors, and for a long time she had wanted to love Malcolm Macpherson. They had met in the Skypoint cafeteria, sitting across from one another, she reading *Outside* magazine, he a book on ravens.

He had raised an eyebrow. "I subscribe to that magazine," he said.

And she had said, breathless, "I like birds, too. Are you a birder?"

"I'm happy birdwatching," he'd replied. "I don't keep lists or anything." And they had started to talk. She was attractive, happy, direct, this latter quality refreshingly different from his brooding ex-wife, who had been as devious as an Italian detour. It might be nice, he thought, looking at her. So he asked Geraldine if she wanted to go hiking sometime and she enthusiastically said yes. He'd picked her up in his three-year-old Subaru wagon, and watched her reaction as his West Highland terrier hurtled over the seat and subjected her to a flurry of wet kisses.

31

"Who is this amazing dog?" Geraldine had said, laughing and squirming.

"That's Bonnie," he said, smiling too. "Scottish for pretty."

"Boy, what a dervish. Any more animal surprises?"

"Clyde." Geraldine groaned. "Hell of a cat, but he doesn't come hiking."

The day was fair, the climb invigorating, the azaleas opening stars of color. Geraldine beamed, and Malcolm found her pleasure in his company flattering. She served on the board of an inner-city organic farming program, he as state lobbyist for the Audubon Society. It should have been perfect.

But when he dropped her off that night, he hoped she wouldn't ask him in. He hadn't gotten the inner signal, and he wasn't going to get involved until he did. They had settled into being frequent companions for a hike or a stroll through the botanical gardens, sometimes Malcolm would rent a small plane and they'd do a round trip up to the Queen Charlotte Islands – a platonic relationship Geraldine had accepted with regret, he with pleasure, mostly. Though being with her reminded him constantly that he had still not found his soul mate, and probably never would.

5

WHEN Malcolm Macpherson got home on Friday he found that his orange Manx had loosened the bungie cord that secured the refrigerator door and knocked out the remains of a chicken, which he and Bonnie had finished off. He had to rush the two animals to the vet, then jump in the car with Geraldine for a mad drive down Broadway to Spruce Hall. They crept in, bringing a gust of wind with them, and took seats at the rear. Everyone turned and stared. Malcolm nodded to Russell Jefferson, one of the few black programmers at Cyberonics, a fellow conservationist, and the best friend he had in Seattle.

"I've been working as an environmentalist for a long time," Claire Davidowicz, of eco-Justice USA, was saying as she slowly paced the length of the stage. Amplified by a lavaliere microphone that traveled with her,

her voice was resonant and warm. "First, as a journalist, then as a researcher-writer, then as a staffer in various NGOs, today as director of an international organization." She was a woman of medium height and abundant curves, in beige linen slacks and a tailored white shirt. Delicate reading glasses were perched on her nose. She had a lot of dark, wavy hair. "For almost that whole time, I soft-pedaled what I knew – whether it was how rapidly the fish were disappearing from the oceans; or how utterly scary it is that it took only four years for genetically modified corn and soy to go from laboratory experiments to more than half of the acres under cultivation in the United States and Canada, and just another four to contaminate the entire North American seed stock and growing fields. Or how really serious the endocrine-disrupting effects of persistent organic pollutants are on all living things including us humans and our babies. It's worse than you know, even if you think it's bad." Here Davidowicz looked at her audience, turned in the other direction, and started pacing again.

"You wouldn't *want* to know what I know about the content of the biological warfare labs. Or about what's happening with nanotechnology, which gives new meaning to the old Star Trek refrain, *It's life Jim, but not as we know it*!"

Macpherson smiled. Davidowicz stopped and threw the audience a dazzling look – part irony, part amazement at the insanity of it all, part wild defiance. It made his body tingle.

"I used to downplay what I knew so I wouldn't frighten people away. Then, in June of 2003, Britain's Royal Astronomer predicted that by 2050 humans will have committed species suicide. We will have, to use his words, 'exploded, imploded or gone to gray goo'".

Macpherson, probably one of the few people in that audience who had read both Greg Bear's nanotech nightmare *Blood Music* and the Royal Astronomer's interview in *New Scientist*, snorted. Geraldine eyed him curiously.

"It's truly a vision to commit suicide by. But hey," Davidowicz grinned, "it showed me what an upbeat gal I really am. Now I tell all those people who suggest I 'lighten up' that I'm a total optimist compared to those brainy scientists. They *know* they're working on instruments of self-destruction, but they can't stop."

"Well," she said, both hands gripping the podium, "I don't hold back anymore. Now I figure the best I can do is give people knowledge so they can do something about what's really happening if they choose to." Great, thought Geraldine. I'm going to leave this place even more freaked out than I already was about the state of the world.

Claire Davidowicz adjusted some papers on the podium, then looked out at the auditorium. "Most of you," she said, "will be familiar with that old Native American adage: Step lightly on the earth. Well, folks, we've stepped anything but lightly on our poor planet. Our enormous footprint, according to UN estimates, takes up 83 per cent of the biosphere for human-related needs and activities. One species; 83 per cent of the space. Wow! Since we've pushed so many of our co-inhabitants out, we're preventing the web of life from renewing itself. The oceans and rivers and trees and grasses and micro-organisms and insects and fish and birds – none of them can perform their tasks of renewal properly anymore. Last year, UN scientists estimated that on average 50 per cent of the world's species face extinction in the next thirty years. In some places, large tropical parts of Latin America, for example, the estimate rises to 84 per cent."

Macpherson groaned. As a nature-loving kid of twelve in Jackson, Michigan, he had joined the Audubon Society's junior division. Since leaving the Air Force he'd reactivated, and for more than four years he'd been fighting to get the organization to renounce its defense of pleasure hunting and concentrate on conservation. Every time he entered the fray, it brought back terrible memories of the fights he'd had with his father on the subject when he was fifteen. He'd never won then, and he wasn't winning now, either.

Davidowicz stopped again at the podium. "As part of that huge footprint, a cloud of aerosols of smoke – made up of gases and particulate matter – hovers particularly thickly over Asia, but, less densely, all over the globe. It's the result of burning rainforests, crop waste and fossil fuels. Well, last year," Davidowicz confided, "a number of scientists met in Berlin. Present were Nobel laureate Pierre Kreutzer and Swedish meteorologist Beno Berensson, former chairman of the UN's authoritative Intergovernmental Panel on Climate Change – the people who brought you all those reports in the late nineties saying that the planet was warming faster than they'd thought. These scientists warned that the aerosol smoke layer has protected the planet – a sort of parasol effect – from as much as 1.8 degrees Celsius temperature rise. Consequently, if the global smoke were to be cleared up – because it damages living things and tears holes in the ozone layer – if it were cleared up *before* greenhouse gas emissions were *radically* lowered we might, literally, fry."

"The IPCC's maximum forecast for global warming prior to that conference," Claire Davidowicz went on, "was a 5.8 degrees Celsius increase over the next fifty years. That alone was enough to have scientists predicting that New York and Vancouver, as well as Montserrat and Shanghai and New Delhi, could be under water, flooded from melting ice caps. That *alone* was enough to predict huge hurricanes, tornadoes, ice-storms, floods, smog inversions, drought – you name the weird weather. Now, though, 'back of the envelope calculations' are prompting worst case scenarios of increases of *7 to 10 degrees Celsius*." There was a collective intake of breath. Macpherson had read about those predictions, but had consciously stopped himself from speculating on what they might mean. Davidowicz did not veer away from the subject.

"Now ladies and gentlemen," she said, "almost no specialist has ever really considered the prospects of life on this planet in terms of these kinds of projections. Let's just say it's going to be as hot – and as violent – as Hades.

"Even though we understand why the web of life is collapsing, and even though – it's the truth – we have the technical know-how to forestall more damage, and eventually repair a lot already done, *even though we have the knowledge to save ourselves*," Davidowicz declared emphatically, "we're still heading to hell in a handbasket.

"Why? Because we *don't* have the subsidies and supports and legislation and enforcement for clean technologies that the dirty old technologies such as oil and gas and coal and nuclear power benefit from. We lack all these prerequisites for the spread of green technologies because our politicians have refused to create them. You say let's make a government program, a public works program to retrofit every building in the country with solar generating materials? You say we'd have good jobs and give the biosphere a fighting chance at one stroke?" Yeah, I'd say that, Geraldine thought.

"Sorry, not possible. We have other priorities. We're going to send our young people to die and to kill to secure oil reserves in the Middle East and indebt our country by half a trillion dollars. Can't be wasting good tax-payers' money on solar panels and wind turbines!" The audience muttered sympathetically.

The hellfire and toxicity of the Gulf War had been the final sharp prods out of the military for Malcolm and he had some painful memories.

Claire Davidowicz's hair gleamed like a beacon in the stage lights. "Did you know that our Environmental Protection Agency and all our

35

environmental laws are being dismantled systematically through a stealth campaign made possible by the Republican control of the White House and both Houses of Congress? It's true. Here's one small example: the Environmental Protection Agency has a computer system to track and control water pollution. It's obsolete. This undermines the entire system of permits and penalties created by the Clean Water Act. It would take about five million dollars to fix it – less than 2 cents for every American for clean water, the very basis of life. But no, the administration has said it's 'too expensive'. Meanwhile, they're supporting a 300 million plus project to get the Army Corps of Engineers to divert water from the White River in Arkansas to subsidized rice farmers, because those farmers have, knowingly, drained the alluvial aquifer dry."

Macpherson watched Davidowicz work to keep her voice steady, though he could sense her burning anger at the hypocrisy and stupidity she was describing. He felt her intelligence as a steady physical pulse of energy washing over him in magnetic waves. He watched her intently. Geraldine watched him.

"Why *do* our mechanisms for controlling environmental damage lag so far behind? I believe it's because the real power to affect which technologies will be used lies outside popular hands. What we're living, folks, is a massive failure in democracy. The World Trade Organization, the World Bank, the huge transnational corporations, our own governments – that's where the power resides. And these institutions tear down environmental standards faster than we can build – or rebuild – them. Our governments function by and large as executive arms of corporate oligarchies."

"Truer words …" Malcolm said bitterly.

"I guess," said Geraldine glumly.

"But if we don't find a way," Davidowicz warned, "we might just as well kiss our world goodbye. Because those transnationals are driven by one imperative – *their own growth*. And, left to themselves, they'll choose that over mere human life every time." Macpherson thought about Kamenev and the Coanda debacle and felt the raw, aching emptiness of all those wasted years.

"Ladies and gentlemen, what we need now are financial resources and political instruments to replace the destructive technologies. Take water as a case in point. One point one billion people do not have access to clean water today. In developing nations, up to 95 per cent of sewage and 70 percent of industrial waste is simply being dumped untreated into watercourses.

Already we're using up 54 per cent of available freshwater supplies annually. That figure is set to surge to 70 per cent by 2025 due to population growth alone, and to 90 per cent if consumption in the developing countries reaches the levels in the developed world. There will be wars over water, and they'll even further ravage parched environments. The number of water refugees – they're cropping up in small towns in the American South and West now, not just in the Sahara – will surpass the number of war refugees for the first time in history before long."

Geraldine recalled a statistic she'd read, that Americans use 270 billion gallons of water every week just to water their lawns. She'd replanted her garden with native grasses and flowering plants and turned off her tap.

"Yet in many places," Davidowicz pressed on, "people who try to do something constructive pay perverse and terrible costs. In Oaxaca a few months ago, the city council had evidence that effluent being dumped in the local river by a Petroco subsidiary was causing birth defects in newborns and other serious health problems, including cancer. The city denied Petroco the permission they'd requested to build a second plant. For this, a NAFTA tribunal slapped the city with a twenty million dollar fine, claiming the municipality had violated Chapter 11 of the agreement and were obliged to pay the company the costs of its 'lost business opportunity!'" A general muttering and a few cries of "Shame!" rose from members of the audience, many of whom had heard about the incident.

"I regret to inform you," Davidowicz finally let her anger show, "that such effective and cruel measures are being taken to put a stop to environmental sovereignty all over the world!

"I suspect that for many of you here in the Pacific Northwest," she lowered her voice again, "where water is so plentiful, the water problems may seem remote. But you will not be immune. Very soon, you will come under tremendous pressure to share your water. There are already at least six plans under discussion with the federal government to ship or pipe your water south and east. And I suspect none of you here knows about even one."

Macpherson's mind, terribly troubled, turned to the world his generation had bequeathed to his children, and the children they might have, though Mike often threatened never to reproduce because of the mess the world was in, and Molly was having trouble conceiving. Don's sperm count was too low, a problem a lot of their friends were having. He felt it like a physical pain, the guilt and sadness for having failed to do the right thing – by his family, his species, his planet. He clenched his fists. And then Claire Davidowicz came back into focus, standing on the platform like an incandescent flame, warm and vital.

"... solve the water problem, it's time to demand and to craft a new ethic that declares water to be an inalienable right for all. And to make that ethic meaningful, we all have to get politically active and take our political institutions back from the super-rich and their hired guns. To survive in the coming years, a system of water governance will have to be built from the ground up — *democratically*. We must make it happen if we're to save ourselves and our children. It's up to you to participate in its conception and creation, and to make it a political issue today, at city, state and federal levels. And to begin thinking about land and air — those other two essential elements — in the same action-oriented, political ways. Please. Do it soon." She took a final breath. "Thank you."

As they left their seats, Macpherson touched Geraldine on the arm and told her that he wanted to ask Claire Davidowicz a question. "Migration patterns and wetlands, birds," he said somewhat sheepishly in response to her puzzled look. He walked to the front of the hall, and took his place in the cluster of people waiting to say a word to the speaker. He knew pretty well what fate awaited the birds in the scenarios Davidowicz had sketched. He had been keeping track for decades and he agreed with Davidowicz's assessments. But he knew she would have something interesting to contribute. And — more — he urgently wanted to see what this woman was like, up close, one-to-one. He watched her. Early to mid-forties he guessed, beautiful skin but bruised with fatigue under the eyes. She was taking questions one at a time, striving to keep her energy up. He saw willed enthusiasm on her face, and wondered whether she was missing her man and her kids back home. He glanced at her hands. Strong, tanned hands, short nails, no polish, no wedding band. His spirits lifted.

The last petitioner made off, and it was his turn. He extended his hand. "That was a very thought-provoking speech." He introduced himself. "I'm the Washington state lobbyist for the Audubon Society."

"Are you?" Their palms and fingers met and held, hers warm, his cool, a sweet feeling hard to let go of when they disengaged. "Pleased to make your acquaintance," she said. "'Thought-provoking' is one of the adjectives I most like to hear." He smiled. She saw clear, steady blue eyes, mischief in the smile, a weathered, handsome face. She noticed long legs in loose jeans, a slender waist, a navy blue T-shirt over a possibly muscular chest, a well-cut jacket in shades of blue and burgundy. Wow, she thought, unaccustomed to thinking such thoughts, how nice. She glanced at his left hand. Double wow.

"Tough on the birds, all this," she said, inviting him to speak.

"Yes it is. Very tough, and that's what I wanted to ask you about." He saw her eyes were hazel and her mouth plum-colored underneath the faded lipstick. "I just wondered whether you had any special thoughts you might want to share on bird-related issues and the environmental crisis?"

"One or two, perhaps." She regarded his eyes – trustworthy and totally focused on her. She was finding it very difficult to look away. And so, though long outside the dance and unrehearsed in its steps, she seized the opportunity she thought he was offering her. "My feet are killing me. I've been on them all day," she said. "Maybe we could talk sitting down, over coffee or a drink?" She couldn't believe she'd done it, but there it was.

"Ah," he said, thinking, *yes!* and then, Geraldine! "I'd love to, but I came with a friend tonight, and I've –" Aw, shit, he thought, as her face changed in the split second he hesitated. Think fast. "Are you still in town tomorrow? May I take you to lunch?"

She smiled, happy again, but warier. "I can probably organize lunch," she said. "Okay." She started to gather her papers, then turned to look at him. "Good posture." She smiled, amused. "You must have gone to a private school or been in the military."

"Your posture's pretty good too," he laughed, skating around it. "Which did you attend?"

She laughed too. "*Touché.* Miss Knight's School for Girls. In Montreal. It's a long, old story. And you?"

Oh great, he thought. "The United States Air Force. Twenty years," he said. Her eyes widened in surprise. Shit! he thought again. "If we can put that aside for the moment," he said, trying to maintain eye contact, "where should we meet for lunch tomorrow? I really would like to talk to you … about environmental impact on birds."

But her hazel eyes looked beyond his and locked on someone else. As pretty, determined Geraldine Morrow pulled up and placed a possessive hand in the crook of his arm, Davidowicz turned formal. "Well, Mr Macpherson," she said coldly, "under the direction of the current military-industrial complex I think we can expect very rapid and violent changes, don't you? And a rate of extinction that will surpass that of the dinosaurs."

39

Geraldine reared her head, surprised by the harsh tone, and looked at Macpherson. He was speechless.

Davidowicz picked up a red sweater, threw it around her shoulders, gathered up her briefcase and waved to some colleagues waiting for her at the door. Then she sighed, visibly composed herself, and turned to them with a strained smile. "Please forgive my outburst. I'm very tired, and sometimes I lose my optimism. Thank you for coming. I hope it's been worthwhile."

6

LATE at night, in his office overlooking the twinkling lights of the lower city, Serge Lalonde considered his options. His hair was disheveled, his blue shirt rumpled, his yellow Hermès tie loosened. He had been reading about water frantically, in the toilet, over breakfast, lunch and dinner, while he was waiting on hold, when he was supposed to be reading memos on other portfolios. He had read just enough about Qaddafi's Great Man-Made River, and the ruinous consequences of the Hoover and the Aswan dams, to know that he was in way over his head. Well, he'd better learn to swim.

Earlier that day, he had met with Pierre Gosselin, a senior government hydrologist and an Assistant Deputy Minister of Natural Resources; a cold technocratic bureaucrat, though not of the *cravate* type, a term devised by Lalonde's wife Nicole for the sort of official both of them despised. True Gosselin was colorless – from the roots of his gray hair to his ill-fitting beige suit. But he was an old-school, heroic engineer who knew the waterways of the province intimately. For seven years, he'd fought the First Nations' claims during the building of the James Bay project. He could handle the pressure of battle.

Lalonde had sworn Gosselin to secrecy, put the American proposal to him and watched his eyes widen greedily. Gosselin saw the possibility of a fitting crown to a career that had begun with promise but now languished in the doldrums. *"Ben, oui,* the dams and diversions are not so big. It can be done without destroying the waterways, why not? Especially if we are able to control the process. That is what you must secure. If you are successful, it can be done."

Lalonde wasn't sure whether this was good or bad news. He said goodbye to Gosselin and ushered in a young hydrologist named Helder Pereira. Helder was the son of his mother's Portuguese housekeeper and he owed his job in the Ministry of the Environment to Lalonde's intercession. He worshipped the ground his benefactor walked on, and loved the lands of Quebec with a passion. Helder had listened attentively, assuming Lalonde wanted approval. Reluctantly, he'd given the project a thumbs down.

"Monsieur Lalonde," he'd said earnestly, "there is no way such a project could be achieved without grave environmental damage."

"Really?" Lalonde replied. "That's not what I hear from hydrologists with more experience than you, Helder. Are you sure?"

Helder's big, dark eyes were apologetic. "Even if it were possible to extract so much water without fundamentally compromising the ability of the system to renew itself – and I am not sure at all that's possible, truly, it could be disastrous, I would need time to study this – even so, it would still be very bad."

"But why?"

"Well, all those diversions and dams, they'd cause a lot of harm."

"But none of them would be very big."

"But Monsieur Lalonde, they would disrupt the breeding of all the insects, fish, birds and mammals in the region."

"Pierre Gosselin said nothing about that."

"But this is now well known, Monsieur Lalonde. In the United States, even the Army Corps of Engineers have been agreeing to use existing dams and diversions to mimic seasonal flows rather than a constant flow to support agriculture. This has caused huge fights between farmers and environ-mentalists. Didn't you read about the big conflicts over the Missouri River?"

"No, as it happens," Lalonde said sourly. "But Helder, surely we could do the same thing? Mimic seasonal flows, I mean."

"Maybe," Helder said doubtfully. "But if the pace of extraction is dictated by the needs of export, that is not really feasible."

After the young man left, Lalonde picked up his phone, and put Helder's objections to Gosselin. He promptly dismissed them. "Of course, you can't make an omelette without breaking eggs. But the bush grows back! The damage can be contained, then healed. He's a starry-eyed idealist, Serge, and he doesn't know what he's talking about."

Lalonde had listened to the sounds of the office as work wound down and people left for the day. His gut reaction was to believe Helder, whose views were more modern and less self-serving. But he knew that with Gosselin's evaluation, there was no way he could avoid giving the government a chance to consider the proposal. So it all came down now to choosing the minister – the most delicate, the most dangerous of choices.

Finally, the only credible candidate is Monsieur Moneybags himself, Serge thought, seeing in his mind's eye the stout body, the gray suit, the generous jowls and the omnipresent cigar of the Honorable Robert Corbeil, provincial Treasurer and Finance Minister. Corbeil would have to approve the project regardless. If he adopted it, no one could object on budgetary grounds or challenge Lalonde's choice of business partners. Cabinet squabbles wouldn't matter in the end if Corbeil wanted to move ahead.

Corbeil had been a fierce supporter of the Free Trade Act, NAFTA and the Free Trade Agreement of the Americas – the treaty that was tying up the whole hemisphere with a big red ribbon. This would already incline him toward the project. Pushing even harder was the fact that the Liberal Prime Minister in Ottawa would gladly negotiate away Quebec's resources. The PQ *had* to take pre-emptive sovereign action on a number of fronts, and soon. Plus, Lalonde noted with grim satisfaction, Corbeil's ego was easily as big as Greele's. He picked up his telephone and left a message for the Minister. Then he gathered his trenchcoat and wrapped a wool scarf around his throat against the damp April night. Nicole's coming home in two days, he thought, as he walked down the quiet hall. Maybe I can put off telling her till it's decided, one way or the other.

A sleety, mid-April rain was melting the massive icicles hanging from the eaves of her house as Nicole Verlaan-Lalonde arrived home from Paris tired and unhappy. Her regular trips to France kept her connected to family and colleagues and gave her the pleasure of time in Europe. But they also left her mind and heart divided, and her body drained.

Serge greeted her with spring lilies, a warm *cassoulet*, a fire in the grate. Yet to Nicole he seemed distracted and jumpy. Her mind was preoccupied, too, by matters relating to work. Hence affectionate but perfunctory hugs were exchanged, instead of the more ardent ones that would normally have followed an absence, and they both fell asleep.

Nicole went to the hospital center early the next morning. The epidemiological studies on persistent organic pollutants she was supervising at Laval University were part of a multi-nation study whose other main center was at the University of Bordeaux. She had met successfully with her colleagues in Europe, but was now behind in her work in Quebec. She came home as the shadows were lengthening. No sign of Serge. Hot food in the oven. Jocelyne gone, back to normal hours.

Nicole changed into a sweater and jeans, poured a glass of wine, and retrieved a ceramic bowl from a shopping bag bearing a Parisian address, to prepare it for mailing to her dear friend Sylvie Lacroix in Montreal. She went upstairs to her study in search of wrapping paper. The bag of materials they kept was nowhere in evidence. She went downstairs to Serge's study, went to the folding doors of the wall closet and opened them. A large plastic shopping bag dislodged from the top shelf, fell on her head, and disgorged a number of rolled-up documents onto the floor. Nicole gathered them up, tried to stuff them back, and saw a bunch of maps. Curiosity piqued, she unfurled one and read *The Watershed and Riverine Systems of Quebec*.

"*Bizarre*," she said aloud as her eye caught sight of the other bag she'd been seeking. Some new interest of Serge's? She put the maps back where they'd come from, grabbed the bag of wrapping paper and returned to her study.

When at length Serge did not appear, Nicole went downstairs to eat supper. She turned on the television that sat on the kitchen counter and flipped to the weather channel. A tall blonde in a very short skirt — what is it with those skirts? Nicole thought — was announcing the conditions across the continent. The jet stream looked like a demented ribbon, dipping wildly down to Oklahoma and Alabama with freezing temperatures, then spiking giddily up through the Midwest to peak over Toronto, where flowers were already in premature bloom. "Despite the mild rain east and north of the Great Lakes this evening," the meteorologist said, "authorities have declared this winter to conform to drought specifications, in the Northeast as well as the Midwest."

This is not what I need, Nicole thought, and clicked it off. She returned to her study, where she reviewed some of the latest St Lawrence River statistics collated in her absence — as bad as the weather.

She thought she heard the front door open, but no call came from Serge. So she made her way down the carpeted stairs. Her husband's coat was draped over the railing, but the kitchen and living rooms were dark and quiet. She heard Serge's voice at the back of the house, and walked towards his study. The door was partially closed, throwing a shadow into the hall.

"... told you that minimal environmental guidelines would have to be part of the package from the outset," Serge said, with an edge to his voice. Followed by a pause. "Well, I have taken advice. The senior hydrologist thinks it's viable, the junior doesn't." Silence. "Yes, yes, I've taken it to the Minister of Finance, and he has given me approval to seek private-sector partners, while looking more closely at environmental impacts." Corbeil had actually told him that if Gosselin said it could be done, it was good enough for him. But Lalonde was hoping to maintain some negotiating power.

"Look at it this way, Bill," he said. "Whatever agreement we draw up may eventually be contested in the WTO or even at the United Nations. We may as well get it right." Another pause. "Of course I'm not threatening you, Bill, I'm just saying that it has to fly here too, and it will not fly if it's pure rape and pillage." What on earth? Nicole thought, alarmed. Another pause. "Do you have children, Bill?" Who was he talking to? "No, but I have nieces and nephews. It puzzles me, really, how a man of such astute perceptions would not care to guard the integrity of the very resource he wishes to exploit."

Nicole's mind was flooded with curiosity, but Serge said, "Very well, Bill," and hung up. As he leaned back and looked out into the moonlit garden, Nicole pressed herself against the wall, ears tingling, mind searching. Environmental guidelines? Rape and Pillage? What was Serge on about? Suddenly ashamed of her lurking, she crept upstairs to wait for her husband to join her, to get undressed and into bed, to give her a hug and tell her about his call. But when Serge finally arrived, almost half an hour later, he only apologized for being delayed by some routine matters. She wanted to ask, but since they'd fought so much in recent months, she didn't want to admit that she'd been eavesdropping. He kissed her goodnight and turned out the light. She lay awake, wondering.

Greele called Bunting Hurst in his Park Avenue apartment in New York. The banker and his wife were reading in bed, and Hurst barely heard the faint ring of his cellphone in his study.

"I've just heard from Serge Lalonde," Greele said, "and they're moving ahead. Lalonde's going to pull together a money-man and a major construction contractor who knows the bush. He's got a senior government hydrologist grooming the proposal for presentation. When those two pieces are done, they're going to take it to Cabinet. And all completely hush-hush."

"My goodness," Hurst said. "That's impressive, Bill. I confess I thought they'd tell us to go stuff ourselves."

"They see the benefits, Bunt. I told you. They have to do this or face someone else doing it for them. Have you done the research you wanted to?"

"Uh-huh. I took the liberty of having a private chat with Gabe Mezulis the other day – just to make sure I had a firm grasp on the subject – and I'm close to completing my assessment of available investment funds. My key question, however, remains the political one. You're sure they're onside for a *private* project? No obstacles?"

Greele let out an impatient sigh. "No obstacles. Some environmental wrangles to deal with, maybe, down the line, but nothing we can't take care of. It's going to be fine, Bunting. Really. So I'm going to set up that meeting in Washington. I'll be asking Vittorio, Rich, and Nick down too. Bernie's going to be in Basel and Wilbur's in Libya, checking out their pipeline technology. Early next week if possible. Time to get the political support we need and move out."

"Bill," Hurst said solemnly. "Before we take this next step. No bullshit, now. No razzamatazz. I need to be a hundred and fifty per cent sure. We're talking billions of dollars and everything that implies. Is this thing really solid?"

"Like a rock," Greele replied.

"All right," Hurst said, releasing a tight breath. "I'll go ahead. If it's solid, it's sensational."

Greele said goodbye, sat in his enormous maroon leather reading chair, put his feet up on the ottoman, and opened the *Far Eastern Economic Review*. But he couldn't keep his mind on his reading. This thing in Quebec was the big one. Really, really big. The very thought of it unleashed a flood of arousal.

His study door opened carefully. "How are you, dear?" Sarah inquired, putting her coiffed head around the door. "Comfy?" To Greele she looked like a gracefully aged Grace Kelly, a porcelain and gold doll, with a virtual "do not touch" sign draped over her shoulders. It had been years since their skin had made contact, since they had agreed to separate bedrooms. She had never been much interested in sex, and truth to tell, neither had he. At one time, once in a blue moon, in Tokyo or Hong Kong, he had indulged himself with the best money could buy. Now it didn't seem to matter anymore. After five years of failing to conceive a child, he and Sarah had stopped, relieved not to have to try any longer. His own relationship with his father had been so tortured, and his feelings about children so ambivalent, that Greele had little regret about the absence of heirs.

When he was a boy, his heart had been repeatedly shattered trying to win his father's approval. For the most part, Greele senior had behaved as though his son were invisible. Only when Bill had returned with his Ivy League economics degree and joined the family business had Henry begun to acknowledge him, then to work with him, eventually to treat him as an equal. Then, in his decline, the son had forced his father to cede to *him*. Henry died of a stroke just weeks after Bill had usurped his role as CEO and chairman of the board. Assuming sole command of the now-colossal empire, William Greele intended to burn into history a legacy of economic brilliance, power, and control that far surpassed his father's.

Sarah had brought invaluable connections to East Coast gentility and political power in Washington. She performed her duties as his chatelaine and traveling companion with impeccable skill. She was a cut-out from *Architectural Digest*, which suited him to a tee.

"I'm fine, Sarah, thanks," he said.

"Well, then," she said. "Goodnight, dear."

"Goodnight, Sarah," he responded from his chair. "Sleep well."

Sarah walked unsteadily up the stairs to her apple-green bedroom suite, her sanctuary. She took a gin and tonic, freshly mixed, to her bath, a nightcap she desperately needed in order to sleep. How long has it been, she wondered, gin and bathwater and tears all sloshing together, since I've said anything more to him than "good morning, dear" and "goodnight dear" and "I'm going to see the Whitneys in Chicago, I'll be back on Tuesday, dear."

She'd never been much interested in men. But she had enjoyed interior design and the physical pleasures of the spa, and since her mother had cared greatly about such things as money and houses, she'd agreed to the match. She shed more tears at the memory of her mother's recent funeral. I know I agreed to it, Mother, she wept. Keep his houses, be his perfect hostess, get what I want in return. But I hate him! She applied a complex layering of expensive creams, then lay in bed like a virgin on a bier.

7

EIGHT o'clock on Friday night in Seattle and Malcolm Macpherson was still in his office. Outside the light was dying, and through a fine mist he looked down over the last of the cherry blossoms. He twirled a pencil between his fingers. The phone conference twenty minutes earlier with Ewen Enright and Jim Orchard, the Coanda plane inventors, was among the worst experiences of his life. When he told them of Nick Kamenev's decision, a stunned, unbelieving silence reverberated hideously over the line. They'd put all their trust in him, and the fruition of their very existence had been hanging on the Brazilian bid. Now their entire lives had crashed and burned. He could still hear how Ewen had gasped for breath, how Jim had been strangled with emotion. "Guys," he'd said. "The rights revert to you now, don't forget that."

"We had those rights for ten years before you came along, Mal. But we didn't have the money to make the damn thing. And you know we still don't!"

"Listen, Ewen, Jim," he'd tried. "If you still want to work with me, I'll be leaving Skypoint as soon as I can." He knew he couldn't stay with Kamenev much longer and he needed desperately to offer them something. "I'll take on finding a new producer."

"What, in another ten years?" Ewen had scoffed.

There hadn't been much else to say. Jim's silence had cut deeper than Ewen's anger. They said they'd get back to him.

He'd been flooded with rage and consumed with remorse. He had tried to get back to work, but his mind just wouldn't engage with the other projects on his desk – stuff he cared nothing about anymore.

He thought about how much money it took to keep one kid in graduate school, and another doing post-doctoral studies, about how much money it took to pay Lucille's alimony, about his cabin in the Cascades, which he hadn't visited in too long. He thought about his place in the military-industrial complex – officially out of the military, still very much in the complex. He thought how much he disliked his boss and, now, hated his work. He thought about climate change and water and drought. He thought about how the rain had beaten down on the corrugated steel roof of the family's Bayport cabin when he was a child, far out in the great Saginaw

47

marshes, the way the cattails and river grasses looked at dawn behind the duck blinds, how the soft, silken ruffle of feathers caressed his ears as the birds took off or came in for a landing. He thought about Claire Davidowicz. He wondered if she liked listening for birds on a glassy marsh, wondered if she had a dog or cat, then thought, Jesus, the animals! He looked at his watch, hastily organized his desk and took off out the door.

Heading to the elevators, he noticed a light coming from the boardroom. That's odd, he thought, and headed in that direction. He heard the Colonel's voice, then others. He slowed his steps and stood in the dark hallway. Through the glass door, he could make out three men. One suit, one leather jacket, one sweat clothes. Something about the childish face in the casual garb rang a bell. Good grief, Malcolm thought, that's Andrew Albert Stiller. He looks just like his photos on countless *Time* and *Newsweek* covers. What's *he* doing here?

"That's a helluva lot of water." It was Nick Kamenev's distinctive voice.

"It's the opportunity of the century," said the leather jacket. "Is what it is. The profit margins are unbelievable."

"Fine, okay, I'm there," Kamenev responded hastily. "No problem."

"I'm cool." Malcolm could clearly see A. A. Stiller talking. "Hell, some-one's gotta do it and it may as well be us. You guys happy with the computers?"

Malcolm turned and quietly walked down the hall. The thought that Kamenev was off investing in some other deal – some secret deal involving water, of all things – when he'd just mortally stabbed two fine men plus his own VP in the back, made him crazy. He took the elevator to the first floor, signed himself out, and took the I-95 north through the fresh spring rain.

Home was a wood shingle bungalow on the northern edge of the university district. He liked the old trees in the neighborhood, the ethnic restaurants on Broadway, the bookstores. Bonnie and Clyde were sitting in the living room window waiting for him with the "you're late" look, so he poured himself a beer and played catch with Bonnie and fetch with Clyde, whose great delight was to pounce on and retrieve crushed paper balls, hanging off as many household fixtures as he could in the process.

He left a message on Molly and Don's answering machine. He'd spoken to Mike the night before, and thought, gratefully, that the only things unhinging his son now were the endless hours at his computer. He worked out with the weights he kept under the bed, which stood under a skylight through which every night he watched the stars or clouds. With an old blue

48

Air Force tie he fastened Bonnie's collar to the couch in the living room to keep her from getting underfoot while he ran up and down the basement stairs twenty times. He poured a second beer, made some pasta, then listened to his messages.

"Wanna go for a walk?" Geraldine's cheery voice greeted him. "Call me."

He got into bed, read a chapter or two of Olivia E. Butler's latest novel. Kamenev's words "it's a hell of a lot of water" reverberated in his head. He listened to the rain.

Malcolm went in very early Monday morning and headed for Cora's deserted desk. He found what he was looking for on the spike she used to keep notes from Kamenev. It was just a few words, "Mezulis, Stiller, Fri. 20:00", but it gave him what he needed. In his office, he switched on his computer and went surfing. The first Mezulis he found was a chemistry professor named Pal, at the University of Massachusetts, Amherst. He had a ten-page bibliography. Very impressive. The second Mezulis, apparently Pal's brother, was Gabor, CEO of a big Seattle engineering firm that did water mega-projects. If that was Gabor Mezulis in the conference room, what the hell kind of project was he doing with Kamenev and Stiller and Greele?

His telephone rang. It was his boss. "I've got a meeting in Washington, Mal," the Colonel said briskly. "I'll stay over till Wednesday, see a couple of old friends. Do me a favor, take my Monday and Tuesday meetings."

This again, Malcolm thought. "What's cooking in Washington, Nick?"

"Not much," Kamenev said offhandedly. "Just some meeting to grease the wheels for the Northwest contract."

He's lying, Malcolm thought. No wheels need greasing. Is he engineering some secret buyout or what? "What do you want me to do?"

"The mayor wants to hit me up for big bucks for a new stadium — corporate box, plus a cash donation. Don't make any commitments. Talk sports."

"My favorite thing."

The Colonel was immune to the sarcasm. "Do the preliminary stuff with Delta. Figure out if we can make it work."

"You've haven't passed that file over to me yet," Malcolm said. "I don't even know what they want."

"My notes are in my laptop," Kamenev replied. "Download them and wing it. And start getting my files ready for my meeting with the Chinese."

He was going to Singapore in August to meet with senior officers of the People's Liberation Army – Liberation, my ass, Malcolm thought. The PLA had been shopping for major muscle to facilitate a huge rearmament for several years. It was an especially odious contract in Malcolm's view.

"I thought we'd agreed I wasn't going to work on the Chinese sale."

"Sorry, Mal. Priorities. We're not doing Varig any more, so you can find the time. Gotta go." The Colonel hung up.

I'd better get that retirement package soon, Malcolm thought. Before I kill him.

Looking around for Kamenev's laptop, Malcolm spotted a computer case on top of the filing cabinet. It was unfamiliar, extremely sleek, very thin. Kamenev didn't mention this, he thought, as he booted up and entered the usual password – Kamenev's boastful "UNO". Nothing happened. A small logo was flashing in the bottom right-hand corner: "CyberKrypt". What the hell is that? Right, he concluded, angry. Nick's got a new password and he forgot to tell me, for Christ's sake.

He considered for a moment, then entered "CORVETTE". No go. He tried the name of Kamenev's Weimaraner – "HANS" – and the computer shut him down. He swore under his breath and rebooted. This time he tried the name Kamenev had given his jet – "SPEED". Nope. Okay, he thought, let's try a more personal tack. He tried Kamenev's wife – "HELENE". Rejected. "NICK JR". Rejected and shut down. What a royal pain! he thought, rebooting again. Chances were that if he didn't get it right on the third round, the computer wouldn't let him try any more.

Malcolm knew something about Nick Kamenev's background. His grandparents had been white Russians who'd fled to the United States, mortified by a cousin's defection to the Bolsheviks and horrified by the revolution. His father had raised his son to be a mighty Cold Warrior. But Malcolm knew that the real war for Kamenev had been the hot one – Vietnam. It was where they had met. Malcolm had coordinated a rescue of Kamenev and his men while doing duty as a weapons coordinator at Monkey Mountain. Kamenev had made colonel there.

So this time Malcolm entered Kamenev's old call sign from Vietnam – "SARGON I" – and abracadabra, he was in! "Hello Colonel Kamenev," the words on the screen said. "Kindly provide your encrypting key."

"What the hell!" Malcolm said aloud. "What encrypting key?"

"You asking me something?" Cora called from the outer office.

"No, it's okay," Malcolm, suddenly deeply suspicious, called back. "It's nothing." He closed the machine and replaced it on the filing cabinet. Obviously, it was no new substitute for the Colonel's Compaq. He continued to search and found the older, familiar laptop on the couch under a pile of industrial magazines. He returned to his office and attended to business for a couple of hours. Then he called Russell Jefferson at Cyberonics.

The lights were low, a saxophone wailed quietly from overhead speakers and the rain poured down the front window of Jaime's Bar. Russell Jefferson sat across from Malcolm. Fifteen years younger, Jefferson was nevertheless the best male company he had found in Seattle so far, whether on a hike or over a beer.

"Nice threads," said Malcolm, eyeing his friend's cream-colored Italian suit. It fit Russell's tall, graceful body like a glove.

"Thanks," said Russ. "Nice babe."

"Oh?" Malcolm looked around, surprised. "What babe would that be?"

"The one you were with the other night, at the talk."

"That's Geraldine," Malcolm smiled. "We're just friends."

"You're kidding!" Russell's eyebrows rose in wonder. Malcolm shrugged. "Let me know next time she comes over for a just-friends kind of visit." It occurred to Malcolm that an introduction would be a very good idea.

"I will," Malcolm said. "Guess what?"

"You know I hate to guess. Tell."

"Kamenev just dropped the Varig contract and killed Coanda."

"*Say what?*" Russell knew every detail of Malcolm's dream. They'd talked about it endlessly over the seven years they'd been friends. Russ had dreamed with Malcolm, had envied his friend the possibility of actually making some kind of contribution to society in his job.

"You heard me."

"Son of a *bitch*!" Russell said. "When? Why, for Chrissake?"

"Last week," Malcolm replied. "And I don't, for the life of me, know why. Just like that. Of course he's getting so fat on DOD contracts, I suppose he doesn't need it. Still, it doesn't make any sense. Thing's a potential gold mine."

"Jesus, Mal," Russell said with feeling. "What are you going to do?"

"Walk, sooner or later. Decided that much. Got to work out my golden handshake."

"I'm sorry, man. For you, and for the rest of us. I'll be damned!"

Neither man spoke for a moment, a silence to honor the dead. Outside, the rain beat a funereal tattoo on the windows.

"Anyway," Malcolm said at length, "what did you think of that Davidowicz woman's speech the other night?"

"Well, I can't exactly say I enjoyed myself." Russ took a swig of his beer. "Toxic pollution, dying species, water running out, the rich destroying the world and we're all gonna fry like ants under a magnifying glass. But I guess she got most of it right."

"Yeah," Malcolm took a long drink. "I find it very disturbing."

"You are a master of understatement."

"Uh-huh. So, I have a question for you, Russ."

"Shoot."

"What's CyberKrypt?"

Russ gagged on his beer. Wow, Malcolm thought. Whatever it is, he knows. Russ took a deep breath and released it slowly. "Where did you hear about CyberKrypt?"

"If you promise to tell me what you know about it, and we both promise not to discuss this little matter with anyone else, I'll tell you."

"A minute ago we were talking *Apocalypse Now*. What the hell does this have to do with that?" Russ demanded.

"Promise?" Malcolm insisted.

"Yeah, yeah, I promise."

"I saw a logo that said CyberKrypt on a computer screen in Kamenev's office, some brand-new Sony VAIO I've never seen before."

"On a *what*?" said Russ, his voice rising. "You are full of surprises today."

"A Sony VAIO, which I found in Colonel Kamenev's office."

"What the hell was it doing there?"

"Precisely what I was hoping you might be able to tell me."

Russ stared at him. "As it happens, you're a lucky guy, Mal. I am one of only a very few people on this planet in a position to tell you that CyberKrypt is a very special encrypting program. It was A.A.'s flying finger to the National Security State. Once the information is in the program, you don't have the key, the information is dead. Buried. Crypt — get it? A. A. thought it was funny. Hah hah." Russ's voice was utterly mirthless.

"And you worked on it?"

"Co-developed it, pal, with Stiller. As it so happens."

"No kidding. So who's using it?"

"Nobody's using it," Russell said. "The government rejected permission to produce. It's based on 128 bits. Which makes it unbreakable. The government can't break it, it's verboten. Last I saw it, it was sitting in Stiller's office, in a bunch of cardboard boxes on the floor. Another one of his pyrrhic victories, the overweening prick." There was a lot of animus in Russ's voice. "I can't fucking stand that man."

This sentiment was not news to Malcolm. "You never told me about that project," he said.

"Top secret. Which raises the point again: what's it doing in Kamenev's office?"

"Search me. I opened it, got to the second screen, then stopped dead when I couldn't produce the key."

"Well, I guess."

"First screen took a preliminary password on my third try – the Colonel's call sign in Nam, if you can believe it. SARGON I," Malcolm said, deadpan.

Russell's eyes gleamed with delight. "The Babylonian warrior king who strewed more corpses about than Genghis Khan."

"Full marks," Malcolm said, smiling for the first time. Russ guffawed. "You are a pleasure to spend time with, my friend. The very monarch. You working on any other top secret projects?"

"Natch. I'm working with Big Boy on a project to turn human DNA into bar codes. And a few other Brave New World computer-genetic fusion technologies that would curl your hair. Literally. Stiller's personal contribution to evolution. And, as usual, no credit to me."

"*Bar codes?*" said Malcolm. Now his eyes were bulging. "Man, how can you do that shit?"

"How can you sell fighters to the Saudis, baby?" A pause while they looked at each other, each man thinking of his family. "You gonna tell me what's up with CyberKrypt?" Russ said.

So Malcolm filled Russell in. About some business deal Kamenev did not want Malcolm to know about that sounded like it included water. About William Greele, Andrew Stiller and some big-time hydrologist called Gabor Mezulis. About really wanting to find out what the bastards were up to.

"I see," said Russ, alert and eager. "A mystery. What do you want me to do?"

"Well, seeing as how you happen to be in possession of the open sesame technology, any way you could instruct me so I could break into Kamenev's little computer? He's in Washington till Wednesday."

"Forget it," Russ said. "Stiller worked with a series of complicated progressions he favored. I did note them" – Malcolm snorted – "but it could be any combination, and you'd have to know how to rearrange them. You'd get stuck for sure. In fact, he may have used entirely new codes, and then even I wouldn't be able to get in."

"Well, then," said Malcolm, increasingly intrigued but stumped.

"Let's have a look at it," Russell said.

"Excuse me?"

"I've got all the formulae we fooled around with at home. We can try them out. We might not get lucky. Other hand, we might. Let's make a little visit."

"Whoa, Nellie. 'A little visit' is known as breaking and entering. We'd be stepping over the line."

"Way, way over," Russ agreed easily, even happily. "Fucker deserves it."

"Hmm." Malcolm was thoughtful for a moment. "You're prepared to do this? It's a big risk."

Russ's face turned serious. "Let me put it to you this way, Mal," he said. "Socratically, so to speak. How much time do you think it takes a high school teacher to earn two thousand dollars?"

Russell's father was a school caretaker in New Paltz, New York. His mother was a nurse's aide. Far away from the urban ghettos, leaving their families behind, they had raised a boy on wildlife, rocks and lakes. Russ had wanted to be a zoologist, but he'd excelled at computers, and computers were the Yellow Brick Road. After coming first in every subject at the State University of New York, he'd gone west, first to Microsoft, then to Cyberonics, to make his fortune. Now he sent home bags of money to parents he loved but could not bear for the weight of uplift they had placed on his shoulders.

"Don't know," Malcolm replied, looking at the anger and pain in his friend's eyes. "How much?"

"Eleven point five working days, a little over two weeks, makes a hard-working teacher two thousand dollars," Russ said. "And that's a lot more than a lot of people make. Especially black people. On the other hand, it takes a partner at a leading law firm eight point six hours to earn that amount. And it takes Andrew Albert Stiller eight seconds."

"I take your point."

"Do I need to repeat for you how much the arms appropriations have been increased since 9/11 and Iraq? What's happening to black single mothers —"

"No, Russ, you don't."

"Okay, so let's just say that the fact that I'm sitting pretty in Bellevue sending money home so my folks can retire doesn't change the fundamental nature of the power structure. It doesn't confuse me or my loyalties one little bit. So I'd like to get back a little where I can. And the universe has seen fit to present me with this truly remarkable opportunity."

"Okay," Malcolm said.

"You seem very calm."

"I'm crapping my pants."

8

THE April sun was glorious as it penetrated the mullioned windows of the capacious study of William Greele's Georgetown house – a wonder of multi-hued leather furniture and mahogany cabinetry, carefully chosen by Sarah. Greele was in full stride, recruiting key advocates, protectors and participants closely linked to the Administration. George Arlington, senior Republican senator for Nevada, sat next to Burton O'Rourke, senior Republican senator for South Carolina, the longest-serving politician in Congress and a menace to any cause not directly supportive of the rich, the male, the white and the near-dead. They were listening intently. So were Diedrick "Duke" Pulaski, a well-dressed bulldog, the governor of Pennsylvania, and James T. MacFarland, the tall, aristocratic governor of Ohio, Republicans both, friends as well as neighbors.

Greele had already held forth about the causes of water shortages in other parts of the world. "Desertification, salinated and polluted aquifers, glaciers melting like ice-cream cones," he was saying. "The Ganges is a mud-bath, the Jordan is a trickle. Qaddafi is mining the great Saharan aquifer at a rate that will empty it in thirty years. The snowcaps on the major mountain ranges are drying up." The three Amwatco members who had come to back Greele up – Nick Kamenev, Bunting Hurst and Vittorio Massaro (an old friend of Arlington's) – had heard this before. The politicians all looked as though their lunch disagreed with them, but they held their counsel until Greele got to the Mid- and Southwest of the United States.

"Here it is in plain language, gentlemen," he declared. "Since the early part of this century, we have abused our lakes, rivers and aquifers mercilessly."

"Hold it right there, Bill," Ohio's Governor MacFarland said sharply. "That's a dangerous thing to say."

"It's true, Governor," Greele replied. "According to reports from the EPA and the American Geological Study, between 60 and 90 per cent of Midwestern rivers are contaminated – with pesticides, with PCBs, DDT that's persisted twenty years and more, with fertilizers, heavy metals – you name it. There's flagrant pollution in every state. In fact, a 1997 General Accounting Office report claimed that over 40 per cent of your state's polluters regularly violate clean water laws. Not much better in Pennsylvania, is it, Duke?" he asked, turning to Governor Pulaski. "And let's face it George," Greele turned again, looking down on the senator from Nevada, "the city of Las Vegas is the world's biggest waste of water, bar none."

Arlington, Pulaski and MacFarland squirmed.

"You believe all that eyewash about our rivers being polluted, son?" Burton O'Rourke asked contemptuously.

Greele's face turned red. "Don't know how you can deny it, Burton," he said tightly. "When twenty-five million tons of liquid hog shit hit the Horton River in South Carolina two years ago, and flooded the whole region with pig feces." He spat the last two words. "I calculate you made about five million dollars in bribes on that one, close to a quarter a gallon, Burton. Pretty good, I'd say, even for an old shit-hauler like you." The intake of breath around the room was palpable. No one had ever addressed the senator in these terms, or spoken openly of O'Rourke's role, though everyone knew of it.

"And each one of you boys," Greele said, turning to look at the three others, "has played some serious hanky-panky with the Federal Energy Regulatory Commission or the Bureau of Reclamation; not to speak of deals you've done with an alphabet soup of other government agencies that deal in subsidies for industry, to protect your big polluters. It's all there, you know," Greele said, somewhat superciliously, "in the public record. In departmental reports and government accounts and court records. If you know how to read them. Which my staff do. Plus I have my personal sources of information."

The politicians found Greele's smug delivery more terrifying than his anger. They exchanged dark looks. Then Governor Pulaski exploded.

"For the love of God, Bill," he cried. "It's the cost of doing business, and you know it! You're paying a building full of lawyers a large fortune every year to deal with the suits from the run-offs from your factories and fields. We're all running interference for you, here in Washington or in our state capitals. So what the hell are you talking about?"

"I'm not judging or laying blame, Duke," Greele said placatingly. "And I very much appreciate the help each and every one of you has given me in the past. I'm just saying we can't afford to buy our own propaganda, gentlemen. We have to get real. And the plan I propose is the way we do it."

The Senator's old eyes flared and his lips opened in preparation for an attack but Governor Arlington spoke soberly from his corner. "Back off Burton," he said. "Let's hear what Bill's got to say."

Thus invited, Greele laid out the consortium's plans and the kind of support that would be needed in DC. He described the complex but generous manner of their proposed remuneration, the place that waited for them on the Amwatco board when they left their political jobs. They listened quietly and carefully.

"Excuse me, Bill," asked James MacFarland, whose state had had seven summers of drought. "I'm no expert. But isn't it expensive to ship Canadian water?"

"No," Greele replied. "Not anymore. Relatively speaking, that is. And 'relatively' is the key word. Relative to need, relative to the costs of other sources, what is expensive now will look reasonable in three years. And after that, well ... within the decade, when capital costs are paid down, it's pure profit."

There was an absorbed silence.

"I thought desalination was the coming thing," said Senator Arlington. "Lots of new facilities being put in in Florida, Atlanta's thinking about it, California –"

"Uh-huh. You'll hear people telling you desalination can be done for about a dollar per cubic meter, and even less, down the line," Greele said.

"That's right."

"Those are the optimists," Greele said dismissively. "'Down the line' is the operative phrase. In reality, desalination technologies are still prohibitively expensive, not least because they're so energy intensive."

"But if they're developed –"

"Listen, George," Greele cut him off. "Desalination is a big fat *maybe*. We do the deal right in Quebec, we rely on bottling and the pipeline and shipping – tried and true technologies. We'll do it better, faster, and cheaper than any desalination project. Nothing theoretical about it."

"I'll check into it. If you're right, I'll support you."

"Can you tell us," Duke Pulaski said, "why this plan is better than the pipelines on the drawing board from Alberta and British Columbia? The President is very interested in those."

"I can," Greele replied. "Two crucial things. First, there's a lot more pristine water to be had in concentrated bulk in Quebec – big parts of Alberta and BC are in water-negative status already. That's *really* important. Second, unlike the provinces of the Canadian West, because of the French thing, there's a political firewall around Quebec." He elaborated on his theory.

"If everything you say is true," Arlington said at length, "we'll put it to the White House. Why wouldn't the President jump at it? His people are all tied up with oil but they know we need water. Why not?" His colleagues nodded, though Burton O'Rourke's mouth was still puckered in disapproval. "But you'll have to get a champion in Cabinet too."

"I'm thinking Jason Stamper," Greele said.

"That's good," Arlington agreed. "Yeah, that's good."

The cleaner's overalls with which Malcolm had supplied Russ to walk the halls of Skypoint after hours covered his midnight-blue Patagonia gear. Two layers of clothing plus high anxiety had Russ sweating like a pig as he labored over the little laptop in Colonel Kamenev's office. Malcolm had closed the outer door but left the door from Cora's office open slightly so they could hear if anyone approached. Russ was trying and retrying long sequences of numbers and letters from a piece of paper.

Both of them were as jumpy as hot oil on a skillet. Russ coaxed the little computer, crooning and cajoling. The sweat was pouring off Malcolm too, every nerve screaming. But on the ninth try Russ finally scored, and scored big. A few files were nestled in a folder called "Water".

"Open it, open it," Malcolm said impatiently.

"Just a minute, Mal," Russ said. "Let me check the passwords. Then we can go back in from my place."

"You audacious devil. But hurry, I'm jumping out of my skin here."

Russ punched in keys, and arcane symbols came and went until he said, "Got it! Okay, let's take a look." Russ clicked on the big file. "Jesus. What the hell is this?"

They scrutinized the screen. It was a memo from W.E.G. – "William Ericsson Greele, probably," Malcolm said – to Amwatco, evidently nine men, among whom A. A. Stiller and Nick Kamenev and Gabor Mezulis were listed. The memo was in the form of a spreadsheet, with price tags attached to items such as bottling plants, a pipeline, a port, a bridge, tanker trucks, roads – clearly the components of a humongous project. The bottom line said fifteen point four billion dollars, and the launch date for the first phase was the following April.

"Fuck a duck," Russ said, scanning the screen. "Three bottling plants. Seven extraction sites. The Pipmuacan Reservoir, wherever the hell that is. There's, what … nine diversion dams and canals. And roads, roads, roads. This is incredible! A tanker loading station east of Tadoussac – I know Tadoussac, we used to camp around there, watch the whales."

"Holy Hannah," Malcolm breathed. Russ scrolled down to page two.

"Check it out. They've got a pipeline route here," Russ said, wiping the sweat from his eyes. "Gonna start at a place called Alma and the Chibougamou Preserve, go through the Laurentian Provincial Park, skirt Quebec City and cross the St Lawrence on a dedicated bridge. Dedicated bridge! Jesus, think of the bucks! Then through southern Quebec, to Vermont, New York, Pennsylvania, Ohio, where it'll branch –"

"Hold it, Russ," Malcolm said. Some instinct pushed him closer to the window. What he saw raised the hair on the back of his neck. Twin halos from a pair of high headlights approached down the drive, and the Colonel's Navigator pulled up like a dark blue shark at the big doors below.

"Holy shit! Kamenev's here!" Malcolm killed the big Maglite, and turned on Russ's pencil-beam flashlight.

"You said he'd be back tomorrow!" Russ was already scrambling.

"That's what he told me!"

"Hold that light still while I pack up, for Chrissakes!" Russ's hands were rapidly pulling cords and packing the case. "What's the plan?"

"Run for my office, code three seven three seven," said Malcolm, holding the tiny flashlight with his right hand, and steadying the case with his left. His mouth was parched. "It's way down the hall to the right. Name's on the door. Hell, run for the men's room. Pray we don't meet security. Wait for him to leave. If we get separated, meet me in my office."

They were breathing hard as Russ finished packing and snapped the case closed. Malcolm snuffed the flashlight and Russ made toward the filing cabinet, but in the dark he tripped over the corner of the desk, stifled a cry of pain, and the computer went flying to the floor. Both men cursed and got down on their hands and knees. Malcolm had just put his hand on the case when he heard the outer office door opening, saw a light go on in Cora's office, sensed a rush of air entering the room and felt something cold, wet and hard press against his throat. He nearly passed out, then realized from the aroma and the enthusiastic panting that it was Kamenev's dog.

"Jesus, Hans, you old son of a gun," he whispered to the Weimaraner, who wagged his cropped tail in the dark, pleased to find his friend down on the floor, ready to play. Malcolm hissed to Russ, "There's a closet in the cloakroom through the doors, next to the can!" Russ went. Malcolm reached into his pocket, found the remnants of a Milk-Bone, and threw it to the far side of the room. "Go get it," he whispered to Hans. Hans complied. Malcolm heard a crunch. He stood up, put the computer on the filing cabinet, then ran for the bathroom himself. He pressed himself against the wall just as the Colonel burst through, framed in blinding light from the outer office. He hit the overheads. Godzilla enters, Malcolm thought. I'm screwed.

"Jesus H. Christ. What's this goddamn door doing open again?" Kamenev complained aloud. "Can't that girl remember to ..." his muttering trailed off. "Hans, what you got there, boy?"

Totally skewered, thought Malcolm. The dog is gonna come right over here. See Dad, it's Uncle Mal! Or Kamenev's going to decide to take a leak. No, he's going to work here for three hours, then he'll take a leak. Malcolm held his breath and stood very still. He heard the thud of something landing on a table, the rustle of documents, and the whoosh of a case being swept from a surface, some unidentified motion, then, "Come on, Hans, let's get the fuck out of here." A door slammed, then another one, and Kamenev, single-minded and swift, was gone. Hope he doesn't notice the laptop's still warm, Malcolm thought, as his knees gave out and he sank to the floor.

*

Somewhere in the wilds of suburbia, Malcolm and Russ ordered coffee and apple fritters. Never had sugar, flour, and fat tasted so delicious, or caffeine felt so wonderful. It steadied their shaking hands.

"I felt like the kids in the kitchen in Jurassic Park," said Malcolm, "with the velociraptors chasing them. Thank God one of them was a dog."

They looked at each other solemnly across the table. Then they smiled. Then they laughed and whooped and high-fived, drawing stares of sullen disbelief from the depressed denizens of the night staring glumly at donut crumbs at scattered tables. Russ pulled out several crumpled sheets of paper.

"We've got it, buddy," said Russ, putting the notes in the center of the table. "But what the hell is it?"

"Well," Malcolm said, rubbing his chin, reading, "looks to me like a plan to get gazillions of gallons of Quebec water down to the US. Is that what it looks like to you?"

"That's exactly what it looks like."

"I've heard nothing about this. You?"

"Not a thing. You'd think it would be all over the media."

"To say the very least. Talk about drinking Canada Dry. But is it illegal?"

"I don't know. Why would it be?"

"I don't know either. But why all the secrecy?"

They considered the conundrum. "Maybe it's not illegal. But I bet it's sensitive as hell politically," said Malcolm.

"Ah," Russ said. "Maybe they want to put all the pieces in place before they go public. Minimize dissent. Strike swiftly and outflank the environmental opposition."

"How can someone organize against something they don't know about?" Malcolm responded.

Russ looked at Malcolm and wiggled his eyebrows.

"What are you suggesting? A little brown-envelope action? We have no documents. Just your notes."

"Why not? I've got everyone's password."

"Oh boy."

"We should be able to hack in. Let's give it a try tomorrow night. I think we should go in as A. A."

"Unbelievable. You're unbelievable, you know that? Talk about insult to injury. Correction," Malcolm paused. "Sweet revenge."

"On the nose. Whatever I get, we can send it out."

"To – ?"

Russ thought for a moment. "That eco-Justice woman," he said. "Davidowicz."

Malcolm didn't reply, though his heart was suddenly pounding.

"She's the one, all right," Russ continued. "Second thought, don't send the stuff, man. Make us both too vulnerable. I mean, you don't know her. She doesn't know you. Take a few days off and go to Washington. Tell her about it face to face. Hand it off and throw it to the environmental winds. To mix my metaphors."

With a pounding heart, Malcolm made a pretext to see Nick Kamenev the next day, to determine whether any damage had been done. He heard Cora's voice in Kamenev's office. "Will you lay off, already!" she was shouting. "I locked it. I told you three times I did!" Malcolm froze. Cora's tone of voice was indignant at the accusation of negligence. It also sounded like Cora addressed the Colonel in a less-than-secretarial manner when they were alone. Check, Malcolm thought.

"As it happens, Cora, you didn't," the Colonel said definitively as Malcolm stepped into the room. Cora was standing there, arms akimbo, furious. Malcolm asked a question about the Saudi contract, thinking it wise to bring the dangerous subject to a close. Cora stalked out of the room, and that was the end of it. Apparently it had not occurred to the Colonel that his office could have been burglarized. Thank God we locked Cora's door, Malcolm thought. Kamenev quickly gathered the papers he'd been looking through into his briefcase. They attended to business.

At his desk that afternoon, Malcolm did a web search for water extraction and export projects in North America. He was able to retrieve information on proposed pipelines and bottling and diversion projects from as far away as Alaska and Newfoundland and as close as northern California and Florida. Nothing on Quebec. He put some keywords relating to Quebec and water into Google, and still drew a blank. Then he browsed various Quebec government sites, the sites of environmental organizations in Canada and the US, including eco-Justice Canada and USA, the Global Watch Institute, the Sierra Club and the River Alliance. Lots of stuff on water, nada on Quebec. He searched the *New York Times* and *Washington Post*, then a number of geographical journals and newsletters. He struck out with every one. He could hardly wait for the evening.

Russ lived in Bellevue. So when he got home, Malcolm invited Bonnie to ride with him in the Subaru, ignoring Clyde's dirty looks. It was a misty night, and he picked up a pizza and drove over the bridge. Russ greeted his friend and accepted the dog's licks with good grace, then went to get plates and napkins. He lived in a small house, built on stilts, overlooking Lake Washington with a spectacular view of the city in the distance. Malcolm followed him through the open living area to a large curved desk fitted into the far corner. There were long trestle tables on either side, loaded up with enough hardware to sink a battleship. Russ gave Malcolm a slice of pizza, and tore up some pieces on a napkin for the dog. She was his forever.

"Let's go," said Russ, throwing the switch on a sleek tower under his desk. A faint, powerful humming filled the air. The dog cocked her ears. "Okay. Let's see if there's new traffic." Russ watched the monitor and held his hands over the keyboard like a concert pianist. Malcolm reached out to restrain him.

"Hold it, Grand Master Flash," Malcolm said. "What if you plug us in to some corporate cyber cabal and leave indelible electronic footprints they can trace back to you?"

"Dammit, Mal, I designed the thing. I know what I'm doing. Okay?"

"All right, all right."

Russ had his notes from the previous evening laid out next to his mouse pad, and started punching a complex sequence of keys. It didn't take long.

"Eureka!" Russ bounced up and down, still punching keys. "I'm in! Well, actually A. A.'s in. He just doesn't know it."

"You get the prize. So?"

"So here's what we got a look at in Kamenev's office last night. Let's print it out." He sent the command. "And something new. Look."

Malcolm read the screen:

MEMORANDUM

TO: **AMWATCO MEMBERS**
FROM: **W.E.G.**

Washington meeting satisfactory. All parties signed on. Proceed as planned.

"Well, no names, but looks like they've got some new muscle," Russ said.

"Yeah. So do you reckon we should share this news? Maybe the environmentalists in Quebec already know all about it?"

"I emphatically doubt it, Mal," Russ said tartly. "You don't get overheard on CyberKrypt. And you don't use it to communicate information that's in the public domain."

9

NICOLE Verlaan-Lalonde hated writing in English, but not as much as her Québécois colleagues, who felt politically entitled to hate the language of their oppressors. So invariably it was she who had to wrestle with illogical grammar and technical vocabulary when English was required. In her sealed, over-heated office on Rue Laurier, she had a splitting headache from the afternoon's mad scramble to get a grant application in to the Pew Foundation in New York. At five o'clock she threw the dictionary against the wall and shouted, "I want to go home!" to an empty office, then packed up her briefcase and left.

Outdoors, a spring breeze tugged at her coat and scarf. She saw snowdrops and crocuses, white, blue, mauve, and yellow, peeking through the last patches of grizzled ice on garden plots. *Ah mon Dieu*, but the winter here is long, Nicole thought. And it could snow again at any minute. In the fields around the big old house where she grew up, southeast of Bordeaux, the poppies would be massed in crimson waves, cyclamen and iris and narcissus growing wild, the sun a honey blessing in a sky of azure blue. *Merde*, it was a lot to give up for Serge.

They had met fifteen years ago, when she, a young research leader on a European Union commission, had made alarming findings about the carcinogenic effects of persistent organic pollutants. Her delegation visited all the capitals, meeting with senior staff in ministries of health, industry and environment. Serge was an Assistant Undersecretary of Industry in Paris.

Like her Dutch father, Nicole was tall and blonde. Like her French mother, she was vivacious and beautiful. Serge was enchanted. He was dark, earthy, highly intelligent, unusually gutsy for a bureaucrat. She recalled with pain how magically they had clicked. He helped her to strategize better in seeking official responses to her research; she sensitized him to health and environment issues, and provided astute advice on ministerial machinations. When the time came for Serge to return to Quebec, Nicole had come with him, eventually building Quebec City into the chief North American site for her worldwide POPs study. Serge enthusiastically plotted with her to get the funding and staff, and she had graciously presided over many a power-dinner as he moved up the ladder to Deputy Minister. It had been very exciting at times. But, increasingly, it had become highly fraught.

About five years ago, new findings shifted the focus of Nicole's research to the endocrine and neurological disruption brought about by trace levels of poisonous chemicals. She became increasingly concerned about the implications for resource and industrial production in the continental northeast. Serge, on the other hand, was working as hard as he could to bring industry to Quebec, and Quebec was competing hard for capital against the likes of Myanmar, China and Vietnam. Small arguments had begun to flare.

Then Serge told Nicole the government was planning to subsidize a big PCB-producing processing plant. All the small disagreements they'd been having coalesced into one huge, toxic blowup. When the explosion was over, they found themselves standing on opposite sides of an ugly, jagged crack in their marriage. Just one or two more fights like that and it would turn into a yawning chasm that neither would be able to bridge. They had been very, very careful since then with how they spoke to one another, what they chose to say. But they found themselves disagreeing more and more frequently, more and more fundamentally. Nicole had an affair in France. It lasted for three visits, then she realized that it didn't solve anything, and that she still loved Serge deeply.

Now Serge's silences, his physical withdrawal, his peculiar telephone calls, distracted looks, all showed Nicole that the problem had moved into a new phase. Not knowing what was far more disconcerting than the substance of any matter he was refusing to confide. Or so she believed.

The matter was very much on her mind as she removed her snow-soaked shoes, called to Serge, heard nothing. She poured a glass of wine and called his private number at the Ministry. He answered right away.

"*Mon petit chou,*" she said. "Still there?"

"Oh yes," he said wearily. "Problems with the goat-cloning experiment in St Zotique. They're behind schedule, and need a couple of million. They say they've perfected the technology, they just need another few months to actually bring the animals to life. Bonafabrica's going to buy them if they do."

"Serge," Nicole said, boggled and sad, "there are times I do not believe what you have to do for your beloved Quebec."

"It's a technology that will help in the manufacture of useful drugs, Nicole," he said both sharply and beseechingly. She was silent. Let's not go down that road again, they both thought. "Anyway, the company needs a bailout. I'm stuck here making calls for the time being, I'll be home around nine. And I've got a meeting about this in Montreal tomorrow."

Nicole hung up. She didn't believe him. A long, difficult moment ensued. While she had never barred Serge from her study, she assumed without question that he would never rummage among her things to spy on her. She had accorded him the same respect. But finally, because his secrecy was a betrayal, she began to search his office for clues to his behavior, and for the bag of maps and charts she had found – and been so surprised by – a week ago.

She opened his closet. The plastic bag was gone. She searched filing cabinets, bookshelves, baskets. Nothing. She went upstairs and looked through the boxes along the shelves of his bedroom armoire, then behind the linens near the bathroom. She searched the whole house. Eventually she found what she was seeking in a cedar chest, in the basement next to the old octopus furnace. A malevolent treasure hunt, she thought angrily, as she took the papers to the laundry room and spread them on the folding table.

"*Mais qu'est-ce que c'est?*" she said aloud after a few minutes, then "*Mon Dieu!*" several times, each imprecation louder and higher, as she read. How could Serge possibly do this, she thought, reading a thin, plastic-jacketed report with horror. At length, she gathered the papers and replaced them in the chest, not caring whether they showed evidence of disturbance. She was going to have words with Serge about this.

But she had something to do first. She went upstairs, picked up the telephone. Cradling her forehead with one hand, she dialed Sylvie Lacroix in Montreal.

"Nicole!" Sylvie's affection for her friend was evident when she answered, but it didn't offset Nicole's black mood.

66

Recounting her home situation with Serge, she felt as though she was at the bottom of a deep well with slippery sides and no way to climb out. "He doesn't want to know about the latest study on IQ retardation and attention deficit disorders from industrial pollutants and pesticides," she told Sylvie. "He cannot tolerate the contradictions." She paused. "Neither can I, anymore. Can you imagine, he says he's working late tonight searching for a subsidy for that company that's cloning goats with human genes for pharmaceuticals. And I'm supposed to just sit there and say, yes *chéri*, good for you *chéri*, I'll keep your dinner warm."

"Nicole, that's horrible." Both women were active in their opposition to cloning. They had originally met at a Green rally at the Sorbonne in Paris, Sylvie having convinced her father, a Montreal lawyer, that she was as much entitled to a French education as her brothers.

"I will have to do something," said Nicole. "Soon. I can't stand it. Suddenly I'm living alone. Last night he fell asleep on the couch in his study. We've barely touched since I've been home."

"Nicole, you know you can stay with us, anytime, if you need a place to go, to think." Sylvie had returned to Canada and taken law exams. She became interested in environmental law, then international trade law as it affected the environment, and now she both practiced and taught her specialties. She was married to a television producer and had a young daughter. Sylvie Lacroix was horrendously overworked. Some days, she thought she would crack from the strain. But she invited Nicole anyway.

"I love him," Nicole wept. "I don't know what's happened to him. We used to plot together to see what we could accomplish. Now he just succumbs to *necessities*," Nicole hissed the word. "That's his favorite word. It's like a drug he can't resist. Oh God ..." Sylvie didn't know what to say, but Nicole began again. For she had realized that before her urge to protect her marriage got the better of her conscience, she had to tell Sylvie of her discovery. Sylvie was a board member of eco-Justice Canada. Nicole told her what she'd found.

There was a grim silence when she finished. Nicole could feel Sylvie's shock.

"Nicole," Sylvie said at last, "it's hard to credit the extent of this. Even for an old cynic like me. Are you sure it's going to happen?"

"I'm not sure of anything except what I read. I told you what it said. I don't know at what stage this whole thing is, but apparently they're planning to take it to the Assembly in the fall."

"What, in six months? Why has no one heard of this?" Sylvie cried, anger and a hint of desperation in her voice. Nicole knew what Sylvie was thinking: Oh no, not another battle royal.

"I don't know. But the secrecy is very disturbing."

"Extremely." Sylvie paused. "So what do you wish me to do with this information?"

"Take it to eco-Justice, I don't know. Take it Eau NO, take it to Denis Lamontagne!" Lamontagne was an environmental reporter at *Le Soleil*, to whom both she and Sylvie had given information in the past. "Take it to someone who will know what to do about it," said Nicole in despair. "I can't do it myself. It's as much as my marriage is worth."

"*Entendu.*"

"And you won't tell anyone of the source of your information."

"Of course not," Sylvie assured her forcefully. "Don't worry. But someone *must* know something about this. It's far too big to remain secret."

High over the middle-class villas of Outremont, up winding streets where gardens full of new daffodils and grape hyacinths were dappled by the young leaves of sugar maples, the houses grew ever larger and farther apart. At the summit stood the mansions of Québécois high society, facing east and north toward the great province. On the other side of Mount Royal, past the park and the old cemetery in Westmount, the grand mansions of the *maudits Anglais* had lost many a resident in the last forty years, as their owners joined the migration to Toronto. In the heights of Outremont, the paint was fresh and occupancy high.

Roch Vezina's house lay at the end of the highest street. Its back gardens joined the parklands so that they seemed to go on forever. Vezina was the owner of Nordicon Ltée, master of the great dams and endless power grids of Quebec, bringer of water to the Arabian Desert, stiller of floods in the tropics. He was handsome in a bland sort of way, self-made and flamboyant with boundless energy for skiing, tennis, sex, and epic projects.

In the cathedral-sized study, Vezina was meeting with Serge Lalonde, Guy-François Langevin, head of the Caisse Laurier and guardian of half of the savings of the people of Quebec, the senior bureaucrat Pierre Gosselin and the very junior one, Helder Pereira. Above a cherry cabinet with a well-stocked bar hung photographs of Vezina with kings and presidents and movie stars. Framing a huge tigerskin rug, four caramel leather couches faced each other over a monkey-wood coffee table. A chafed silver humidor, two marble ashtrays the size of dinner plates, and a stout, old-fashioned, silver lighter sat proudly in the center. The air was blue with the smoke from Vezina's large Havana cigar and Serge's cigarettes.

Lalonde had chosen Vezina because he was clearly the best-qualified major contractor in Quebec. He had chosen Langevin because the banker wanted to modernize and go global while bypassing the hated Toronto Bay Street banks. Langevin had been instrumental in urging the Parti Québécois to bring the Canadian NASDAQ exchange to Montreal, to invest heavily in the high-tech, biotech and aeronautics industries. But as one of the oldest banks in Quebec, his institution also had tremendous depth in resource extraction – the bread and butter of the non-urban Quebec economy.

"*Messieurs*," Lalonde said, "you may be aware that for some years a case concerning the export of water was held up in the British Columbia courts. San Francisco's Southbelt Properties sued the BC government for reneging on a deal to export half a billion acre-feet of water to California. Recently their suit failed. Southbelt will challenge under NAFTA. When that happens, Ottawa – I stress *Ottawa* – will be compelled to address the enormous question of the Americans' thirst for Canadian water. And the Prime Minister and his gang of thieves will decide the terms." For a moment there was respectful silence at the dreadful prospect.

"It's imminent," he continued. "The Americans are very thirsty already, and it's going to get a lot worse. Another American firm has entered negotiations with Newfoundland. There are two plans in front of the BC and Alberta governments for water export. And the new Prime Minister wants to do business with that *cochon* of an American president. If we do not define our own terms for the exploitation of *our* water – and *soon* – the PM will deal with the Americans." Serge paused and then added, "The group that has approached me." The two businessmen stared at him.

"William Ericsson Greele – you know Greele Life Industries? – Greele and his consortium want to export two and a half billion acre-feet of Quebec water to the United States over the next ten years. They believe they can make a mutually beneficial collaboration between themselves, the Quebec government and certain 'local partners'. That would be you, if you're interested."

"*Mais, oui!*" Vezina practically leapt from the sofa. Langevin followed with "*Bien sûr!*" He loosened his tie and licked his red, rather fleshy lips until they were shiny. Then both men hurled an avalanche of questions at Lalonde.

"Can we assume Pierre's approval by his presence?" Roch Vezina turned to Gosselin, whom he knew well. Gosselin nodded and uttered some brief words of reassurance. "Good," Vezina said, "since we can also assume he has carefully scoped out the plans. Which I would like to see right now."

Serge spread a huge map on the table and pulled out a report of several pages. "Before we discuss nuts and bolts, however," he said, "I think it's important that you hear Mr. Pereira's thoughts on the possible dangers of the project."

Helder Pereira, in his chinos and short-sleeved checked shirt, was very nervous about the short presentation he had been asked by Lalonde to make. Gosselin had advised Lalonde to cut Pereira loose. But Lalonde respected the young hydrologist's judgment, and he wanted some independent counsel and a clarification of certain issues. He wanted to ensure that some ground was laid for pushing back on environmental considerations if need be later on.

He nodded to Pereira. Helder's throat was parched, but he finally croaked, "With our own water levels lower than they've been in a hundred years, *messieurs*, I am not at all sure that the degree of extraction currently suggested is, ah ... sustainable."

An uncomfortable silence gripped the room. "It's perfectly sustainable," said Pierre Gosselin irritably, "if done properly."

"I, ah, begging your pardon, Monsieur Gosselin, really, I am not sure that is true. Let me explain." Helder painfully stuttered out his objections, one by one. His little speech evoked not a word from Vezina or Langevin or Gosselin when he had done.

"Thank you, Helder," Lalonde said when the silence became uncomfortable. "I appreciate your honesty. You needn't stay for the rest of the meeting." Thank God, Helder thought, backed out of the study, flew down the staircase, and burst out of the house, taking in huge gulps of air when the doors had closed behind him. Oh shit, he thought, what have I gotten myself into.

"Gentlemen," Serge turned to the group. "While we will surely bow to Monsieur Gosselin's superior judgment, I thought it important that you hear these reservations. We shall have to attend carefully to environmental considerations as we go along." He received a chorus of placatory harrumphs in response.

Mindful as always of listeners, Sylvie Lacroix placed several calls to Quebec City from a colleague's office down the hall from her own. As generally as possible, she queried a lawyer in Industry, Trade and Technology, an assessment officer in Environment, a hydrologist in Quebec Hydro, an engineer in Natural Resources. No one knew anything about any plan for bulk exports of water. Disturbed, she placed a call to an unlisted number in Toronto.

"Hello, Sylvie, you legal terror," said James Amanopour affectionately. "How are you?"

"Thank you, I am as well as my schedule permits. And you?" She could see his cinnamon-cream complexion and liquid brown eyes as she spoke. She had witnessed grown women, accomplished and happily married, unconsciously start to pant when they stood next to him. He was as gracious and playful as his job as Executive Director of eco-Justice Canada allowed.

"James, I need some information, but on a secure line."

"All right," he said. "Give me your number, I'll call you right back." He hung up, took the elevator down six storys from the office and stepped into a telephone booth on Queen Street. "What's up?" he said when Sylvie answered.

"Do you know anything about plans for a major water export project in Quebec, the Lac St-Jean region, northeast of there?"

Amanopour was surprised. "BC, Alberta, Newfoundland, yes. Quebec, no. What's this?"

"I'm not sure. But a reliable … informant, let's say, has just told me that the PQ is negotiating an unbelievable project. Huge. Bottling plants, shipping, a *pipeline*, if you can believe it. To the US. If it's true, why doesn't anyone know anything about it? But I've checked in Quebec City and drawn a complete blank."

"It's news to me. Huge *and* secretive? That's not good. I'll investigate and get back to you."

"Please. But given the sensitivity of the identity of the informant, do it without letting on what I've told you, okay? For the time being."

"Will do."

"*Salut*," Sylvie said.

"*Ciao*."

10

BERENDT Vogel was nursing a brandy, gazing out over the Fifth Avenue skyline from the balcony of his Central Park West apartment – a flawless art deco restoration resplendent with his beautifully hung collection of Klees, Kandinskys and de Chiricos. Vogel was waiting for Bill Greele to come and finalize the financing for the project. Later he had a date with a Columbia computer science professor with a mind like Einstein and a body like a porn star. Yet he did not feel the usual thrill.

He was weighed down by troubling strategic questions for Bonafabrica. He'd pushed very hard into biotechnology in the late nineties, just like Novartis and Monsanto and GenSysCo, and was, at this moment, in negotiations with a small firm near Montreal to buy a cloning method that promised to overcome some of the persistent unforeseen problems. He'd pushed hard into xenotransplantation, matching Novartis's hundred million dollar budget to breed the better pig. He maintained an expensive cadre of science and computer nerds to mine the Human Genome Project. And he'd sunk big resources into botanical genetic engineering, working with Greele's Techniplant, to launch a huge new line of "nutriceuticals". Personally, he thought the whole strategy brilliant and comprehensive and thoroughly twenty-first century.

But instead of welcoming these heroic inventions, Europeans, *his own people*, had turned paranoid en masse. First, those stupid, filthy Brits, with their mad cow disease. And then the revelations of that cursed Hungarian Arpad Pusztai in Scotland, doing research for Monsanto, for Christ's sake – claiming genetically modified potatoes could damage the immune system! Then that bastard Wilmut, coming out and saying that all those aborted clones, those obese and prematurely aging clones, indicated that cloning might not work after all.

The Greens were cleaning up on the continent. They'd won compulsory labeling of food, and now they were going for outright bans on the most promising new organisms. Their whinging "experts" were on the news, long-haired morris dancers were pulling up experimental petunias, the supermarket chains were telling suppliers they wouldn't stock their stuff if it contained GMOs. Public health doctors were blathering on about cross-species disease transmission. And eco-Justice and the World Wildlife Fund and every other environmental organization was screaming to put genetic safeguards into WTO treaties.

Berendt Vogel put his drink down and massaged his temples. God in heaven, he thought. Has everyone taken leave of their senses? Until this summer he had hoped that he might win acceptance of GMO crops in the US, then use trade law to impose them on the rest of the world. But even here, several food chains had gone GMO-free. Thank God Americans had been diverted by those crazy Arabs. Nevertheless, Vogel badly needed some insurance.

The buzzer sounded, and the doorman announced Mr Greele and Mr Hurst. While they were on their way up, Mr Massaro arrived. Soon, the four men were sitting around the Alvar Alto dining room table, reviewing documents.

"We've got our game plan," said William Greele. "We need ten billion from our side for the first phase, maybe ten and a half. Quebec companies get the lion's share of the on-site construction contracts, say 70 per cent, and Quebec banks will finance about 30 per cent of the whole project, bringing the total budget to fifteen billion.

"As long as we own most of the facilities when they're done, and have strong controlling interest on the board, we'll achieve our objectives. Consortium companies will still get paid for the high-dollar services we provide at the planning, drawing and supervisory stages. Plus we're positioned to compete with Vivendi, Suez, Thames, Danone, Coca-Cola if water can be privatized in Quebec itself. Plus access to the rest of Canada and the US eventually. Plus, of course, the profits." Satisfied nods communicated everyone's approval.

"The meetings in Washington went very well," Greele continued. Bunting Hurst and Vittorio Massaro remembered the remarkable moment when the imagined stench of twenty-five million tons of liquid pig feces had hung over the room and smiled. "Okay. Time to commit. What have we got?"

Massaro had conferred with his uncle, the senior family member and a man with a driving need for a place to launder money. He'd promised him at least 18 per cent profit margins and received a huge infusion of cash in exchange. Massaro offered 400 million dollars plus a team of top supervisors to work with Gabe Mezulis and the local people. Greele was pleased.

Next Greele looked to Bernie Vogel. They were facing a lot of the same issues, watching the whole ship of genetic engineering founder in heavy seas. It was a struggle with a still uncertain outcome. Hence he was pleased, if not surprised, that Vogel offered 800 million, half from company coffers, half from his personal fortune. He was covering his corporate behind, Greele thought, and why not?

"Nick is in at 600 million," Greele informed the men, "and A. A. is in at an even one billion. He's got a lot of cash just now. Wilbur's putting in 500 mil plus technical expertise. Rich Franklin's given 250 million plus media support. That brings us to roughly three point five billion dollars. We need eleven billion total for our side. I'll be contributing three and three quarter billion." He paused to let that sink in. It was a great deal of money, even for him, and it had taken some effort to liberate it. But it would make him the largest single shareholder, and that was important. "I'll also collect a little slush fund of contributions from our political friends in Washington. They'll be well rewarded. But for the duration I want them to feel very highly motivated about this project." The others appreciated his point.

Greele turned to Bunting Hurst. It was the moment of truth. Hurst knew it, looking around the room and drawing out the suspense, till Vogel finally exclaimed, "Come on, Bunting! What's your position?"

Greele sensed that Hurst was still holding back and felt his blood pressure begin to rise. An angry flush was starting to creep up from his collar. To have come all this distance, only to be foiled by that fat little self-important –

"Three and a half billion dollars, as promised," Hurst declared. "It's there, along with my personal reputation, and that of my bank. Here's to our great and common success." He lifted his Scarpa coffee cup in a toast in which the others hastily joined. That moment of doubt had made Greele ill with fear. He played me like a violin, he thought savagely. Still, he smiled for appearance's sake. They were in business.

Claire Davidowicz was going crazy in her office, trying to produce a report while fielding all her other responsibilities, when the receptionist buzzed and dubiously told her that some guy who wouldn't give his name but said something about a Miss Knight's School for Girls was on the line wanting to talk to her. She straightened up. Handsome Mr Audubon from Seattle? She had not forgotten him, their conversation, her moment of shining hope and then her embarrassing outburst. It was the only time in living memory she could remember mentioning her old school. But he was calling anonymously. "Put him through, Troy," she said.

"Whatever you say, Ms D," the receptionist replied.

"Thanks for taking this call, Ms Davidowicz," said Malcolm, "spy versus spy notwithstanding. But I have something important to discuss with you and I'm sure you will understand my caution."

The last words were spoken slowly and deliberately. He has something he doesn't want to share with whoever might be listening, she thought. He knows the government, so why shouldn't he be at least as prudent as we are? Equally, he could be a nutcase agent provocateur setting me up. But such a nice-looking nutcase. "All right," she said. She felt glad to be speaking to him again.

"I'd like to meet with you," Malcolm proposed, hoping he didn't sound one-tenth as nervous as he felt. "At your convenience sometime next week, if possible, to tell you about something important I've recently learned."

"Something that concerns me or eco-Justice?" she asked.

"Something that concerns the environmental health of this continent."

"I see. Something very weighty."

"Very. I can come to Washington."

"I'll be in New York most of next week," she said, "at an NGO conference on endocrine disrupters."

"I can come to New York," he said. "If you can find the time."

She considered the prospect. "All right," she agreed, intrigued. "Come on Friday, a week today. Things will be winding down. Can we make arrangements by phone now, or do we need to be more devious?"

"I'm sure it's overkill, but for the time being, let's use caution. I'll stay at the Wellington, on Seventh at Fifty-fifth. I'll be there by mid-morning. Can you get a note to me there?"

"Why not?" She spoke with nonchalance, but could feel her heart beating.

One week later in New York, at the peak of lunch hour, El Miro was crammed. Malcolm made his way down the stairs from street level and searched the sunken outdoor terrace, then scanned the front room. He nudged his way farther in through the din of the crowd and blaring jazz, looked into the back room and recognized Claire Davidowicz sitting on the far banquette. She was leaning over the table, her body tense. The back of the booth obscured her interlocutor. She was speaking rapidly and she looked angry.

Malcolm was hesitant to interrupt, and stepped back outside. He waited five minutes, watching the New York flora and fauna in wonder, then went back in with as much purpose as he could, intending Davidowicz to see him. As he pulled up to the table the cacophony reached its peak and subsided as it will from time to time and he heard her say furiously, "...ever, under any circumstances condone it."

"Ms Davidowicz?" he said. Her face was pale, and two hot circles burned on her cheeks. She looked up at him. "I can see you're busy, would you like me to come back in an hour or so?"

Davidowicz was flustered, but she rapidly refocused. "Oh, Mr ... no, not at all! How do you do? Please sit down. My friend here was just about to leave." She turned to face her companion. "Weren't you?" she said icily. Brrr, thought Malcolm. The two men looked at each other. Nearly blew my last name, Malcolm was thinking. Glad she caught it.

"Um, Malcolm, meet Jeffrey," Davidowicz said awkwardly, introducing a big man with dark-blonde hair and a ruddy complexion. He had broad shoulders and powerful limbs and wore a denim shirt, jeans, and cowboy boots. Not exactly a New York native.

Malcolm reached out his hand.

"Howdy," said the other man, accepting it but making no move to leave.

"Jeff is here for the conference," said Davidowicz. "He collaborates with people to monitor the occurrence of hermaphroditic frogs west of the Mississippi, and up in the southern regions of the Canadian Prairie Provinces. Isn't that right, Jeff?"

"One of the things I do," he allowed, sulking.

"What else do you do?" Malcolm asked.

"Most of the time I work with the Canada–US Wolf Release Program," Jeff said proudly. Ah, that's more like it, thought Malcolm. Wouldn't want to spend too much time with those faggot amphibians. He had noticed the killer-wolf identification in a lot of macho men. Evidently it worked for Jeff too.

"Where are you based?" asked Malcolm. He was standing at the side of the table trying to figure out what was going on, and waiting for the boorish man to leave or make room for him. He was getting fed up.

"Montana," Jeff said flatly. "Missoula." Then he turned to Davidowicz and said, "Well. If you change your mind, you know how to reach me." He stood to his impressive height, said, "Nice to meet you," to Malcolm in a tone that implied just the opposite and walked out.

"Please sit down, Malcolm, uh Mr Macpher –"

"Malcolm, please."

"Claire. I'm very sorry about that."

"Are you all right?" he asked.

"Yes," she said, "I guess. Jeff and I go back some way in the environmental movement, and we sometimes disagree. I'm really sorry you got caught there." Some disagreement, Malcolm thought, but let it go. "How was your trip?" she asked. "Would you like to order something to eat?" The restaurant was beginning to empty. The afternoon light played in the stained-glass windows and bathed tables and patrons alike in mellow colors.

"I'm ravenous," he said. "What's good?"

"Everything." She stretched, ran her hands through her hair and rubbed the back of her neck. And gave him a smile. "I'm very curious indeed to hear what you have to tell me." Malcolm smiled back, delighted. Then he assumed a more sober expression, opened his briefcase, and pulled out a slim manila envelope.

"No question, exporting this amount of water will do horrendous damage to the whole ecosystem," Claire said when he'd finished his explanation. "Yes, compared to the American states they want to serve, Quebec's got a lot of water. But not compared to its own traditional levels. I don't understand why I've never heard of this project before. Clearly, they're going after Canada's weak link. Quebec, I mean." She thought for a moment. "I guess they want to buy the land more or less stealthily. Then, if they have to, use Chapter 11 of NAFTA and the WTO to enforce the deal."

"Chapter 11?"

"Among other things, it provides the grounds to judge environmental considerations as, quote unquote, impediments to business, rather than legitimate reasons to stop development. Also, if this group succeeds in buying the land and then someone tries to stop them, they can demand incredible compensation, like what happened in Oaxaca. The Southbelt people who got shafted by the British Columbia government a few years ago are asking for ten *billion* dollars, can you imagine? But – and this is the scariest part of all – once water is commercialized anywhere in Canada, which includes Quebec of course, it's open season in the rest of the country. That's truly terrifying."

"How do they expect to get away with it?" Malcolm felt sick.

"This is an incredibly powerful group, one. And two, most ordinary Americans are blind to Canada."

He raised an eyebrow. She liked the eyebrow. "You're not," he said.

77

"I grew up in Burlington, Vermont, quite near Quebec. I have family in Montreal and went to school there." She smiled. "And I'm not exactly your mom-and-apple-pie American either." God, what an understatement, she thought.

"What does that mean?"

"Well, my parents are European – I mean *really* European. They love opera and theater and anchovies, and believe me, that made them very strange in Vermont in the 1960s. And they dragged me to Montreal, Manchester, Paris, Jerusalem every holiday, summer and winter. I developed a different perspective on the world."

"That's how you ended up in school in Montreal?"

"More or less. When I was fourteen I begged to be released from Burlington. I mean, I love it now, I'd be happy to live there, but it was a backwater then, and I wanted out. My parents agreed to send me to Miss Knight's, just a few streets away from my Aunt Elizabeth's house in Westmount." She'd got a good formal education there, and a pretty good informal one too. She remembered the joints her Lebanese friend Zaida Nahal used to smuggle in and smoke with her in the washroom, the dates they'd sneaked out for, the demonstrations they'd joined, and other crimes and misdemeanors they'd committed with glee.

Malcolm watched her face, and found he couldn't take his eyes off her. She caught him staring. "Back to the matter at hand," she said hastily. "I don't mean that most American environmentalists are blind to Canada, or for that matter, most Americans living in the border states."

"I grew up in Michigan," Malcolm said. "Spent part of every summer on Long Beach, other side of Lake Huron."

"So surely you've noticed that to the rest of America, Canada is a big, cold, blank space populated by polar bears and igloos. Or the fifty-first state. Do *you* see the American people rising up as one for the right not to water their lawns in the desert or fill their swimming pools? Give us a few more years of global-warming droughts, maybe that'll change. But right now the majority of Americans would back that consortium all the way to the World Trade Organization."

"You're saying Americans won't care if corporations take over northern water and wreck the continental environment when they do it? Come on!"

"Not exactly. I'm saying the minority who understand and care a lot are small and weak and have huge agendas and no money. They'll support a Quebec campaign with small gestures. But they're not likely to throw their precious resources at a cause they think they can't mobilize on or win." Claire looked grim. "That's the way it is."

"I see." The lines around Malcolm's eyes tightened in dismay. But he did understand. He'd been a protagonist often enough in debates over scarce resources in conservation groups, and there was never, ever, enough to go around.

"I intend to try my best to get something going, though," she said. "It's incredibly important. The affected ecosystem is a central part of the continental canopy, and if it's irreparably damaged, the consequences could affect the entire hemisphere. *And* it's in my own backyard."

"Vermont, you mean?"

"Actually I have a little place across the border, close to Sutton and Abercorn, where they're planning to run the pipeline."

"Hell's bells," Malcolm said. They were silent. In an attempt to dispel the bleak mood, he told her about his cabin in the Cascades. This set off an exchange about the beauties of old and new mountain ranges, about eco-fitting and wildflowers and duck marshes. He looked at her face, saw her warm, full body, imagined her on a blanket in a meadow of alpine wildflowers. She was thinking of him, blue jeans and blue eyes, striding upward through a ponderosa pine forest, gazing out from the summit. They both reined in their Harlequin reveries at the same moment. Military, she reminded herself. Volatile, he said to himself.

"So where do we go from here?" he asked.

"I'll make some calls, ask around. Nothing this big can stay secret long. Someone else must have heard about it in Washington by now – ditto for Quebec – maybe someone knows something that can give us a legal, official opening to act."

"Okay."

Claire watched him across the table. "Obviously, in the next few months, this plan will become public," she said. "Maybe sooner. So you'll be cleared. But meantime, you took a tremendous risk in getting this information." Malcolm thought he heard admiration. "It could get you fired, possibly sued, possibly worse."

"I don't think my boss ever needs to find out," Malcolm said, fervently hoping this to be true.

"Maybe not," Claire replied, "but I'd really like to know what motivated you to bring me this information."

"Both my friend and I are environmentalists," he said, careful not to name

Russ. "He was at your lecture too. Once we had this information in our hands, we felt we had to do something with it. I've got a background in geography. But you don't need one to see that this could be a real nightmare."

"I see," Claire said thoughtfully. He certainly didn't seem like an agent provocateur, even a clever one. He seemed smart and brave.

Malcolm looked at his nails. "As it happens, I also find myself troubled by apocalyptic fears these days. I keep seeing everything around me ten, twenty, thirty years from now, completely fucked up." Just a few hours ago, driving into town, he'd gazed at the New York skyline. He'd read that hawks and seagulls had taken to using the buildings as vertical culs-de-sac to herd, then kill, tens of thousands of songbirds, and now the fabled sight made him furious. Far too frequently these days he looked upon the works of man and saw not triumph but hubris. "Anyway," he continued, "I think about my kids."

Oh dear, Claire thought. A wife too? "How many children do you have?" She asked it as casually as she could.

"Two. Both in their twenties. Their mother and I separated about ten years ago." Was that relief in her eyes? "Anyway, I think about my kids, and their kids – I mean the ones they're probably going to have, I'm not actually a grandfather yet – and I feel terrible. I guess that's a factor of sorts."

"I know those feelings. Eco-anxiety. Doing something is about the only thing that helps, in my experience."

They were quiet a moment.

"Will you let us know if there's more information?" she asked.

"Sure I will. I'd like to establish some way to communicate securely. I'd really like to be kept informed if something does happen." He was aware that the topic was fast running out, and that he would soon have to leave.

"Yes, by all means." She looked at him. "I'd like to stay in touch."

Touch. He looked at her. He took a breath and held it. "You wouldn't by any chance be free for dinner tonight, would you?" he asked. "What with your conference and all?"

"I'm done this afternoon." The words tumbled out so fast she blushed. She had a dinner loosely scheduled with colleagues, but she could cancel. She remembered the beautiful woman who'd been with him in Seattle, his military background, and hesitated. And then she thought, what the hell, he doesn't seem dangerous. "I stay in Kensington, near Prospect Park," she said. "Can you come to Brooklyn? I'm really tired of restaurant food."

11

THE gargoyles on the old, gothic wing of the National Assembly looked down on the Grande Allée. In the Ministry of Finance, the Honorable Robert Corbeil had been conferring non-stop since Monday with every important Cabinet minister and with the sitting members whose constituencies would be affected.

For the whole week, Serge Lalonde had been mad with anxiety. Apprehensively, he absorbed Corbeil's daily reports. Things at home were frigid. He was sleeping on the couch most of the time now. He knew he was at fault, and Nicole was moving farther and farther away. He was hoping against hope that when the Cabinet approved the venture, he could finally present it to her as an assignment to be carried out, not a project he had initiated. Maybe they could repair the damage. They could go away for the long-promised weekend.

The telephone finally rang at four o'clock. "I have the indications of a strong majority in favor," Corbeil barked. "We have a Cabinet meeting on Wednesday. I shall present a motion and we shall take a vote. Unless something untoward happens between now and then, I am reasonably confident it will pass. My colleagues understand the need for maximum ..." – Corbeil searched for the right word and Lalonde wondered what it would be – "... smoothness."

"I am extremely gratified to hear this," Lalonde responded, with a dignity that hid his agitation.

"We will not, however," said Corbeil, "make any official announcement, as we discussed, until every I is dotted, and every T crossed, on our part and on the part of Vezina, Langevin and Co. And until supportive legislation, approving the appropriation and sale of the land and the construction of the necessary infrastructure, is drafted and ready to move swiftly through the Assembly and committee."

"Of course," said Lalonde.

"I make that moment to be in early October, more or less. It is inevitable, however, that when it arrives there will be opposition. The usual suspects. For the moment, of more concern to me is that our window of opportunity is very narrow for such an enormous undertaking."

"You're referring to the fact of next year's election?"

"*Précisément*. We have to push this through by Christmas. We simply cannot afford to risk opposition too close to the campaign."

"I understand. We must bend every effort, then."

"*En effet*. I have spoken to your minister, and told him that if this passes Cabinet I'm seconding you to work on the project in my ministry, reporting directly to me. I thought it best to minimize friction."

"I appreciate that very much." Lalonde was immensely relieved to avoid crossing swords with his boss, and to have the most senior politician in the government willing to take the flak. "Thank you very much, Minister."

'Not at all. It makes sense. You have done a superb job to date, Lalonde. If you continue your performance, I shall see you are well rewarded. Perhaps Consul General for Quebec in Paris?" Corbeil said tantalizingly. It was the equivalent of an ambassadorship – *the* ambassadorship – and would thrill Nicole. Maybe it would heal the fresh wounds that his withdrawal had opened up.

William Greele was flying to San Francisco, and Sarah was flying with him as far as Los Angeles, to join a friend for a spa weekend. Half an hour before they reached LAX, she cleared her throat and said, "Bill, you're very tied up these days. I'd like to stay on for a while." Greele lifted his head from *The Economist*, looked at her blankly.

"With Magda," Sarah explained. "Henk's away for a couple of months, I think she could use the company." Sarah was lying. Magda's husband was a Shell Oil executive and he was in Kuwait, but Magda wasn't the least bit lonely. Sarah simply didn't want to be in Indian Hill anymore.

"Fine," said Bill, and went back to his reading.

Wearing a blue Dolce and Gabbana scarf around her hair, orange spandex pedal-pushers and a screaming, patterned Versace shirt, Magda met Sarah in the Rolls. The air was a blast furnace. Inside the car, all was serene and cool.

"My God, the things you wear out here," Sarah said.

"Oh darling," Magda replied. "Relax. Time to enjoy yourself."

High in the Berkeley hills, the buttery rays of the setting sun illuminated a white, stuccoed house, all low lines and rising horizontal planes. Energy Secretary Jason Stamper, in a yellow polo shirt and brown chinos, showed William Greele through a large living room, then a family room, where a monster television screen was showing what appeared to be a *West Wing* rerun. "I love watching that show," Stamper said, turning it off. "Talk about fantasyland! Oooowee!"

He stepped out onto a large terrace, gestured Greele towards a wrought-iron table and armchairs scattered around a sparkling turquoise pool. It was a scene straight out of David Hockney. The only thing missing was a young man or three, draped like designer clothing over the expensive patio furniture. The Secretary's taste did not at all run to boys, Greele knew; though his much-traduced wife hobnobbed with artists and art curators, including several young men happy to visit her pool when her husband was in the nation's capital.

Jason Stamper, originally from Arkansas and educated at Stanford on a basketball scholarship, could easily look Greele in the eye. Still handsome, he was somewhat florid and heavy now and his hair had turned to snow white. Over the years he had developed such good working relationships with the whole energy sector that the President overlooked his ungodly personal proclivities. He was a demon for free trade and privatization and had reorganized his entire department to work to those ends.

Greele, his usual scotch in hand, took some time to explain what was on his mind. Stamper knew all about the problems with water, so he didn't have to waste much breath on that. "So," Greele summarized his intentions, "we want to import two and a half billion acre-feet from Quebec."

"Boy howdy!" The Secretary's astonishment was tinged with hostility. "That's a lot of water! How the hell you propose to do that when Southbelt couldn't get a quarter of that out of BC?"

Greele told him, chapter and verse. The Secretary's negativity was evident in the questions he threw at Greele and in the way he nervously jiggled his right leg while Greele spoke. Stamper's attitude came, Greele suspected, from two sources. He was afraid of losing his potential sovereignty over the entire continent; and he was green with envy. Greele's research unit had informed him that Stamper held shares in Southbelt, though under a complicated arrangement that masked his conflict of interest. So Greele persisted in the technicalities, and then he played his trump. "I've come for your support, Mr Secretary. And, if you're interested, for your active participation. I'm inviting you to become part of Amwatco. We can craft a suitable arrangement," he said meaningfully. "And, need I remind you, if we can commercialize water in Quebec, we'll open up the *whole* country." It was a masked allusion to Southbelt, but clear to both of them.

83

Stamper sat back in his lounge chair, his leg came to rest and in a matter of minutes the project had switched from "hopelessly unrealistic" to "jim-dandy".

Satisfied, Greele asked for Stamper's intercession at the White House.

"Sure," Stamper said. "Hell, he'll get a get a hard-on the minute he hears about it. He really hates the Canadians since they refused to support us on Iraq." Stamper thought out loud. "He won't want to have a big public blowout with Ottawa, but he'll get a kick out of this. I don't think Ottawa's gonna give us a big fight if they have a done deal in front of 'em. Anyway, their new Prime Minister wants to win back some favor."

"That's an essential part of our political calculation, Jason," Greele said unctuously. "Good. I'm delighted. What about the Trade Rep.?"

"Not a problem. His job, to support American business. A little extra incentive?" Greele nodded. "Okay. I'll set up lunch in a week or two. How's that?"

"Perfect."

"Yeah, okay. We don't even need legislation. We just let it happen, ride shotgun. But we're gonna need some serious coordination this side of the border. Can you get your plans to me Monday?"

"Absolutely. We were hoping you'd help us there too. Could you assist us in working out jurisdictional matters with the Bureau of Reclamation and the Army Corps of Engineers? My sense is that it would be best if you activated those connections from inside, at the top, instead of me going to those guys directly. Then our head engineer, Gabe Mezulis, can take it from there. But I'm open to your thoughts."

"I'll set things up in DC, let them know your people will be in touch."

"Good."

"The state capitals are another matter." Stamper rubbed his chin, thought for a moment or two, his right leg started its dance again and he made figure-eights with the wet rings from the glasses on the patio table. Greele tensed.

"You know what's happening," Stamper said at last. "Trend to smaller-scale solutions and dam reclamation projects all over the West. Imagine for a minute the God-awful howls of protest by local environmentalists over a major new pipeline, even if the source is in Canada."

Greele's face was a blank.

"Think about the thing for a minute, Bill," Stamper insisted. "You'll see my point. Now, you get buy-in from the other governors yourself, just like you did with Pulaski and MacFarland. *Of course* you'll have the approval and support of the Administration, and once I've got the green light from the President, you can make that entirely clear to them. We'll signal Quebec like I said, and line up everyone in DC. But it would be *much better* if I didn't show up in governors' offices in person, and didn't have to use the federal override to impose the purchase of rights of way."

"I don't know why, Jason," Greele said coldly, eyes flashing. "You've done it plenty of times in the past."

"The less fuss made about this project the better, Bill." The words were soft but the tone was steel. "Why antagonize anyone we don't have to? The River Alliance has more than three thousand member groups now, did you know that? And they don't like this Administration, do they? Don't want to create a national freak-out. So you do the work, you keep things as quiet as you can till the last minute, and you catch the flak when it comes. No one can fire *you*."

Still Greele said nothing.

"Listen, Bill. I'll check the plans Monday. I'll tell you when Washington's solid. You let me know when you have the governors on side. We'll coordinate." Stamper got up.

But Greele stayed seated. "I think I can handle New York," he said. "But I'm not prepared to go ahead if I can't call on you for Vermont." He was taking a huge risk, but he was resolved not to take one more step along this path if Stamper wasn't going to back him all the way.

The Secretary glared. Greele stood up. "Do I have your word?"

12

AT twilight, bronze currents of light played in the darker streams of the East River. Brooklyn, America's second largest city until New York imperiously annexed it early in the twentieth century, was bathed in the same liquid fire, warehouses and factories and archaic water towers black against the sky. Malcolm's cab threaded its way to a little street of higgledy-piggledy houses on the southwestern edge of Prospect Park.

Bottle of wine in hand, he rang the doorbell. The house was modest, clapboard, two-story. Claire explained that she spent almost half her time in New York, and had held on to the first-floor apartment which she had rented and sublet for more than ten years. She now shared it with a toxics campaigner who was regularly in Europe and Asia. Malcolm saw straw-yellow walls, bright white woodwork, a red sofa and chairs, bookshelves everywhere. A radio was on somewhere in the apartment. "… mangroves sustained irreparable damage," the familiar voice of NPR newscaster Corey Flintoff was saying, "and local marine fauna have almost disappeared. But the Thai government has rejected the demands of a coalition of environmentalists to halt the shrimp farming, citing World Trade Organization rules."

"Jesus Christ," Claire said bitterly, popped into one of two small bedrooms, and turned off the radio. Then Malcolm followed her into a bright, tiled kitchen that gave on to a tiny patio shaded by a leafy grapevine.

"Thank God for Italians," Claire breathed the open air and gestured to the vine. "That thing is fifty years old. *Viva la terra.* Would you like some wine?" He lost track of her words. She was wearing black cut-off pants, a white T-shirt and red sandals; small garnet earrings, a sparkly bracelet, a little eye make-up. Her skin was lightly tanned. Her cologne smelled of limes and crushed leaves and something sweeter, maybe lavender. "Or something with gin, or vodka or scotch?" she was asking.

"Wine is good," Malcolm wanted to keep his wits about him. Back in the kitchen, Claire found that her hands were trembling at the intensity of her attraction to this stranger. Give me prudence, give me *restraint*, she pleaded with a libido she had all but forgotten, but which had risen up suddenly like a tropical storm rampaging through her protective barriers. I barely know the man, she told herself. He's been a professional soldier, for Christ's sake.

"How do you like living in New York and DC?" Malcolm called to Claire through the open door. No answer. He thought she hadn't heard. She came back with a tray, bottle, corkscrew and glasses.

"I don't," she said, kicking the screen door closed. "I live in cities because I have to. For the usual reason – work that is. But I'm getting very tired of it. Not to say scared. Just over that horizon, there's a big hole where two huge skyscrapers used to stand."

"Of course," Malcolm said. They both let a moment go by, remembering.

"It's just that I'm not a big-city girl at heart. I want to be somewhere green and mountainous. More and more as I get older. Sad but true." As it happened, she was looking anything but sad. She was looking radiant.

"Now tell me about yourself," Claire said to Malcolm, noticing the tracery of blue veins on his well-formed hands as he lifted his glass in a salute to her. "You're working for Skypoint." Malcolm nodded. He was organizing his thoughts, an explanation of his current, untenable situation, when she said, "Sort of out of the military but still connected to its economy?" God, she thought, why did I put it like that? Not formally killing innocent people, just functionally.

"My skills and my contacts developed in the Air Force," Malcolm said dryly. "It was a natural move over to aeronautics when I left. My boss knew me and respected my abilities – and he had a good job to offer me. I had an ex-wife and two kids in college to support. I needed the job." There was much more to it than that, but he wasn't quite sure where to start. "I'm responsible for weapons control technology in our military production, which I had hoped would end with … Anyway, I also advise Nick Kamenev on corporate strategy and major contracts. He trusts my judgment and knows that I'm not one of the knife-wielding VPs who's out to usurp him."

"Still," she said, looking at him critically, "pretty well right up there."

"It may seem so," Malcolm replied wearily. "But that's not how it is. Kamenev and I live in different universes. I make 250 thousand dollars a year. I support four adults on that, after taxes. I'm not complaining. By national and global standards I'm a very privileged person. But Kamenev is a billionaire with all that implies. We're not friends. Especially recently."

"Point taken," she said. "But you do contribute to corporate direction. Which these days must include a hell of a lot of military work." Shut up! her libido told her. Stay clear, commanded her higher self.

"Yes," he said, "but again, not the way you seem to think. When I joined Skypoint, I brought access to a revolutionary new aircraft design – and I do mean revolutionary, it's capable of yielding fuel economies twenty to forty times greater than today's planes, so you can imagine the environmental implications."

"Fabulous," Claire said. "I've never heard of any such thing."

"It's real. Anyway, it's a long story – persuading Nick to try it, getting the rights, waiting for the right contract to bid it, but we were getting there. Then September 11 happened, the money from the Department of Defense started pouring in like shit from a broken sewer. Which allowed Kamenev to keep putting off bidding any contracts. Then Iraq happened. More postponements. But then we heard that a company in Brazil was looking to build a new short-haul fleet. It was the perfect contract and he finally agreed we'd go for it. I was so happy, so were the two guys who invented this thing, it was, truly, my dream come true. Then, just before you and I met, for no reason whatsoever that I can discern, Kamenev killed the project."

Claire flinched, imagining his pain. "You must be devastated."

"Yup," he replied. "I am. With all that military money obviously Nick has no incentive to try anything new. Besides," Malcolm paused, took a healthy sip from his wine glass, "something I have to face, Nick's got, how can I put it … he's got a sexual relationship with fighter planes. It's really all he wants to build. Deep down." Claire's eyebrows popped up. "I'm not kidding. He loves those planes with a physical passion that's embarrassing. Way more than his wife and kids."

"Tell," she prompted, amused.

"He did his second tour of duty in Vietnam, out of Ubon RTAFB. He flew with the 8th Tactical Fighter Wing – the Wolf Pack, as it was known then. When he talks about those planes and those sorties – which I assure you he does frequently – his eyes glaze over, and I feel like I should leave the room. He has a thing for his car too. It's a 1958 Corvette – Inca Silver, 283 cubic inch fuel-injected V8. Nice car. Polishing it is an erotic act for him. I've seen him, and it's excruciating to watch."

"So he wants the company to make sexy war planes."

"Oh yes indeed."

"So what rank were you when you retired from the Air Force?" she asked.

"Lieutenant colonel."

"Hmm," she reflected. "So I'm really curious. How could a person of your evident intelligence, sensibilities, and morality survive twenty years in the military?"

It had been a small eternity since Claire had fallen in love. Sensing that possibility now, her sense of self-preservation was spitting like Xena the Warrior Princess roused unexpectedly from a nap, foul-tempered and brandishing her spears.

Malcolm searched for words. He understood why Claire wanted to know. But he was also taken aback by how quickly and directly they had gotten to it.

"I'm sorry," Claire said, abashed. "That was rude. That's a very personal question and I have no right to ask it." She paused. "It's just that I have never known a person of such elevated status in the military – I know you're not *still* in the military, but you know what I mean – who I could relate to and trust."

Trust. The idea of it reverberated like a soft gong in the night air as a cricket started its song somewhere. It sounded much more intimate than she'd intended. Oops, she thought.

"It's okay, Claire," Malcolm said. "I'd want to know in your shoes, too. And I want you to know." The shadows lengthened. "If what you're asking is how I managed to reconcile my participation in the military with my personal value system, the short answer is I didn't." He cleared his throat.

"I started out patriotic and idealistic, a small-town Michigan kid. My dad was a mossback Republican. Am-Vets was the center of his life. Still, by the time I was due to be drafted, I really didn't want to go to Vietnam. I had some awareness. I'd graduated from Michigan State, been accepted by three schools to do a master's degree in geography. The ghettos were burning and the students were marching. But what was the alternative? I couldn't see myself going to Canada. I was the oldest and I was a good boy. And I still believed that America, whatever that was, could stand for something good. I was offered officer training in all three services. I chose the Air Force. Most science, least paperwork."

The distant hum of the city droned on, the cricket chirped, a siren wailed. Claire watched him. A breeze ruffled the young grape leaves.

"I went to Officer Training School at Lackland Air Force Base in San Antonio, Texas. I graduated top of my class in all the technical stuff, and thanks to years of duck hunting I guess, started pulling decorations for marksmanship. By then I'd reread *Catch-22*, and I was beginning to grasp the true nature of the institution to which I'd just committed the next five years of my life." On his first day off after nearly two months of intensive training, he'd headed for the zoo and hung with the animals for about four hours, just for a hit of sanity. Then he'd visited the Alamo, and walked around, wondering what was going to become of him – and mankind.

"They sent me to train as a weapons director at Tyndall Air Force Base in Panama City. That's where I met Lucille – General Offley's daughter." He recalled the moment as though it were yesterday. He'd been walking along the shore, performing his twilight ritual of spotting marine birds. Lucille had come strolling down the beach, arm in arm with her mother. She looked like Botticelli's Venus rising from the foam, gorgeous, the tendrils of her blonde hair gleaming in the last rays of the sun. And she had cast him a sly but bold glance as he passed by.

"We got married six months later, and not a week after that, I was deployed to Okinawa," Malcolm continued, his voice low. "Lucille was forced to wait behind for six months. When she finally joined me, we both discovered how fundamentally incompatible we were. I was reading eastern philosophy and hanging with the local fisherman. She wanted to know why I wasn't going to barbecues with the base brass. One afternoon she caught me reading *The Tale of Genji* and smoking a joint. She blew her top. I should have left right then, but people didn't divorce the way they do today. And we were in the middle of a war."

"Oh brother," Claire said, not knowing what else to say.

"I was assigned to Monkey Mountain in Vietnam in 1970. I'll spare you my Vietnam tales for now. My father-in-law had me yanked home only one year later. He wanted me back and climbing that promotional ladder." He paused. "I wanted to leave the Air Force after Vietnam in the worst possible way. And I did leave, for three years, while I finished a master's degree and completed all my coursework for a Ph.D. in Physical geography. We were living in Bend, Oregon. I was training to become a state environmental officer." He cleared his throat again. She could hear it constricting.

"But Lucille, she wanted back in," he continued. "Badly. She did not like life outside the military. And she was pregnant. She made her wishes known in painful ways and for the sake of the new baby I decided I had to go back." He paused again. "Four years after Molly was born, Michael came along. My kids mean a lot to me. At that time, there wasn't anything more important. So I stayed with Lucille and I stayed in the Air Force."

He looked at her across the little table. "I asked for and got good assignments – Japan and Korea, three years in Vicenza, Italy, three tours in Saudi – Riyadh, mainly. Always wanted to go to those places when I was a kid. I chose defensive operations and got them. A small, personal issue with me – hardly an effective political gesture. I knew I'd retire relatively young, so I stuck it out. Left the marriage and the military when the kids finally left for college. Now I'm supporting them all from Skypoint. But not living with any of them."

He took a deep breath, reflected. Claire did not interrupt. "One pragmatic decision after another," he said. "Today I don't know if I did the right things. I wish I was living in Bend now – I'm not a big city-boy at heart either – and instead I'm in Seattle at Skypoint, with my kids far away and my work in ruins."

Claire waited a moment, but he'd come to the end. "That's some story," she said softly, assimilating the things he'd told her. "Are there a lot of other people like you in the military?"

Malcolm smiled sardonically. It was wonderful, she thought, the way his face crinkled when something pleased or amused him, the mischief in his eyes. She could see that he'd smiled a lot. "No," he said, matter-of-factly, "since you ask, there aren't. There's a logic to the institution that makes it hard for most people with my views to do well."

"Ah," Claire said. "I was just thinking, listening to you, how stupid stereotypes are. You know, the sort that a person like me might have."

Malcolm laughed. "Oh yeah," he said. "I think I know. I did find some good people here and there, made some good friends who still mean a lot to me. But on the whole you won't find many people who think like I do in the armed forces."

"Then it must have been very hard for you," she said quietly.

"In many ways, yes. After all the gore – gore's bad, no getting around it – the worst of it was what happened to a number of my close friends over the years. In Vietnam, I had a buddy, a brilliant young officer, who became a conscientious objector. If you can believe it, right there in Da Nang. They put him in the stockade, and then they court-martialed his ass. *That* was really hard."

"Must have been awful."

"Uh-huh," Malcolm said. "He did the right thing, and I simply couldn't accept what they did to him. Something in me just snapped. As they say. And I got a great big, ugly hit at the end too. Had to train weapons controllers that went over to the Gulf, and watch some of my closest friends go back into combat. One of them – he was deployed to Iraq – he's gone totally to pieces. I adopted his dog a few years ago because he couldn't take care of her anymore." Remembering Jim Gregorian in his wheelchair, tears pouring down his ravaged face as Bonnie looked longingly at him out the back window of the car, Malcolm choked up.

"Was he injured?" Claire asked gently.

"Gulf War Syndrome," Malcolm said. "Hellacious case. Immune system shot, suppurating rashes, cold sweats, black depression, gastrointestinal disorders from his mouth to his anus, a complete wreck. He went to war. I stayed behind. He was sacrificed, I was spared. Plus," and now Malcolm swallowed and struggled even harder to speak, "when I saw the footage of those fires burning in the desert, and the oil slicks and the dying birds,

I knew that was it. I had to get out. And I did. March, 1991."

"I'm sorry," she said.

"That's okay," he said. "My marriage was bad too, and all wrapped up in the thing. Got free of them both. "

They sat in silence for a moment. At length Claire said, "Thank you for explaining. It helps a lot." She smiled and stood up. "I'm starved. Let's get some food on the table."

"Yes, ma'am," he said. "Want some help?"

The telephone began to ring. "Give me a minute," Claire said, and disappeared into the apartment. Malcolm took in the evening air – the smells of growing things and urban pollution blended together. He knew very little about Claire's personal story, but it felt remarkably, amazingly good to be with her. He could feel that she wanted to get closer to him, despite her aggressive questions. Be cool, he told himself, *piano, piano*.

"Hey Malcolm, you coming in?" Claire called presently.

"You bet," he said, stepping into the kitchen. She was standing with a distracted air at the door to the hall. A blush of pink showed on her tanned breastbone, warm against the stark white V-neck of her T-shirt. Her dark hair billowed around her face. Her curves sang to him and her red sandals winked at him. He felt a surge of pure testosterone. Down boy! he commanded himself.

"That was James Amanopour," Claire said with a peculiar expression on her face. "He's the executive director of eco-Justice Canada. Guess what he was calling about."

"What?" He looked at her. She looked very serious, raised her eyebrows. "Really?" he said, "Water Incorporated?"

"Earlier this week a board member in Montreal called him about something very bad she had just learned. He did some research, couldn't find out a thing. He thought it best not to discuss it over the telephone, other than to say that it concerned water and 'my people' as he likes to put it."

"Dang," Malcolm said. "Great timing."

"James said the board member is organizing a meeting in Montreal late tomorrow afternoon with a committee of water activists in Quebec, and wondered if I could fly up."

Malcolm's disappointment was like a falling rock. "I see," he said. He'd been hoping that she might agree to visit the Metropolitan Museum of Art or the American Museum of Natural History with him, maybe eat supper in a quiet restaurant somewhere.

"I was planning to head out tomorrow for a few days to my country place. In Somerville," Claire said.

"Right." A sadness out of all proportion to the time he'd known her overtook him. She looked at him, standing in the doorway to the garden framed by the blue satin of the night sky and she could see that the news of her departure upset him. She didn't want to say goodbye to him either.

"Well, then." She went to the fridge, pulled out a large bottle of gazpacho, cold chicken, some vegetables that had been cleaned and cut up. She got a wok from the cupboard, and started stir-frying onions and red peppers. She lifted the lid on a small pot and checked on some rice. He could tell she was working herself up to say something so he waited. The clock ticked. She added some snow peas to the wok, opened the refrigerator again, retrieved a salad.

"So who's the gorgeous redhead?" Claire blurted, turning back to the stove and stirring the vegetables to hide her flaming face. Mamma mia, how could you ask such a thing, one of her voices excoriated her. But what's the point of taking the chance if it's doomed from the beginning, shouted another. She put a hand to each temple and shook her head. He watched her with fascination, not knowing what was happening.

"The – gorgeous – redhead," he repeated slowly. "Oh, Geraldine!" He got it. He smiled at Claire but winced inwardly at the thought of his friend. "She's just a good friend. Honestly."

"She didn't look like 'just a good friend'." Xena was riding hell for leather.

Malcolm moved closer to Claire and looked into her eyes. "It's possible that there's an imbalance in our feelings for each other. But Geraldine and I are *just friends*. I'm a free agent."

One mad flash of paranoia seized her. "But not an agent."

"No." He didn't mock her. "I know what you mean. I'm not."

Claire took a deep breath. She turned the stove off. "Well, then," she said, "maybe you'd like to see where the pipeline will go through. In northern Vermont and southern Quebec."

"The pipeline?" Once again he was disoriented by the change in subject. "Of course, the pipeline!" he recovered, and nearly hyperventilated when he realized the nature of the invitation she'd just extended him. "Yes, I'm immensely curious to see where it will go through."

"We could drive up together to my place tomorrow, then from there to

Montreal and back on Sunday. Head back down here Monday morning. If you can swing it."

"I can swing it."

"Just to be clear," she said, "I'd like to take it step by step. I don't quite know how to say this, but I think it would be better for my equilibrium if we … well, if we didn't get too physical too fast." Christ, she thought, I'm forty-five years old, I can say the word sex. And what am I doing, refusing it?

"You mean not sleep together?" he said.

"I can sometimes ignore my better judgment when I bond with someone sexually. Has that ever happened to you?"

Twenty years of Lucille flashed before his eyes like the visions of a dying man. "You don't know the half of it," he said.

"Or if it's too strong, or happens too fast, I get scared and run away –"

"It's okay, Claire," Malcolm said, reaching to take her hand in his. He squeezed it gently. She felt herself melting under his warm, smiling gaze. I'm crazy, she thought. But he's awfully nice to make it so easy.

He continued. "Just know this: I'm interested. *Very*. But you lead. Okay?"

In the taxi on the way back to his hotel, Malcolm had a moment of anguish when they passed through Times Square. Gone was the grungy glitter of the sex-shows and porn palaces. But what he saw now was scary in a different way: dazzling, multistory, electronic billboard images that moved without sound, in slow motion, dwarfing the humans and cars below, celebrating the great corporations: GAP, Disney, Sony, Coke. It's *Bladerunner*, Ridley Scott's post-apocalyptic Los Angeles minus the constant rain. Then the traffic jam broke and the cab drove on.

"Russ?" he said to his friend's answering machine when he returned to his hotel room. "It's Mal. There's been a change of plans." He thought for a moment. "I want to extend my trip by a day." How to explain? That would have to suffice. "How are you doing with Bonnie and Clyde? Maybe you can drop them off at Geraldine's?" He gave Russ her number. "Good excuse to call her, buddy. I'll try to track you down tomorrow when I'm on the road. Thanks a million."

New York Governor Edward Caccia was a man with a face like a potato and a mind like a razor. William Greele had asked for a quiet, discreet meeting to discuss something very important, and the Governor had agreed to receive him in State House in Albany on Saturday morning. So at ten o'clock Greele was accepting bad coffee and making a florid little speech appealing to the patriotism of the Governor of the Empire State. He mentioned that Vittorio Massaro, whom the Governor knew well, was a partner in the consortium for which he was asking support, and named the other members. Impressed, Caccia leaned back in his overstuffed chair and gave Greele his full attention.

Greele spent ten precious minutes detailing the ways in which New York's waterways were polluted: extensive acidification of lakes and streams, even in Adirondack State Parks; the enormous amounts of PCBs deposited in – and not yet removed from – the Hudson. He demonstrated that he was intimately familiar with the nature of New York's pollution problems, named the names, detailed the deals that had been made over the years. Greele's research wing in Minneapolis had done, as usual, a superb job. Caccia continued to be impressed, though less happy. Greele was rattling his saber because ideally Amwatco wanted 300 miles of pipeline right of way in Caccia's state. And that meant the Governor would have to run political interference, possibly very heavy, to assist in procuring the land swiftly and quietly.

Stick brandished, Greele waved the carrot: the same arrangement he had offered the other governors and senators. "So I'm hoping, Mr Governor," Greele concluded, "that you'll want to join and support the venture."

Caccia leaned back so far in his chair it creaked. "I'll tell ya, Bill," he said, calculating, fully aware that without New York there would be no pipeline. "In principle, I can see the merit of the project. Makes a lotta sense to think ahead. Us politicians, well, lotsa times we're just planning for the next election, the … howddaya call it, the 'contingencies of the moment'." You can say that again, you pompous ass, thought Greele. "It's good we got far-sighted types like you, Bill, thinking ahead for all of us. And I hear ya, I do. I know New York's got a lot of pollution problems. Hey, who doesn't? Still – and here I'm gonna be honest with you – I'm not sure about the costs versus the benefits to the people of New York."

Greele heard the coded message and responded. "I think that participating in this project will show your electorate just how visionary and patriotic a politician you are, Governor." Which would be awfully good for the next election, of course. "And I'm entirely sure we can help to spread that perception. A few stories in *The Times*, a profile in *New York Magazine*, maybe a *Newsweek* cover when the time comes." Greele spoke these words carefully, but the look he gave the Governor also conveyed a more sinister meaning – "do it, or face my enmity."

Caccia considered the implied blackmail. "You get Putnam's consent to take the pipeline south to Manchester or somewhere, through Vermont, so I only have to find a hundred and fifty miles of right of way in New York, Bill, and I'll back it. Got a lot of them green types with their shorts in a knot over acid rain and global warming and tire dumps and God knows what else. Group up in Plattsburgh's driving us crazy. Not a good time right now. You need to trust my judgment on this." Meaning, you've got no choice, big boy. He stood up. "We don't want to sink the thing same time we're trying to launch it. Am I right?"

"I take your point." Greele, angry and insulted, stood and looked coldly down on the Governor. "I'll fill you in as things proceed."

"Good, good," said Caccia. "Get your plans to me. I'll get someone to start looking at them, liaise with Massaro. Someone I trust. If it looks better than I thought, I'll get back with you."

William Greele walked out. Ed Caccia watched the door close and smiled. Got that fucking stuffed shirt, the Governor thought. And got some goodies too.

13

NEW York receded behind them, a brown, noxious smear against the blue summer sky in the rear-view mirror. Malcolm had had his wake-up call at six, splashed water on his face, and taken a taxi to Brooklyn. Claire was waiting on her front porch and got in. They picked up a car rental then stopped for a latte to go. "Oh boy. Road trip," Claire said. They headed up the Palisades Parkway to 87 North and the New York Thruway, talking about the state of the world and the environment, comparing perceptions and hopes. After the turnoff northeast at Albany, Malcolm asked her to tell him more about herself.

"What would you like to know?" she asked.

"Everything. Start at the beginning." He watched her, in red shorts and a black T-shirt. Nice legs, he thought.

"The very beginning?" she said. She was glad to have someone to share the driving after so many trips alone. She found it hard to account for the profound ease she felt with him, she knew him so little. But the feeling was intoxicating. She watched the sun glint in his hair, brown feathered with silver, traced the line of his biceps, his abdomen, through his shirt. He was so fit and trim. She thought he might not like her generous proportions.

"Start with your parents," Malcolm suggested. He was imagining her without her clothes and thinking of Goya's *Naked Maja*.

One reason Claire had stopped dating was because she was so tired of having to explain her complicated family, her complicated choices. "All right," she said. He was worth it. "As I told you, I'm not exactly classic New England stock. My father's family left Warsaw in the 1920s, some to New York, some to Paris, my grandparents to Jerusalem. One great uncle stayed behind in Poland. His family perished at Auschwitz. My father is a reconstructive surgeon, retired now. He worked in England – in Manchester – during the war, where he met my mother – not Jewish. They tried Israel for a few years after the war, but it just didn't work. Too much anti-goyism …" Claire enjoyed Malcolm's smile.

"My mother's sister, Elizabeth, had married a Canadian and moved to Montreal – Montreal was the leading city in those days, not Toronto. My father had relatives in New York and a surgeon Dad had worked with during the war invited him to come to the military hospital in Plattsburgh. So my parents moved to Burlington, close to work and to relatives on both sides. Mom had me six months after they arrived. My brother Eric came along three years later. He's great. He lives in England.

"You know the in-between part. After high school, I studied botany at McGill University, then journalism at Columbia. And when I graduated, I got a job as a reporter with the *Detroit Free Press*. Of course, there was nothing free about it. I wasn't able to write honestly about the environmental problems of the city. Surprise. But I got to know people who were starting to research the drudge at the bottom of Lake St Claire, in Windsor as well as Detroit. Yuck! My first exposure to the problems of persistent chemical toxins. The Detroit gang asked if I'd like to work for them as chief researcher. I leaped at the chance. Since then, I've worked as a researcher and policy director for quite a few organizations and government agencies.

Did a six-month stint in Brussels with the World Health Organization. Another year in Paris with UNESCO. I took the job with EJI five years ago. And here I am."

"Lucky for me," he said. He meant it.

"Me too," she rejoined. They'd both turned to look out their respective windows, thinking, oh my God.

They cruised along. "You haven't said anything about husbands or children or lovers," Malcolm said. "How come?"

What to tell? thought Claire. He's Captain America and I'm the Rebel Girl. "Well," she said. "No kids. Never had the right situation. Not sure I could have brought kids into this world, anyway. But maybe, had the right person come along. Lovers – let's see. At McGill, I had a Québécois boyfriend, an artist. He was very talented, very passionate, very political. No big scars from that one really, a lot of good memories. Improved my French, too." She paused.

"And?"

"At Columbia, there was a lawyer. We were together for two years. He had just moved to New York to start his career, which was already stellar, in some Wall Street firm. It ended painfully." Claire paused and looked out the window. "When we met, he was hanging with progressive types because he couldn't stand his own associates. Used to tell lawyer jokes all the time – you know, what's twenty-five lawyers at the bottom of the Hudson? A good start. Fooled me at first. I thought he was on our side."

"He wasn't?"

"Nope. He believed the rich would always triumph because they had power, which they would do anything and everything to keep. He was from a poor family, and he wasn't going to 'swim upstream,' as he put it, all *his* life. He was on the fast track to money, and he took it. I was on the fast track too – in the opposite direction – into a life of resistance, really. And we disagreed, violently, about sexual politics – monogamy, for instance. He was against it. It was horrible."

They drove in silence for a few moments.

"I was single for quite a few years after him, and then I met Jeff." Malcolm looked at her, and she nodded sheepishly. "At a conference on endangered species. Eighty-nine, I guess. He was EJI's reigning specialist on the topic then, brilliant and committed. His last name's Brannigan, by the way. He really liked me, and he swept me off my feet. We seemed to agree politically. Or so I thought at first."

Malcolm watched Claire's face darken and she fell silent. "Didn't work out?" he prompted.

"To say the least. Ironically, we fought over politics — strategy and tactics, if not general goals. Constantly. It was poisonous. We were very much on-and-off because of our jobs anyway — both back and forth to Europe. Christmas 1996 we had a very big argument about the future of environmental politics." She paused, searching for the words.

"Let me guess," said Malcolm. "If it isn't being too presumptuous."

"Go ahead," Claire said with a grim smile. "But if you want to take this particular topic any further, I'll have to swear you to secrecy. I mean it."

Malcolm looked at her. "You've got it," he said. "Which reinforces my guess. I'll bet he favored a form of 'direct action', as you folks call it, that went beyond what you were comfortable with." Malcolm thought of how Brannigan had waved the wolf symbol at him.

"*Very* perceptive," Claire said. She remembered the poisonous battles they had had, how she felt she was drowning in Brannigan's rage. "Yes. We disagreed fundamentally on the use of violence in direct action. Jeff parted company with me and the organization simultaneously."

"But you still talk to him?"

"Oh yes. I see him at conferences all the time — let's say he lives parallel lives, one of which is as a well-known environmental activist. He is vastly knowledgeable. He has an amazing database he's been cultivating for years, and he's been helpful in the past. Hey, *this* is some coincidence. Jeff lives near Missoula. Your big water honcho — Greele — has a huge ranch up there, though apparently he's never in residence, just in hunting season. He's definitely at the top of Jeff's Global Evildoers list. Anyway, I — we — eco-Justice that is — have *nothing* to do with Jeff *politically*, let me make that clear."

"It's clear."

But instead of feeling better, Claire suddenly felt as though she had betrayed her former lover. It wasn't as though Malcolm Macpherson had spent his life as a pacifist working for the Red Cross. "Just so you know," she said. "Jeff's not in favor of violence against *humans*. Let me be unequivocal about that. Though I often felt that he considered *Homo sapiens* a lesser species. Let's just say that he sees property of various forms as a legitimate target."

"I hear you." Malcolm watched her face for telltale lines of stress or sorrow or longing. There weren't any. He decided that's all that mattered to him. "Anyway, since then I have lived a near-chaste existence," Claire said, with a small, self-deprecatory smile. "I had a couple of affairs, but I stopped. I can't seem to get physically involved without becoming emotionally involved, and those men weren't right for me."

"So how's chastity?"

"It's supposed to be its own punishment, I know," she said. "And I can't say it's been easy." My God, what an understatement! That aching loneliness, and the despair at the thought that she'd had all her chances and blown them. "Fact is, though," she said, "once I finally got used to it, I found it's easier to be alone than to have a relationship that constantly made me sad or crazy. Though I do get tired sometimes, just having to deal with everything life throws at me on my own."

"I know what you mean. On both counts." Neither said anything for a moment.

"If I find a man who's right," she said, "I'll go for it. I'm talking about true compatibility, though – mind, heart, values, expectations and, ah … chemistry. Otherwise, for me, it just isn't worth it."

He smiled at her and she smiled back, her face bright. The mountains, fields, and forests had grown taller and wider and more expansive. For a while they rolled along, each marveling at the beauty of the world.

"How much do you need that job at Skypoint?" she hazarded at length.

"I'm getting out," he said. "That's a given. I just have to figure out how to do it with a decent severance package." A drop in Lucille's standard of living won't kill her, he thought. "Next year, Molly and Don should both be teaching. Michael's nearly done with his Ph.D."

"Wonderful," she said with feeling. He turned on the radio, and there was Jennifer Warnes singing "Ain't No Cure for Love". He hummed along as they drove north.

A gazebo stood surrounded by late spring flowers in the village square of Somerville, Quebec. Claire took Malcolm into the Boulangerie Peregrine's Peak, where she bought croissants and exchanged greetings with its proprietors, Benoît and Simone, French expatriates who had fallen in love with the Eastern Townships and settled there. Then they headed south, out into open farmland. "I can't believe the green," Malcolm said. "It's so intense."

"They didn't call it *Vert Mont* for nothing," Claire replied. They turned up a poplar-bordered drive that led to a small white farmhouse, shielded at the front by a thick hedge of lilacs. A solar panel sat on the roof, and a windmill and well were visible in the field behind the house, where several acres of meadow rose gently toward a wooded peak. They got out and stretched in ankle-high tangles of buttercups and clover, overlooking the quilted fields and forests of the Missisquoi River valley, grazing cows, the huge blue sky with clouds like fat lambs. For a few moments they just stood, breathing deeply. They unloaded the car, went for a walk to the covered bridge a mile down the road where the border divided Quebec and Vermont, then got in the car and headed to Montreal.

Outside the limestone townhouse on Rue du Parc Lafontaine, residents of East Montreal were taking their ease around the fountains and ponds. A young family strolled by as Claire got out of the car, the children eating ice creams and the parents trailing the smell of Gitane cigarettes. The tall windows of the houses facing the park were thrown open to the May sun.

Armed with a city map and sightseeing suggestions, Malcolm watched Claire stride toward the green lacquered front door, then pulled back into traffic. Sylvie greeted Claire and invited her in. Ten or so people were seated in the living room. James Amanopour got up to greet his US counterpart.

"Hey pardner," he said, giving her a hug. "Good to see you."

"James, you old heartbreaker," Claire replied, returning the hug. "What a treat. How are you?"

"Good," he said, "I think. But this isn't welcome news."

Sylvie presented Claire with coffee, and called the meeting to order.

"*Bonjour, chers amis*," she said. "Claire, this is the Eau NO group. We work together on water issues in Quebec. I have told everyone what I have learned, though I am not at liberty to reveal my source at this point. Maybe you can begin, Claire, by telling us what you know. Then everyone can add what they've heard. Please everyone, introduce yourselves as we go. Then we'll talk strategy."

"Gladly," Claire agreed. She proceeded to reveal the consortium's members to the extent she knew them, the amount of water targeted for export, the means for extraction and the progress the consortium had made securing political protection in Washington, DC. A long moment of appalled silence followed.

A thin, intense man in a tan suit, with a long black braid and a belt with exquisite beading, introduced himself. "I'm Ovide Obansawon, a partner of Sylvie's," he said. "I've provided legal assistance to the Cree in James Bay for more than ten years. This is the first I've heard about this water business." The sallow skin and the tension around Obansawon's eyes bespoke years of gritty struggle. "You should know that large parts of the land the consortium wants to drain in the project's second phase are ancestral to my people. They can't have them."

"*Bof*!" snorted the middle-aged man sitting next to him. "They will take them! And without consulting you, or any of us!" He was dressed for golf, from his checked trousers to his cleated shoes. He spoke with a Parisian accent.

"I'm René Dubois," he explained to Claire, "and I teach engineering at the University of Montreal. I'm a hydrologist. Like Ovide, I hadn't heard a thing about this before today. But I'll tell you categorically. If this goes ahead, the regions involved cannot sustain the drainage. You have to understand that Quebec Hydro has already been drawing down the reservoir system drastically to sell electricity to the Americans. In the late 1990s, Quebec's reservoirs were already more than half empty. And the snow pack the last few years has been small. This is madness."

"I can't believe this government," Sylvie exclaimed. "The *hypocrisy* of their so-called patriotism!" What she really couldn't believe was that her friend Serge Lalonde was involved.

"Get real. They're all the same." A big woman with salt-and-pepper hair, big glasses and big gestures waved Sylvie's comment away. "Lorraine Beckman," she snapped. "Canadian Public Employees Union. I'm here strictly as an individual at this point. But I'll report back to national executive on this, and recommend whatever action seems sensible. Some action seems sensible. Urgent, actually."

"You're lucky, Lorraine," said a stocky, balding man in faded blue jeans and a gray T-shirt. He turned to Claire. "Henri Scott," he said. "I live in Chicoutimi and work in the Lac St-Jean region. I'm a health and safety official for the Power Workers at Quebec Hydro there. My people are desperate for work. If these Americans agree to negotiate union contracts, my members will be leaping into their arms."

"Union contracts, it's a bad joke!" It was a derisive snort and it came from an exceptionally lanky, long-faced man with a peculiar accent. "They're not going to want union labor!"

"I'm sure you're right, Olaf," Scott replied wearily.

"So maybe we'll have a chance to fight it. But maybe even that won't make any difference." The man introduced himself as Olaf Gunderson, head of the Committee to Save the Verchère. Gunderson was a Swede who had fallen in love with Quebec on a winter camping trip in the late seventies. A penchant Sylvie thought insane, if admirable. "A local company has already built one diversion dam on our river," he said. "Tiny compared to what you're describing. We've seen some of the damage these things can do first-hand." He leaned over and handed Claire some photographs.

Claire said, "Jesus!"

"The same company wants to build two more of these things," Gunderson continued. "We have a strong committee fighting this. Support across the province. But we didn't succeed in stopping the first one. And we have only now won a proper hearing on the others."

"I'm very, very worried," said Sylvie into a brief silence. "The levels of the St Lawrence River and the Laurentian lakes are lower than we've ever known them. By margins of 40 and 50 per cent. And the temperatures keep climbing season after season. I hardly have to tell you. And those stupid Americans think water is plentiful here."

"They don't care, that's clear," said a young woman whose black hair bristled in a short buzz-cut. Her dark brown eyes shone with outrage. She was dressed in lime green and black cycling gear. "My name's Diane Molyneux. I'm an engineering student at the University of Montreal, and a member of the student council. In the Townships the ponds are already dropping, and it's only May. What is my generation going to inherit? Scorched earth?"

The last person to speak was Michel Herriveault. With calloused hands and a body hard from years of outdoor work, he had come from Abitibi for the meeting. He worked with the Cree in the boreal forest and had developed alternative economic activities to logging and hydro damming. "Look," he said. "The PQ is only seven months away from an election year. If we and others make a big enough stink about this for long enough, the government won't be able to push it through before Christmas. After that, they'll lose their nerve. That's what we have to focus on."

"In theory, making a big stink is fine." Sylvie ran a tired hand through her dark bobbed hair. "In reality, everyone's overextended, everything's about to shut down for the summer, everyone's budgets are locked in for the year. It will be impossible to get the degree of mobilization necessary to stop this thing."

"Same for us," Claire said. "No budget, no staff allocations, no communications budget, yadda, yadda." She looked bleak. "I'll seek out some of my colleagues in other national environmental organizations in DC. I'll alert the River Alliance and the Sierra Club. Try to get some national press."

"I'll approach the Canadian Environmental Network and the Coalition of Concerned Canadians – those folks are rabidly opposed to bulk water exports," James Amanopour volunteered, "and we can both speak to eco-Justice International, in Brussels. The lobbyists working on the ongoing rounds of WTO meetings have to put North American water on their agenda."

"My group will push the Finance Minister," Olaf Gunderson said.

But it wasn't nearly enough, and they knew it. Then Herriveault had an idea.

Malcolm and Claire took a walk up the back meadow behind Claire's house and surveyed the valley, the clouds stippled with lavender, rose and gold. Then, for the sheer joy of it, they ran down through the sweeping fields to the house. It had been a wonderful couple of days.

"I'll miss you."

"I'll miss you, too." He took her hand, and he could feel his whole body responding. "When would you like to get together again?"

She squeezed his fingers. "Soon. As soon as possible." She looked at him, and the sweet smell of his fresh sweat intoxicated her.

He brought his forehead close, so it was touching hers. "*O, Claire de la lune*," he whispered in her ear. She gave him a lingering kiss which he returned with urgent pleasure. He said in a husky voice, "Just as soon as possible."

Claire's limbs felt as though they were dissolving. She put her arms around his neck, he put his arms around her waist, and they kissed again. She couldn't believe how good he tasted.

"I think you're wonderful," he whispered in her ear.

"You're pretty nifty yourself," she whispered back and pulled him closer.

When Malcolm returned to Seattle, Russ came over for a beer and to catch up. He congratulated Malcolm on his new relationship, and on helping to provoke an organized resistance to the water export project. Malcolm said, "Everything go okay with the animals?"

"No problem. I called Geraldine, we got together Saturday."

"And …?"

"And we ended up spending the weekend together."

"You don't say?" Malcolm smiled. "Fast work."

"I'm crazy about her," Russ said plainly. "I think she likes me, too."

"What's not to like?" Malcolm replied, grinning.

"I told her about your trip, the situation."

"Did you now?"

"She's your good friend, and if she's going to be my … well … I thought she should know."

"Fair enough. What did she say?"

"Watch out, brave warriors."

Malcolm's smile turned wry. "Good advice. With a little luck, the whole thing'll be out in the open soon. So. What more from the back door of Greed Incorporated?"

"They've got Jason Stamper – Energy Secretary – and they've got Edward Caccia."

"Governor of New York Edward Caccia?"

"Yup."

"Geez Louise." Malcolm felt a surge of anxiety as he watched the rain pour down his kitchen windows.

PART TWO

14

"VEZINA'S office is worse than a priest's on Sunday afternoon," complained Josette, his assistant. "When one group leaves, another arrives. I've never seen so many engineers and lawyers in my life!" At the new division of the Caisse Laurier on Rue Peel, Langevin's PA was sympathetic. "Things are crazy over here too. Monsieur Langevin is moving money around like he's Rothschild. What's your boss going to do with all that cash, Josette?"

There was a pause on the other end of the line. Josette whispered, "Jacinthe, I had to sign a paper that said I wouldn't speak with anyone about what we're doing. All those people who come out of Vezina's office looking like they just got their Christmas presents early – the ones who are coming down from Jonquière and Chicoutimi – I have to make them sign something too."

"Me too. I signed something when I was first hired." Another pause. The offer was clear: I'll show you mine if you show me yours.

She got no uptake. "Listen," Josette said. "I have to go. The mayor of Chicoutimi just walked in. *Salut.*" She hung up, acknowledged the visitor with a nod of her well-coiffed head, picked up the phone and announced him to Roch Vezina.

Royal Gagnon was quickly ushered in and Vezina gave him a tantalizing but limited version of the projects. After all, many of the sites were well north of Gagnon's bailiwick. Vezina stressed that the government fully approved in principle, and that the Caisse Laurier would be financing. "Let me also stress," Vezina said, at his huge desk with all of Montreal in the plate-glass windows behind him, "that we are asking all the people involved in this exploratory stage to maintain discretion. It's important that we are able to develop the plans in a comprehensive and satisfactory manner."

Pure merde, Royal Gagnon thought. By the time he stepped from the air-conditioned office tower to the stifling street below, he was a deeply troubled man. Okay, he said to himself, we'll have a five-year boom, okay, we need it desperately. But how many good jobs will it leave behind? And what will it do to the beauty of the region? This could sabotage our plans for serious ecotourism. Some months earlier, Gagnon had attended a day-long workshop for municipal leaders co-sponsored by the Committee to Save the Verchère and Eau NO, and he had seen the "before" and "after" photos of a small diversion dam that was already in place. The pictures were frightening. Assurances that the government was overseeing environmental considerations were laughable.

But he knew that the voters would be pounding the ground in the other direction if there were jobs. He decided to call Henri Scott. Also that Swedish fellow, Gunderson. And the mayor of Tadoussac. He was going to need help on this one. And he would have to tread very carefully if he didn't want to shoot his reelection campaign in the foot.

Returning in June from a meeting in Montreal with Vezina and Langevin, the Honorable Robert Corbeil was horrified to find a hundred demonstrators shouting and waving placards on the sidewalk in front of his office. The placards demanded a moratorium on water projects in the province, and were signed by the Committee to Save the Verchère. Olaf Gunderson personally handed a letter to the Minister detailing their demands. Then Corbeil reached his office and found that his communications director had patched through a call from the *Le Soleil* reporter Denis Lamontagne, who wanted to know about the demonstration and a rumor he'd heard about American companies being given the right to bulk export water. Corbeil vociferously denied the rumor, hung up and went crazy. When Serge Lalonde arrived as summoned, the Minister was pounding his desk and shouting about leaks from the Cabinet. Lalonde tried to reassure him, the result of which was an order from Corbeil to initiate telephone surveillance on Gunderson and the Verchère Committee. "Someone leaked that rumor to that punk Lamontagne," Corbeil shouted. "And I want to know who it is before they leak some more!"

The venetian blinds were turned down to keep the fiery sun out of the huge boardroom on the thirty-fourth floor of New York's InfoMedia Tower on Fifth Avenue. Richard Franklin had called a national meeting of his senior editors and producers. He looked particularly handsome in a blue silk blazer and striped shirt with white spread collar, the silver at his temples gleaming, his manicured hands eloquent as he spoke

"As you know," he said, addressing the thirty-seven men and four women who'd gathered from all over the country, "we like to have consistency in our approach to key issues. National editorials help. But two or three times a year, we look ahead to some of the issues we're anticipating, to give you guidance, to give *us* continuity. So let's see what's coming up this summer.

"Of course," he said, "number one, we'll be continuing our policy of support for the Administration's efforts to defeat terrorism – at home and abroad. Freedom of speech is one thing. An important thing. But comfort to the enemy is something else altogether. We've got national security considerations here, as you know. The government will draw certain lines for us where they have to. But we have to exercise our own judgment too, be responsible.

"Another important theme we'll be dealing with this summer is the weather. We all know it's already hotter than hell." Uncomfortable laughs around the table. "But it won't help if we fan the fires." He smiled at his little pun and the corners of thirty-eight obedient mouths turned up in return. "It would be irresponsible of our outlets to feed into hysteria about global warming. So keep your stories strictly factual, and avoid a lot of unnecessary speculation about causes and effects. And for Christ's sake don't give special interest groups a soap-box to foment panic." Everyone in the room understood the code for "kill environmental weather stories". Only one person had the nerve to challenge him.

"Listen, Rich," said Elias Hazen, editor of the *Los Angeles Star*. "Climate, heat, drought – we want our audience to buy our papers, we gotta do some stories. These issues are huge right now, and we can't just pretend they're not."

"Do your stories, Eli," Franklin said soothingly. "Report on the weather, what people are dealing with. Do some human interest stuff, do some stuff on weather cycles. Just don't become a mouthpiece for the environmentalists."

"There's no way we can just omit all the active environmental groups from our coverage, Rich. Half the time, they're *making* the story."

"Jesus, Eli, haven't you ever heard of negative spin?" Hazen lifted a skeptical eyebrow. "Eli, I'm not suggesting we take no responsibility for helping Americans deal with the consequences of this weather change. I've been made aware that a number of state and federal politicians are working on solutions, and we'll be ready with thorough coverage when they release their plans to the public. Okay?" Hazen considered Franklin's approach bad journalism. But he wanted to keep his job. He nodded his compliance.

"I've got the tape of a paid ad on my desk," said Samantha Everden of the Albany station WNEP, close to the Canadian border. "Sponsored by the River Alliance, something about the need for new ways to deal with water through cross-border, US–Canada planning, that sort of thing."

"Don't run it."

"But it's a paid comm —"

"I said, *don't run it*!" Franklin was categorical, and he intended to put a stop to any other network running it too, as soon as the meeting was over. He'd complied with a similar request for a cross-network boycott of an ad campaign for a green car not one year before, and he was going to call back the favor now.

"Now as you know," Franklin continued, "InfoMedia's got some pretty heavy investments in Canada. You're aware how crazy it is up there with the French nationalists. We want to make sure our outlets are voices for stability. So let's not give any wild-eyed idiot a spoon to stir that pot, either. Let's leave them alone. If they see that nobody's paying attention to their silly tantrums, maybe they'll just stop having them." Some of the editors and producers exchanged puzzled glances. But Franklin had laid down the law.

On June 21, an article by reporter Kazim Hachemi appeared in Canada's leading newspaper, the Toronto *Globe and Mail*. Hachemi, thrilled with his appointment as the new Washington guy, had been present at a White House press conference for foreign correspondents, and had nearly fallen off his chair when the US President broached the topic.

US PRESIDENT LOOKS FORWARD TO TALKS ON CANADIAN PIPELINE

The President of the United States declared yesterday that he wants to explore possibilities allowing the export of Canadian water to the "parched regions of his country." The President said, "The idea of a pipeline is especially promising." He declared that the US was in need of a comprehensive water replacement strategy, "especially looking forward to population growth in the western states," and that he was "ready to discuss the idea of a pipeline at any time."

In Ottawa, Liberal Minister of Natural Resources Herbert Osler was not available for comment. Dorothea Engler, the leader of the New Democratic Party, said, "It appears the President wants us to go back to being a resource extraction economy – for the United States. He pulled his country out of the Kyoto Accords and is promoting an agenda of rampant consumption with no regard for conservation. Parliament must say no."

On the other hand, Brian Stockard, leader of the Canadian Conservative-Alliance Party, warmly welcomed the proposal. "If we negotiate for the necessary environmental safeguards and achieve fair remuneration, there's no reason why Canada shouldn't trade water," he said.

The Prime Minister is in China on a tour promoting Canadian business, and could not be reached for comment.

For three days, the story dominated the English Canadian press. Various pundits dismissed the idea of a pipeline as unworkable and too costly from an environmental point of view. A reporter from the *Vancouver Sun* finally tracked the Prime Minister down. "Canada's waters are not for sale," the PM said from Shanghai. "But sooner or later, we'll have to help our neighbors to the south, and we'll have to face that reality in the near future."

James Amanopour called Claire and told her about the brouhaha. Claire called Malcolm. He spoke from a telephone booth and she from a friend's loft – just in case people were listening in routinely on her office, home and cell phones. She wasn't sneaking out to make her other water-related calls, which were very much in the line of duty, though she was circumspect about what she said. But neither of them wanted Malcolm involved.

"There isn't a word, not one *word*, about the press conference in the US media." The frustration rang in Claire's voice.

"How do they do that?" Malcolm said. "It's as though the whole thing were completely orchestrated."

"Don't let me shatter your illusions, Mal. But it could very well be. We've been told by our friends in the media often in the last five years, around a number of issues, that instructions have been sent to editorial boards to provide no coverage of eco-Justice, or, where this was impossible, to provide negative coverage. It's been a recurring problem."

"That fits," Malcolm said. "The Seattle papers only write about eco-Justice to rant about how destructive it is."

"My point. In Europe our corporate markets events make the front pages, and many of the big newspaper chains have joined the boycott. But here we can't get one positive column inch. We've consistently published alternative economic strategies for the forest communities, for example. Not *one* of them has ever been reported in the mainstream press. Instead the media keep on howling about how eco-Justice cares about bears and trees and owls, but not people."

"Freedom of the press belongs to those that own one," Malcolm said. "As A. J. Liebling once said. Still, it's hard to credit."

"Why? Monopoly, sponsorship, cross-ownership ... What else is new?"

"Remember that incredible media conspiracy to defame those seven wildlife scientists in Washington, to get the lynx delisted as an endangered species and push through that big development in Utah?"

"How could I forget," Claire said. "The heads of the US Forest Service, the US Fish and Wildlife Service and the Washington Department of Fish and Wildlife held press conferences and wrote letters to the media refuting the lies about the scientists, and not *one* retraction was ever printed. Oh God," she said. "Sometimes I wonder what's the point."

"So I gather you've made no progress getting media uptake yourself?"

"Zip. Nada. *Rien*, even from my usual stalwarts. The River Alliance, bless them, tried to take out a paid TV commercial about the need for cross-border water planning, and every network station in the country turned them down. I've talked with the Sierra Club, the Nature Conservancy, the World Wildlife Fund, and the Global Watch Institute. Everyone says they're willing to put information on their web sites. But a serious coalition and campaign is out of the question unless, as they keep telling me, the issue gets some 'profile' down here."

"Meaning, of course, the ever-elusive media coverage?"

"Which I can't get without some hard information. And that is either not available officially, or, well, stolen. Sylvie says her information indicates that the project is moving forward at a terrifying pace. We need that profile fast. Maybe I'd better make some news myself."

15

THAT year, North America received less precipitation than in any preceding month of June ever, and temperatures all over the continent broke records. By July, farmers from Oklahoma to Saskatchewan, holding dusty, friable clods of earth with stunted, puny seedlings in their hands, squinted up at the hot sun, and shook their heads. Beef cattle went thirsty and hungry, and emergency rail and truck trains ferried hay across the continent to help farmers rescue their animals.

Small rivers ran dry, large rivers sank to unknown levels, the Great Lakes plummeted. Lake freighters had to offload their cargoes or face becoming mired in the canals. Their owners went bankrupt; the people who relied on their passage fees went on unemployment insurance. Forest fires that had started as early as May raged across the continent. From Atlanta to Toronto generating stations pumped out fossil fuel emissions at record levels to power the continent's air conditioners. Masses of smog roved the continental skies, covering regions the size of large states, choking babies and old people. It was the hottest summer of the hottest year since people began keeping records more than one hundred and forty-five years before.

The weather was front-page news, week after sweltering week. Who could ignore the hundreds of people dropping dead in apartments that had turned into ovens in the poor neighborhoods of American cities? Then Europe got blasted with coke-oven temperatures too, along with forest fires run amok and tens of thousands of deaths. Much was made in the media of annual variations and periodic fluctuations and tropical currents. But, though frantic reports from the United Nations, environmental organizations, scientific associations and even government agencies were sounding alarms about greenhouse gases and climate change – alarms that received a few column inches in the press, or a little air-time on the weather and Discovery channels – the mainstream media seemed determined to avoid tying these reports of global warming to the heat and parched conditions everyone was suffering through.

The lesson was not lost, however, on the men of the Amwatco consortium, on both sides of the Canada–US border. Nor was it lost on the people who had begun to fight them.

In July in the large upstairs room of the Bear Pond Bookstore on Montpelier's State Street, Claire sat at a microphone, ready to speak to the two hundred or so people who had come to hear her on "Vermont and the Crisis in Water". Reporters from the *Burlington Free Press*, WVMT television and Vermont National Public Radio were in attendance. The air conditioning labored noisily and uselessly against the blistering heat outside and the hot television lights indoors. Malcolm, who had flown in for the event, noted beads of sweat on Claire's upper lip and lines of strain on her face. But she still looked wonderful and her voice was strong.

She detailed the causes of the country's water crisis – fertilizers from factory farming that fed pools of deadly organisms, medical wastes, derivatives from gasoline and industrial effluents that created hideous toxic soups. She spoke about the 700 thousand miles of deteriorating water pipes, the documented increase in gastrointestinal illnesses, even cancers, as a result of back-up and debris and toxic accumulation in municipal systems. You could have heard a pin drop. The list was long and overwhelming, and few in that room had ever heard it itemized in quite that way.

As the audience struggled with the heat and the bad news, Claire gave some examples of big-time environmental criminals, dating back to early in the twentieth century. "Rockwell International, ladies and gentlemen," she said, "manufacturers of universal joints for automobiles, from 1910 on, discarded lead, arsenic, cyanide, and other toxins directly into Michigan's Kalamazoo River. Eventually this turned into a Superfund site. Multiply this sort of thing all over the country. We have a lot of Superfund sites, though since 1995, Congress put an end to the original 'polluter pays' policy. General Electric factories, dating from 1946 to 1976, dumped two million pounds of cancer-causing PCBs directly into New York's Hudson River. Six hundred thousand pounds remain. GE spent two and half million dollars on advertising campaigns persuading the Hudson Valley residents that dredging the river would make the situation worse. Which the environmental experts hotly deny – though without the two point five million dollars to tell their side of the story." The tension in the room rose perceptibly.

She then provided some words of encouragement. "In 1972," she said, "America passed the Clean Water Act, which, for a time, lessened the most flagrant forms of water pollution. Note, my friends," she slowed her pace so no one would miss her message, "when polluters resisted the change and the federal government refused to properly enforce its own laws, it was local citizens' groups who played the essential role in pressuring them to comply. As a result, the water quality of many rivers improved. This example of the power and potential of strong local action still shines brightly. It is the example that I hope will be taken up by the citizens of Vermont today."

Claire had a number of related points to cover in short order. "Did you know," she said, "that bottled water is the source of a twenty-two billion dollar a year industry worldwide? And did you know that, where tap water is still up to standard, bottled water is often no safer or healthier? That's because bottled water is largely unregulated. Yet if affluent people buy bottled water all the time, they remove political pressure from authorities to guarantee clean safe water for everyone. Eventually, as public systems deteriorate even more, only the well-off will have safe water. This is already the case in many parts of the world today, and folks, it's where we're heading in the USA."

"One point five million tons of plastic are used every year by the bottled water industry," she went on, "with the toxic chemicals posing a threat to the environment at both the manufacturing and the disposal stage. And the transport adds significantly to greenhouse gas emissions." By the stunned expressions on every face, it was obvious no one had ever thought the innocuous act of drinking bottled water had such heinous consequences. Many looked guiltily at the water bottles they were guzzling from.

"With the damage that's been done already, is it any wonder that American business interests, supported by our federal government, are today seeking ways to bulk-export Canadian water by pipeline and tanker from Quebec down to the American Mid- and Southwest? Yes, folks, this may be news to you. But this proposed project demands a whole new level of vigilance and action."

"Although bottling water on a large, industrial scale can damage aquifers, lakes and rivers, moving it out in a pipeline and supertankers accelerates that damage immeasurably. The havoc wrought by the construction of roads, the clearing of rights-of-way, the installation of port facilities – these have the potential to disrupt whole regional ecosystems – and, eventually, their neighboring regions." Claire paused. "That would be here, in Vermont."

There was much shifting and shuffling in the audience.

"So what does this mean for us?" Claire threw the question into the hush, paused for breath and went into the home stretch. "The answer is *not* privatization. Which is what this White House is pushing hard, along with the World Trade Organization and the IMF and the World Bank. I've brought a hand-out for anyone who's interested." She waved a sheet of paper. "The average annual rate for water in our cities in 2002 was $47.50. In municipalities with privatized water systems, that figure went as high as $100.17. And just ask Atlanta how responsive their private provider has been.

"No. We need to create public, continental bodies capable of managing and guarding our water. The International Joint Commission that governs the Great Lakes, though far from perfect, gives us the *beginnings* of a model. We need something stronger than that. And we need it soon."

Coverage appeared in the *Burlington Free Press*, on Vermont NPR, and on WVMT. All three reporters mentioned Ms Davidowicz's claim that plans to bulk export Quebec water through Vermont were afoot, but noted she had been unable to provide sources with which to confirm the story, other than to refer the reporters to the Ministry of Finance in Quebec City. Upon being reached, the communications director there said no such plans were in place, though the government was in the beginning stages of developing a water management framework, and would be announcing some contracts for development in the region north of Chicoutimi in the fall for major Quebec firms. Asked whether bulk exports were on the agenda, he said it was premature to comment.

Claire and Malcolm sat at the picnic table in the meadow of her Somerville house, breathing the sweetgrass, finishing a glass of red wine.

"Would it offend your feminist sensibilities if I told you I find you incredibly exciting when you give a great speech?" He took her hands in his. "Giving a speech, driving a car, sitting in a chair doing nothing - come to think of it, I just find you incredibly exciting."

He got a low laugh in return. "I'm not offended in the least." She was blushing, but the fading light hid it. "Since my feelings are entirely reciprocal." Her heart was racing and she felt slightly breathless. "I mean, not that I've heard you make a speech …"

Malcolm leaned over and whispered in her ear. "Ready to see if the chemistry works?"

With every conversation they had had, and with each of the long, personal, revelatory letters they'd exchanged in the weeks since they'd first met, Claire had come to like him more and more. He made her laugh, he made her think, he made her happy. And she felt trust too. The more she learned about his life and choices, the more she appreciated the loyalty and commitment of which he was capable. To a woman with Claire's history, this was an aphrodisiac in itself. Plus he was gorgeous.

"Ready," she said, leaning against him. He put his arms around her – strong, steady arms, she thought with delirious pleasure – and they kissed for a long time. "I have no doubt at all," she said, barely willing to stop for breath, "that the experiment will succeed brilliantly."

The first Saturday in August was a scorcher in Montreal. Still, by six o'clock a fresh breeze began to blow in from the northwest. By eight o'clock, crowds were thronging west to the park at the foot of Mount Royal. The side streets were jammed with cars, and the sidewalks with concertgoers, vendors, jugglers, fire-eaters, and clowns. At nine o'clock, on a stage at the base of the mountain, Inuit Dream, the warm-up band, got a driving rhythm going. As the huge crowd swayed, the band initiated a call-and-response, elevating the audience and taking it higher. When, at ten o'clock, Luc Morin himself finally appeared on stage, the crowd went nuts. Morin had a pelvis that moved anyone and everyone on the sexual continuum. *Pur laine* – that is to say, pure Québécois – he was like Ricky Martin in French. A long-time campaigner for the boreal forest, he was every young Quebecker's patriotic idol.

Morin leapt into a sequence of pulse-racing numbers that soon had fifteen thousand people dancing, stomping, clapping, and whistling. For an hour and a half the mountain shook. Then the music slowed, and Morin took up his guitar. He sang Gilles Vigneault's love song to Quebec, its proper anthem, "Mon pays n'est pas un pays, c'est l'hiver", – my land is not a country, it is winter – a song known to every single person in his audience, and they joined in the choruses. Many faces shone with tears.

When the last strains had subsided, Morin paused for a moment of silence. Then, in the poetic and political rhetoric of Quebec's nationalist movement, he addressed the crowd.

"What, *mes amis*," he called out, "what defines winter in Quebec?"

"*La neige!*" they called back in unison, happy to be thinking on that hot night of skiing and carnival and cool, white fields of snow.

"*La neige!*" he repeated. "Soft, white, frozen water, that blankets our land and feeds our lakes. Water that swells our rivers and nourishes our fields and our souls. Water in abundance, changing its beautiful form with the seasons. Well, *mes amis*. Our water and our land are in danger!"

The crowd stilled.

"Pollution, hydroelectricity, irrigation, global warming are destroying the planet's water as its population and its industries grow. The world is growing thirsty. And the water we have here in Quebec is turning into blue gold. Well, *mes amis*, our own government has plans to sell *our* water to American companies, without our consent!"

Shock tingled electric in the air.

"They will make it impossible for us, the people of Quebec, to have sovereign control over this most vital of resources!"

Boos started up, and people stamped their feet. Morin held up his hand. Quiet returned. He looked beautiful under the spotlights, sweat dripping down his chest, dark hair tousled, brown eyes sparkling with the thousands of lights strung around the stage. The people listened.

"Friends of the environment have asked me to bring this issue to you. They have asked me to tell you about Eau NO, their coalition, and to ask that you support their demand of a moratorium on all sales of water in Quebec until we can establish public management of our precious water." Applause started up and grew louder. "Yes, *mes amis,* please show them your support."

The applause swelled in waves, and then took up a regular rhythm. "Please," said Morin, addressing the committee members sitting in the front row. "Come up and take a bow." As Inuit Dream picked up their refrain again and the rhythmic clapping grew louder, the group that had met at Sylvie Lacroix's house mounted the stage and waved to the crowd. They were wildly cheered. Michel Herriveault took the microphone, thanked the people, and directed them to tables set up where they could sign petitions and volunteer lists, and find information packages for themselves, their communities and their political representatives. He announced a mass demonstration in front of the Montreal offices of the Environment Ministry to be held in September. Luc Morin had agreed to perform again.

Every entertainment writer in Montreal, and all the environmental reporters who had been tipped off that afternoon, madly scribbled notes, grabbed the coalition's material, and jumped into cabs to rush downtown and file their stories. The crowd itself stampeded to the information tables. On Sunday morning, Luc Morin's plea was all over the front pages of Quebec, in both official languages, and Eau NO, ecstatic with the success of their brilliant idea, was collecting boxfuls of signed petitions.

"Hello, Bernie," William Greele said, breathing hard and mopping his forehead in his workout room Sunday morning. "What's up? You calling from New York?"

"I am in Switzerland, Bill. I have just received a call from my director in Montreal. Also I have just sent you an e-mail. I thought you might be in Europe still."

Greele had gotten back from Essen in the small hours and gone straight to bed. "Just got back. Haven't had a chance to download yet but – "

"Have you heard about the concert?"

"Concert? What concert?"

Vogel explained.

"Excuse me, Mr Greele –" Jurgen had his head around the door.

"Just a minute, Bernie –" Greele was feeling stunned.

"Sir, there's an urgent call from Mr Franklin on line two. I told him you were occupied, but –"

"Bernie, I'll call you back," Greele said. "Rich is on the other line." He punched the button for line two. His voice and his hands were shaking.

"You don't have to tell me. I just heard about it." The news was sinking in and he was beginning to flush with rage. "What the hell? Who are these people?"

"I don't know, Bill," Franklin said. "I asked one of my guys to scan the American Sunday media. The good news is no one covered it."

"Of course no one covered it. I told you, no one cares about Quebec. But get your people to do the same tomorrow, too. Just in case." He saw the light for line one light up.

"Excuse me, Mr Greele." Jurgen was at the door again.

"Just a sec, Rich. What now, Jurgen?"

"Mr Mezulis on line one –"

"All right, all right," Greele snapped. "Get back to me on this tomorrow Rich. Got to go. Gabe's on the other line." He punched the other button. "Yeah," he said, breathing hard, "I know all about it. Bernie and Rich have just called."

"Roch Vezina just called me," Mezulis said. "He says half of Montreal was there. He also says he thinks the environmentalists have trumped the PQ's Quebec card by playing it first. He doesn't think it's decisive. But it's a blow."

"No kidding," Greele said savagely.

"Sir?" Jurgen was back. "Mr Hurst is on line two."

"Tell him I'll call him back!" Greele shouted. His face was an alarming shade of red and the sweat was pouring off it. Jurgen hesitated to contradict him.

"I did sir. He said he had to speak to you immediately – "

"Godammit!" Greele was on the verge of exploding. "I'll call you back, Gabe." He punched the blinking light and felt the blast in his ear.

"I've just invested in the fucking Titanic!" Bunting Hurst roared at him without so much as a greeting. He was calling from Martha's Vineyard. His wife and kids were on the beach under a clear blue sky, and Hurst was in his study ready to throw up his breakfast. "Isn't this just what you said wouldn't happen?"

"Get a grip, Bunting," Greele said harshly, imposing on himself a calm he did not feel. "Just *cool it* until I've spoken with Lalonde or Corbeil. Nothing, absolutely nothing, was reported in our Sunday papers. So far no damage has – "

"Bull*shit*!" Hurst shouted back. "That was a very sophisticated maneuver they pulled. They're going to reach out to US environmentalists. Mark my words."

"It's a tempest in a teapot, Bunting. There's a *cordon sanitaire* around Quebec. As long as Ottawa doesn't care and there's no movement in the US, it doesn't matter how much noise they make. As long as the PQ government is prepared to use their majority and pass the enabling legislation."

"But that's the point, Bill." Hurst's tone could have corroded steel. "They won't pass that legislation if it's political suicide."

"I think they will," Greele said stonily. "I'll call you back after I've spoken to Quebec City. I'm not going to waste my breath on speculations." And he hung up. He knew he had added insult to injury by cutting his banker off like that, but he was feeling sick with fury, and wasn't able to keep talking. His blood pounded in his veins. He considered placing a call to Quebec City, but, reining himself in, stood up and threw open the French doors. A hundred and three Fahrenheit degrees with ninety-two per cent humidity hit him like a sledgehammer, and he slammed them shut again.

He had guaranteed that no effective opposition could develop in Quebec. He'd staked everything on it. His face flushed an even deeper crimson at the prospect of the humiliation, and he went to the intercom and called for ice-water. He was having trouble breathing when Jurgen found him a few minutes later, legs askew in the chair, fists clenched. "My God, sir, what's happened?" the butler demanded, helping his master to drink. "Shall I call the doctor?" He had never seen Mr Greele in less than the pink of health. But by an act of sheer will, Greele regained his breath, drank the water, and waved Jurgen away. He sat in his air-conditioned room, and considered his options.

16

WHEN Robert Corbeil had tasked Serge Lalonde with developing telephone surveillance of Olaf Gunderson and his committee in June, Serge found the assignment problematic as well as odious. It seemed a very, well, American way to proceed. And he was reluctant to call on the Sûreté, the provincial police, because the Commander's office leaked like a sieve. But as it happened, he had a good alternative that had been provided, albeit inadvertently, many months before by Staff Sergeant Jean-Luc Perrinault, head of the Montreal police force's computer crime unit.

In his routine perusal of the underground hacker boards one winter night, Perrinault had found a dossier of page-long postings describing the cash subsidies and tax breaks that Quebec's Ministry of Industry, Trade and Technology had awarded hundreds of firms. It was an impressive catalog of corporate welfare. It was also an unbelievable breach in government security. The next morning, he'd gotten in touch with the Deputy Minister responsible – Serge Lalonde – and was duly instructed to bring down the hacker, who went by the handle Radisson.

The fearsome demon "Radisson" turned out to be young, scrawny, pierced Victor Paquette. True, he had a massive, home-made super-computer that snaked into every corner of his bedroom and beyond. It ran on UNIX code artfully lifted and modified, and it turned out to be as powerful as any government mainframe in the Quebec system. On the other hand, he was just an idealistic kid of twenty-two who'd grown up in suburban Longueil, with a gargantuan IQ and no one to talk to. So he'd built a machine to provide him with companionship.

Victor was sent to the lock-up for almost six months to await trial. His parents were hysterical. But Perrinault persuaded the Deputy Minister and a Superior Court judge that the hacker could best repay his debt to society by building firewalls for the ministry he had violated. Victor had felt himself snatched from the jaws of disaster and placed on a plush velvet cushion.

Victor very rapidly developed an intense loyalty to the men who'd recognized his talent and saved his butt from certain annihilation. Serge had grown to like Victor quite a lot, and even invited him to dinner at home, where he entertained Nicole hugely. It made perfect sense to ask Victor's advice.

"You just want logs of calls, homes and offices?" Victor had wanted to know.

"At this point, yes. Let's see who's talking to whom."

"Fear not, *chef*. We can do it alone. Believe me. It's just the *telephone* company." Victor's tone implied that if he couldn't pull records from the telephone company, he might as well resign from the Society of Hackers.

Victor Paquette had a cycling holiday planned for the last two weeks of June. So he didn't begin until early July. Each morning he visited the telephone company's mainframes, looked for the numbers Gunderson and his committee members had called the day before, cross-referenced and traced them. Ten days into the exercise, he'd collected hundreds of numbers. He continued to watch for those that recurred, while tracing the names and other important details for the people he'd found. Over the next two weeks, he noticed that Gunderson himself spoke regularly with several people in different parts of the province who were not members of his committee, his family or his work network. Three and a half weeks into the exercise, as Victor was checking the calls that these people had made over the weekend, and reviewing the calls they had made in the previous couple of weeks, he found something that made him leap from his chair and put in an urgent appeal to his boss. But unaccountably, Serge had gone AWOL from the office and did not return his calls.

Serge Lalonde was at the front window in his living room, regarding with a sharp pain the movers leaning against the van parked outside, drinking coffee from paper cups. Serge, normally dapper and energetic, looked like he had just come off a heroin jag. He'd had four days of anguish since Nicole told him she would be leaving on Monday, and twenty-four hours to consider how seriously the weekend's concert was going to screw things up and how ugly Corbeil would be.

Nicole had rented a small apartment. But to put some distance between them, for the rest of August, she was going spend her holiday time in Sylvie's country house in the Eastern Townships. Serge had nearly gagged on his toast when he'd seen the photo of Sylvie on stage at the Morin concert in Sunday's *La Presse*. A shrill alarm had gone off in his head, but he had silenced it. Now the telephone was ringing, but he let it go. Eventually it stopped, and Nicole came down the stairs. She looked limp and wrung out and her eyes were red from crying.

"That was your secretary," Nicole said. "She says Corbeil wants you in his office immediately." She and Serge had exchanged only eloquent looks when he had opened the Sunday paper. "She said Corbeil wants the *telephone* records."

Serge covered his eyes with his hand.

"It's going to be bloody, you know," Nicole said. "You're not going to get away with this without a very big fight. Maybe you won't get away with it at all."

"Nicole, can we not start on that again, please?"

"You're right. No point."

"I have to call Victor. Give me a minute." Nicole watched despairingly as her husband picked up the phone, and instructed Victor to prepare a report he could show Corbeil in an hour. When he hung up, Nicole placed her hands on her husband's shoulders and put all the urgency and passion she could summon into trying, one final time, to change his mind. "Serge, my darling. I beg you to reconsider …"

"Reconsider what?" His voice was sharp and his gaze was bleak.

"Everything, Serge. Reconsider everything."

"My job, my career, my best judgment – that kind of 'everything'?"

"That's right, Serge, that kind of everything. We don't have to live in a big house, you have skills you could use for so many different purposes …" She looked at his face and trailed off.

"This is who I am, Nicole. Accept that."

"But I fell in love with a man who is not the one you say you are."

They looked at each other, and both began to weep.

"I'm going to wait six months, Serge," said Nicole. "I undertake now to do that. I won't find anyone, I won't sleep with anyone. For six months." She walked to the door, waved the moving men in. "And then I'll go back to France. Think about yourself, and me, and try to imagine a different future for us."

Serge picked up his briefcase, they embraced one last time. "*Je t'aime*," Nicole whispered in his ear, and he headed out the door. He drove the car around the corner, parked, and broke down for ten minutes.

Robert Corbeil's chief of staff had presented the Minister with petitions containing more than fourteen thousand signatures. This was but the first installment in a major petition drive, the covering letter from Eau NO announced, demanding a meeting with the Minister. To Corbeil's shock the letter itemized a list of the Amwatco consortium members and a brief but accurate summary of the project, which they threatened to release to the press if a response was not forthcoming within forty-eight hours.

Corbeil's substantial stomach heaved. It would be almost impossible now to present the water project as a great victory for Quebec sovereignty and national maturation, when these people would frame it as the sell-out of the century. They still had the jobs to offer – and that gigantic *bonbon* still might outweigh all other considerations. But the going would be much tougher. And now he had the telephone records in front of him.

"Have you examined them yet?" Serge shook his head no, horribly aware that he had been avoiding his task. His distaste for the things they were doing to bring this project into being was growing into loathing, but he knew he could not evade his responsibility any longer. Together they read Victor's report.

It revealed that several of the people Olaf Gunderson called regularly matched those in the photo of the Eau NO Committee in *La Presse*. Each of these people had been making calls to other individuals and organizations who might conceivably be involved in organizing against the water project – mayors of regional towns, local and national trade unions, environmental and citizens' organizations. Sylvie Lacroix was also in regular touch with eco-Justice USA offices, and the home of its director, Claire Davidowicz. This was underlined in Victor's report.

"But this is appalling!" Corbeil thundered, eyes bulging, skin almost purple with rage. "They're already organized! Why didn't you tell me this before? We've been humming along, thinking everything was splendid, and they've been covertly organizing an opposition for the last two months!"

"This is the first comprehensive report I've had," Lalonde replied testily, badly shaken. "It took us three weeks to get the technician and the surveillance system set up, for pity's sake. Victor just banged out this summary a few minutes ago." But Lalonde knew he should have been on it and answered Victor's summons, that he had let precious time go by because of his own ambivalence.

Mercifully, Corbeil's communications director knocked at the door and saved him further abuse. He had scanned the *New York Times*, the *Wall Street Journal* and the *Washington Post*, and checked the US wire services, and found absolutely nothing about Morin's concert. He noted a short item under "Entertainment News" in the *Globe and Mail*, which simply reviewed "the Quebec environmentalist rock star's" musical performance and omitted his speech. There was no other English Canadian coverage. Outside Quebec, the damage was close as dammit to zero.

Corbeil and Lalonde talked for an hour, and then Corbeil said grimly, "I'm going to see the Premier. I will be back in an hour and a half. We'll call Greele." The Premier's going to go crazy, Lalonde thought. Frothing, screaming nuts. "And afterwards," Corbeil told him, "I want you to meet with that creature from the black lagoon you hired to prepare this," he swiped the telephone report with his big hand, "and I want you two geniuses to figure out how those *salops* in the committee got the names of the consortium. Only you, I, the Premier, Vezina, and Langevin knew all those names. I want live taps on the whole committee, every single one! Tell the Sûreté to give your boy whatever he needs to do it. And tell him to put a live tap on that *Le Soleil* reporter, Lamontagne, too. He had wind of this two months ago. We have to know who he's talking to." The Minister stalked out the door.

Serge felt a bleak, cold draught sweep down his back.

The fiery voltage of Greele's fury scorched the telephone lines. "I want to hear from you now that our deal is binding, and that we will have enabling legislation from your government by December at the very latest! Nothing moves forward without that assurance. And we're not going to start moving backward!"

The Minister said coldly that the government was still committed, and that they were going to proceed to ensure that the battle went as well as possible. "We will announce," he explained, "a structured and controlled public consultation on a master water plan which *we* will provide. We will announce that we are having exploratory meetings with firms capable of bringing it to fruition. If, in the meantime, that stupid committee gives out the names they have, we will say that these may or may not be among the firms we are considering. No more. We will tell the people of Quebec that if we do not strike a separate deal with the Americans over our water soon, the terms will be negotiated by Ottawa. The Premier is ready to lead that fight and go to the wall on it. *We* will set the terms of the debate. *We* will organize individual hearings, and *we* will position our opponents as amenders of *our* plan! And we are willing to legislate by end of the fall session."

"I don't like it," Greele said. "It'll only give the enviros a chance to scream and maneuver."

"Well, Bill," Serge interjected, doing his best to sound matter-of-fact. "I recall discussing with you the importance of decent provisions on environmental considerations from the beginning. Our senior engineers assessed your plans this morning in light of the weekend's events, and they do not believe that they can make it through public scrutiny. I have instructed them to develop an estimate of the nature and projected costs of necessary revisions. It's clear now that the project has to be at least minimally environmentally respectable." Lalonde had his one happy moment of the day as he delivered this news.

Greele was contemptuous. "Your opponents are going to say that bulk water exports per se are damaging. They're not going to go for your plan, even with cosmetic changes. And I'm telling you now, they'd better be cosmetic."

"All the better," Serge came back. "If they reject the whole thing, we can show how ridiculous and unrealistic their approach is, how it robs rural Québécois of their right to a decent living." Corbeil was nodding approvingly with every phrase. "Given the Morin concert and its consequences, and how that has shaped our options, it's much better to have the environmentalists trying to improve *our* plan – it will undoubtedly cost you some profits, but not the bulk by any means – than to have a multi-party revolt in the back benches of the Assembly because of huge demonstrations in the streets. Then we couldn't impose the legislation even if we wanted to."

Serge could hear Greele breathing, dragon-like. "Believe me – us," Serge said, trying once more for agreement, "we know how to do this. It's better to co-opt than confront."

"What the hell is this committee?" Greele demanded, off on a different tack. "How did they get so well organized?"

"They are exactly who we would have expected to oppose the plan," said the Minister. "But they're at least three months ahead of schedule," he added angrily.

"Where the hell did they get their information?"

"Ah," said Corbeil icily. "I can assure you, Mr Greele, they did not learn this information from any of us. We have pulled the telephone logs for all the committee members." Greele gave thanks that at least the Quebeckers had thought to initiate surveillance. "We see certain patterns of communication here in Canada, but none that suggests to us any source of information. We do see, however, that regular calls are being made by some committee members to the Washington, DC and New York offices of eco-Justice USA. We don't know yet whether these calls concern our project. But you should be making sure that no information is leaking on *your* side." Corbeil's lips were blue with rage.

"Put live taps on the key people," Greele said.

"In place," Corbeil replied, stretching the truth.

"I'll take care of eco-Justice here," Greele said. "Cat's out of the bag anyway."

"Listen," Corbeil hissed. "If you want to see this project complete, you will continue to control the flow of information rigorously! You must find out who was prompting the Montreal group to get organized. Who knows what other information these parties might have, and what damage they can do!"

"Right," said Greele tightly. "Send me down your security reports. I need to reflect on matters for a couple of days. I need to know what this is going to mean to the bottom line. In the meantime, I am leaving this conversation with the assurance that you are committed to passing legislation by Christmas. I warn you, I may insist you move it through first thing in September!"

Serge sat in his study with Victor Paquette as the sun set, drinking a beer called *Fin du Monde* and smoking Victor's Gitanes. Serge was glad for the company, but he was also insane with anxiety. Handing over the envelope of telephone logs that morning, Victor had said accusingly, "I've left some stuff out you better know about before the day is out. I *tried* to reach you."

Victor put Sylvie Lacroix's June and July telephone logs in front of his boss. Wordlessly, he drew Serge's attention to the calls highlighted in yellow. Serge looked at the page, and tried to refocus. It didn't work. He was looking at his own home telephone number, repeated about twenty times, in calls made from Sylvie to Nicole and Nicole to Sylvie over the last two months. The anvil that had been hovering in the semi-conscious zone over his head for weeks dropped. "Nicole and Madame Lacroix have been close for many years," he croaked, attempting a casual explanation of the yellow lines.

Victor looked at him and said, *"Mon oeil."*

"It's true Victor. They're good friends. I have no reason to suspect that Nicole tipped anyone off about the project." Liar, he thought. "She knew very little about it – certainly not the facts that Eau NO had today."

"Then why are you so scared, Serge?" Victor demanded. "You're shaking like a leaf."

"Because the big boss in the US wants our telephone records for his own security people – so they can work on linkages down there. How do you think it's going to look? Especially when they find out she just left me this morning."

"Who left you this morning?"

"Nicole. She moved out. She's gone."

"But why?" Victor was horrified. His idea of successful yet cool Serge included his smart, beautiful wife.

Because, Serge thought, she thinks I'm a sell-out and a renegade. He evaded the question. "Victor, forgive me. I don't have the heart to speak of it now." His exhausted adrenals hurt, his head pounded, and he could taste panic in his throat. He put his head in his hands. "What am I going to do?"

"Don't worry about it, boss." Victor thought, the guy's in mortal agony here. The least I can do is help him out. Victor had absolutely no loyalty to the bureaucracy or the government, who would gladly have thrown him to the wolves. But he really loved Serge. "Hey, take it easy, no one has to see this. I've already deleted her from the report for Corbeil. She's not the source of the leak, so it doesn't matter if we just take out those calls. What they don't know won't hurt them."

"You can do that?" Serge raised his head. "What if they go back to the originals, at the telephone company?"

"Jesus, Serge, they're not gonna do that. It wouldn't occur to them."

"You don't know these people."

"I'll take care of it. Right now." Victor turned to his laptop. He plugged into the telephone line. "Turn your back if you don't want to witness the commission of a crime, and I'll pay a little visit to the master computer at mère Bell, I've got a little macro written here that should do the job ..." Serge heard whirs and clicks, and presto! the calls were gone from the mainframe records. Victor took the yellow-lined pages of telephone logs, folded them into accordion shapes, burned them in the wastebasket, and dumped an ashtray full of cigarette butts on top of them.

Serge felt a great weight lift off his shoulders. "That's it? It's really gone?"

"There's the original tape back up, in a climate-controlled room in Pierrefonds or St Zotique or somewhere. But you'd have to break and enter to get that. No one's gonna look there. It's gone," said Victor.

"*Merci, mon ami*," said Serge feelingly. "For that act of true friendship."

"*De rien*," the younger man said, abashed. "And I'll run the tapes from the taps by you before I do anything else with them." Oh God, taps! thought Serge.

17

SARAH Greele was on a two-week retreat at an old Santa Cruz mansion turned exclusive spa. It featured a diet of the liquefied extracts of every edible leaf and vegetable the planet had to offer, plus chi kung and tennis, personal workout coaches for aerobics and weight training, and daily massages. She was enjoying the feeling of warm, oiled hands sliding over her toned and tingling body. Face down on her table, Sarah acknowledged to herself that for years now, her sensual life had consisted entirely of massage, performed by countless young women with strong, searching hands. Now, her bonds to her husband loosening, she allowed herself a sound that acknowledged her pleasure. The young masseuse felt a shudder pass through her client's body.

In Indian Hill, William Greele called the spa and left a message for Sarah. Then he flew west with the dawn.

Though the Midwest was burning up and the Northwest was short on water, a cool ocean breeze greeted him in Seattle. As a hotel waiter set out coffee, rolls and pastries in his suite at the Westin, Greele turned on CNN to catch the morning news. A vast throng filled the screen. "Yes, Brick, it's another monster rally," the reporter was saying. "I'm in Buenos Aires, as you can see, and every gaucho and his gal have shown up to support GO KYOTO —" Her words were drowned by an immense cheer, as a building-sized banner was unfurled.

"The process hasn't lost any momentum, I see," said the anchorman.

"You're right, Brick, if anything it's —"

Greele heard a knock at his door, clicked off the television, and welcomed his guests. They quickly got down to business. He summarized the conversation with Quebec and concluded, "I told them point-blank that we had to have their assurances now that they will pass this legislation by Christmas, whether it's popular or not."

"Good," Nick Kamenev affirmed vigorously. "It's the precondition for proceeding, far as I'm concerned."

Greele said, "They have this ridiculous notion that if they conduct a controlled quote unquote public consultation they'll be able to use it to rubber-stamp the plan and push it through by Christmas. I think we should tell them to ram it through in September."

"Well," Gabor Mezulis said. "They're bright boys. Their plan gets the project and an unblemished chance to form the next government without provoking a huge fight. Which would be the best outcome for us too."

"You think so. But listen to this," Greele came back. "They told me that if they try to ram it through next month in the face of a loud popular opposition, apparently junior Assembly members could break party discipline, cause a revolt, and the legislation could fail. Could something like this really happen?"

Everyone looked at each other and shrugged. "Maybe," Mezulis said. "If they say so, I guess."

"So, Gabe," Greele said, "if the consultation does not go well, despite their best-laid plans, if a big opposition develops, say, over the fall, what's to stop a revolt at Christmas?"

The room was quiet. "Jesus," Mezulis said.

"My point," Greele returned. "We can't possibly risk waiting until Christmas if we don't know one hundred per cent it's in the bag. I'm not willing to let the fate of the project be decided by some risky political maneuver that could backfire as easily as succeed!" No one contradicted him.

"Okay," he said. "I've got another matter to talk to you about." As his associates listened, Greele explained the security leak. "Corbeil thinks it would have taken the Montreal group a couple of months to organize that concert, which suggests the leak took place about – well, only a few weeks after our Washington meeting."

"It's pretty hard to imagine any of those guys barbecuing the golden goose." Andrew Albert Stiller articulated the general sentiment.

"Why would they agree and then sabotage the project?" Mezulis said.

"The people in your company know more about the scope of the project than anyone else. Could you have a whistle-blower on your staff?" Nick Kamenev asked Mezulis.

"It's possible," Mezulis replied. "I'll make inquiries. But really, no one comes to mind."

"So," continued Stiller, calculating, "two months ago – not our political friends, not our employees. If that's true, it would have to be one of us."

Kamenev straightened up and his eyes narrowed. He looked at Stiller and Mezulis, and thought of the others – Massaro, Franklin, Vogel, Hayes, Hurst. "Frankly, Bill, I can't see it," he said. "What would be the motive?"

It didn't feel right to Greele either. He had hand-picked his group, and not one comment or incident since their initial meeting had led him to doubt their faithful commitment to the project.

"I suspect somebody has found something, seen something," Kamenev continued, thinking out loud.

"How?" said Stiller. "We've got no paper trail. I mean everyone's companies are working on some aspect, but the high-level information you're talking about isn't known to the employees." He stopped, struck by a thought. "Has anyone made hard copies of our correspondence?"

Kamenev looked pained. "You didn't," said Stiller, with deep dismay. "For Chrissakes, why? Who knows who might have seen them?"

"I just did it once," said Kamenev. "In May when we were working up all the specs. I burned the papers the same day. In my study, at home."

"I print out all the e-mails I send and receive," Greele said. "I keep a central file in Indian Hill. The papers never leave my office. I make no apologies. No one comes into my office there."

"No one saw mine either," said the Colonel. "My question, could someone be reading our correspondence electronically? I mean, off our computers?"

"Absolutely not!" Stiller retorted, affronted. "It's got thirty-four decillion possible keys. *No one* can break into it. Look somewhere else." He tossed his long hair.

"Thank you gentlemen," Greele said, rising. "I'll take your views under advisement. May I assume, however, that all of you are still committed to going ahead?"

"Jesus Christ, Bill," said Mezulis feelingly. "How can you even raise the possibility of not going ahead? We've already broken ground for roads." The others voiced agreement.

"All right," said Greele. "But I'm still not sure about our electronic security."

"Be sure," said Stiller, regarding Greele with the insolence of the self-confirmed genius. "Be very sure. No one can break CyberKrypt."

"Very well," said Greele. "Thanks for your counsel. Goodbye Gabe – I'll see you for dinner to discuss our position on the revisions they're going to want. And consider their threats to our bottom line. Nick," Greele said, laying a heavy hand on the Colonel's shoulder as he opened the door, "stay back a moment, won't you. I'd like you to take over our security."

At a telephone booth in suburban Tacoma, Malcolm punched in the home number for the curator at the Smithsonian who had been lending her telephone to Claire. Visiting her friend Andrea Baretti's downtown loft was a regular part of Claire's life when in Washington.

"Hey," Malcolm said.

"Hey yourself." Claire paused to bathe in the warm, melting sensation she experienced when she heard his voice. "Everything set for this weekend?" she asked. She was going to meet him in Portland and visit his cabin in the Cascades.

"Yep," he said. "I can hardly wait."

"Me too." Another pause, which said even more than the words. Then Malcolm told Claire about the exchange of angry e-mails he and Russ had monitored on Sunday.

"It was brilliant," Claire said. "Using nationalism to pit the people against the government, maybe even the sitting members against the Cabinet."

"Well, congratulations," Malcolm said.

"Thanks. But you know, Mal, there's been nothing here, not one word. The talk I gave wasn't picked up by anyone outside Vermont. There's still no profile to the issue, and no outing of Greele and Co., which we need desperately if I'm going to make any headway building a campaign. I don't believe they can win alone in Quebec."

"Still no journalist willing to write about it?"

"Not so far."

Reluctantly, Malcolm broached another topic. "They're very worried, Claire. I suspect they'll be launching surveillance on the Montreal Committee, if they haven't already done it. When they get to looking at the telephone logs, they'll find the eco-Justice USA connection. I wouldn't be surprised if there's a live tap on your office phone by the time you get in. Home too. That's in addition to the ones I imagine the FBI and the NSA keep as a matter of routine."

"Right," she said grimly. "Most comforting."

"So for the time being, darlin', no calls without precautions. Not even cellphones. We can talk about how to communicate when we see each other this weekend. Better safe than sorry."

"Okay," Claire said, suddenly uneasy and anxious. Her shoulders hunched forward, and she shivered. "But what if we need to talk again this week?"

Malcolm considered the problem. "We both need to get cellphones in someone else's name. We should have done it a long time ago, in retrospect. Can you do that?"

"Yes."

"Do it then. Leave the number with Andrea, and ask her to call it to Geraldine Morrow. I'll give Geraldine mine, they'll exchange them, then we can talk without worrying. And if anything comes up beforehand, have Andrea call and leave a message with Geraldine. And don't worry about inconveniencing anyone at any time, Claire. Call if you need to."

"Okay," Claire said. She wrapped her arms around her chest.

"Hey, sweetheart." She smiled at the endearment and longed to be with him. "It's gonna be okay. It's all going to come out in a matter of days or weeks, and we won't have to hide anymore."

"Okay," she said. "See you at one o'clock Friday, at the airport."

"Wild horses, baby."

Claire let herself out of the loft, and headed on foot to the office. The lid to a Pandora's box of paranoid terrors had somehow been pried open. More than anything, she was overwhelmed by dread at Malcolm's vulnerability. She urgently needed to know whether Eau NO had succeeded in finding a way to identify the consortium independent of him. She also needed to blow the story open in the US, in a way that wasn't traceable to Malcolm. Had the water project been an organizational priority, she might have been able to assign her assistant to local intelligence-gathering. And that would surely have yielded one concerned bureaucrat somewhere who was willing to talk or help. But Juniper Diaz was overworked as it was. Claire stopped, thought for a moment, and turned back to Andrea's loft. When she got there, she made two calls.

18

DOUGLAS Boyle stood in front of the wall of mirrors, contemplating the muscles he would target in his morning workout. He still regarded the worm-like scars over his cut pectorals, the result of building muscle at unnatural speed when he was competing, as badges of honor. He padded to the kitchen in bare feet and jockey shorts and drank a tall glass of cranberry juice, unsweetened. Then he headed down to the family room, which was filled with Nautilus equipment and free weights. He attacked each station with one hundred per cent concentration, as the sweat poured down his face and body. No pain, no gain.

He dressed in his usual polo shirt, chinos, aviator shades and expensive shoes. Then he drove his black GMC Typhoon to Skypoint, arriving at eight forty-five, looking and feeling like one mean motherfucker.

At two in the afternoon, he got a summons from his boss. "Let's take a walk outside, Doug," Kamenev said. That's new, Boyle thought. They met at the main doors, and headed into the park-like gardens.

"I won't beat around the bush," Kamenev said at last, "I didn't bring you out here to talk business as usual." No kidding, Boyle thought. "I need a job done. Not a Skypoint project, at least not directly." Kamenev glanced at Boyle.

"Go ahead," Boyle said. "I'm listening."

"Good," said Kamenev. "I'm part of a resource extraction deal up in Quebec – very, very big. It needs to stay out of the media and away from the environmental groups here – I mean the US, not Seattle per se – for a couple of months, minimum. Ideally three or four."

"Political work," Boyle said.

"Yeah, that's right. And sensitive," said Kamenev. As they patrolled the lawns, he described the project and the breach in security.

Doug Boyle presided over Skypoint's corporate security – the muscle and the espionage. He was a graduate of Caltech, the Air Force and the National Security Agency, where he had headed an aeronautics intelligence-gathering branch. There he had become familiar with every form of surveillance technology, from spy satellites to the tiniest of cameras and microphones. All these he had deployed primarily for the United States Trade Representative, the NSA's major client. When BMW was going to outbid McDonnell Douglas in Pakistan, say, or Airbus was going to outbid Boeing in Spain, Boyle's intelligence had given stateside firms a chance to … refine their approaches.

Boyle's identity had been forged in the performance of his job. It didn't create much of an inner life – or a family life – but it created an obsessive, goal-oriented security chief for Kamenev. In addition, his ongoing contacts with the NSA were unparalleled.

"Most immediately," Kamenev said, "we really need to know what this eco-Justice USA connection is about, and how far it's gotten. And we need to know very fast." Kamenev made him an offer. Boyle was delighted.

"I'm honored that you've chosen to call on me, sir."

Malcolm's doorbell sounded, loud and unexpected in the summer night. Clyde hissed and arched his back, looking like the spawn of a carrot and a porcupine. "Your objection is duly noted," Malcolm told the cat. He looked through the peephole and saw the shoulders, neck and chin of a big man wearing a cowboy shirt. Familiar but not identifiable. He opened the door, and had to fight to keep the astonishment from his face. There, looking even angrier than the first time Malcolm had met him, stood Jeff Brannigan. What's *he* doing here? Malcolm thought. Come to kill the competition?

"Hey there, Jeff," Malcolm said. "What a surprise. What brings you here? Bonnie, be quiet." The dog was carrying on.

Brannigan was frowning, but he bent the long, long way down to the Westie, put out a huge, weathered hand, and in a moment he'd made friends with her. Malcolm liked him for that. "Come in, why don't you," he said. "You must have something very important on your mind."

"I do," Brannigan said, moving toward the living room and sitting down in Malcolm's reading chair.

"Any point asking how you found me?" Malcolm asked.

"None." Whatever Brannigan had come to say seemed to have stuck in his throat. Damned if I'm going to make it easier for him, Malcolm thought.

Malcolm sat down on the couch. Brannigan's blonde hair had not had the benefit of a professional barber for some time, though his clothes were clean and his body strong. His large, slightly protruding blue eyes were bloodshot. He fixed them silently on the other man. Oh get over yourself, Malcolm thought. "You're a long way from home, Jeff. Let me ask again, to what do I owe the pleasure?"

"Claire may be putting herself in serious danger."

"Come again?"

"I saw Claire. This water thing could be very, very bad for her health."

"Oh yeah?" Malcolm felt a bolt of fury at the thought that Claire had told Brannigan about him and the water project. "How would you know?"

Brannigan saw the anger. "Look, Malcolm – can I call you Malcolm? I'm going to level with you. I came here because of what I've pieced together, from what Claire told me, and from what I can see for myself. So you tell me if I'm right, and if I am, I'll tell you why it's dangerous. If I'm wrong, you get to curse me out for being an interfering son of a bitch, and I'm gone."

"Go ahead," Malcolm said. "I'm listening."

"Claire and I had a coffee together. There's something I'm doing that I wanted her support for. She's not giving it, didn't want to talk about it. So we talked about other stuff. I asked her about you." Malcolm made a face. "I knew you were crazy for her when I saw you that first time. I also noticed how glad she seemed to see you. So I asked. And she blushed. She refused to answer my questions, you'll probably be relieved to know."

Malcolm was ashamed of the transparency of his feelings, and didn't want Claire talking to Jeff Brannigan about anything, let alone him. But looking at the big, tired man, now sitting forward in his chair seeking some sort of connection with him, he suddenly realized something. He said, "You're still in love with her, aren't you?"

Brannigan winced and said with dignity, "I care for her a great deal. That's why I'm here."

"Okay," Malcolm said at length. "What's your problem?"

"It's her problem, and it's called William Ericsson Greele."

"Claire told you about *him*?" Malcolm was dumbfounded.

"Told me what?" Brannigan asked, smiling for the first time.

"You tell me, Jeff."

"Okay. Claire asked me what I knew about Greele. Claire knows that we're neighbors, kind of …"

"Claire mentioned that."

"Not very discreet of her." It was Brannigan's turn to be angry.

"She didn't tell me anything of significance, don't worry."

"Yeah. Anyway, Greele owns ten thousand acres, I have a hundred, so we don't socialize much. But I'd know about Greele anyway. He's the single largest pesticide manufacturer in the world. And he's also funding some of the most dangerous genetic technologies under development. On behalf of his companies, as well as Monsanto and Bonafabrica, the Trade Representative's office has been fighting initiatives by India, Thailand, half of Africa, all of Europe, to keep out genetically modified foods and terminator seed technology."

"Claire told me you do a lot of research."

"I do. I keep a database on the activities of the most important start-up companies doing the really dangerous cutting-edge work in animal-to-human technology transfers and on about fifteen of the big transnationals that buy and fund and trade them." It was obvious from the way he spoke that Brannigan was proud of his research. "Course they merge and morph and monopolize like mad. There were forty in 1990, when I started my database. Now we're down to fifteen or so really big ones. I've got access to … well … let's say information comes to me from a variety of different but excellent sources. You'd be surprised."

Malcolm thought that if other people were as uncomfortable with the directions their corporate bosses were taking as he was, he wouldn't be at all surprised if a whole network of whistle-blowers was silently at work across America, quietly holding down their jobs to pay the rent while sending out wave upon wave of brown envelopes so they could sleep at night. "How do people know to send stuff to you?" he asked.

"They generally send it to some mainstream environmental organization. And then someone inside sends the material on to me. Sometimes, they also send the name and coordinates of the contacts, I get in touch with them, we establish a relationship. I have amazing regulars." I believe it, Malcolm thought. "Claire knows all about my database. That's why she asked me about Greele."

"So what kind of profile have you seen?" Malcolm was fascinated. "What's he like?"

"Brilliant and ruthless."

"How?"

"Well, he jumped faster than any other transnational on the bio-technology bandwagon. And now no one's smarter when it comes to using government muscle to help his business. He's a huge player in the biotechnology cartel behind the US's push to use trade rules to outlaw the banning of GM crops. He moved a lot of his industrial production to Asia – India, Indonesia, China – ten years before anyone else. And he's a dangerous bastard close to home too. Six men were killed in the seventies trying to bring a union to some copper mines he owned in Montana. The working conditions and emissions in his US chemical plants are notoriously bad and the disability rates set records decade after decade. His lawyers have fought compensation suits with more success than any other chemical giant."

Brannigan shifted his shoulders and lowered his voice. "Since we started the Alberta–Montana wolf release program, his ranch foreman has led the opposition. Apparently Greele lost a few head of cattle to a pack, and the wolves are eating the deer he likes to hunt. Two federal rangers have died since then. One from a driving 'accident'. The other, from an arson bomb planted right in his office. Can't seem to get any new staff."

"I see."

"I asked Claire why she was interested in Greele. She told me that he's leading a consortium of people trying to buy bulk exporting rights to water in Quebec, that it's still effectively a secret, and that she's trying to help the environmentalists who are fighting it."

Once again Malcolm felt burned and his expression must have conveyed it. Jeff said, "Look here, Malcolm, I may have some other qualities Claire doesn't appreciate, and some views she doesn't share. But one thing she doesn't question is my ability to keep a secret. Or my environmental dedication." Malcolm's lips stayed tight, but he nodded.

"Now listen, I don't know any more than that. I don't know how you're involved. I told her to be careful, that it was dangerous to mess with Greele. She told me she could take care of herself. But I gave the matter a lot of thought, and now I'm here to tell you. You're her guy now. Watch her back. And if you're in this in any way, watch your own too. You do any military time?"

"Twenty years in the Air Force. Retired in ninety-one. Why do you ask?"

"Because Claire's a very sophisticated lady, politically speaking," Jeff replied. "But she doesn't understand jack shit about violence. Far as I'm concerned, she's committed to denying how big a part it plays in the real world. You worked for the wrong side, buddy. But you've been a warrior. At least you know how things really stand. And I'm telling you now – Greele thinks he's a kind of emperor, and he won't hesitate to use a mercenary Praetorian Guard if he thinks he has to."

Malcolm took all this in. Claire's own deep unease showed she was not naïve. But the evidence that Greele would not restrict himself to legal or economic means in fighting back, though not surprising, was sobering. "Thank you, Jeff," was what he finally managed to say. "You've given me very important information, and I really appreciate it."

"Good," Jeff said dryly. "Got any information for me?"

"Uh-uh. Not right now." Claire might trust Jeff but Malcolm didn't know him, despite this rather scary gesture of good will.

"Right. So I'll be on my way. Here's two numbers where you can reach me." Jeff reached into his pocket, pulled out a small notebook and started writing. "First one's a normal line, case you want to go sight-seeing or anything. Second one's secure. Just in case. Call only from a secure line." Jeff handed Malcolm the sheet of paper, made for the door, said goodbye, and was gone.

19

DESPITE Corbeil's protestations, Serge Lalonde excused himself from the office mid-week and drove down to the Eastern Townships, to Sylvie Lacroix's country house. As the hills began to swell, he rolled his windows down and let the warm, humid air, laden with the scent of sweetgrass, soothe his tight, anxious face. The miles sped by and at one o'clock, he found himself winding south down Route 245 into the little town of Bolton Center. He turned and drove a couple of miles east into the hills. Nicole's red Honda Civic was parked near a small wooden house. He parked his silver Peugeot behind it, and walked up to the front door. Before he knocked, Nicole flung it open. He said, "Nicole, we have to talk."

Nicole turned silently into the house and Serge followed her to the kitchen. Torn between anger and longing, her hands shook as she squeezed lemons and assembled sugar syrup for lemonade. They exchanged tense pleasantries. Finally, when Nicole recognized he was not there to apologize or seek reconciliation, she said, "Why did you come, Serge?"

"Corbeil is tapping the telephones of the Eau NO Committee."

"I gathered as much when he wanted the *telephone logs*," she replied acidly.

"I mean, he's ordered live taps now. But as for the logs, obviously you know what's in them." He spoke bitterly.

"You mean all the calls between me and Sylvie?" Shakily Nicole handed him a cold glass. The ice cubes clinked madly.

"How *could* you?" Serge demanded.

"How could I what?" she shot back, very angry. "How could I talk to my best friend?"

"What were you talking *about*, Nicole?"

"I really don't see what right you have to ask me that, *chéri*." Nicole was squinting with pain. "Since you have chosen to keep so many secrets from me."

"Secrets you have evidently seen fit to share with others."

"What secrets would those be, Serge?" she demanded belligerently.

"I told you about the project right after Cabinet decided to proceed," Serge replied. "Not a week later there was a demonstration in front of Corbeil's office, and questions from your pal Denis Lamontagne to Corbeil. Jesus Christ, Nicole!" his voice was rising.

"As it happens, Serge," her voice rose even higher, "I found your maps and charts when I got back from Paris. I waited and waited for you to tell me, but you lied to me! So yes, I told Sylvie about it. *Before* you told me." Serge was ashen and his eyes burned with fury.

"However," Nicole added quickly, guilty and frightened, "you should know that very soon after that, Sylvie learned much more from someone in the US – through the eco-Justice network. My information was minimal compared to theirs."

Serge stared at Nicole. There *is* someone in the States, he thought. And Nicole stared back and thought, uh-oh, maybe I shouldn't have said that.

"There's nothing I could say to explain those calls that wouldn't compromise me impossibly," Serge said, "absolutely *nothing*. And nothing that wouldn't put you in line for criminal charges for breaching government confidentiality, if Corbeil wanted to take that route."

"He won't." She knew the last thing Corbeil wanted now was a scandal involving the secrets of the project. "And not that you'd cooperate." Nicole ventured this more with bravado and hope than conviction.

"No." Though you deserve it, you bitch, he was thinking. "But if Corbeil finds out about your calls to Sylvie, it could ruin me, and drive that pig Greele into outright bloodlust."

Nicole didn't know what to say.

"So the calls have been deleted," Serge finally said.

"Deleted? What do you mean?"

"Deleted. From the master records. By Victor."

Despite her distress, this information brought a smile to Nicole's face.

"But Nicole, listen. Corbeil and Greele are completely enraged about the security leak. They want to know how the information slipped through to the environmentalists. From now on, they'll be listening to you talk to Sylvie." He paused for a beat. "You can't talk to her, Nicole. Not just about this. About anything. You can't phone her from here. She can't phone you." He wanted Nicole to move out of her country house, to never see Sylvie again, but could see Nicole was on the verge of a gale-force eruption. He suggested they move outdoors.

At a table under the shade of a spreading sugar maple, Nicole tried to speak calmly. "Serge, how can you do this? Sylvie and Georges are your friends too. You're tapping your friends' telephones!" Serge looked stricken. "I know you, Serge. You hate this. You hate it because you know it's wrong. And dangerous. Think about what these methods signify –

about Corbeil, about your American partners." In the distance, the faint buzz of a chainsaw could be heard.

"Nicole, I want you to tell me you won't be exchanging information on the telephone with Sylvie from now on. Will you give me that?"

While Nicole considered, they heard a car laboring up the hill. "I won't talk to Sylvie on the telephone, Serge, not for the time being, I will give you that. But I do intend to talk to her in person. I'm not giving up my best friend for this despicable madness." A beige Nissan turned into the long drive.

"*Calice*," said Serge. "What's she doing here?"

"I don't know. It is her house."

"I'm leaving."

"Do what you like," Nicole snapped, "but for heaven's sake, be civil."

"When can we speak alone, in person? There's more we must talk about." Sylvie's car stopped a generous distance behind the silver Peugeot.

"Come down Friday afternoon if you must. Sylvie and Georges won't be coming down until Saturday. But after that, Serge, don't you dare come back unless you have something good to tell me. I left because I couldn't stand being around you. Don't bring that pain down here." The car door slammed. Serge took out his car keys and walked to the Peugeot, exchanging cold nods with Sylvie as she passed. He drove off, making the gravel fly.

"*Désolée, chérie*," said Sylvie as she saw Nicole's tears. "I'm so sorry I intruded."

"What a fucking mess," said Nicole, rubbing the tears away with the back of her hands, "what a fucking mess. Sorry. I didn't know you were coming."

"Ah," said Sylvie. "We think it prudent to assume that we are under active surveillance since the concert. And I have something important to discuss."

"Hah!" Nicole exclaimed. "You *are* under active surveillance!"

"Serge told you. So our suspicions are confirmed." Sylvie looked grave.

"I agreed not to speak with you by telephone."

"I see. It's wise, I think. For all parties concerned. Most especially for your Serge."

"Sylvie, I'm worried. We were fighting, and he was accusing me of leaking the information, and I admitted to talking to you in the spring.

I couldn't lie about that to him. But he was so, so furious, and I didn't want him to be so ang – well, without thinking about it ..." Nicole found she couldn't finish her sentence.

"What, *chérie?* What?"

"Sylvie, I blurted out that there was someone else, that I wasn't the sole source of information, that there's someone in the US who had more."

"Ah," said Sylvie. "Just so. Oh dear."

"That was stupid, wasn't it?"

"Maybe," Sylvie said to Nicole. Absolutely, she said to herself. "Listen, Nicole, I spoke with Claire Davidowicz on a secure telephone yesterday." Nicole knew Claire from the anti-POPs network. "She's very worried about her informant, his safety. She feels we must find a way to make this project public so that people who know about it are no longer in danger."

Nicole, shuddering, began to walk toward the house. "Come in for some lemonade. Oh God."

Sylvie followed her friend through the back door. "If her instincts are right, then she may be in danger too. And I don't take Claire's concerns lightly. Your confirming this person's existence to Serge won't improve that situation."

"*Mon Dieu,*" said Nicole.

"What we really need right now is an independent source to tell the hidden part of the story," Sylvie continued, "someone who's not connected to you or our other informant down there. Someone who'll motivate a journalist to write about the situation here, so we can build opposition to what's really happening here, and so others can pick it up in the States."

"What we really need is for the Opposition in the Assembly to fight to the death to prevent this insane project," Nicole replied tartly. "Have you spoken to André Ducharme?" Nicole was referring to the leader of the Liberal Party, hungry to return to power.

"I did. And he stands exactly where you'd expect someone to stand who was an architect of the Free Trade Agreement when he was a Cabinet minister in Ottawa. He laughed at me. He told me he could hardly oppose a project he'd initiate himself if he were elected Premier. And yes," Sylvie said, "I've felt out a number of other members of the Assembly as well – it's delicate as you know. And no," she concluded, "I haven't made any headway at all. A few of the usual greener ones are opposed, but they're not breaking party discipline at this point, and that's all there is to it." She took a long, thoughtful drink. "You're the one who knows Quebec

City, Nicole, the bureaucracy. Can't you think of anyone who could help us?"

Nicole sat at the kitchen table and let her mind review a parade of the many faces she had come to know among *les cravates*. At length, however, the image that came to mind was of a Montreal apartment over a shoe store on Rue St Laurent. She saw the shining face of Fernanda Pereira presiding over a table laden with freshly baked cakes and homemade wines, thanking Serge for arranging the hiring of her only son by the Ministry of the Environment.

20

"IT'S pretty amazing, Paula, you'll have to admit," Claire said. "Look where we are now."

"We're in Halversen's, as far as I can see," Dr McIntyre replied sardonically. "In the middle of the hottest summer Vermont has ever had."

"Always the smart-ass," Claire said with affection. When seven-year-old Paula McIntyre had shown up with her immigrant's English accent in Miss Snedden's second-grade classroom, they had been the brightest kids in that class, then every class up the elementary school ladder. They'd become best friends during those years. Then Claire went away to Montreal and beyond, and they never got a chance to reconnect. Though Claire hadn't kept in touch, her parents had provided her with gossip and newspaper clippings. So she knew that her old friend had become a doctor, specialized in public health, and had gone to work for the city, then the Vermont state health department. A year or so ago, she had learned that Paula had accepted the position of public health policy advisor to Governor John Putnam.

"You know perfectly well what I mean," said Claire. "We've chosen to live similar lives, for similar purposes."

Paula was a tall, broad-shouldered woman with thick auburn hair beginning to gray in streaks. She had a well-defined jawline, and the radiating facial lines of a mountain climber. But Claire saw only the tall girl with whom she had shared her early years at school, if calmer and more collected, in a cream shirt, pleated tan slacks and sensible brown walking shoes.

Claire had spent most of the night getting her work in order. If she was going to be away for more than a day or two in Vermont, much had to be rearranged and delegated at headquarters. Thanks to a number of small blessings, it was a fairly calm moment in the campaigns. Before heading for the airport, Claire had checked with Juniper Diaz to make sure that the affidavit concerning Malcolm Macpherson and the water project, sealed and to be opened in the event of misadventure, had been couriered to the lawyers.

"It's wonderful to see you, Claire. It really is. You look great. But you didn't call me up out of the blue to reminisce, did you? Heard you were speaking in town while I was away. Does this have something to do with that?"

"Yup," Claire said. "I need help with something important. I've tried a lot of other avenues."

Paula raised her fine eyebrows.

"I need to find someone who will confirm, publicly, that a pipeline carrying Quebec water is going to cross the Vermont border at Richford, south of Sutton and Abercorn, and travelling south to Manchester, where it's going to turn west into New York state. Destined for the Mid- and Southwest."

"Go on," Paula said. Claire continued. "I need someone who is willing to raise questions about the provenance and the wisdom of the project. I believe it's very dangerous ecologically – and so do a whole slew of Quebec environmental groups who are organizing to fight it. But if I don't find this someone soon, I'm afraid it'll be too late to stop it."

Paula looked at Claire and opened her mouth to speak. In that instant Claire recognized a fleeting but familiar expression on her old friend's face. It was the look of studied innocence Paula used to assume when she was going to spin a big whopper to some unsuspecting teacher, one that would have the two girls flying off the school grounds to play hooky at the lake. Claire cut her off.

"Don't," she said. "I won't do anything with any information you give me without your consent. I swear. Just don't lie to me. And hear me out about why this thing is so dangerous and so ill-conceived, please."

147

"Not bad, Davidowicz," Paula said admiringly. "You caught me right off. And you know what?" Paula leaned over the table, so Claire could see the familiar flecks of brown in her pale blue eyes. "You haven't changed either, kiddo. And I can see you're on your high horse now. So you tell me what you know and why you're so worried. Then I'll tell you what I know. And then we'll see."

Claire thought better of querying the "high horse" comment, and set about telling Paula the main lines of the story. When she finished, Paula sat back. She raised her hand to signal the waiter, ordered a Labatt's Blue, and looked in Claire's direction. Claire knew any alcohol would knock her out within the hour, but thought it better to relax the atmosphere. She ordered some white wine.

"Okay," Paula said. "I know about it. Or something like it, anyway. There's a guy staying in Montpelier, buying right-of-way property for a pipeline, from Quebec down the western part of the state. But he's a Fed I think – as far as I know, the Feds are overseeing the project. We're not doing it. I've never heard of any consortium, and I've certainly never heard of any Greele Life involvement. I thought it was a public project."

"There's nothing public about it," said Claire. "Didn't somebody have to sign off on the sale of state lands? Or for licenses? What about complying with Act 250?"

"Putnam signed off himself, far as I know," Paula replied. "It's beyond the scope of 250 – that deals with small- and medium-scale development, I think. But, hey, it's not my thing. I had the impression it came from Jason Stamper's office. I was away when all this happened, and I don't know much about it. Gordon Pellerin, Putnam's chief of staff, mentioned it at a team meeting just last week. Otherwise I might not even have heard about it."

"No discussion?"

"It wasn't up for discussion. But I did ask Pellerin about it afterwards. He said we were facilitating for the Feds, but it was just in the early stages, or something. Anyway, Pellerin said neither he nor the Governor saw any major negatives. Doing our part for our fellow Americans." Claire snorted. "What's wrong with that? There's going to be horrendous shortages – you know that. What's your problem with sharing the water?"

"Nothing," Claire said, "in principle. Water should be shared – not owned. But it should be shared in ways that conserve it, keep it clean, above all keep it circulating through its natural cycles, in ways that ensure its ability to renew itself. You know that as well as I do, *Dr* McIntyre. And the bulk exports involved in this project are so big they're going to jeopardize that possibility. Simply put."

"Is that right?" Paula countered, wearing a familiar expression of disputation. "You know, Davidowicz, I'm not persuaded. From what I read, the big threat isn't bulk exports. It's the terrible damage all those huge hydroelectric projects have created in Canada. The Canadians have done a shitty job of managing their own water. They've dammed and diverted more water than any country in the world, and the scale has been devastating. That's the problem, not bringing a little water into the US."

"Well, McIntyre," Claire said, sitting back and grinning. "It's nice to get a well-informed objection. I see you know something about it after all."

Paula smiled back, pleased by the compliment. "I keep up, toots," she said. "We hike a lot in Northern Ontario and Quebec." So there's a "we", Claire thought. "Anyway, it's my job to know about environmental health impacts. And water's key."

"It's an excellent point. But it doesn't cancel out mine. I don't think Canadian bureaucrats and engineers should be allowed to screw it up for the rest of us. There are *no* effective instruments of regulation, nothing like enough remediation of existing damage, either side of the border. Not nearly enough conservation, drip irrigation, waste water recycling, desalination, assorted other technologies. I'm hoping to help get a campaign going for alternatives to bulk export."

"Well, that's a good idea," Paula said. "Makes sense to me. I'll join."

"Join what?" said Claire. "No profile. No story. No culprits to organize around. No campaign."

"Ah. I see." For a moment Paula dropped her gaze.

"You get the picture," said Claire. "Right now I'd settle for a simple public debate about the matter. We need to show the public the destructive scale, the need to think ahead. But I can't even find anyone who'll publicly admit that this particular project is happening."

"Why don't you release the story yourself?"

"I don't have documentation I can show, and the reporters I've spoken to have declined to write speculative stories. Even though I would have expected some of them to go after it."

"So how do you know all this for sure?"

"The usual way. Someone told us. Someone reliable, close to the project. Someone who can't go public."

"I see." For several minutes Paula reflected, but showed no inclination to volunteer any further comments.

"Okay, Paula." Claire pressed her. "Think about this. You agree we need a sustainable continental water strategy, right?" Paula gave a grudging nod. "Who's going to make one? A private consortium going for the bottom line for its members? Or publicly mandated commissions? The latter, right?"

Paula nodded again.

"Putting Quebec water into the hands of private American corporate entrepreneurs – and all that'll mean in terms of opening up the Canadian north to commerce in water – that's going to foreclose on the possibility of managing water properly by specialized public authorities. And, when the water gets here, there's no public accountability over its distribution. Water to the highest bidder, not for the public good. So it disempowers Americans too."

Paula shifted in her seat.

"You know what happened in England, when they privatized water under Thatcher," Claire said. "The corporations gutted the public utilities. The people in Yorkshire were going to rusty public taps, for Christ's sake, to get their drinking water, because the infrastructure collapsed. In South Africa, after Vivendi took over one water system, ten million people were cut off because they couldn't pay the rates. Here's the fact-sheet I presented at the Bear Pond bookstore – take a look at what's happened in this country."

The health advisor to the Governor of the State of Vermont looked down, then squirmed.

"Listen," Claire said urgently. "If you throw in waste water services, sanitation as well as drinking water, privatized water operations are in more than a hundred countries now. They're doing 500 billion dollars worth of business. And this project – I'm telling you, this isn't Ben and Jerry here. This is Greele Life Industries, and their pesticides and transgenic plants." Claire looked at her. Paula dropped her gaze. "Gotcha," Claire said.

"Huh," Paula grunted. "I hate that biotechnology shit. The boys with their chemistry sets. Look ma, look what I did – oops! Only the oops comes ten years later with hideous irreversible consequences."

"So help me, Paula."

"I don't know what I can do. It may be complicated." Paula played with the dregs of her beer. "Look Claire, I can't talk anymore right now. I have to get back to the office. Why don't you come by the house tonight? You can meet Ramona."

Ah, thought Claire, the "we" is revealed, and it's a she. "All right," she said. "I'd like that very much."

Dr Paula McIntyre had a good relationship with Governor John Putnam. He was an independent, and in her exacting opinion, had a decent understanding of public health issues. He had helped her move a number of initiatives through – a vaccination outreach project, a water-purity monitoring project, pre-natal assistance and food for poor expecting mothers. She had four new initiatives planned, and they were stacked up like jets at La Guardia. They meant a lot to her. Also, because she had a girlfriend instead of a boyfriend, she knew there were lots of politicians who wouldn't have her on staff. So she thought John Putnam a good man by any standards, and a gem by political ones.

"What's on your mind?" John Putnam asked when she pulled up a seat, his long, craggy face and bushy eyebrows, his stork-like limbs, crammed into a chair behind his desk. He liked and respected his public health advisor, and it was obvious she was seriously troubled.

"I've been asked by an old friend –"she began hesitantly, "an environmentalist friend – about this water-pipeline project. I don't know much about it, and I wondered if you'd fill me in."

"Ah," said the Governor. Paula noted the shadow that darkened his eyes. "And what would you like to know?"

"Well, my friend tells me that there's a private consortium behind it." She waited for Putnam to say something, but he didn't. "Sir?"

Putnam looked away, then looked at her again. "Paula, I have two choices now. I could lie to you about this, or at least stonewall you, and keep the lid on it for the time being. Then you could do some snooping on your own, and find out what's happening, and lose respect and trust for me. Or I could tell you the truth up front, but maybe risk ... well, destabilizing the situation."

Great, Paula thought. So I have to promise to keep my mouth shut if I want him to level with me. "I think I'd like to know what's going on directly from you," she said slowly.

"Right," said the Governor. "Well, I'll count on your confidence then." Looking at Paula's earnest face, the Governor felt frustrated and angry. John Putnam had gone into politics to undo dirty business and now he was in the middle of it. He'd grown up on a farm in the mountains of the Northeast Kingdom, and from as early as he could remember, the bank's threatened foreclosure was an annual ritual. Every February, his father would be called into Newport to be told that he had two months to make his overdue payments or face losing the farm. John would ride with him in the front seat of the Chevy pickup, more rusted and battered every year, with a pain in his own gut caused by the tension that distorted his father's face. When April came, every penny from the sugar bush went to the bank, and nothing was ever left over to fix up the barn, or replace the chipped crockery in the kitchen, or buy him something decent to wear to school. His long, skinny limbs always stuck out of his frayed clothes.

John had understood early how the bank was supported by policies crafted in Washington, DC. His father had explained it to him on every drive to Newport, and each year he had been able to absorb and understand a little bit more. It stuck with him, the gross injustice of rich, powerful, faceless people, far away, squeezing his parents for every penny when they broke their backs from dawn to dusk to make ends meet. Eventually, his feelings became his motivation for entering politics. But Putnam also understood the relationship of forces – a phrase he was fond of using. It was why he had succeeded so well in politics, despite his independence. He was a pragmatist who preferred to bend and get something done rather than break and stay ideologically pure. Still, something about how this particular issue had unfolded stuck in his craw.

"It's like this, Paula," he said. "In June, I got a call from William Greele – the CEO of Greele Life Industries – about a project he was leading. We met. Greele's pulled together a consortium and they're planning to pipe water down from Quebec. They need to put their line through Vermont. Pipeline's supposed to go through New York, down into Pennsylvania and Ohio." Putnam unfolded his long, bony frame and stood up, walked around the desk, and folded it back into the chair beside her.

"I wasn't thrilled at first, I'll have to admit," he continued. "And Greele made my skin crawl, he was so arrogant. But he made a strong case, and told me bluntly me he had the Administration's support. Big water shortages coming in the next ten years. Crisis for American agriculture. He promised that Jason Stamper's people would oversee the appropriations process, if I didn't want the State to do it – which I categorically don't – and pay for the whole thing too. Got a follow-on call from a banker who's helping finance a new cheese co-op in Enosburg Falls. Decent guy, name of Bunting Hurst." It wasn't the whole story, Paula thought, but it was a start.

"Then why all the secrecy, Governor?" she asked. "And why the smokescreen – why do people here think it's the Feds when it's a private consortium?"

"Oh, Paula," Putnam said, shaking his head slowly from side to side. "You're the one who usually gives me lectures on *realpolitik*. Greele asked me to keep this quiet until the fall. It has to do with getting all the pieces in line up in Quebec. Says they don't want premature hassle about it before they've got the whole thing designed."

"Please. If they're buying right of way, sounds pretty well 'designed' to me already."

"It's politics, Dr McIntyre." The Governor reminded her of her political position. "This project has protection right into the White House."

"Then why isn't the US government doing it?"

"That's not how it's done anymore. You know that," Putnam replied. He got up and went to gaze out the large, leaded windows over the lawns. "Governments now exist to 'facilitate' the private sector. We're their pimps, not their regulators."

"You don't believe that," Paula said.

"I don't believe that's the way it should be. Of course I don't. But who am I? A nobody."

"What do you mean, a nobody? You're the governor –"

"Of one of the poorest states in the union," he interjected, "with no clout in either party. Look Paula, I told you, it goes to the White House. The Trade Representative has already drafted briefs to slap on the Quebeckers in the NAFTA and WTO tribunals if they change their mind. Greele told me. Stamper gave me a little call and he told me too."

"You're a governor with a strong constituency that's a lot more conscious than most. Let's debate the thing publicly, for Chrissake. Give your people a chance."

"I don't think that's a very good idea, Paula," Putnam said sadly, once more assuming his seat at his desk. "Even though I sympathize. In part. I'm just not prepared to have a big, ugly fight we can't possibly win."

"I see," said Paula, thinking, but through a glass darkly. "You said you sympathize in part. What part?"

"I prefer to see big undertakings like this debated. I'd like to see water managed as a public trust. I'll give you that."

"But?"

"We're going to need the water. For the Midwest, maybe other places.

Bad times coming, as you know, and for all the talk about green ways of doing things, no other technology to deliver fresh water in significant bulk is on-line. Isn't that true?"

"I really don't know the answer to that question, Governor," Paula replied. "But my friend thinks there are better ways, and she's got a list. "

The Governor grunted.

"At the very least, Governor, the impact of this pipeline on the environment should be publicly debated."

"Whose environment would that be?" Putnam asked, eyebrows like two caterpillars over his dark, bright eyes.

"Why, all of ours, John. We're right downstream of Quebec. And their water levels are incredibly low! Ours too for that matter."

"Hmm ..." Putnam mused for a moment or two. "It's going to take a long time to get some intelligent continental water management structures in place."

"Exactly what my friend said."

"And who might your friend be?"

"You don't really want to know right now. But she is knowledgeable, and she says that if this project is completed, it'll foreclose on the possibility of that kind of policy." She filled Putnam in on Claire's main arguments.

Putnam looked troubled. "I can't stop it, Paula," he said at length. "I just can't. And neither can the people of Quebec."

"What about the people of Vermont *plus* the people of Quebec?" she asked, pushing hard, deeply upset and confused.

"You undertook to keep my confidence," John Putnam reminded her.

"Can I at least not deny what my friend already knows?"

"Have you already let on that it's happening?"

"I didn't know it was a secret, Governor," Paula said, quietly but angrily. "I also didn't know anything else either. So I didn't give much away."

"We're not hiding it," said Putnam. "We're just not saying much about it for another few weeks. It'll all come out soon. People can debate it then if they want to."

"This is wrong," Paula said as Putnam scribbled something on a piece of paper, handed it to her.

"That's the way it is," he said. "I'm sorry, Paula. I'd rather have them pay for the land than give it up to a federal override. Now, if you'll excuse me, I have a lot of work to do before I can pack up for the night."

Stung and bewildered, she headed out the door through the now-empty reception office, into the hall. She stopped and read the chicken scratches on the scrap of paper in her right hand. "Charles Emerson", the writing said, then, underneath, "Northern VT/Land use Planning Commission". When she understood, her eyes filled with tears.

21

THE minute he got into the office, Doug Boyle sat down to study the logs that had arrived by overnight courier from Victor Paquette in Quebec City. Only one significant communication path from Canada to the US, and it stuck out like a garter belt on a marine. He picked up the telephone. Why reinvent the wheel?

"Hey, Jeb," he said. Jeb Angell occupied Boyle's old desk at the NSA.

"Hey, Doug," said Angell, recognizing Boyle's voice immediately, "long time no hear, see or speak."

"Need a favor," Boyle said. "Need it fast, too."

"I'll help if I can, Doug. Tell me what you want."

"Okay. I need to know whether a certain project is about to develop a dangerous case of environmentalitis. It's not Skypoint, something else."

"Who're you tracking?"

"eco-Justice. Got some private time for me later today if I fly in?"

"Make it tomorrow, and there's no problem. Come to the office. No harm in that. A friendly visit. I'll bring in one of our field experts, Jorge Echevarria. Young. Good."

By eleven a.m. the next day, with hundred-degree temperatures and a smog alert outside, Boyle was alone in Angell's office with Jorge Echevarria. Echevarria's Los Angeles street rhythm didn't mesh well with Boyle's military march. He wore cut-off jeans and a Hawaiian shirt and his long, black hair was in a ponytail. He was a hip nerd and looked every inch the part.

"So what can I tell you?" Echevarria asked Boyle.

"What eco-Justice is up to, how much you know about them."

"What do you know about them already?"

"Assume nothing," Boyle said. Why waste time?

"Okay. They're an interesting organization, one of the most sophisti-cated. Run multiple campaigns on multiple issues. Last few years, they've done a lot on forests – big confrontations over old-growth temperate rainforests. Big campaign in the Amazon – illegal mahogany trade, other stuff. They do a lot on transgenic engineering and pharming, too, that's with a 'ph' – raising animals to use their blood, milk, tissues, and organs for human drugs and transplantation."

"Jesus," said Boyle. He felt queasy. Mixing genes in a soybean was one thing. The thought of a pig's liver replacing his steroid-toxic original made him nauseous. He'd rather die. Well, on the other hand ...

"And," Echevarria continued, "they do a lot of climate change stuff. I'd rate them as exceptionally skilled in pulling off 'direct witness' actions – the ones where they climb smokestacks or board ships or stop nuclear convoys –"

"Ecoterrorists, then," Boyle stated.

"Ah," Echevarria said, "no. I wouldn't say they're ecoterrorists. Some-times we confuse direct action with terrorism and –"

"There's terrorism against property too, Echevarria," Boyle growled, thinking, the kid's soft, what's he doing here?

"I know," Jorge said, holding his ground. "But they never use violence. It's in their charter –"

"Who initiates new campaigns? And what role does their executive director play?"

"Campaigns are decided by senior staff – usually head campaigners and executive directors – from the offices of all the national organizations. They meet every year, then work together internationally. The US ED is a smart woman named Claire Davidowicz. Long-time toxics expert and policy wonk, here, Brussels, Paris."

"You keep live taps on their lines?" he asked.

Echevarria hesitated, but he knew Boyle had been the boss around here. He was a legend, if not a pleasant one. "Right now, we're monitoring their biotechnology guy with a live tap. Monsanto, Dupont, Techniplant, GenSysCo, Bonafabrica, Novartis – they're all screaming that their biotech dream is going to hell. eco-Justice is playing a big part in the demos and negotiations in Europe. So yeah, we have one open on him right now.

We're monitoring their forest campaigner too."

"What about the executive director?"

"Well, we can get her telephone logs, no problem, but we don't have tapes or anything –"

"These guys talk about water?" Boyle pressed.

"Not so's we've noticed," said Echevarria.

"Would you be in a position to know if they're planning some sort of campaign on water?" Boyle pressed on.

"Hmm…" Echevarria rubbed the two-day stubble on his fine-boned chin. "Well, water's involved in everything they do, you could say," he mused. "I talk to the guys who do pulp and paper and oil and gas pretty regularly. They haven't mentioned anything."

"Ask," Boyle said.

"Ask?"

"Ask. About water."

"Yes, sir," said Echevarria.

"I also want your records of their telephone logs and your analysis of them asap. Review ECHELON data – I want to know what they're communicating on – phone, fax, e-mail – anywhere in the world. Search on each campaigner, the executive director, key words: water, pipeline, Quebec."

"Jesus, Mr Boyle. It's gonna take forever!"

"Correction. It's going to take you no more than a few days. Get it all together and get it to Jeb. He'll get it to me," Boyle commanded. "Dismissed."

The coffee and brioches on Lalonde's conference table were cold. Gabor Mezulis had come down from Chicoutimi to hear Pierre Gosselin, head engineer for the Quebec government, discuss the reevaluation of the project required to address environmental concerns. Gosselin had never become comfortable in English, but the American spoke no French.

"Dis evaluation, it will require from us tree weeks," Gosselin declared. "We cannot arrive at a dollar value accurate in less time dan dat." Gabor Mezulis scowled. "Must I to remind you dat we are speaking of ten proposals, dam and diversion, tree plants for de bottling, numerous places for de aquifer extractions, installation for de supertankers, clearing of a long route for de pipeline – it has required six monts to develop de plans jus' to dis point. It would be irresponsible completely even to attempt dis reevaluation in less dan tree weeks!" He stopped, humiliated and exhausted from wrapping his tongue around impossible syllables.

"Three weeks is out of the question," Mezulis said categorically.

"*Anyting less* is out of de question!" Gosselin came back again. "You should be understand of dis."

"I may understand it, but it doesn't change the fact that the consortium has to know sooner. Mr Greele won't wait three weeks to make a decision." The two engineers glared at each other.

"Tell me, Monsieur Mezulis," said Serge Lalonde, freshly shaven and properly dressed for the first time in days. "Exactly what decision is Mr Greele going to make? Of course we will take his guidance and advice under consideration. But ultimately, we are the ones who have to make this real, and we will have to ferry it through the turbulence ahead."

"Mr Greele has final say as to whether the additional costs are acceptable, Mr Lalonde," Mezulis said coldly. "And you damn well know it."

"With respect, Monsieur Mezulis, this is not a unilateral decision. We are confident that the venture will still be profitable, if not to the same degree as before." He looked at Pierre Gosselin, who nodded agreement.

"With respect, Mr Lalonde," Mezulis echoed him, "the degree of profitability is exactly what's in question. And three weeks is too long to wait."

Lalonde and Gosselin exchanged looks. "We will meet wit de Montreal Committee next Monday morning," Gosselin said. "When it is over, we will know better deir concerns – dough I am sure we can prevision many of dem. Why do we not consult togeder Monday afternoon?"

"Not good enough," said Mezulis. "I need a figure now. Not a fully accurate figure, perhaps, but a ballpark figure that we can work with."

"Monsieur Mezulis," said Lalonde, drawing the line. "We do not have such a figure today. And we are not going to make one up. And I further want to remind you that at every stage of this process, I have told you and Monsieur Greele that environmental impacts had to be addressed."

Mezulis snorted in disgust. "I'll give you one day after your meeting to put your heads together and come up with a summary of the major hot spots and the amount of money – ballpark figure, like I said – it's going to take. We'll meet again here next Wednesday." He rudely pushed his chair back. "And until we meet, do not, I repeat, *do not* make any promises about public consultations or anything else." Mezulis stalked out. Lalonde and Gosselin stared at each other.

"Get to work," Lalonde said dully, and Gosselin left, rolling his eyes. Lalonde sipped absently at his cold coffee. If Greele wasn't prepared to live with a pared profit margin – what? He would call the deal off? It was practically unthinkable, considering what he'd invested. Maybe find some way to compel them to comply with the original plans. But how? If he went public with the story of the government's complicity, public sentiment would turn against the Americans as well as the government, and neither they, nor their Liberal successors if they lost the next election, could force the Assembly to accept the project. Then they'd have to go to Ottawa and the NAFTA tribunals, which would take years. And be disastrous for Greele's beloved short-term profits. So if not political blackmail, then what?

22

A NEW wave of forest fires in Northern Quebec had smothered the entire northeast, from Quebec City to Boston, in a brownish haze that filled the emergency rooms with asthmatics, babies and old people gasping for breath. Claire felt her eyes smarting as she pushed open the front door of the Vermont Land Use Planning Commission. A plaque on the wall of the Victorian-era complex said that it had originally been an insane asylum; now the corridors were quiet and sedate. On the glass panel of the small reception area, a note informed visitors that the secretarial staff was on holiday until August 31. Claire consulted the panel listing the people who worked in the building, and saw that Charles Emerson, Officer, was in room 206.

Over margaritas the night before, at Paula's refurbished farm house with its pale-blue shutters and wraparound verandah, Paula had begun by announcing she couldn't help Claire officially. However, she hadn't denied the information. She'd encouraged Claire to check back in a month's time. She'd also suggested the filing of freedom-of-information papers – "Way too slow!" Claire had protested. But then she'd handed Claire a piece of paper on which she had typed the name that Governor Putnam had slipped to her, and the address. "Don't tell," Paula said. "Don't ask. Please don't even comment."

Now Claire climbed the stairs and found the room at the end of the hall. The door was closed and on it was posted more letterhead attesting to the fact that Emerson worked for the Natural Resources Agency, Northern Office; then, in neat handwriting, a note: "I'm on vacation until Monday. Please leave a message in my mailbox downstairs. Or send me an e-mail. I will respond on my return. C. E."

"God dammit!" Claire cursed aloud and kicked the door. I'm going to have to come back. It's going to screw everything up.

It would take five hours and many stopovers to get her back to DC, then a frantic rush to the office, to her apartment, to do laundry, pack, back to the airport – all to be in Portland looking fabulous and feeling happy in twenty-eight hours. The euphoria she'd felt as she had opened the big door downstairs evaporated as she retraced her steps. She was tired and discouraged. And, over and around and underneath it all, she was still frightened. She drove back up South Main and stopped at a payphone at a 7-Eleven. First, she called Andrea at her Smithsonian office, and got a telephone number from her. Then she rummaged in her satchel and pulled out a cellphone. She sat in her car and keyed in the number. "Malcolm, hi, it's me."

"Hello, darlin'. How are you?"

"Hot. Sweaty. Frantic. Can you talk?"

"I'm just sitting at my desk trying to plow through some overdue paperwork. It's okay. Where are you?"

"I'm still in Vermont. Waterbury. I've got a lead. But he's away till Monday."

"Bummer."

"Is it ever. I've got to get back to DC, then fly to Portland, then come back here …" She didn't groan but she might as well have.

"I get the picture," Malcolm said. "Why don't I get on a plane and meet you in Burlington tomorrow? Just do our thing, but at your end? We can spend a couple of days in Somerville, eat a lot of *pain au chocolat* from Peregrine's Peak. Not exactly a hardship. I can drive you down for your rendezvous."

"But your cabin, and the animals, and –"

"Don't worry, Claire. It's not a problem. Russ and Geraldine will look after the animals. You'll see the Cascades some other time. They'll still be there. It's okay. I just want to be with you."

"It would be so much easier," she said, her knees sagging with relief. "And it makes me so happy to have you here."

"No problem. I gather you've got your new phone?" he asked.

"Yup," she said, and gave him the number for the mobile, obtained in record time by Juniper from a cousin who sometimes engaged in less than legal goings-on and had a variety of untraceable hardware. Malcolm's telephone was listed under the name of a person pulled from the "recently deceased" files of the US government, courtesy of his son Michael. At least they could talk.

"I'll call you when I know my arrival time," Malcolm said.

"Wonderful," said Claire, energized and happy. "Fantastic. Thank you, thank you. Speak later." She hung up, closed her eyes, breathed deeply for a few moments. Then she used her old cellphone to call Juniper, and gave her a long list of things to do. She stressed that no one on staff should give information about her whereabouts to anyone she didn't know personally. Returning to the store phone, she fished out her telephone book and dialed the number for Ron Benholz, a science writer who, on several occasions, had actually taken a lead she had given him, investigated the story, and broken it on the Reuters/Yahoo wire. Breaking the story nationally, rather than through a local paper or television station, would be best.

"Ron Benholz here." Claire heard his message for the umpteenth time. "I'm on assignment in New Mexico." Claire hung up but didn't leave a message. Instead, she punched in a number she knew by heart in Los Angeles.

"AT&T," said the female cyborg voice. "It's seven a.m. where you're calling." If she's there and asleep, Gemma won't like this, Claire thought. Too bad. I can't take a chance on missing her. One ring. Claire pictured her friend sprawled over her pillows in the big bed, sleeping off some substance or other. Gemma's dead-to-the-world posture might look incongruous on the Pulitzer Prize-winning beauty. But likely she'd been writing till four o'clock in the morning, and Gemma ingested whatever it took to meet her deadlines. She was one of the best environmental journalists anywhere and an expert on the ecology of California's Central Valley – the breadbasket of the state and the country she had happily adopted when she fled Britain in her twenties. Three rings, four rings, pick it up, Gemma, Claire willed. Five rings. The machine answered. Claire hung up, redialed. Three, rings, four rings – damn! – and then, *finally*, deliverance.

"Hullo for Christ's sake!" Gemma Richardson croaked.

"Gemma, it's me. Claire. Wake up."

"What the buggery bollocks are you doing calling me at seven in the morning?" Gemma demanded hoarsely.

Claire assumed the unchecked profanity was a sign of friendship. "It's nice to hear your voice too. I've got something for you to write about."

"At seven in the morning? You can't be serious. I couldn't write my own name at seven in the morning!"

"Listen, Gemma, I'm on the road. Get out of bed, take a leak, take an aspirin, make yourself a cup of coffee. I have to talk to you now."

"Half an hour?" Gemma begged blearily.

"Please," said Claire. "It's important, and time is a factor."

Gemma grunted. She sat up in bed, rubbed her throbbing forehead, pulled back the covers. "So what is it?"

"It's the water story I called you about a few weeks ago —"

"Excuse me, darling. That wasn't a story. It was a rumor." Regularly employed by the *Los Angeles Star*, Gemma also freelanced frequently, and was sometimes able to persuade editors to let her follow leads and stories they would not have given to less enterprising or skilled writers. When the *Star* said no to her suggestions, as it had increasingly done in the last couple of years, she wrote for *Outside* or *National Geographic* or *Mother Jones*. She got as much into print as she could. It was a lot more than most.

"It's a story now," Claire said emphatically. "I think I have someone you can talk to. Someone who's actually working on it. A Vermont land use officer. He can show you where the right of way is going through. And more, probably. I won't know for sure till next week though. Which gives you time to pitch it to your editor. Which is why I'm calling now."

"I'm going to the valley today, and Eli's not interested, I told you."

"Get him to change his mind. *You* can do it."

Elias Hazen, the editor-in-chief at the *Star*, was a big personal fan of Gemma's, and they had a high-drama, on-again, off-again, extra-curricular relationship of some duration. It had been off for a few months now at Gemma's insistence. Eli was married, which violated her ethics, even as it reinforced her libido. She loathed herself when she had sex with him. But single men were such a turn-off. They all wanted to get married.

"Watch it, sweetie. You know how things stand just now. In any case, I don't think I can." Gemma felt her way along the kitchen counter toward the coffee pot. She tripped over her computer wires and stubbed her toe on a tall stool. "Ouch," she exclaimed.

"Put your slippers on."

"Piss off."

"I know Eli wasn't interested," Claire persisted. "But this is for real, Gemma. This guy officially knows about the pipeline, where it's coming from and where it's going to. Tell Hazen that."

"I still don't think he'll go for it." Gemma ladled several tablespoons of French triple-roast into the coffee filter, and put the kettle on the stove. "He had negative interest in the story."

"Refresh my memory, please."

Gemma groaned. "I pointed out the California/Southbelt angle. He blew me off. Informed me they were working to 'stay responsible' this summer about climate change and related matters. Isn't that rich? He also gave me some blather about going easy on the Canadians and especially on Quebec – 'not to fan the flames of separatism', he said. 'Help out our Canadian friends'. A million Canadians in the Los Angeles area. Some bullshit. But, as you will remember, I didn't have anything hard to tempt or push him with. And it's not as though I don't have enough to do."

"Go back to him now."

"What? You're daft. I'm in the middle of a story, remember? Clandestine releases of a new strain of genetically modified strawberries in the Valley. I'm working on the second installment, and lucky to be able to get it published. I can't bloody well drop everything and waltz off to Vermont." Gemma poured boiling water over the coffee, then gratefully inhaled the aromatic steam.

"Does that mean you'd do it if you had the time?"

"No, no, no darling – not so fast." Gemma poured the coffee as steadily as she was able, took the first sip of black ambrosia. "No commitments till you have the evidence in hand."

"I'll get it for you Gemma. Meanwhile, think about this: if this project happens without public debate, it's going to set a precedent under Chapter 11 of NAFTA and World Trade Organization conventions for privatizing all the waterways of North America. *All* the waterways. That means Canada, that means the US, that means Mexico."

"That's some edge-of-the-wedge, darling."

"Well, that's what's at stake, Gemma. I mean it. So I'll do my part and you do yours. I'll get back to you with the information. Call me on my cellphone when you come to your senses and agree to write it. I may be out of range for a while, but leave a message and I'll get back to you."

"You do that. I'll get back to bed."

Gemma finished her first coffee, then made a second and took a shower. The caffeine woke her, the hot water soothed her stiff muscles and cleared her mind. She thought about what Claire had told her. She took two aspirins and drank two large glasses of bottled water. She looked at the label. Naya, it said, produced in Mirabel, Quebec. An hour later, she stepped out of her cabin in a white T-shirt, denim coveralls, hiking boots and a weather-beaten straw hat. She was slathered in sunscreen, on her way to trek through fields with the United Farmworkers' representatives where they would show her the territory they believed had already been planted with the demon seed, and the territory that had been inadvertently contaminated. In her prized white Miata, she headed down the hillside to the freeway, still pondering.

Lightning had crackled over Montreal, black thunderheads had released a tremendous downpour, intense and brief, and now the air was sticky with smoky particles and hard to breathe. Headlights and taillights shimmered in the late afternoon smog. Nicole Verlaan-Lalonde ran up the worn marble steps, slimy with the toxic soup, of the government building on Rue Sherbrooke and paused beneath the wrought-iron canopy. Then she pushed open the tall glass doors, walked through the musty foyer and up a large circular staircase. She took the hall leading west. At the very end a door stood ajar. The sign read "Quebec Ministry of the Environment, New Septic Technologies Study". Brochures tacked on a bulletin board advertised a plastic webbing seeded with bacteria that ate septic waste, and a peat installation that transformed it into fertilizer, both manufactured by small Quebec firms. The tinny sound of fado music came from a bad radio.

"*Pauvre petit*," said Nicole to herself, as she knocked on the door.

"*Entrez*," said a small, bored voice. Helder Pereira turned from an old desk in the corner of the room. Through the narrow window, the wet gray wall of the adjacent building was visible. "Madame Lalonde!" he exclaimed as he rose, his transparent features showing surprise, pleasure and confusion.

"Helder," she said softly, stepping in and closing the door. "*Bonjour*. I need to talk to you."

He offered Nicole his chair – the sole chair in the room. She accepted and sat. He noticed, not for the first time, how gorgeous she was, a Viking Amazon, if ever there was such a creature. Monsieur Lalonde was a lucky man. Several different shades of gold were visible in her French braid, and they gleamed dully in the glow of his desk lamp. Helder stood against the wall.

"It's so nice to see you again," Nicole said. "I've missed you. What are you are doing *here*?"

"Oh. Well. Those septic systems in the brochures out there. They're two green technologies Monsieur Lalonde and the Environment Minister helped to fund. I'm, um, supervising a long-term study on their relative merits."

"Excuse me, Helder," Nicole said. "You're a hydrologist. You do rivers, not septic tanks. *N'est-ce pas?*"

"I was transferred," he said, his voice and body conveying imprisonment. Helder had always loved to be outdoors. When he was fourteen, he'd seen a poster for a nature camp at the local YMCA, and begged his parents to send him. Fernanda went to the administrator and begged for a subsidy. When Helder had stepped off the bus in Abitibi, in the black spruce wilderness, he thought he'd died and gone to heaven. Then he'd hauled boxes on a market stall every Saturday, through the freezing rains of November, through the snows of December, January, February, and March, and saved enough money to go back to camp. Fernanda and Tony Pereira had no idea where his love of the bleak, cold north came from. But they were content when his science, geography and maths grades improved, and his teachers started talking about scholarships. Many boys were taking drugs in the backrooms of the billiard bars on St Laurent and getting their girlfriends pregnant. Helder was reading university-level geology and going camping. At eighteen, he knew he wanted to be a hydrologist. Now he was twenty-seven and the rivers and lakes were a receding dream.

"Why didn't you protest?" Nicole said, reading his eyes.

Helder looked at her mutely. Did Madame Lalonde know about the water project? That Monsieur Lalonde had consulted him at the beginning, still visited him, late at night or on the weekends, and asked what he thought of this or that installation or plan?

Nicole regarded the spreading panic on Helder's face. She doubted that a routine bureaucratic transfer was responsible for the dread her question had elicited. She hated to add to his misery, but her guilt and fear about revealing the American informer to Serge propelled her. "Helder, I know the government is in the process of finalizing a deal with a large American consortium to buy huge tracts of Quebec land for its water, and ship the water to the US."

"Naturally Monsieur Lalonde has spoken to you of it." Relief shone in his eyes.

Aha! thought Nicole. "No, Helder. In fact, he's told me very little." She let that sink in. "But I found out about it anyway."

"Oh."

"And I left Serge over it last week." Nicole dropped that bombshell. Helder looked stupefied. He had a thousand questions, and couldn't put one of them into words.

"Helder," Nicole said. "Please. I told you a painful truth about my life. For the sake of this land, which I know you love dearly, please be honest with me." Helder just looked at her miserably. "You know who the Americans are, the ones who own the consortium?"

"Some of them," he said, his voice raspy. "I know some of them."

"Do you know who the main people are? William Greele, Greele Life Industries?" He nodded. "Who else knows the whole story?"

"I-I-I, ah, I don't know," Helder stuttered painfully. "Not m-many people. Monsieur Corbeil certainly. They-they've set up a special office in Finance."

"I see. You've seen the plans?" Helder nodded. "All of them?" He nodded again.

"So now, tell me. What in your view is the environmental responsibility rating of this project?" She saw the answer in his face, though his lips were sealed. "*D'accord*," she said. "Disaster. As my friends have informed me."

"Your friends?"

"Eau NO. I'm helping them to try to stop this project. We're desperate for someone who will help us prove what's really going on. I have no idea where else to turn. I'm begging you, for what you know is right, please, to speak with Denis Lamontagne at *Le Soleil*. Anonymously, of course. We have learned about this consortium, but we can't prove their existence. And Lamontagne isn't interested unless we have someone who can swear from first-hand experience that it's happening."

"Madame Lalonde," Helder was shocked. "Surely you understand it's impossible for me. How could I do such a thing to Monsieur Lalonde? He's been my benefactor, my mentor. He's been my *friend*."

"He's been *my husband*, Helder. I don't want to harm him. But keeping this secret is wrong. We both know it." Nicole's tone was kind, but she did not relent for a moment.

Helder was turning green. "My mother would kill me." The wrath of Fernanda was, by a slim margin, the worst of the awful consequences he faced.

"She may not need to know. But if she does, tell her to think to the future of her grandchildren. Tell her I begged you to help."

"Oh, Madame Lalonde," Helder said, running his hands through his dark hair, "I don't think I can do it."

"You must," she said. "Somehow you must find the inner resources, and help your community, your land. I'll come back on Monday." He looked at her bleakly. "And Helder," she said striding to the door, "I have it on good authority that there is much high-level surveillance being employed right now. So I won't call you. And don't tell Serge I came. Don't tell *anyone* I came. And until you tell me it's okay, I won't tell anyone about you either." He nodded his head. He looked like a lost, abandoned orphan. On an impulse she walked back and gave him a big hug. "*Courage, chéri*," she said, and was gone.

"Denis?" It was Nicole's fourth attempt from an anonymous telephone to reach Lamontagne. She was relieved to finally have him in person at his desk. "I have something important on the water project you've been in touch with Sylvie about. Someone who knows about it first-hand. He is very, very reluctant to talk, even though he thinks it's going to be bad for Quebec. I'm working on him. What I need to know from you is what kind of confidentiality are you truly prepared to offer?" She listened. "Think about it for a day or two. Don't try to reach me. I'll call you on Monday. Yes, we'll take it from there. *Au revoir*."

23

GEMMA drove into town, punching in Hazen's number on her cellphone. A pale green silk pantsuit clung to her long limbs, and white Italian sandals showed her aristocratic feet to perfection. Her blonde hair was gathered in a shining ponytail, and she had steamed and moisturized her skin back to velvet, then applied just the right shade of coral lipstick to make her green eyes shine.

"Gemma," Hazen gasped when she opened the door. Mojo working, she thought, as she took a chair. Hazen cleared his throat. "Nice to see you," he said, trying for sarcasm, but he couldn't pull it off and it came out more like the moan of a hungry man. I bet, Gemma thought. Still, it was good to see how much he still cared. Or whatever it was he did.

"I've been trying to reach you, as you know damn well," Hazen said, looking at her with sharp brown eyes behind narrow rectangular glasses. "Messages all over the building, on your phone and e-mail. Where the hell have you been?"

"Avoiding you." Gemma looked him straight in the eye. He flushed.

"I'm your *boss*," Hazen said. "When I call you, you're supposed to call me back." But his tone came out beseeching rather than angry. He sat back in his chair and crossed his arms behind his head, stretching and flexing them, and reminding her how nice his chest was, and all the parts it was attached to. She smiled. "Well," he asked, "who goes first, me or you?"

"I'd like to look into the story I mentioned a while back, Eli," Gemma said. "About the plans for a US consortium to import water from Canada – Quebec – to the US."

"Would you now?" Hazen leaned forward, so she could see the desire in his eyes and smell the pheromones he'd released an hour ago on the squash court. "You got something new?"

Gemma's delicate nostrils flared for a moment. "I'll know for sure next week." She sat back in her chair. She had a nice chest to show off too.

"What is it?" Hazen asked.

"Someone in Vermont, connected to the project. Until I know for sure, I'd rather not say more. But Eli, I wouldn't tell you it was a good lead unless it was."

"Look," Hazen said, with effort. "I can't play this out to a mutually satisfactory conclusion. I'm not interested in that story. This is Los Angeles, remember. Not Canada. We don't do stories on Canada."

"You told me there were a million Canadians here," she protested. "You do stuff on Canada all the time."

"We're talking Canadian comedy takeover, sweetheart, not Canadian resource extraction. Where's the link to LA?"

"Southbelt. I told you last time, and I was right. Don't call me sweetheart."

"Southbelt's suit is proceeding. There's no news. What does this have to do with it?"

"It'll set a precedent, it'll lock it —"

"Gemma," he said, interrupting her. "I'm not gonna do this story. I'm already in very serious doo-doo because of your strawberry story. That's right," he affirmed to her skeptical expression. "Now it's my turn, warrior princess. So you listen up. Techniplant is suing the paper over your last piece. You'd know if you'd returned my last three calls."

"Litigation? You don't say." Gemma was unmoved. The freedom of the press belongs to those who can fund an army of lawyers. "Over what, precisely?"

"Over unsubstantiated and false allegations of illegal release of transgenic organisms."

"Let them sue," she said contemptuously. "The United Farmworkers had the DNA analysis done. Our stuff will stand up in court. We're talking Techniplant's own proprietary blend, for God's sake." Hazen looked baffled. "It's Techniplant's *patented* strawberry/flounder combination. The Flounderberry, or alternatively, the Strawfish — whichever you like. Yum yum."

"That's revolting," Hazen said. "Why are they doing that?"

"So the berries will be more resistant to frost. Officially."

"I'm not even gonna ask for 'unofficially'."

"Coward."

"There's no frost in California."

"It's for growing in colder climates."

"For Christ's sake, can't they think of better things to do with all that science?" Hazen said angrily, looking seasick.

"It's good to see you upset, Eli," said Gemma. "Nice to know there's a caring human being behind the mindless rut."

"You have such a way with words," Hazen said hungrily, aroused at the image. "Yes to that. Yes, yes, yes. But no to the Canada story. In fact, my intrepid, not to say luscious reporter, you have to help the lawyers draft the letter of response to Techniplant. No second installment for you until it's cleared up. Maybe I could join you for a long liquid lunch on Monday, between sessions?"

"I don't think so, Eli," said Gemma. "I'll tell the UFWA people to call. They have everything your people need." She got up and made for the door.

"That's it?" Hazen said. "You come in here dressed like that, and you leave, and that's it? You don't even like single men!"

"That's it, love," Gemma said lightly, turning to face him. "I'll take care of the lawyers on Monday. But starting next Tuesday, I'm on a leave of absence. I'm going to sell the story to somebody else."

"Not to any big dailies, you won't," Hazen said knowingly. He stood and leaned in her direction. "Or the big weeklies."

"Oh," Gemma said. "And what makes you so sure?"

"Word from New York. Couple of months ago."

"Is that right?"

"That's right."

Gemma walked back toward him, until they were face to face. "All that stuff about being responsible about global warming, all that crap you gave me about being good friends to Canada? All pure blarney?"

He looked her in the eye. "You got it. Word from on high. InfoMedia is watching you," he said, moving his eyebrows up and down. He could smell her perfume and her body's own fragrance. His hands itched to grab her.

Gemma brought her face very close to Hazen's. She could feel his breath come faster. "I still think you're hot too, sweetie," she said. "But if people can't write about a project like this it's not really a democracy any more. Is it, darling?" She kissed him lightly on the lips. "And I don't do it with totalitarians."

"Stay in touch," Hazen said as Gemma walked out the door.

Malcolm had spent the day in transit. That, the heat, and the constant sweat he was in thanks to uncontrollable fantasies of seeing Claire again made him feel grungy when he spotted her across the barrier at the baggage carousel. She was wearing a fresh white shirt, olive-green shorts and those red sandals that drove him crazy. His glandular system had taken complete control, the way it had when he was seventeen.

Claire looked solemnly at him for a moment, as if to register that he really, truly existed. Then her face lit up, and they embraced. He buried his face in her hair. She breathed him in, felt his heart beating. The strength, the completion she felt when their bodies met was something she had never felt before.

"I can't tell you how good it is to see you," Claire said, as they walked toward the parking lot. There were tears in her eyes.

"What's wrong? Are you upset?"

"I got so frightened, this last week," she said. "I had a feeling something dire was going to happen." She looked at him searchingly. "I was afraid I wouldn't see you again."

"Whoa," Malcolm said, putting down his suitcase and holding her tightly. "I'm here. And so happy to be here. It's okay."

"I know, I'm so glad to see you," she said, her eyes still full of fear.

"You're really spooked," Malcolm said.

"I am. Believe me, I'm not usually like this. Really. I'm a tough cookie."

He looked at her again. "Come on," Malcolm clutched his bag in one hand and took her arm with the other, "we'll talk in the car."

It was already something they had done for many hours together, and Malcolm and Claire settled into the drive north to Somerville with pleasure. She told him about Gemma's possible interest in the story.

"Gemma Richardson?" Malcolm asked. "*Outside, National Geographic* Gemma Richardson?"

"My old friend and partner in crime. I stress maybe, however. It's contingent."

"On what?"

"On the willingness of a certain Charles Emerson in the Vermont Land Use Planning Commission to be the source."

"Aha!" Malcolm said. "You've been a busy little environmentalist."

"Aha is right, but again, maybe. He's the one who'll be back Monday. Don't know what he'll say yet."

"How did you find Mr Emerson?" Malcolm asked and Claire told him about Paula.

"So if he agrees, Ms Richardson will speak with him?"

"She hasn't committed. But if I know Gemma, she's going to have a hard time resisting her guilt and sense of duty when she finds out more abou —"Claire's words were interrupted by the ringing of a cellphone. After a humiliating scramble, and two wrong phones answered, it turned out to be Claire's old cellphone. She huffed "Hello!" on the fifth ring.

"It's me, darling, what took you so long?" Gemma Richardson demanded impatiently. She sounded very wide-awake and very sober.

"Gemma!" she said. "Hi. What's up?"

"Isn't that just the question!" Gemma retorted. "Just took a meeting with Eli. Pitched the water story again."

"What did he say?"

"Just so you know, sweetie, I was maximally tempting in my presentation."

Claire laughed. "I can just imagine. You're the kind of woman wot gives feminists a bad name. Was he salivating?" Macpherson raised an eyebrow.

"Foaming at the mouth."

"You bad girl."

"It's good for my ego."

"But still no go?"

"Dead in the water, darling. And guess what, you old conspiracy wonk, you. Months ago InfoMedia properties *were* issued policy advisories to keep mum about global warming stories, and – get *this* – to stay away from stories about Quebec."

"Wow," Claire said.

"Why are you surprised, darling? You're the one who's always talking about the corporate control of information and – how do you put it? – 'the awesome power of omission'."

"I'm not *surprised* surprised, Gemma. It just always floors me when I see it in action. Thanks. Thanks a lot. Change your mind about the story by any chance?" Claire held up two crossed fingers.

"Yes. In a word." Claire signaled thumbs up. "If you have something real I can hang it on, that is. And if you e-mail me background information, so I don't have to put in a couple of weeks of research. Can you do that?"

"I can send you the notes on my laptop later today. But for the rest, you'll just have to wait until Tuesday. I can't get back to the office before then. I've got something important to do." Macpherson raised his eyebrow at her.

"*Really* important?" Gemma teased. "Is the sister going to renounce her veil at last?"

"I did already, Gem. Just haven't had a chance to tell you. But I'm going to do it again as fast as good grace permits. *If* you give me the time."

"I've got to make some calls. I'll go to *The Nation*, I think. It's minimum three months' lead-time on the monthlies. Or maybe the *LA Weekly* or the *Village Voice*. Anyway, you get me the goods. And good luck to you."

"Check your e-mail. I'll call you right after I speak to this guy on Monday."

"Should I make reservations to fly up Tuesday?"

"Do it. You can always cancel if you have to."

Claire was so much cheered by her conversation with Gemma that Malcolm decided to get the Brannigan news out of the way. Claire's eyes popped when he told her he'd had a late-night visit from her former lover and repeated Brannigan's warnings about Greele. She was very distressed.

"I didn't tell him about your involvement, Mal, I swear!"

"It's okay, I know you didn't."

"I'm worried too," Claire said. "Worried sick."

"I noticed." He paused. "Would you say that, for a civilian, you've had a fair degree of experience with, ah, operations?"

"You mean direct action?"

"Yes. Planning and execution of."

"Yes, if you put it that way. Yes on both counts. And for many years too."

"Well, you get spooked the way you are now when you do that stuff?" Claire looked at him hard. "Never."

"So do you think your present frame of mind is a function of uncontrollable endorphins and androgens and estrogens going crazy inside you, like all my hormones are, since we met? You know, men's sex hormones make them aggressive and reckless, and women's sex hormones make them protective and weepy?"

Claire laughed out loud. "I think some of my fear did have to do with you – finding you," she said, looking away, "then maybe losing you." She thought about it for a minute. "But no. I've just got a very bad feeling about the situation."

Claire Davidowicz and Malcolm Macpherson bonded like crazy glue. They made love on a blanket in the upper meadow, shaded by a huge umbrella and serenaded by goldfinches. That weekend they saw rose-breasted grosbeaks and evening grosbeaks, bluebirds, barn swallows, tree swallows, five different kinds of woodpeckers, purple finches, a flock of blue jays, a pair of Baltimore orioles, and one flaming scarlet tanager. At night they sat under the stars and pointed out constellations in the deep blue dome above. Contemplating the Milky Way, for the first time in their lives neither felt alone.

They began to talk about finding a way to live together – a way for Malcolm to exit Skypoint and come east. Both were astounded at the rapidity of their connection but neither could deny it. They had stepped into a groove of belonging that felt, finally, right. Yet, now that they had met, they began to fear losing each other. Many times fate had snatched a goal, a possibility, the life of a friend from Malcolm. Claire had her own catalog of painful misses and losses. "'At my back I always hear, Time's winged chariot drawing near,'" she quoted. "And this time, the chariot driver is William Ericsson Greele."

PART THREE

24

WHEN Victor Paquette heard Madame Lalonde's voice during his routine check of the tapes of Denis Lamontagne's tap, he gagged on his falafel. He put in an urgent call to Serge, told him he was cycling over. When he got to Rue des Braves, Serge was in shorts and sandals in his study, drinking Armagnac out of a beer mug. Victor sat down next to his boss, pulled a cassette recorder from his bag, switched it on. Serge looked like he'd just seen a ghost.

"I wonder who it is," Serge said. "Her contact." Serge was shivering despite the heat. His head was full of screaming paranoid fantasies about the people working on the project in the special office at the Ministry.

"Don't you think you'd better find out?" Victor asked.

"Maybe I should go see Nicole again —"

"You gonna tell Corbeil?"

"Tell him what, exactly?" Serge snapped.

"Take it easy," Victor soothed. "Just trying to stay with you here. Want me to destroy this tape?" Serge looked at the young man, took in his loyal gaze and determination. "I can dump it, no problem, Serge. I don't give a shit about Corbeil." He looked hard at his boss, swallowed. "I'm beginning to believe you're on the wrong side of this one, though."

"Ah! I don't know what to do," Serge blurted, and buried his head in his hands. "Give me forty-eight hours."

At sixty-five, William Greele had lost the ability to deal with the kind of failure he now admitted was a possibility. When he had returned from Yale to take his place in his father's business, the cruel indifference he'd felt as a child changed. His father never actually warmed to him, but he did begin to treat his son as a partner in the businesses that expanded hugely in the seventies. By the end of that decade, Bill was Henry's equal. With his East Coast education and hundreds of millions of dollars behind him, Bill's ego mushroomed in overcompensation for the deprivation of his childhood. The moment finally came, one morning, when Henry, white-haired and confined to a wheelchair, legs covered in fine mohair blankets, had looked up for the blessing of a greeting from his son.

And William, with iron in his soul, had refused the gesture, turning his back on his father as his father had once done on him. Day after day, the ritual was repeated, until, in a matter of months, William had mounted a coup in the board and usurped his father entirely. Henry died of a stroke within weeks of his overthrow, while his son's psyche contorted in an ambivalence of agony and ecstasy.

Since then William Greele's wealth and power, and the way he chose to deploy both, had protected him completely from any painful emotions. After thirty years of total insularity, of privilege and command, he had no words or resources to deal with what was happening to him now. His climbing blood pressure was a flood of rage and frustration. He felt his identity, his very manhood, would be shattered if the project failed. "It's not possible," he repeated mentally as he paced. "That kind of betrayal. Not possible." And certainly it came to this: his was an empire whose economic enterprises had taken hundreds, quite likely thousands of lives, indirectly. He would not flinch from taking one or more directly, *if* that would solve his problem. But – and here his blood pressure rose again – *would it?*

He waited in his air-conditioned study in Indian Hill to hear from Kamenev in Singapore, who was waiting to hear from Boyle. He occupied his mind by determining his permissible profit margins and considering his options.

On Friday, Sarah Huntingdon Greele's masseuse had asked her client if she wanted to get together off-hours. Sarah, astounded, had agreed to meet her in Santa Cruz at the kind of hippie café where she could count on meeting no one she knew. She did not return until lunch on Saturday. Overnight, her universe changed. It was as if she had been resurrected from the dead.

The papayas in the bowl at the spa looked more delicious, alive, pulsing with color, than all the fabrics and furniture she used to care about. She called her husband and told him she was staying on for another round of treatments. He barely took the time to say fine.

The Eau NO manifesto, published in both official languages in *La Presse* and the *Montreal Ga\(\zeta\)ette* on Monday morning, was signed by "The Hundred" — an impressive list of people and organizations, including fifty notables in the arts and sciences, and fifty groups ranging from city-gardening cooperatives to women's, consumer and farmers' groups, to national unions and labor federations.

QUEBEC'S WATER IN PERIL

Today, in several provinces in Canada, provincial governments and courts are involved in various stages of negotiation to effect bulk sales and exports of water to private American enterprises. Though the government of Quebec persists in hiding the names of the American corporate interests, we have learned that our own representatives are on the verge of abandoning the patrimony, the legacy, and the future of this great province — its water.

The members of Eau NO are not opposed to continental water-sharing. But the potentially severe water shortages that are approaching, and our continued indifference to the diversion, pollution, and waste of water here in Quebec and throughout North America, demand that we treat water as a common heritage, governed by the principles of public good and sustainability, not private profit.

Internationally, the United Nations must begin now to lead in the development of an international system of water governance if we are to safeguard our water in the early decades of the twenty-first century. If it does not, the principal source of human life will be used as a strategic resource — rare, precious merchandise in a new, highly lucrative market.

Here in Quebec we must develop a water policy that sustains us and future generations on this continent. With leadership in Quebec and North America, we could assist the United Nations to lead on a global basis so that the crisis in water does not become, in the decade ahead, a fundamental crisis of human civilization.

We are asking for your support in calling for a moratorium on all bulk water exports in this province, and a democratic public consultation on provincial, national and continental water policy.

The Honorable Robert Corbeil, who had been stalling the committee, was not amused by the breadth of the coalition. But he noted the absence of key energy and construction unions with great satisfaction. The boys wanted the jobs, and they were holding out. If they exerted pressure on their National Assembly members, the backbenchers wouldn't dare to vote against them.

Corbeil knew he would get an avalanche of letters and faxes. So what? No further revelations had been made, and his communications director had already told the press there would be an announcement on water policy within the next two weeks. His chief of staff had called Sylvie Lacroix and arranged a meeting for next Friday between government planners and René Dubois, the committee's engineer. Meanwhile, Lalonde and Gosselin were cleaning up the plans as much as they could without provoking the terminal wrath of the consortium. Corbeil turned to their preliminary assessments, and tore up a pink message slip asking him to call Denis Lamontagne.

Claire found the land use planning officer sitting at a long desk against the far wall of his office. A large, framed photo of Emerson with his arm around a tanned, auburn-haired woman, both wearing hiking gear and backpacks, was perched near a towering stack of papers and reports. The walls were completely obliterated by maps and aerial photos. A big bookshelf was crammed with more documents, books, and a dusty rock collection. Emerson sat in the midst of it all like a benign bear – blond, bearded, with feet shod in Mephisto sandals and an orange T-shirt bearing the words "Don't Californicate Oregon".

"Hello there," he said, regarding her curiously. "Can I help you?"

"Mr. Emerson, sorry to intrude," Claire stepped toward him and extended her hand. "My name is Claire Davidowicz, and I'm with eco-Justice USA."

"You are?" he said, quickly rising to pump her hand enthusiastically. "Gee. Aren't you the executive director?"

"Well, yes, I am," she said, very pleased that he knew.

"Gosh, hi! Please sit down." Hastily Charles Emerson cleared a chair of papers, and motioned her toward it. He beamed. "I'm a monthly donor. To eco-Justice that is. Put in a year on the early forest campaign on the West Coast, couple of years after college. It's great to meet you."

"Thank you very much," said Claire, flattered and touched, thinking that, perhaps, at last, the Goddess had given her a break. "How wonderful." And she beamed back at him.

"So Ms Davidowicz," Emerson said, sitting back and crossing his hands over his stomach, "what brings you to this neck of the woods?"

"Call me Claire, please. I'm up here looking for help. It's about a project that I understand you know something about."

"Which one?" Emerson's kind face grew curious.

"The new water pipeline that's slated to go in down the west side of the state, to New York, Pennsylvania, Ohio ..."

"Sure. Isn't *that* a coincidence!"

"How's that?"

"Well, as it happens, I've got some questions about that project myself. I briefed the Governor on some of them a couple of weeks ago, before I went on vacation. I asked him to, well, to consider the ecological wisdom of the plan for Vermont. I thought it was important to ... But ..." His words trailed off.

"You have questions," Claire prompted.

Emerson regarded Claire and pursed his lips. "Yes, I do."

"What's wrong?" Claire asked. "You're uncomfortable talking with me?"

He ran his broad, rough hands through his curls. "Yeah," he said, regarding her seriously.

"Well, if it helps," Claire said, "I'm not sure who exactly, but I've received the impression that you ... well, let's say you've got some friends in high places. Friends who directed me here. I doubt you'd get fired for speaking to me or a reporter, for that matter, about this. Needless to say, I would add my own voice to the hue and cry if you suffered any consequences."

"Hmm," he said. "Well. I'm really worried about this project. And I'm intrigued. So explain what's going on and what you need. And I'll tell you if I can help."

For twenty minutes, Claire told Charlie Emerson everything she knew, omitting only Malcolm's identity and place of employment. Emerson listened attentively, asked a few questions.

"I didn't know it was a private, for-profit venture," he said. "But I certainly figured out that the scale of the thing would be disastrous, and I said as much to Governor Putnam. Jesus, how could it be anything but, the volume they're planning to bring down, the disruption the site installations will cause! Totally scary to think people in Quebec have no idea about the ownership or the scale of the thing."

"Yes," Claire said. "And we can't get a US campaign going to stop it because no one knows about it, or has any understanding of its implications."

"Oh brother," Emerson sighed, shaking his head. "So what kind of help do you want from me?"

"We need someone, officially connected to the project, not someone like me with information obtained by questionable means and heading a 'special interest group' as the press always says – someone legit to blow the whistle to a journalist who'll write this story."

"That's harder than talking to you. I'm not supposed to say anything to the press till I get the green light – that's standard procedure, by the way. We often wait until there's a good opportunity, tie an announcement to some issue in the public eye."

"But in this case," Claire said, "as you know, the function of the secrecy is to make something a fait accompli without any public debate, something that desperately needs debating." Claire felt sick about pressing Emerson. But she'd come up with nothing else, and the stakes were a lot bigger than his job, or hers, for that matter. She'd lost several jobs over the years by doing the right thing. She wasn't asking anything of him she wouldn't have – hadn't – done herself.

"Don't you think, Charlie, that the people of Vermont specifically, as well as the citizens of both countries, deserve a chance to discuss what's going to happen to the watersheds directly to the north?"

Emerson trained his large brown eyes on Claire's face, and slowly twirled the thumbs on his broad hands. For a long time he said nothing. She waited. For a few more moments, his gaze turned inward. He was weighing his civil servant's oath against the ethical responsibility he felt. Even though his body barely moved, somehow Claire discerned, under the teddy bear exterior, the real bear, wary, strong, ready to fight. Watching him, Claire knew he would be a truly great partner to have on any camping trip, on any mountain, up any smokestack.

"Fair enough, Claire," he said, coming out of his meditation looking clear and decided. "You've made a big effort to get here, haven't you?"

Claire nodded. "And I agree with you this is very serious. So I'll make an effort too. Well. What reporter do you have in mind?"

25

"OKAY, Mr Boyle," Jorge Echevarria said on the video link, "here's what we found. We did the ECHELON search for eco-Justice. Nothing relevant on 'pipeline', a useless avalanche on 'water', a few things on 'Quebec' related to boreal forest stuff. Total waste of time." Boyle grunted. "Now the eco-Justice telephone logs. We looked for Toronto and Montreal area codes for June and July, and focused on Davidowicz. It looks interesting. From her DC office, home and mobile phones, New York home number, total calls: twenty-two. Total calls the previous year to those area codes: four."

"We knew a woman called Sylvie Lacroix, in Montreal, was calling her during those months," Boyle said.

"Yeah. She's the one in Quebec Davidowicz calls all the time. Calls the eco-Justice guy in Toronto a lot too – a James Amanopour. By the way, did you know there's a cluster of, like, four calls to Quebec at the end of *May?*"

"No, I didn't," Boyle said. "End of May. That potentially pushes the date of the leak back even further. So who else is she calling?"

"She makes hundreds of calls in the US. About a dozen calls on her own or her assistant's line to the River Alliance. On over twenty occasions she has personally called numerous reporters in the last couple of months. Which is highly unusual. Normally the communications department organizes relations with the media. She's tried the Reuters/Yahoo science writer Ron Benholz about five times and she was in touch with the *Los Angeles Star* writer Gemma Richardson a couple of times in June. Called up both *their* logs. Found something odd – both of 'em received calls last Thursday from the same payphone in Waterbury, Vermont, of all places. Turns out it's outside a 7-Eleven near a big state government office complex. Offices for natural resources, land use, that kind of thing. The call to Benholz's line lasted thirty seconds. But Richardson's conversation with the person in that booth lasted fifteen minutes. I've prepared a briefing on Richardson."

"That's weird," Boyle said. "Where's Waterbury?"

"Between Burlington and Montpelier. Burlington is Davidowicz's hometown, parents live there. Finally, on the other side of the country, we were able to identify two calls in June and July from her mobile phone to a couple of telephone booths near the university in Seattle. So it made us wonder, why's Davidowicz calling telephone booths there?"

"Good question." Boyle mused. Mezulis and Stiller are both based in Seattle, he thought. Was one of their operations leaking?

"Find out if either of those journalists called Davidowicz again after Thursday, and report to me. See if she *received* any calls from telephone booths in Seattle – or anywhere in Seattle – on any of her phones. Maybe that'll tell us more. And for now, give me home and office numbers for Richardson."

"You got 'em in the briefing, download your e-mail."

Boyle hung up, did as Echevarria told him, then dialed Richardson's home, prepared to hang up if she answered. He got a recorded message, in a refined voice, informing him that she was out of town for a few days. He then called the *Los Angeles Star* and was routed to the features editor, who said that Richardson was away, but that he'd be happy to pass on a message when she got back. "It's very urgent," Boyle improvised. "I ... I have some news of her family ..." Rapidly scanning the briefing on his screen, he hoped his hesitation would be read as diffidence. "Her younger sister ..."

"I don't know where she is," the features editor said. "The story's not for us. New England, somewhere, I think. New Hampshire, Maine, someplace like that."

"Vermont?" Boyle suggested.

"Yeah, maybe Vermont."

"Thanks, I'll see if I can track her down." Boyle hung up promptly. The features editor held the receiver for a moment, gripped by the image of a leopard and a gazelle.

The phone rang and it was Echevarria again. "Found a call from Richardson to Davidowicz's mobile phone on Friday, and again on Monday afternoon. Direct hit, Mr. Boyle."

"Good," Boyle said, the thrill of the hunt rising in him. "Now tell me if

Richardson has been on, or has booked, a flight to Vermont in the last twenty-four hours." Boyle held, and held, and held, and turned over myriad scenarios in his mind.

"Yeah," Echevarria said at last. "She flew out of LAX at seven thirty this morning on American. As a matter of fact. Changing at La Guardia to Continental – a commuter flight – arriving Burlington seventeen hundred hours this afternoon."

"Right," Boyle said. "Thanks." He hung up and dialed again. "Hey, Marco," he said. Boyle's best operative was sitting in a café across from the eco-Justice office on L Street in Washington, DC drinking a double espresso to stay awake. "How's it going?"

Marco and Tiffany Mostyn, a husband and wife team and hot industrial spies, hadn't done much better than three or four hours sleep a night for the preceding three weeks on a job in Switzerland. Before he'd turned around and shot them off to DC Boyle had promised them a three-week leave, all expenses paid, after this job was done.

"I've got to get to a doctor soon, Mr Boyle," Marco said. "This thing I picked up in Jakarta really hurt me in Europe and it's getting worse. I think it's maybe a parasite. Anyway, it's quiet here. Davidowicz is still in her office."

"Where's Tiffany?"

"At the hotel, sleeping."

"Wake her up. Tell her to take over. You're going to Burlington, to find a lady reporter called Gemma Richardson. Hot on the trail of the story we don't want her to have. She's flying in from New York at five. Be there. Charter something if you have to. Check in when you've got her. You're getting backup from the NSA."

"But I haven't gotten in to Davidowicz's office, Mr Boyle," Mostyn said.

"Tell Tiffany to do it. I want you on Richardson's tail."

Mostyn rubbed the back of his neck with his hand, said rude things to himself in Polish. Out loud he said, "I am on it, boss."

Doug Boyle placed a call to Jeb Angell, arranged for backup for Marco in Burlington and Tiffany in DC, and was pulling the final picture together to update Nick Kamenev, when Echevarria called a couple of hours later.

"Calls received by Davidowicz on her cellphone show three additional calls *from* payphones in Seattle. But not the same part of town. Tacoma."

Boyle jerked upright. "Tacoma?"

"Yes, sir, where you are right now."

"Thank you," Boyle said frigidly. "I know where I am. What else?" But the sirens were wailing in his head.

"She calls her parents in Burlington, of course, and she calls some woman by the name of Andrea Baretti a lot. Decided, just for the hell of it, to see what *her* telephone records look like, and I found several calls out to Seattle telephone booths, and another Seattle number. It belongs to a ... Geraldine Morrow, 625 Arbutus Street."

"Who the hell is Geraldine Morrow?" said Boyle, while Echevarria entered her name into the NSA data banks.

"We show nothing on her, sir."

"Pull her Visa application."

"Okay." Echevarria punched his keys. "Wait, wait, wait ... No Visa."

"Try Mastercard." Boyle waited some more.

"Got it! Address, telephone number, social security number, credit limit $5,000, employer –" and his voice stopped dead.

"What?" Boyle demanded into the silence.

"Ah, well, actually sir ... shit. She works at Skypoint Industries, sir."

Boyle's adrenals went into overdrive. "She's our deep throat! Just a minute, Echevarria," he said grimly. He accessed Skypoint's personnel files, found Geraldine Morrow in marketing. Her smile was out of a toothpaste commercial.

"Let's just pull up Morrow's calls before we call it a day, Echevarria," Boyle said. "Initiated and received."

"Okay." Echevarria punched in his request. Presently, a long list of calls appeared on their screens, but aside from the Baretti number, none were familiar to their eyes or to a quick computer scan for repeat numbers from the lists they had already compiled.

"I'll have to work on these, sir. Put her numbers together with names. I've got some urgent work to do, so I won't get to it before tonight."

"Make it now," Boyle snarled. Then he called down to Human Resources.

Blasts of hot, humid air mixed with jet exhaust blew into Burlington airport every time the doors opened. Inside, two men watched the luggage pick-up area. One was Marco Mostyn, gaunt, his eyes red-rimmed, badly in need of a shave. The other was Baily Cummings, special NSA agent, black, taller even than Mostyn, much heavier. The first passenger off the Continental flight from New York had just picked up his suitcase. But Gemma

Richardson had brought only overnight and computer cases, and was already leaning over the Avis counter. The two men spotted her and nodded to each other across the carousel. Both of them were thinking how superbly she filled those blue jeans as they followed her out.

Gemma didn't notice the light blue Toyota Camry and brown Chrysler minivan following her to the Holiday Inn on Church Street. Once in her room, she called Claire, who was still at her desk in DC. "I'll be heading out in five. Just wanted to let you know I've arrived," Gemma said as she put her bag on the bed and her laptop on the desk. "I've worked on the notes you sent. I think the background piece is almost done. Thanks so much, sweetie. They were perfect."

Gemma washed her face, freshened her lipstick, headed downstairs and out the door. She grabbed a Phad Thai to go in the Church Street mall and drove out of Burlington, eating with a plastic fork and glancing occasionally at the map as she made her way to Charlie Emerson's place, up in the Green Mountains. The Camry followed.

For four hours, Marco sat at the bottom of the drive, taking regular breaks in the bushes and trying to keep tabs on the conversation he'd miked. The microbial companion he'd brought back from Asia was partying like crazy in his gut. He was seriously dehydrated, trying to cope with the impact of a dozen time zone changes and hundreds of fast-food meals. And now, in these godforsaken hills, he was sitting at eleven o'clock at night on a road someone had actually named Apple Tree Lane. Marco thought Americans suffered from terminal sentimentality, which insulated no one from the truth of their brutal social structures. His cellphone hummed in his breast pocket.

"Bingo!" Baily Cummings crowed.

"What have you got?"

"Lots. When I wired her room, I took a look at her laptop. She's got an almost finished piece on North American water that ends in a promise to blow a big story about the northeast soon. She has a 'Vermont' file with the address and telephone number of one Charles Emerson, who, according to the Vermont Government Directory, is an officer of the North Vermont branch of the Land Use Planning Commission."

"I'm sitting down the road from his house. He's telling her all about this pipeline. The route for the right of way. His attempts to warn the Governor. I'll check in as soon as I come back. Which better be soon. I can't take this much longer."

Mostyn didn't have to wait long. He heard Richardson get ready to leave. He waited until she had started back down the mountain roads, retrieved his bug, then followed her to Burlington. As soon as she was in the hotel, his phone hummed again. "Come on over," Cummings said, like he was inviting Mostyn to a barbecue. "You can listen in."

"Sure," Mostyn replied, though all he wanted was a proper toilet and a decent bed. He walked slowly over to the van in the far corner of the parking lot. He felt the warm, humid night air as a blessing on his skin. Stepping into the air-conditioned van he felt a chill, like a nasty cold coming on.

"She's talking with Davidowicz," said Cummings. "Check it out."

Richardson was saying, "We're going up to the border, to Richford. He said there was some land for the right of way he thought a community of Abenaki people might refuse to sell, violation of aboriginal rights, that sort of thing. Also that when the environmental impacts to the north become known, you won't lack for allies." Davidowicz gave Richardson the number of some Indian in Quebec to get to talk to the Abenakis. Davidowicz sounded happy.

Mostyn reported to Boyle, and was assigned to stay on Richardson's ass. If he hadn't been so bone weary, the thought would have warmed him.

26

IT was midnight in Seattle but three o'clock in the afternoon in Singapore, and Colonel Kamenev, on the terrace of the Snooker Bar at Raffles Hotel, was schmoozing General Hu Zhenyu. PLA officials were buying foreign avionics and weaponry technology like kids in a candy store. Everyone was selling. The US had imposed an embargo on such sales after Tiananmen Square – which is why Kamenev couldn't meet the General in his boardroom in Seattle. But many Israelis were happy to provide cover for US contractors. Kamenev was contemplating a tremendous profit, and was annoyed to be interrupted by a call.

"Sorry, sir, I think you need to hear my report as soon as possible."
Kamenev did not miss the tension in Boyle's voice. He excused himself.

"Jesus H. Christ," Kamenev said, when Boyle had filled him in on the
situation in Vermont. "Shit. I mean, well done, Doug ... But Jesus, that's
bad news about the journalist. Terrible. Give me a minute to think."

"Yes, sir."

Slowly Kamenev massaged his forehead. He had learned that you could
afford to ignore a lot of things. Some article in a local green newsletter, for
example, even packed with facts – no problem. Even a headline in the *Post
Intelligencer* in a big Metro edition, if it was about something local, rarely
went national. Like "Poor Seattle Moms Now Over 20 Per Cent", or "Coast
Showing Extensive Marine Damage". But when a big, splashy article in the
national press connected with widespread sentiment in the population, a
small ripple could turn into a tsunami, spin control or not. Like the GO
KYOTO campaign, which should have been a dead letter, but wasn't. And
there was a lot of simmering discontent with this Administration on environmental issues.

"If she transmits her material before we get to it, we're fucked," Kamenev
said. "So I suggest you make sure she can't transmit from the telephone
line in her room."

"She may have a wireless modem, sir."

"Oh great."

"Do you want Mostyn to break into her room now?" Kamenev didn't
answer. "And that's not the worst of it, sir."

"What? What the hell do you mean?" Kamenev felt his stomach clench.
"That's pretty fucking bad."

Boyle told him about the Geraldine Morrow connection and put his
fingers in his ears while the Colonel blew.

Kamenev bit the bullet and called Greele in Indian Hill. He briefed him the
same way he'd rip off a bandage, hard and fast, rather than endure the pain
of taking it off slowly.

"How did that woman find out?" Greele yelled.

"We honestly have no idea, Bill," Kamenev replied. "She's in *marketing*,
for Chrissake." He heard Greele's labored breathing and waited. Greele
was sitting on his rage because he needed Kamenev now. Finally he spoke.

"I've had a very bad feeling for days, Nick. At least we know what's
happening now. What do you recommend?"

"A warning to the key players, delivered immediately."

"Maybe," Greele replied skeptically. "Though if we warn them, we give them a heads-up, they place the story even faster. Only kind of warning we can afford to give is one they can't – and I mean *really can't* – afford to ignore."

"We're together on that," Kamenev said. "I don't think it's a good idea for Ms Richardson to publish her articles for the foreseeable future. I'm proposing we do something about that immediately."

"Agreed. And I don't think," Greele came back, "it's a good idea if all the other people working on the project in five states and in Quebec read about this pissant Vermont whistle-blower."

"Plus I don't think it's a good idea to have anyone inside our own companies passing on information. I'll discuss operations with Doug Boyle. I'll have more information after daybreak."

"That's good, Nick. Thanks." That telltale dizziness meant his blood pressure was up. "Meanwhile, you'd better brief Vittorio. He'll have resources we can call on if we have to. We may have to bring Wilbur in eventually too. But right now, let's leave it at Massaro. And not a word to the others. Need to know only."

"Roger and copy," Kamenev said.

"Be thorough, Nick. And whatever you do, do it fast."

"Mr Boyle, it's Jorge Echevarria." Boyle was in his office, working the phones. He'd called Vittorio Massaro, then a security company in LA he'd used with success a number of times in the past. He was in a black mood, caused by an ambivalence he didn't deal with well. He'd been told to hit. But how hard?

"I found something I thought you'd want to know right away." There was a hint of something in Echevarria's voice, something Boyle didn't like.

"Go ahead," he snapped, grabbing a pad of paper and a pen.

"I'm matching Morrow's numbers called to names, then doing background checks. By the way, seems she's on the board of some local organic food organization. An enviro. So that fits. Anyway, I've found two names that'll knock your socks off, sir. Well, maybe that's not the right way to –"

"Just tell me, Echevarria," Boyle said nastily. "Spit it out."

"Okay. Morrow calls a guy called Russell Jefferson a lot. Looked up his tax return, he works at Cyberonics." The name of Stiller's company throbbed like a nuclear reactor in Doug Boyle's ear. "Jefferson's name sounded familiar to me, so I looked him up in our high-tech hotshots file. Turns out he's been a co-developer, with A. A. Stiller, on a number of genetic and encryption apps. Doesn't get the credit for it, but everybody knows —"

"Save it!" Boyle snarled, feeling his adrenaline start to pump. "Who does Jefferson talk to?"

"Not too many people. Sunday calls to New Paltz, New York, hometown, his folks. Main number of interest from our point of view, besides Morrow's, is a guy in your outfit. Name of Malcolm Macpherson. You know him, Mr Boyle?"

Boyle felt the wolf leap in his heart. Macpherson, that son of a bitch! Boyle would bet the Typhoon it was Macpherson and this guy Jefferson who were the real leaks, Morrow a secondary person, a mutual friend or something. If the two men had access to information, maybe hacking into the consortium's e-mail and funneling information through Morrow to Davidowicz and Richardson, the journalist would have much, much more information than they could afford for her to have. Ambivalence resolved. Boyle's concentration focused sharply.

"Forward the addresses, telephone numbers, and all biographical material you can get on Macpherson, Jefferson, and Morrow," he commanded. "I want to know the coordinates for their parents, lovers, siblings, children. And I want it *now!*" Echevarria was shaken by what he heard in Boyle's voice, and hung up fast.

When Gemma got back to the Holiday Inn after a long day with Charlie Emerson she had only forty-five minutes to pack, check out of the hotel and check in at the airport. She threw her toiletries into her case, grabbed her laptop – she thought she'd left it closed, but didn't stop to think about it – and checked in at the gate ten minutes before takeoff. A tall, fair, gaunt man rushed to the same counter to check a long, leather bag. He looked vaguely familiar. She fell into her seat, exhausted. Though she often worked on long flights, this time she read a novel and dozed, wiped out by her marathon forty-eight hours. Eyes closed, she reviewed what she had learned. A huge new pipeline practically a done deal before it was debated. It was audacious and it was simple, and she figured the consortium was counting on the backing of the American people: their sense of profound entitlement to water and, even, to Canada itself. Manifest Destiny made truly manifest. One of the least attractive features of her adopted country as far as she was concerned.

As she saw it, her job was to persuade Americans that the damage would eventually have an impact on the US and that planned cooperation by public authorities was better than corporate appropriation. It was a big job, and she rubbed her eyes at the prospect. She saw the blond man sitting at the rear of the aircraft when she went to the loo. She saw him again waiting at the Hertz counter at LAX, along with half the passengers on her flight. She picked up her Miata, and made her way through the freeways and up into her canyon, top and windows down. At home, she put away her things, checked her messages, put out some stale crackers and dry cheddar, and poured herself a double scotch. Then she lit a cigarette and switched on to CNN for the late news.

"... Nations Global Environmental Outlook today released a report endorsed by twenty-three hundred leading scientists saying that global warming was accelerating much faster than predicted," the announcer said. "If unchecked, the UN claims that climate change will bring catastrophic consequences for agriculture and human health in the coming decade. The UN is warning that the number of environmental refugees will put an enormous stress on national and international systems. Our UN reporter, Barry Fitzgerald, filed the story."

"This is the eleventh such report released in the last ten years, each predict –" Gemma turned the TV off with a wrenching twist. "Oh my God," she said through clenched teeth. "Will someone fucking *do* something?" With drink in hand, and a second wind, she decided to put her notes down while they were still fresh. She placed her laptop on the kitchen counter, plugged it in to recharge her batteries, and booted up.

Instead of her familiar screen saver of blue hydrangeas, however, an unfamiliar series of lines appeared:

```
BIOS message
VGA BIOS
Memory check
Plug 'n Play BIOS
CPU type
```

A list detailing the amount of memory, the hard drives, and parallel and serial ports in use appeared, followed by the following words:

```
Non-System disk or disk error.
Replace and press any key when ready.
```

"Bloody hell!" She checked her floppy drive and found it empty. "What the buggery ..." she said as she went to her desk and got her startup disk, so she could boot from the floppy and check out her system via the DOS prompt. What she found horrified her. The computer hardware was working, yet all the files on the hard drive were missing. That could mean only one thing: someone had tampered with her computer.

Gemma remembered her open laptop at the Holiday Inn and let out a sound that was part moan, part scream. "Oh no," she said. "Oh no." She returned to her desk in the tiny alcove behind the bedroom, booted up her desktop machine. Once again the hardware was healthy, but all her files utterly destroyed. She reached into her desk drawer for the backup tapes, and found them gone. A slight acrid odor drew her nose and eyes to her trashcan, and she saw a hideous mass of goo, with bits of tape sticking out.

"*Oh no!*" she shrieked, as terror overtook rage. She'd been inclined to accuse Claire of paranoia, but my God! This was worse than even Claire had feared, and they – whoever "they" were – had been in her house and in her things. Had wiped out her entire working archive of electronic files. She kept her archival stories and research files on Zip disks – she looked frantically in the chest where she kept such things, they were there – and her accountant had her tax files. But all her working files on the Flounderberry story, Claire's files on the water story, and her own stories, as well as a year's worth of professional correspondence, projects in development and many extensive notes for a book she was planning on the Central Valley – gone, *destroyed*.

Suddenly her beloved solitude seemed like appalling isolation. She ran back to the kitchen, reached for her cordless phone and punched in Claire's number at home. As she waited for her friend to answer, she went back to her closet, got her overnight bag out, and started frantically to repack.

"Hello, Claire!"

"Gemma?" Claire sounded sleepy. "What's wrong? It's three o'clock in the morning."

"I've got a frigging disaster here," Gemma said grimly, ready to explain why she was getting ready to hightail it down the canyon to a hotel with good security in West Hollywood.

"What?" Claire said, waiting. "Gemma, what is it?"

But Gemma had been suddenly struck dumb by the certainty that if her house had been broken into and her computers trashed, surely her telephone, and Claire's, were being monitored too. Gemma froze when she heard a sound at the front of the house. She put her head around the divider. The gaunt man from the airport was visible through the upper square of glass, pushing at her front door. Gemma stepped behind the kitchen partition. The fear was like a punch in the stomach. She could hardly breathe. "Someone's breaking into my house, Claire!" she gasped. "Call the police!"

Gemma dropped the telephone, grabbed her purse and keys and ran out the back door. Her feet felt like lead, her legs like rubber, the way they did in bad dreams when she was trying, trying to get away. Glass shattered and the front door gave as she scrabbled around the side of the house, looked around to the front. He was in. In seconds he would find the back door. The Miata seemed ten miles away. She saw him outlined in the light as she somehow crossed to the drive. She willed her legs to move, fell, somehow scrambled to the car, started the ignition. The man came running out on the front porch as she reversed at speed.

Gemma made for the canyon road, fighting tears and hysteria. "Oh my God, oh my God," she repeated as a small, clear voice inside told her to get a grip and focus. She fought hard to control her breathing, steady her hands. A minute later, she was blinded through her rear-view mirror by the high beams of a large vehicle that came careening up behind her. Jesus, if he caught up with her he could run over her little car with his bumper and squash her like an apple. She hit the gas. The road whipped back and forth like an alligator's tail. Gemma was fueled by the desperation of the damned, she knew the curves by heart, and she pushed the Miata to its limits. A stream of curses and prayers flowed from her lips. Slowly she extended the distance between them. The five minutes they snaked down the canyon seemed like an hour and she was feverish and bathed in sweat. But she couldn't extend the gap far enough. He's going to get me on the straight-away to the freeway, she thought. I don't want to die.

In the rented, souped-up Chevy Suburban behind her, Marco Mostyn was feeling foul. His eyes were gritty, his mouth felt like a gutter, and his intestines were on fire. His Suburban went into a hideous skid. He fought to hold the pavement. They were coming down to the feeder road leading to the freeway. He could see his chance. But, fuck your mother, coming from the opposite direction was an LAPD police car, siren wailing and cherry twirling, pushing ninety. "Ah, fuck, fuck, fuck!" he shouted. The Miata's horn started blowing, she was turning her car into their lane to make them stop. The cops screeched to a halt, and Richardson sprinted for their car. Mostyn held on to the steering wheel and forced the Suburban to pass on the right. In the side mirror he could see his near-victim, talking through the window to the police, pointing after him.

One hour later, Mostyn sat in the bushes outside Gemma Richardson's house again, watching the police swarm over the scene of the crime. He'd parked a half-mile down, off the road, and skulked through the eucalyptus trees until he could see the cottage. Two more cars arrived, and a couple of women officers. He could see Richardson leading them around, showing them her computers. Was there any possible way to wait until they left, then try again to take her out? The excruciating pain in his gut made it hard for him to think straight. He put the gun down and reached for his cellphone, but before he could key in Doug Boyle's number, Richardson stepped out on the front porch. All alone. She stood there and took deep breaths of fresh air. An easy shot, Christ! Even though he was almost seventy-five yards away he reached for his weapon. She looked beautiful through his scope, lit up like an icon under the porch light. Slowly he brought his weapon to bear on his target. No one inside would hear his shot thanks to the integral silencer.

Gemma Richardson stretched her arms. Mostyn selected two-shot burst mode to ensure a fatal wound, and used the 5X scope to aim at her center of mass. He worked against the pain to control his breathing, and, as his Polish sniper training had taught him, prepared to pull the trigger between the beats of his heart. But just as he took his shot, his intestines clenched in fierce agony. In that split second his aim went low and the two bullets fell short of their target. Richardson crumpled like a rag doll just as her front door opened. He was pretty sure he hadn't killed her, and hoped she would bleed to death before the ambulance came.

27

IN her apartment in Fairfax, Claire very nearly lost her composure trying to explain the situation to the LAPD and persuade them to take an emergency call from halfway across the country. Then she'd waited in terror for an hour during which she felt reality shifting from normalcy, in which struggle was a constant, yes, but bearable, into a dimension where she and the people she loved were face to face with evil. She shuddered repeatedly, tried to warm herself with a couple of brandies. When she called the police back, the sergeant told her what had happened, and the hospital where she could find Gemma.

Wracked by horror, grief, guilt and fear, Claire went in search of her cellphone to call Malcolm. Then she stopped dead. If they knew enough to trace Gemma, she thought in a panic, what if they had microphones in her apartment and were listening in on her every word? Was that what Gemma had realized when Claire had picked up the phone, what silenced her?

She suddenly found thinking straight very difficult. The word "camera" popped into her head and she nearly jumped out of her skin. Where would they put one? Are they watching me even now? She had to warn Charlie Emerson. She had to warn Malcolm. I'll slip out the back, she thought. What if the car's wired too? How far do I have to walk to evade a parabolic mike? Where the hell am I going to walk at four o'clock in the morning, talking into a cellphone, in Fairfax, for God's sake?

Okay, she told herself, pull yourself together. She straightened her bed, plumped the pillows and turned down her blanket, then turned on the radio and adjusted the dial to a station playing soporific classical music. She went through her dark living room into the unlit hall, stepped into the well-lit kitchen, put a kettle on to boil for tea. For the benefit of whatever microphones might be lurking, she turned on the bath and let the water run. Then she slipped into the darkened living room, and looked out the window. Ten or fifteen vehicles on the block. Halfway down, a white, commercial van of some sort with aerials. Lots of them. She grabbed the file on a side table and stuffed it into her briefcase, walked quietly into her darkened study to grab her laptop, placed both items near the front door. She returned to the kitchen, and made a leisurely show of making tea. Then in the dark hall she took her emergency bag from the front closet.

If it was infrared technology, and they'd placed cameras throughout her apartment, they'd be having a ball watching her get ready to flee. If they had someone watching from the street, on the other hand, or an ordinary camera, they wouldn't be able to see anything except in her lit bedroom and kitchen. In the hall, she got dressed as quickly and quietly as she could. She placed the bag by the door, with her keys and purse, and slipped the latch. She put her nightgown on over her clothes, returned to the bathroom, turned off the water, made splashing sounds, brushed her teeth and flushed the toilet. In the bright kitchen, she finished making tea. She turned out the kitchen lights, went back to her bedroom, got into bed, and made a pretense of sipping and reading for ten minutes, remembering all the wonderful times she and Gemma had spent together, praying they would have some more. Then she turned out the lights.

"I'd give a lot to know what you're thinking right now, Miss Greener-than-thou," said Tiffany Mostyn, sitting in a borrowed white NSA van with the stenciled name of a dry cleaner. She watched the lights go out in the apartment. Not as much as I'd give to be home asleep with Marco, though, she thought wearily. She pinched her cheeks to stay awake. She had listened to and recorded every word between Gemma and Claire, and Claire and the LAPD. She had heard from Boyle that Marco had failed to kill Richardson, but left her critically wounded. Boyle had told her not to lose Davidowicz or else. She kept one eye on the bright windows of the apartment, and another on her unrevealing video monitor.

Tiffany wondered how Marco had missed. This thing he'd gotten in Asia, she was really worried about it. She pulled her sweatshirt around her shoulders, slunk down lower into the seat. Davidowicz would be making an early start. Goddamn, I'm tired, she thought, as "Eine Kleine Nachtmusik" lilted softly in her earphones. Her eyelids felt heavy. She shook herself awake. She listened carefully to Davidowicz's apartment. Quiet. Just the music, and the soft beat of the locator device on Davidowicz's stationary car.

To the strains of Debussy's "La Mer", Claire eased her body off the bed and onto the floor. It had been a wild thirty minutes, her mind a storm tossing her back and forth between certainty that she was under surveil-lance, and certainty that she was a certifiable nutcase performing a hallucinatory charade for her own ghosts. It took her ten minutes to exit the apartment soundlessly. No one was in the hall, so she headed to the laundry room.

First she tried Charlie Emerson. No answer. Then she called Malcolm. Bonnie was barking in the background. "Malcolm, don't say anything," she whispered. "Get dressed very quietly and go for a walk. Far away from your house and car. I'll call you in fifteen minutes."

Fifteen minutes in a dark laundry room seemed like hours. She kept an eye on the van in the street and continued to review what she knew. She found Malcolm in an all-night diner, and told him about Gemma.

Malcolm said, "Maybe she was upset about something to do with the story, but that had nothing to do with whoever shot her, Claire. Didn't she say anything else?"

"Nothing. But she was really, *really* freaked out. I could hear scrabbling sounds and a door opening, then banging and wood tearing. Oh my God! And the guy came back and shot her when her house was full of cops!" Claire's voice was hoarse with shock.

"Jesus Christ," Malcolm said. "That's no garden variety armed robber."

"And I think there's a surveillance van outside my apartment. Mal, if Gemma was shot because of the water story, they must know about her because of me. How else would they have targeted her?"

"Maybe Emerson spoke to someone about his meeting with her."

"Maybe. But I really doubt it." She thought about it for a minute. "Their Quebec surveillance, which Sylvie told me about, for sure they'd have spotted a relationship with eco-Justice. And if they decided to go looking with a fine-toothed comb in *my* telephone records, they would have found my calls to Gemma. And to Paula."

"Uh-oh."

"And if they looked hard enough it's possible that they've found out about you. Maybe even Russ and Geraldine. Malcolm, you could be blown. Right now. And they have somebody out there shooting people."

"Holy cow. Okay, I think I'd better do an emergency evacuation, get Geraldine and Russ to do the same."

"Agreed."

"I think we should go underground for a couple of days, think this through, contact lawyers, so forth."

"I've got to go see Gemma, Mal. She may not make it through the next day. Can you meet me in LA?"

"Claire, we need time to regroup, think this —"

"I'm not going to let her die without seeing her."

"Okay, all right, I'll meet you in Los Angeles. But call the local eco-Justice lawyer, and be ready to run if there's funny business with the LAPD."

"What funny business? I mean at least there's evidence of –"

"Of what? It's going to be hell to prove anything connected to –"

"Malcolm, let's stop talking! I'll meet you at Century City Hospital as soon as you can get there. We'll figure it out from there. Only thing ..."

"What?"

"I don't know how to make it to my car without being followed."

They shared a sardonic laugh. "They may have a locator bug on your car," he said. "I wouldn't drive it, personally."

"That's reassuring."

"Shit! Is there a back door? Does it give onto a street, or what?"

"Yes. It opens on a parking lot."

"Call a taxi. Get him to pick you up out back, tell him to turn off his lights, you're running away from an abusive husband, whatever. Can you do that?"

"I think so."

He heard the doubt in her voice. "Listen, I know it's not much of an idea. But it's better than going for your car."

"Okay. I'll meet you at the hospital."

"There'll be cops all over the place. I don't know if they'll help, but I guess the shooter won't go after us while they're there."

"Listen to you! They just tried to do it to Gemma!"

"I don't think they'll do it in broad daylight, in a hospital. I've got to get to Russ and Geraldine."

"I tried calling Charlie Emerson. Just now. There's no answer. At five thirty in the morning!"

"Try again."

"I will, as soon as I get to the airport."

"Claire?"

"Yes?"

"It's going to be okay. Maybe there's another explanation. I'll be with you soon and we'll deal with it together. Okay? I've got my phone, call me if you need to. Bye, sweetheart."

As he walked the dark streets towards home, Malcolm made a call to an old friend from his AWACS days, a man with whom he'd lived through many trials and tribulations and with whom he had forged strong bonds. Frank Spinnaker was asleep in his bed in Midwest City, close to Tinker AFB where he still worked, but now as a civilian consultant. "Hey Frank," Malcolm said to the sleepy voice, "sorry to wake you. Yeah, I know it's late, but this is an emergency. I need your help. Yes, now. It involves lending me the apple of your eye for about twenty-four hours. I need you to get it to Los Angeles by tomorrow, late a.m. No, I'm not joking. No, not even a little. Yes, I'll sacrifice my first born if it comes to any harm. Yes, I'll tell you exactly where to leave it. No, absolutely not, there's no way you want to know why ..." They argued for a few minutes, but Spinnaker finally agreed to Malcolm's plan as Malcolm turned the corner of his street. Oh hell, Malcolm thought as he hung up. Gotta find a way to get those animals to the vet.

Claire managed to get to Dulles by six thirty. As Tiffany Mostyn finally woke and saw with relief that Claire's car was still parked out back, Claire flew out of the capital exhausted and burdened with dread.

28

CHARLIE Emerson sat on a rock at the edge of the small orchard behind his house. It was six thirty, the air was fresh with a premonition of fall, and Charlie was marveling at the news he had received last night from his girlfriend in Brattleboro: she was pregnant, and willing to come to live with him. The feeling of deep, spreading contentment was a sweet balm and he wondered whether they could put an extension on the cabin without cutting down any of the orchard. He heard a car lumber its way in his direction from a mile or so down the road. For a moment, he found himself hoping that the information he had given Claire Davidowicz and Gemma Richardson would be used to the good, and not to deprive him of his job, just as he was about to become a father.

He said a little prayer of thanks as the sound of the engine came closer, indeed came down his driveway, and stopped. He saw a big, dark green SUV, and a tall man in black jeans and a T-shirt step out. The man dragged a contraption from the front seat. Emerson recognized it as a crossbow. The man hoisted it into position and began to scan the field. Even more than his weapon, the expression on the man's face told Emerson all he needed to know. In that instant, the man's eyes locked on Charlie, and in one fluid motion, he pulled back his arm and released a poisoned barb. It caught Emerson in the calf, and the searing pain was followed almost instantly by paralysis and lethal suffocation.

The killer put the crossbow back in the vehicle, donned leather work gloves, grabbed some cloths from his trunk, and walked over to Charlie's body. He placed the cloths around the leg to catch what little blood seeped from his wound. He removed the barb, hoisted Emerson's burly body over his own beefy shoulders and staggered into the house. A small fire already burned in the wood stove, underneath a coffee pot. The man stoked it mightily, draped Emerson's body over the wood pile, threw the cloths on top, arranged kindling and logs artfully. He went outside and, with a large branch ripped barehanded from an apple tree, carefully covered over the tracks he had made in the grass. He backed his car onto the road, and smoothed the driveway. Then he walked up the flagstone path back to the house, which was dry as kindling thanks to the lack of rain. Outside, he threw some barbecue starter on the place where he'd cut the telephone wires in the night. Inside, he removed the top from the wood stove. With the tongs, he removed four burning logs from the fire and set them down in each corner of the small cabin, applied barbecue starter strategically and ran. The house caught fire with a mighty whoosh.

It took the nearest neighbors the better part of twenty minutes, first to smell the fire, then to go outside and realize there was a hellish blaze on Charlie Emerson's property, then to call the fire department. When the fire brigade arrived, the house, the front yard, and half the orchard were burned to ashes, and the corpse was reduced to a few greasy cinders. No telltale casings. No strange footprints or blood. No one suspected foul play, and no official questioned the finding of death by domestic fire accident when it was delivered by the Waterbury chief of police that afternoon to Emerson's heartbroken parents.

"I owe you, Mr Massaro, thanks," Doug Boyle said over the phone. "The Colonel is very grateful."

"Our man is one hundred per cent dead. What about your target?"

Boyle grimaced silently. "We're confident. I'll keep you posted."

"You do that," Vittorio Massaro said. "Listen, Boyle, I'm worried about

Quebec. I was up there last weekend doing some work for Gabe with Vezina, at his place in Sutton, and there's banners about water draped over the stores, petitions in the supermarket parking lot. And Roch Vezina said there was a long article on water management in one of the French papers last week – guy called, let's see," Massaro rummaged around his desk, "Dennis Lamontagne."

"Our people have a live tap on that guy's telephone. We're on it. However, I appreciate your concern, and your information."

"Yeah. Well. Just don't concentrate so hard on the situation down here that you lose track of the big mess up there."

"Roger," said Boyle, thinking, grudgingly, he's got a point. "And if we need your help again ..."

"Just call, and we'll get it done." He couldn't resist a final needle. "Clean. Professional."

Boyle gave a silent sneer, hung up, and gave the matter some more thought. He got Echevarria on the line, and an hour later he was downloading a list of calls made to and from Lamontagne's office in Montreal in the last two months. Aside from Sylvie Lacroix, whose name appeared on the Montreal Committee list and who called eco-Justice a lot, Boyle had absolutely no idea who these people were that Lamontagne talked to. Without someone to interpret the list, all those Quebec names took him no further.

He called the number for the weird guy the Quebeckers had doing their phone taps and asked him to get the tapes for Dennis Lamontagne. The young man jabbered on about not knowing where the tapes were, and generally gave Boyle a hard time. Which at first pissed Boyle off. Then it made him suspicious.

Serge Lalonde was in his office struggling with Gosselin's final figures for environmental upgrading. Greele would scream bloody murder when he saw them, and even so, Pereira would tell him that the environmental impacts would be intolerable. Serge jumped when his private line rang.

"Mr Lalonde, Doug Boyle here."

Serge swallowed hard. With as much bravado as he could muster he said, "Yes, Mr Boyle. What can I do for you?"

"Understand some reporter's been writing about water up there recently, by the name of Dennis Lamontagne. That right?"

"Yes, Mr Boyle, that's *Denis*, not Dennis," Lalonde said, dry mouthed.

"In last weekend's *Le Soleil*." No way he could deny it. "But it was a general article. He's got nothing on our project."

"According to the list you supplied me with last week, we've got a live tap on this guy, that right?"

"Yes … yes, we do."

"Why him?"

"Why him?" Serge parroted, perspiration breaking out on his brow. "Because he's the best environmental reporter in Quebec, and he writes for an influential newspaper."

"I see. Well?"

"Well, what?"

"Well, have you got anything from the tap, dammit!"

"No. We don't."

"I'm looking at a bunch of names and numbers here, Mr Lalonde. Downloaded it a couple of hours ago."

Serge Lalonde's stomach went into free fall. He said nothing. Boyle pondered the silence on the other end. It didn't feel right. "You know, Mr Lalonde, I'm not sure your surveillance guy is really on the ball."

"Oh? What makes you say that?"

"He told me he lost the tapes to Lamontagne's line."

Mon Dieu, Lalonde thought. Victor must have nearly shit himself. *I'm really beginning to believe you're on the wrong side of this*, he'd said a few days ago. Last night, his words had been harsher: *How can you endanger her?* "Victor Paquette is very competent, I assure you," Serge said firmly, even coldly, in his best bureaucrat's tones. But he was shaking inside.

"With respect, Mr Lalonde, tell him to find those tapes. And to cooperate with me in making sense of Lamontagne's telephone logs. This is very serious, and I've been instructed to tell you that the success of the whole enterprise depends on your cooperation." He was improvising, but he was sure the Colonel would approve.

"No problem," Lalonde said, purposefully using a phrase that would mollify the American. "And how does your search go in the United States?"

"Just fine. We've identified the source of the leaks, and we're taking measures." Boyle wasn't sure whether he should bring Lalonde in on the situation or not. Something felt peculiar.

There was a pause. "What measures would those be?" asked Lalonde, sitting very still.

Something about Lalonde's voice made Boyle question whether Lalonde

really wanted to know. "No measures you need to be concerned with, sir."
He was testing.

"Are you sure there is nothing we need to know?" Lalonde asked,
stretching hard for authority. But his tremulous voice betrayed the split
between his desire to know and his desire to be entirely out of it.

"Not a thing, sir," Boyle said, absolutely sure this time. "I'll be in touch."

29

"LISTEN, Detective Lenoir." Angry, exhausted, haggard, and frightened,
Claire tried to appease Jack Lenoir, the Los Angeles Police Department
detective who had been assigned the investigation of Gemma Richardson's
shooting. "I understand your frustration. But my lawyer's on her way from
San Francisco. She'll be here in two hours. For reasons I'm sure you'll
understand later, I don't feel safe saying anything until then."

"Makes no sense." He'd been pushing, and now he pushed harder.
"You're not a suspect."

"Of course not," Claire said. "But very powerful people are involved in
this attempt on Gemma's life. I want a witness to what I say —"

"Claire!"

Malcolm stood in the doorway, holding an overnight case in one hand
and a small laptop case in the other. Claire's body went nearly limp with
relief as he walked to her side. "Jesus Christ," he said, looking at Gemma,
silently suspended in her bandages and traction apparatus.

"Her spine is shattered," Claires's voice was raspy. "So is her right hip."

"Good God," Malcolm said.

"And you would be?" Lenoir asked Malcolm.

"Malcolm turned to Lenoir. "Name's Malcolm Macpherson. You?"

"Jack Lenoir, detective, LAPD. You a friend of Ms Richardson's?"

"Ms Davidowicz, as it happens. I'm here to help her out."

The two men eyed each other. "She's had a terrible shock. Would you
be willing to give us a couple of minutes together?"

"Sure. If you can get her to talk to me."

The instant Lenoir had gone, Claire and Malcolm embraced like drowning lovers. Almost as quickly, they started arguing about how to handle the detective.

"You said yourself that Gemma's shooting is tangible evidence of malevolent intent," Malcolm said. "I think we should tell him, see his response –"

"Fine, after the lawyer gets here."

"We don't have much time. Two hours is too long." Claire gave him a look. "Listen Claire, with the protection this consortium has, I'm sure any minute now someone's gonna slap a national security seal on us. Probably kick the case to the Feds."

"That *strengthens* my approach ..."

Malcolm took her hands. "I think we should get our story out to this guy, have at least one LA police officer we've spoken with. We may have to run, soon. But I think it's important for us to be seen to be cooperative and we've got to test the waters. So let's tell him –"

"By all means," Lenoir said, walking back into the room. Claire and Malcolm regarded him stonily.

Lenoir sighed wearily. "You too?" he said to Malcolm. "Joseph, Mary and all the saints."

And then a new visitor opened the door. Lenoir raised his droopy eyebrows as a wiry, well-groomed man with narrow glasses entered holding a huge bouquet of flowers. He looked suspiciously at the three people around Gemma's bed. His eyes were red and his features drawn. "Who are you?" he snapped.

They introduced themselves. Lenoir showed him his ID. "And you?"

"Elias Hazen." The words were curt. Hazen walked in and deposited the flowers on the dresser. "That's one of my best writers wracked up on that sputnik. I heard what happened. What kind of frikking department are you clowns running?"

"It was inexcusable, sir," Lenoir said. He was disgusted himself. "The only thing I can say is that we've never had an experience like this – the assailant returning to the scene of the crime and committing another crime while the police are still present." Lenoir watched Hazen's face and wondered whether he cared this much about all his writers. "Tell me, Mr Hazen, do you have any idea why someone would want to harm Ms Richardson? The officers saw evidence of a violent forced entry, computer tampering."

"Absolutely none."

Liar, Claire and Malcolm thought in silent unison.

"Isn't she in hot water with some huge biotech company right now?" Lenoir asked. "Wrote some stories for your paper about illegal releases of genetically engineered plants in the Valley? I read them. Maybe they don't want her stirring up any more trouble." Hey, thought Claire. Our boy is on the ball. She caught Malcolm's eye.

"Bonafabrica?" Hazen scoffed. "They don't need to attack her. They have pockets the size of the Grand Canyon." As it happened, he'd just been informed that InfoMedia was going to pay the settlement, for which Richard Franklin had extracted from him a reaffirmation that *The Star* would do no stories on water. Which made Hazen curious as hell about the story Gemma had been researching. But equally determined to tell nothing.

"Excuse me, Mr Hazen." Claire spoke up. "I think you may know something about why she was shot."

"Oh?" Hazen looked at her like something the cat dragged in.

"I believe she was shot because she was working on the Quebec water story. Ask him about that," she said to Lenoir.

"Nonsense," Hazen said contemptuously. "She had no such assignment from us!"

"Because you told her there was a blackout on the story and you wouldn't run it," Claire shot back.

"What the hell are you two talking about?" Lenoir demanded angrily.

Hazen walked to the door. "I really don't know what Ms Davidowicz is saying, Detective. But I'd be pleased to speak with *you* at any time. Privately. Good day." The air crackled and he left.

"Am I gonna find out what that was all about, or what?" Lenoir demanded.

"We'll tell you," Claire decided.

"At last the lady relents," said Lenoir. "Well. I know it's going to be long, complicated, and horrible. So let's go to the cafeteria and get something horrible to eat."

"I'll meet you there," Claire gathered her bags. "I want another moment alone with Gemma. And I have to call Charlie Emerson."

The din in the hospital cafeteria was overwhelming as Malcolm laid out the story for Lenoir. A malodorous haze of stale french fries and coffee pots left too long on their burners turned his stomach and the fluorescent lights acted like strobes on his tired eyes. "So what it comes down to is," Lenoir summed up, "we got a stealth pipeline, and Ms Richardson was attacked to keep it a secret." Malcolm nodded agreement as Lenoir made notes, and saw Claire approaching. She reached out to a chair for support. She was pale and trembling and he took her hand in a strong grip.

"That's a wild story, Mr Macpherson, Ms Davidowicz," Lenoir said.

"Well, it just got wilder. Charlie Emerson – did Malcolm tell you who he is? – well, I just called his office. Some secretary was taking his calls. She told me," and here Claire fought hard with rising hysteria, "she told me his house burned down this morning and he died in the blaze." She felt like weeping and screaming, but she made an enormous effort to keep her voice level. "They were together yesterday, Detective Lenoir. Gemma and Charlie."

Lenoir looked from Davidowicz to Macpherson. This was a strange, crazy, scary story, and he wasn't sure what to do with it. He asked some more questions, then told them he was going to call in to his chief.

"What about Russ and Geraldine?" Claire asked when Lenoir had gone. "Are they safe?"

"*They're* safe," Malcolm responded tensely. Claire saw that the lines around his eyes had deepened, and his cheeks were hollow.

"Meaning?" she said.

"Meaning that their families, and mine, are being threatened –"

"What?"

"Yours too, I'm sure. I'd show you if we had someplace to take your computer online."

"My computer's wireless. I use my cellphone as a modem."

"Do it, then," Malcolm said. "Fast." Claire had thirty-seven new messages in her in-box. Buried between "ENN Newswire", subject: "New connections shown between POPs and mental retardation" and "Eric Davidowicz", subject: "I'll be home for Thanksgiving" – was an anonymous e-mail, subject: "READ THIS NOW".

Claire opened the message and saw a split screen. On one side was a color photo of Eric, laughing with friends in a pub. A copy of *The Times* lay on the table among a cluster of half-pint mugs. On the other side of the screen was a photo of her parents in their backyard in Burlington. The photo must have been taken from the roof of a neighbor's house. Her father was sitting on a garden chair, reading the paper. Her mother was wearing her gardening hat and tending to her roses. Claire found the detail of the velvety, particolored petals of the prize flowers in their full August bloom terribly disturbing.

"Oh no," she said, overtaken by vertigo. "Is this what …?" Her words trailed off as he nodded.

"The Jeffersons, in New Paltz, on Russ's e-mail. Geraldine's mother, sister, and nephew in Buffalo on hers. They were there this morning, before we all split from Seattle. My mother, my kids, my brother and his family."

Malcolm sat down and put his arms around her, but he had a furious, murderous look in his eyes.

"Where have Russ and Geraldine gone?"

"Montreal. They were going to drive to Vancouver, fly to Ottawa. Pay cash, false names. Then take the bus to Montreal." Malcolm took her hands. "If we're going to fight back, and we don't get help here fast, we should join them. That's what I suggest. Here he comes," Malcolm looked toward the cafeteria doors. "Let's see what he has to say."

"Funny thing," Lenoir said in an odd voice when he sat down. "Told Chief Willet I'd been talking to you, Ms Davidowicz, as the person who had put in the call, and to you," he nodded to Macpherson, "her friend who'd come to give her support. I also ordered twenty-four-hour police protection for Ms Richardson. Officer should be in place in half an hour."

"Good," Claire said.

"Yeah, well, wait for it. Chief told me to bring you both in along with your statements and any computers or documents you may be carrying. Says you're wanted for theft and environmental terrorism."

Claire let out an involuntary cry. "They're out of their minds!"

"After which," Lenoir kept going, "I get to hand off the file to the Feds. Willet told me that the US government had ordered the case sealed to everyone but the NSA due to 'national security considerations'. He got the order from DC half an hour ago, he said."

"Right," Malcolm lifted his eyebrow at Claire. "Check this out, Lenoir," he said, and showed him Claire's computer screen.

"My brother and my parents," Claire said.

Lenoir took a long look.

"I've got some excellent photos of my mom, my kids and my brother and his family on my laptop," Malcolm added. "Our colleagues have some too. We didn't take the pictures."

"I'll be damned," Lenoir said quietly. It was blaringly obvious that the two attacks and the macabre e-photos were highly professional and costly.

Also the ballistics report was beyond suspicious: a homemade .22 caliber bullet, made for something like a Heckler & Koch MP5SD with an integral silencer, weapon of choice of military and professional assassins. But he was puzzled. "If this consortium is so worried, why haven't they already taken you two out?"

"Who knows?" Malcolm said. "Maybe they're afraid that Russ and I had direct access to their communications, that we've filed copies of their e-mail with a lawyer. Which we have. We'll get that stuff to you, too. At least it'll prove –"

"Those documents are stolen," Lenoir stopped him. "And you'll be giving the Feds the excuse to apprehend you." What have I just said? he asked himself.

Malcolm took a deep breath. "I know they're stolen, Detective. But they prove we're not lying. Also, Claire here has a little organization that would turn her into a planetary martyr if she got killed. So I conclude that their strategy is to stop the immediate leaks – Gemma, Emerson – and intimidate the shit out of us."

"Which this certainly does," Claire said, her jaw tense. The three sat quietly for a moment.

"So," said Malcolm. "You planning on turning us over?"

"Those are my orders." But Lenoir just sat there looking morose. He didn't know how this case had arrived out of the blue to fuck up his life. He'd never even considered trying to reverse a national security classification before, but he didn't believe it could be done. After a lifelong career in intelligence and security he trusted his instincts. Davidowicz is a terrorist like my daughter is a terrorist, he thought. Macpherson's an aviation executive, for Chrissake, hardly a threat to national security. Besides, it was obvious. The fix was well and truly in. The speed and efficiency with which he'd been shut down frightened him more than anything else about the case so far.

Lenoir needed more time to weigh the issues. But he realized that time was in short supply for Davidowicz and Macpherson. They watched him play with his stir-stick. He was thinking of his pension; he'd put up with untold amounts of garbage for it. He was thinking of his daughter, a marine biologist at Wood's Hole, an environmentalist, and of being able to say to her, I stood up for what you believe in, for you and for that goddamn grandchild I'm counting on you for.

"Okay," he said, deciding. "I just remembered I've got an emergency root canal scheduled this afternoon. I'll pick you up at your hotel at five o'clock." They registered the significance of what he said. "I told Chief Willet you were being very cooperative. You're not suspects as far as I'm concerned. You were both thousands of miles away. You had no motivation. You're not carrying any documents or computers, so how could I bring them in with me?" He paused, sighed, looked up. "Can't very well postpone the dental surgery. Infections of the bone can be very serious."

"What about our lawyer?" Claire asked. "She'll be here in an hour."

"We'll call her office when we're out of here," Malcolm said, giving her a stern glance.

"Right," she replied. "We'll be at the … ah …"

"Marriot Courtyard," Lenoir supplied.

"Absolutely." She and Malcolm stood.

Lenoir scribbled in his notebook, tore off a page, gave it to Malcolm. "Here's my home e-mail address and telephone number, plus my work coordinates. Good luck. Stay in touch. On a clean line, needless to say. I'll keep you posted via e-mail if you tell me how. I gather you've got some genius geek working with you. Just so you know, the Feds will consider you fugitives from justice at about five fifteen, when I call in and say you've disappeared."

"Thank you," Malcolm said. "Very, very much."

They started to walk away, when Malcolm turned back and asked, "Can you give me your pad a minute?" He bent over a table, started writing. "If you're willing, contact this old friend of mine, he's Interpol, Brussels, corporate crime unit. Ask him if he's got anything nasty on any of the partners in the consortium. I won't be able to contact him for at least twenty-four hours, and that's a long time right now. Will you do that?"

"Your intention?"

"Pressure."

"*Pressure?*"

"Blackmail, then," Malcolm said. "Maybe it can cut two ways."

"Check in tomorrow."

30

"THERE'S a national security seal on the case," Jeb Angell reported to Douglas Boyle, "and the Los Angeles police have just handed over the Richardson shooting to us and the FBI. We've got one of our people leading the team."

"Excellent," Boyle said.

"That's the good news."

"Yeah? What's the bad news?"

"We don't know where Macpherson and Davidowicz are."

"*What?*"

"Apparently the cop released them, told them not to leave the city. He thought they were at the Marriot Courtyard. But they're gone."

"He *released* them?" What a stupid motherfucker. "What did their statements say?"

"No statements. Apparently they agreed to meet him in their hotel lobby at five, after his dentist's appointment. But they didn't show."

"*Dentist's appointment?* What is this?" His voice was menacing.

"We didn't have surveillance on those people, Doug. You did."

Boyle wanted to kill someone. Angell could hear him growling over the line.

"Hey!" Angell was heartily sick of this whole thing. "We're just helping out here, Doug, okay? Not my fault your gal lost Davidowicz. Or that your guys got to your Seattle people too late. So give me a break."

Boyle bit his tongue. He needed Angell's good will and help. He had to get more staff. This thing had gone Tango Uniform way too many times.

"Want me to put out an alert for them on the usual channels?" Angell offered, meaning air, rail, bus, and car rental companies, police forces and customs and immigration barriers at all points of exit.

"Immediately."

"You got it."

Boyle made a call to the security specialists he used in Los Angeles, then to Tiffany Mostyn. "Get your ass to LA and finish what Marco fucked up."

It was after ten o'clock when Jack Lenoir finally parked his rusting Saab outside his small, salt-corroded bungalow in Long Beach. He walked up the peeling wooden steps, reminding himself for the fiftieth time that the railing and the second step from the top were both dangerously loose. He had an image of himself paralyzed by a broken hip, calling vainly for help and cursing himself for laziness one of these days. He went out onto the deck and breathed deeply of the tangy ocean air. He'd been badly jarred by the situation which, like some snarling demon, had just clawed its way into his life.

I gave it my best shot, he consoled himself. He'd spent an hour trying to convince the Chief and the Commissioner to pursue a parallel investigation. Commissioner Haig – a small man with sharp white teeth and so many facial peels that small children burst into tears when he smiled at them – had said, absolutely not. And Chief Willet – with his huge gut, furrowed brow and tired blue eyes, a tough old cop who understood his place in the chain of command, and wanted to keep it – had said, ditto.

Haig had toyed impatiently with his solid-gold Rolex while Lenoir made his pitch. He rolled his eyes at the end. "It's a *national security* issue, Jack," he repeated. Meaning: don't fuck with this. "Continental trade, future water supply for the whole country, how are we gonna keep our way of life in the next ten years? You think these people are helpless victims? Well they happen to be national traitors. Ecoterrorists, Jack. We don't fool with terrorists anymore, now do we?" Chief Willet's right shoulder was twitching like a mad thing, so Lenoir knew it was all bullshit.

"These people are not terrorists. You know it," Lenoir had said. "They're respectable middle-class professionals."

"Forget it, Lenoir," Willet had returned flatly. "For-get-it."

"Someone's gonna call for an investigation, you know," Lenoir hazarded. "Like her newspaper, for one." It was his last gambit.

"I *really* don't think so," the Commissioner said. "National security seal applies to the media. Besides, Elias Hazen called this afternoon and said that due to the lawsuit they're under, from that biotech company, he didn't want any damaging attention at this time. He'd appreciate our co-operation."

"*Damaging attention?*" Lenoir heard his voice jump an octave. "You can't be serious!"

"Dead serious," Haig said, snapping his Rolex back on his wrist. "Goodnight, Jack."

Lenoir knew if he challenged them any further or continued to investigate the case openly, Willet would have him suspended, fired and discredited quicker than you could say cashiered. He'd lose his pension. As he left the office, he heard the Chief on the phone, canceling the watch on Richardson's room as of eight the next morning.

After a few moments gazing at the lacy surf, Jack walked back inside, threw his shirt in the wicker laundry basket and donned an old gray T-shirt and navy surplus shorts. He made a ham and cheese sandwich with the pungent, grainy mustard he'd become addicted to when he had been stationed in Germany decades ago. He opened a Heineken, and sat down at his desk overlooking the beach. A photo of his daughter, sleek as a dolphin, diving in the Marianas Trench for sulfur-based life forms, stood to the right. Sipping his beer, he gazed at it for five long minutes. Then he booted up his computer.

As it warmed up, he reached down to the lowest drawer of his desk and found the battered Schimmelpenninck box, the one that had held the sweet little cigars he used to buy at the BX. In 1973, while stationed in Cambodia, he had traded tobacco for the greater, if more episodic, pleasures of an occasional reefer. One hit of Thai stick, offered around the office late one steamy night, had made neurotransmitters flow and synapses pop, and they had solved an insoluble problem faster than you could say, "good shit". He extracted a joint from the tin box, lit up, took a toke. Then he launched Netscape Navigator, and for two hours he visited web sites and databases, reading material posted by the environmental groups. Thanks to his daughter, he was no longer naïve about the extent of environmental damage in the US. Even so, his search left him very perturbed. On the River Alliance's Newscentral site, for example, he read the following:

INDUSTRIAL WATER WASTE RISING

In 2002, the North American Commission for Environmental Cooperation released a report documenting that industrial pollution dumped into US and Canadian lakes, rivers and streams rose 26 per cent from 1995 to 1999, overshadowing an almost equal reduction in toxic air emissions. There was a 25 per cent jump in on-site releases to land, a 35 per cent surge in off-site releases – mainly to landfills, many of which will eventually leach into groundwater and aquifers …

His eyes scanned the text.

Industries are required to report pollution releases and transfers in Canada and the United States, but that is not yet mandatory in Mexico.

In that case, Lenoir thought, it's a lot worse than this.

Almost 3.4 million tonnes of toxic chemical waste was produced in 1999, the Commission said, roughly 1 million tonnes of that released on-site into the air. Almost 8 per cent of total releases included chemicals known to cause cancer, birth defects or other reproductive problems.

Virginia Tangredi, Commission director, said that the Great Lakes region is producing far too much pollution. Top polluters were Texas, Ohio, Pennsylvania and Ontario, though the problems were widespread across the continent.

Guess these folks have no enforcement power, Lenoir thought. Just the power to put reports together, sound the alarm.

In 1999, almost one-third of total releases were metals such as lead, chromium and nickel and their compounds, largely produced by steel, aluminum and other metals makers. Electrical utilities were again the biggest polluters.

Just 15 of the 21,500 industrial facilities reporting, or less than 0.1 per cent, accounted for 7 per cent of the waste produced. The top 15 included MagNes Corp. of America in Utah, The Pintero Group, Inc. in Arizona and Montana, GTL Steel in Pennsylvania, Agrichem Corp in Minnesota and Ohio, United Haulage of New Jersey, and the lone Canadian entry, Sani-Sure Ltd. in Ontario.

Shaken, Lenoir went on to research the Amwatco consortium. By midnight, he had a pretty good idea of the players. He knew full well the kind of power men like William Ericsson Greele – fewer than two hundred of them on the planet – wielded with governments. Power that was all the greater for being silent and invisible.

He remembered as though it were yesterday those classified documents he'd seen in Germany on his first assignment with US Naval Intelligence in 1968, and his first shattering loss of political innocence when he realized that Ford was making vehicles for the Nazi war machine when his father and Uncle Donald were already fighting in Europe. Not long after, he'd become convinced that Dupont's need to market napalm, and the US government's desire to create a market for it and for other arms manufacturers, had been at least as important in causing the Vietnam War as geopolitics, ideology, and the so-called domino theory. Same thing now. Screw the women and children, man. Screw the ecosystem. We've got product to use!

In the mid-1960s, in the deep freeze of the Cold War, he had been in officer training and compelled to study some of the writings of Karl Marx. Know your enemy, and all that. Jesus and all the saints, what clanking, bombastic, ponderous prose! But one sentence out of all that verbiage had stuck with him. Now, as he stretched out his stiff legs and wriggled his bare toes, it leapt to his mind. Behind every great fortune, a voice in his head intoned, lies a great crime.

"Well, let's see if it's true," he said to no one in particular. He typed an e-mail message and pressed send.

William Greele, cloaked in a striped silk robe and fine Egyptian cotton pajamas, paced the polished floors of the Indian Hill mansion as the great grandfather clock chimed three o'clock. The huge television screen in his study cast its ersatz light out into the hall. Periodically he would go and watch CNN for a few impatient minutes. He was suffering from insomnia. An unusual, a horrible feeling of lack of control had profoundly unbalanced him.

Greele looked at the telephone sitting in a pool of light cast by his desk lamp. He punched the numbers for Sarah's spa. Because this was the twelfth time in two and a half days, he knew it by heart.

"Mrs Greele's room," he said darkly. "It's Mr Greele."

On the sixth ring, the clerk's voice cut in. "Mrs Greele is not answering, sir. Would you like her voice mail?"

"I don't want her voice mail, young lady, but I'll take it," he said shortly. "Where the hell are you, Sarah?" he snarled after the pre-recorded message. "I've been trying to get you for two goddamn days! Call me!" His fingers drummed a tattoo on his desk.

A horrible thought occurred to him: maybe something bad had happened to her. That's all he needed. He dialed again, and this time demanded to speak to the night manager. "This is William Greele. My wife, Sarah Greele, is a registered guest with you."

"That's correct," she said politely.

"I've been trying to reach her for two days. Do you know where she is?"

"No, sir, not if she's not in her room. I'm sorry." She had watched Mrs Greele leave with Matty Dalgety the masseuse at six thirty every evening since Monday. But this was not something she thought it politic to share.

"Check carefully, see if she's left any information – about a trip somewhere, whatever." He heard her moving things around in her office.

"I'm sorry, sir, I have no idea."

"Well, Ms whoever-you-are, has it occurred to you that something serious may have happened to my wife?"

"No, sir, it hasn't –"

"Well maybe it should have!" Greele shouted. "If you don't find her in one hour, I will personally call the chief of police in San Francisco, and have a carload of the city's finest walking through that boudoir of pampered whores you're running. Is that clear?" A part of him registered that his behavior was completely over the top, but he couldn't stop himself. He hung up and forced himself to breathe deeply.

The night manager called Matty Dalgety's place to give her the message. Twenty minutes later the telephone rang in Indian Hill. "Hello, Bill." Sarah's cool voice greeted him as though she were saying hello a bridge partner.

"Where the hell are you, Sarah?" Greele yelled. "How dare you not call me back for two days!"

There was a long ominous silence. "I'm not coming home, Bill. I'm sorry."

Greele was losing all his bearings. Sweat popped out on his forehead and dripped furiously under his arms. "Sarah, what kind of crap is this? Has Magda had you reprogrammed by some fake guru?"

"No one's kidnapped me, Bill," Sarah said. He thought he detected the sound of a stifled guffaw in the background.

"Who — was — that?" Greele said, attaining a whole new plateau of fury.

"Bill, calm down." The hysteria and rage that frayed her husband's voice were new to Sarah. "Don't be upset, you never loved me. You don't need me. And, actually, Bill I don't need you. I want a divorce."

"You're insane. Where are you? I've got your number on the call display here, Sarah. I can have it traced. Who's ..." he squinted to read, "M. Dalgety?"

"I don't know what's going on with you, Bill," Sarah, suddenly frightened, evaded his question. "You sound very stressed."

Greele held the receiver at arm's length and looked at it. She had just asked him for a divorce, in the middle of everything he was going through, and she wondered why he sounded stressed. Was she completely out of her mind? "I need you here, Sarah," he said, as slowly and deliberately as he could. "Things need taking care of. I'm having a big meeting tomorrow afternoon and we'll have guests tomorrow night, maybe the night after. I refuse to even discuss the topic of *divorce* on the telephone. I'm sending the jet. Be at the airport in three hours and we'll talk about it after my guests have gone."

Sarah sat up against the pillows. She stroked her lover's hair, marveled at its corn-silk consistency, looked lovingly at Matty's sparkling eyes. She thought it wrong to comply with Bill's commands — she wasn't his any longer to command. But what she heard in his voice was very ugly. If he thought she would make him a laughing stock, he could be exceedingly dangerous.

31

AT first the drone of the small plane over the disused airstrip just north of the Vermont border was no louder than the buzz of a dragonfly. As it approached and the propeller's pitch deepened in descent, cattle and sheep sleeping in the neighboring fields woke to the unfamiliar sound. The sky was starry and clear, and the small plane made a bumpy but satisfactory landing. When the propellers had come to a stop, Claire and Malcolm tumbled from the plane door, and dragged their stuff down after them.

"Sorry for the landing," Malcolm said, groaning as he stretched. "Couldn't see a goddamn thing."

"We're here, that's what counts," Claire said. "And thank you for that."

The red and white Mooney that Malcolm's friend Frank Spinnaker loved like a baby had been waiting for them at a small, private airport in Bakersfield when they'd fled from the hospital. Spinnaker had made an exception to his "no one but me flies this machine" policy for Malcolm, not for the first time. And he had even agreed to fly up to Montreal, then bus and taxi down to pick up the plane from the old airstrip off Somerville's Airport Road in exchange for the whole story, which, he'd conceded, Malcolm was free to deliver at his convenience rather than in the middle of a red alert.

"It's good to have friends in the military-industrial complex," Malcolm had said to Claire when they climbed into the cockpit many long hours ago. He'd raised a wan but grateful smile from her.

"No argument," she'd said.

Mal was utterly drained from fourteen hours of flight, broken only by a couple of refueling stops at obscure airstrips across the country. The noise of the engines had made conversation difficult, so they'd had many hours to contemplate their predicament. Reviewing the last few months, Malcolm realized that though he'd hardly registered it, he had stepped over so many old lines that he was, in a very real sense, a new person. Or rather, that the person he had been for his whole adult life had cracked, like a large shell, under the weight of gross disillusionment, and a different Malcolm Macpherson had stepped out, fully formed. Now here he was, on the run from the armed forces of the country he had served so loyally, prepared for civil disobedience and much, much more. The fact that he had undergone this transformation without becoming hideously embittered, even psychotic – he thought of the Unabomber and shuddered – had everything to do with his love for the remarkable woman beside him.

They had never expected this to cost anyone's life. Now the enormity of what they were up against blew his circuits and made strategizing difficult. How can we get at them? he kept asking himself, over and over again. And the answer always came back: *Hurt their bottom line*. But how?

In the fragrant stillness of the early country morning, they contemplated what lay ahead. "Let's walk," Claire said. Her house lay just to the south and she thought longingly of it for a moment, but they made their way north to the road and began the trek to Somerville.

At first every step hurt her muscles, cramped from the tension of their long flight. But the moon lit their passage between swaying trees, and dust mingled with the dew and night air, creating an aroma as reassuring as childhood. Her body began to uncoil, and then the tears followed, tears for Gemma's broken body, for wonderful Charlie Emerson. She wanted to fight for the Earth, had fought for it all her life. But she could not think how to do it now, in face of the terror that had been unleashed on them.

Doublethink, that's what they called it in *Nineteen Eighty-Four*, and that's what it was now. They were being pursued by the naked terrorism of the corporate sector. But that terrorism would be framed by the media as civic service, while their non-violent methods would be twisted and framed as ecoterror. She didn't know how she could possibly counsel the Montreal Committee to continue fighting, when doing so meant potentially signing their family's death warrants. Not to speak of her own, and Malcolm's. This was the wall of fire she came up against every time her mind tried to move through the situation.

Malcolm saw the wet tracks on her cheeks. "It's okay, baby," he said to her softly. "We'll figure something out."

Claire smiled, even though they both knew they were up the proverbial creek. "Sure we will," she said, as they reached the point where the road dipped down and crossed the Missisquoi River, to the Boulangerie Peregrine's Peak, and the house of Benoît Mandel and Simone Pelletier.

Jack Lenoir, who'd dozed off in the chair, picked up the phone on the first ring.

"*Eh bien*, Monsieur Lenoir!"

Interpol on the call display. "Mr Aubin? Good to hear from you."

"That was an e-mail most interesting you sent me. Malcolm is in *trouble*? What a bizarre notion. He was always a very good boy!"

"It's a long story, Mr Aubin —"

"Jean-Marie, please."

Jean-Marie Aubin met Malcolm when both were attached to NATO in the early eighties in Europe. Aubin was a French chauvinist and rabid anti-American, though he had liked Malcolm's freethinking attitudes a lot and enjoyed his company. Malcolm had thoroughly enjoyed Jean-Marie's acerbic wit and non-conformist views. Both were fish out of military water and both had marital woes, so they'd grown close. "So," he said. "This information you have asked for will help to clear Malcolm of these ridiculous charges?"

"I hope so," Lenoir didn't know Aubin, so he didn't repeat the word blackmail. He suspected Aubin could figure that out. It did improve his spirits, though, knowing that he was collaborating with at least one other justice official.

Aubin rifled through the papers on his cluttered desk. "I did a little research," he said. "Do you want your answers over the telephone?"

"Sure. Thanks. What have you got?"

"*Alors*, I have done a scan most preliminary," Aubin said briskly, "on Greele and known properties and subsidiaries of the GLI companies, for corporate financial crimes. Clean. By the usual criminal standards that apply to global corporations, of course. There is no record of the laundering of money or other financial crimes historically or actually."

"Hmm ... Anything else?"

Aubin hesitated. "Perhaps we may say, not yet. The first thing to comprehend is that in the last ten years, Greele Life Industries have practiced a strategy very common among the very big corporations, that is offloading ownership – though not, of course, control – of their production facilities. You know, for example, the manner in which operates Nike?"

"No. Tell me."

"Nike Corporation really is a design, administrative, financial, and advertising organism that contracts out its production all over Asia – Korea, Vietnam, China. A network of factories produces the goods, which are then sold in Europe and North America at roughly twenty times what they pay the factories. Nike don't have to submit to international labor standards, because legally they hold no responsibility for the factories. Do you see?"

"So Greele Life has been going in this direction - organizing production via contractors in countries other than the US?"

"Yes. For some long time now. They still have installations in their own name throughout the world, *bien sûr*. But for the past few years, they appear to have been contracting out some of their genetic research and a great deal of their agricultural chemical production. Also, Mr Greele himself sits on the boards of maybe fifteen or twenty global corporations, so there is a wide range of possibilities there. I see that you mentioned the United Construction Company in your list of his associates."

"My informants supplied the name."

"*Bien*. This company is very well known to us. It is a conduit for massive laundering of the money, money from the drugs and arms and gambling. The major base for their cash flow is Catania, in Sicily — which has had severe drought, by the way, for several years. Ironic, *n'est-ce pas?* But we have never been able to actually – how to say? – nail them. In any case, the significance is that the real record is very far from complete. It would require a country-by-country search to match up the independent producers with one of the core companies, Agrichem, or Techniplant or GenSysCo. To go the next step – to look at the records of the contractors and their links to other companies – *merde*, forget it. Even were you to find links to corporate crimes by these contractors, you would encounter difficulties most grave in winning for Greele Life or its subsidiary liability in an international court in the current climate. A climate I naturally abhor."

Lenoir took this in. "I know you must be busy, Jean-Marie. But your friend is in one desperate situation. Do you think you could look a little further?"

"Of course," Aubin replied quickly. "But I caution you. All the information will not, underline *not*, be on record. Nevertheless, I agree."

Lenoir brushed his teeth, stripped to his trunks, climbed between the sheets. He had only a couple of hours of sleep before he called in sick, and returned to Gemma Richardson's room.

32

CLAIRE awoke violently from a hideous nightmare. She had been inside the body of a large, thirsty bird, looking down on mountain ranges that should have been green with trees and meadows, but had turned to cracked ocher instead. She had soared over riverbeds flowing with parched sand instead of water, plains strewn with skeletons, the devastated land deserted, the streets of towns filled with desiccated garbage, wind-blown newspapers and rusted, abandoned cars.

The aroma of baking bread brought her back to reality. She parted the lace curtains and watched the dawn rise pink, blue and gold over Somerville's village square. Beside her, Malcolm stirred. Tears came to her eyes as she looked down at him. Tenderly, she traced the tiny, light brown freckles spattered like stars across his muscled shoulders as he lay face down on the bed. The possibilities of loss overwhelmed her. "I love you," she whispered.

"I heard that," Malcolm replied sleepily. "I love you too."

"Good," Claire said fiercely. "That's very, very good." Malcolm turned over and grabbed her, pulled her down beside him, held her arm, her lush body close. "What is it you said about time's winged chariot?" he whispered in her ear. He understood why people made love after funerals.

Stuffed with flaky croissants and several cups of Benoît's superb coffee, Malcolm booted up his laptop and read an exotically routed message from Russ, telling him where he and Geraldine were staying. He and Claire hugged Simone, said goodbye to Benoît, and got on the eight o'clock bus to Montreal. It was already ninety degrees outside. From the Berri Street bus terminal downtown they took a taxi west across the core of the city, then south into the old working-class neighborhood of St Henri. The driver was grizzled and taciturn. He had his radio on to the Canadian Broadcasting Corporation's hourly news.

"The drought that has plagued the central corridor of the continent has been officially declared to extend to the eastern seaboard of the United States, from Maine to Georgia," the newscaster was saying. "Atlanta has been particularly hard hit. For the first time ever, water for essential functions has been rationed. Global warming and fossil fuel emiss —"

The driver flipped to a French pop station. Truculently, as though it were his passengers' fault, he said, "*La planète*, she gonna dry right up."

The rows of small, redbrick houses and stylish new brick condominiums were punctuated by corner grocery stores and steepled churches. The cab stopped in front of an aging triplex. Marigolds, petunias, snapdragons and dahlias grew in the postage-stamp front garden and Virginia creeper climbed up the front stoop, twining around the tiny second-floor balcony. They pressed the doorbell, felt themselves scrutinized by a shadow behind the lace curtain, then Russ opened the door with eyes alight.

"Damn, it's good to see you," Malcolm said, embracing his friend.

"You don't know how good, man," Russ punched Malcolm lightly, then extended his hand to Claire. "Claire, good to meet you. Come in, come in." Russ led them down the hall, and told them the apartment belonged to a musician cousin of the eco-Justice toxics campaigner. The house was old, the plumbing doubtless clanked in the winter. But, like Claire's homes, to Malcolm it felt more alive, in its brightly painted rooms and woodwork, plants and folk art, than all the vast, pastel living rooms and grand solariums of the rich and powerful he had had occasion to visit over the years.

"I've looked forward to meeting you for months, Russ," Claire was saying. "I'm so sorry it has to be under these circumstances."

"Who ever thought it would come to this?"

They followed him outdoors. Geraldine, masses of red-gold hair falling over her face as she weeded a patch of tomatoes, stood up to greet them. Malcolm gave her a warm hug, then she turned to Claire. She had not forgotten their first encounter but love had made her generous. She gave her a nervous smile. "Oh, Geraldine," Claire said, embracing the younger woman.

They sat at a small blue table on assorted rickety chairs, shaded by the huge maple tree that served three backyards. Having ascertained that no one had received further communication from the consortium, they exchanged news.

"We met with Sylvie Lacroix last night," Russ concluded. "She's getting in touch with the committee today, and there's a meeting tomorrow afternoon at her house."

"We can't go, obviously," Malcolm said definitively. "They're under surveillance."

"So let's decide what we're going to ask her to convey," Claire suggested. For a moment they just looked at each other. Claire spoke again.

"I've dealt with many kinds of threats before, including government intimidation and union thugs. But this is something else entirely. None of us wants anyone harmed again. This group has already killed once, tried to kill twice. I'm not willing to fight them openly if it means more deaths. Malcolm agrees." Russ and Geraldine nodded vehement accord. "So the question becomes – what can we do to stop them now, stop the killing and stop the project. Or are we going to have to settle for the first – no more deaths?"

"There's only one way we've been able to think of to stop both," Malcolm followed. "We need to make it more expensive for them to proceed with the project than to back out. Only catch is, we have no clue how."

"Good one," Russ said. "Any other brainwaves?"

"Maybe we can find something to hold against them." Malcolm explained what he'd asked Lenoir to do.

"Nice idea," Russ said. "With a snowball's chance in hell."

"Hold on," Malcolm replied. "There's a huge universe of information out there – and a lot of it is in computers," Malcolm said. "As you are aware."

"Do you know what you're looking for?" Russ demanded.

"No," Claire said.

"If you don't know what you're looking for, you don't know where to look."

"So what do you propose?" Malcolm said.

Russ shook his head. "Do you think if we step out of this thing now we can get out of the line of fire?"

"Russ," Malcolm said, "can you see Stiller and Kamenev, let alone Greele, letting us just walk away? I mean, really, does that fit?"

Russ said nothing, but he moved his head to indicate Geraldine, who had her arms around her folded legs and her head low, picking at some obscure weed in the cracked patio. Malcolm got the message.

"I'd like to step out of this nightmare too," he said. "But we can't. It won't let us. So can you patch us through to that policeman in Los Angeles, Russ? Find out if he's heard back from Brussels?"

Serge Lalonde was a nervous wreck. He was missing Nicole more and more every day, and with the hot fire that Yankee predator Douglas Boyle was breathing down his neck he was beginning to feel the snap, crackle and pop of the seams that held his sanity together.

He and Victor had concocted some story about garbage bags and cleaning staff to account for the missing tapes. The story had cost him Boyle's trust. Boyle would doubtless sound an alert that would reach Greele. Then it would travel to Corbeil and the earth would shake. Whether he had half an hour before Corbeil came for him, or a couple of days or a week, Serge did not know. In the meantime, the compromise proposal on greening the water project would make Greele furious. He figured it for about 7 per cent of total budget in additional costs – around 840 million dollars. He also knew this compromise – which, once accepted by Amwatco, would be the basis for the "public consultation" – would be branded by Eau NO as a cosmetic attempt to mask an environmental disaster. But, *calice*, the profits Greele could make were still rich by the standards of any mere multi-millionaire. And if the people of Quebec had to sell their water regardless, at least he'd pushed for environmental improvements. So he consoled himself as his report zipped through cyberspace to Indian Hill.

Wouldn't it be wonderful if a popular uprising forced the next government to nationalize the whole fucking thing, he thought. Oops, he was slipping ideological gears. He didn't dare go there.

33

BILLOWING in the August wind in one hundred and five degree temperatures, the old, deep-rooted trees of Cincinnati's Ault Park were still mostly green. But the grasses of the valley below were yellow and brittle, the flowerbeds along residential streets were colorless and lawns were scorched brown. Governor MacFarland of Ohio and Governor Hicock of Kentucky had issued a lawn-watering and car-washing prohibition to conserve water in July, and the vegetation had shriveled and dried in the blistering heat of August.

The Greele mansion off Muchmore Road was, somehow, exempt, an oasis of flowering gardens and green lawns. The swathes of exotic grasses near the helipad, Greele's favorite place to walk, waved invitingly.

The provisions for the meeting – Sarah had placed her order to a caterer from her husband's Gulfstream somewhere over Denver at seven a.m. – were not as lavish as usual, but still impressive. Wilbur Hayes and Nick Kamenev noticed something a little peculiar about Sarah, though. It took a moment but both men identified it: her hair was loose instead of in a chignon, and she was wearing those hideous flat German sandals their wives would rather die than be caught in.

Something was not entirely the same about Sarah's husband either. He was flawlessly groomed as usual, in his pressed khaki safari suit and handmade shoes. He had shed a few pounds and hardened his profile. In truth, he had been exercising to lower his blood pressure, which had risen to 200/120. He'd cycled for hours, hit the heavy bag, lifted weights. Yet when Jurgen put the blood pressure cuff back into the cabinet before he left for his holiday, he said this was a very serious reading, and to consult a doctor immediately. Greele thought, screw that, and hit the gym again. There was a flushed, reddish tone to his complexion over an underlying pallor that hadn't been there before.

"This is it, boys," Greele said, slapping the document. "Those big figures on the bottom line – 850 to 950 million dollars – represent Gabe's best estimate of the additional costs to 'green' the project to that little shit Lalonde's satisfaction. You don't have to be a mathematical genius to understand that this will cut our profit margins in Phase I by up to 8 per cent of total. That means we're at 11 or 12 per cent altogether, not 19 or 20.

"Of course, I'd like to hear your reactions. But I've decided that it's simply not acceptable. I'm going to demand that whatever arrangements the Quebeckers make, they restore our margins."

A. A. Stiller and Nick Kamenev, who were looking to the water project as a form of diversification, told Greele that they could live with 12 per cent if they had to. That didn't seem to please Greele. Wilbur Hayes, sweating profusely despite the air conditioning, said he had expected something closer to 20 per cent, and didn't see why he shouldn't get it. Vittorio Massaro had promised his uncle at least 18 per cent, was hoping for 20, had even fantasized 22. "I don't like it," he felt compelled to say.

Greele grunted. "We're not a charity, gentlemen," he pronounced. "And why should I pull three and a half billion dollars' worth of assets already earning 12 per cent or more out of my other enterprises just to finance this operation? I want our 20 per cent, and we're going to get it. It isn't just the money. *They* don't get to change the terms, and *they* don't get to call the shots. We don't have that kind of trouble with our own politicians, and we're not standing for it from them." And I'm not going to eat crow with Duke Pulaski and George Arlington, either, Greele thought, or Jim MacFarland, or Ed Caccia, or John Putnam, or Jason effing Stamper.

Massaro and Kamenev exchanged worried looks. Their role as warriors didn't trouble them. If prudence called for outright aggression, they were willing to do the necessary. But they wanted such acts decided on by a calm, rational mind, and at the moment, Greele's did not entirely fit that bill. The silence following Greele's little speech was uncomfortable.

Greele broke it. "The Quebec legislature goes back into session the day after Labor Day, and we're going to tell them that not more than thirty days later the enabling legislation has to be passed. Forget Christmas. Forget consultation. It's October 7 now, no ifs, ands or buts. Right. Let's get some lunch."

Seated around the dining room table eating cold cucumber soup, they were joined by Douglas Boyle, whom Kamenev had brought with him. Introductions were effected all around. Andrew Stiller, his mouth full of soup and bread, asked Greele, "How are you going to force the Quebeckers to do the thing by October 7?"

"We're sending them a message today. I don't believe we'll have any trouble afterwards."

"What kind of message?" Hayes asked. Greele didn't answer directly, but told Hayes and Stiller about how they had plugged the Richardson and Emerson leaks.

Stiller's eyes opened like saucers, but Hayes exploded like an overripe melon. "Why the bleedin' bejesus didn't you tell me?" he shouted. His face was the color of beets, his spittle flying.

"Didn't have time for a group consultation, Wilbur," Greele said matter-of-factly. "We're telling you now. Richardson was on the verge of transmitting her story to *The Nation*. The Vermont guy could have stepped up and screamed foul when he heard of her death. Is she dead, by the way?"

Douglas Boyle said, "In a coma. Prognosis uncertain."

"I trust that will be corrected as soon as possible. Wilbur, we were going to be blown too early. And we couldn't take that chance. *Could* we?" Greele glared at Hayes, and Hayes glared back.

"No," Hayes finally conceded, his heavy jowls trembling with anger. "But why the *hell* didn't you consult me?"

"Wilbur, I told you, there was no time. I acted instead." Well, thought Boyle, actually *I* acted, but why quibble. Stiller, judging by his pallor, was amazed but unprotesting.

That Greele had underestimated the complexity and the difficulty of the undertaking by quantum measures was a thought that occurred to all his colleagues, but no one wanted to speak it. What they wanted was Hayes's buy-in.

"All right, all right, dammit," he said, mopping sweat off his face with a huge white handkerchief. "You did the right thing. But don't make any more decisions without me."

"That's why you're here," Greele said grimly.

Hayes's eyes flicked from man to man. "Why aren't the others here?"

Greele sighed. "Rich is vetting a big story that'll appear in *This Country Today* on Monday, and setting up more. He's got his job to do. We've got ours."

"Bunting will pop a blood vessel when he hears. So will Bernie."

"They won't hear," Greele said. He'd just decided.

"What? You're going to keep this from them? I can't believe it!" Hayes's voice rose hysterically again.

"Believe it," said Nick Kamenev. "This and that little message we're planning for the Quebeckers." He knew what Greele was thinking, and he supported him.

"You're going to do it *again*? Who the hell you gonna hit this time?"

"Another journalist, a Quebecker," Doug Boyle answered. It was his job.

"We've got a plague of goddamn journalists," Greele growled.

Boyle continued. "We put our own tap on his line twenty-four hours ago because we got some strange vibes from Lalonde. Turns out he's on his way up north to check the story, has an informant in the Quebec operation who's going to help him. He's planning to write it all up."

"It's a no-go, Wilbur," Greele said. "And it's serendipitous. Because right now the people in Quebec City need their chains rattled. Hard."

"Look, Bill, Nick, Vittorio ..." Hayes appealed to the hard men. "You know I'm no pussy. But this could backfire on –"

"We've always had the best of security when you and I have collaborated in the past, haven't we, Wilbur?" Greele cut Hayes off. "This is no time to start complaining. And Andrew here knows how to keep his mouth shut." Greele gave the man who'd said no one could break his encryption code a deadly stare. "Don't you A. A.?" Stiller nodded. Personally, he hoped Boyle would find a way to kill that fucking traitor Russell Jefferson too.

Claire listened to the voices of her friends going back and forth in the café they'd ventured to for a little air conditioning. Sylvie Lacroix and James Amanopour, who'd flown in from Toronto, were arguing with the others in low, urgent voices. She ceased registering the words, only the pain, fear, anger and frustration.

"Hey, gang." Claire interrupted the exchange and their voices stopped abruptly. "Let's try something else. James, could you compose an e-mail to all the eco-Justice executive directors worldwide, also head campaigners and toxics campaigners in every national eco-Justice office. Ask them to send us information about any *major* petrochemical, toxics disposal, pesticide and biotechnological disaster in the last five years, including the names of the companies responsible, the cost of clean-up, the long-term effects, the efficacy or otherwise of action taken – all the dirt. Nothing under a billion dollars' worth of damage. Over five billion is more like what we need." The e-J people looked at her blankly. "Thanks to Malcolm's friend in Brussels, we now have a list of Greele Life's holdings and links. Let's ask how fast he can come up with a similar list for the other major players. Maybe – just maybe – we can find some *bad* environmental disaster to tie to Greele or the partners –"

"I hate to break your bubble, Claire," Amanopour cut in, "but that is the longest, I mean the most impossible shot ever. Forget it. Talk about a needle in a haystack."

"I think we should do it, James," Sylvie said. "We have nothing to lose."

"Nothing to lose?" Amanopour was incredulous. "The time, the effort –"

"What it comes down to, James," now Claire cut him off, "is that we have nothing else. And collectively eco-Justice knows a great deal that isn't public information."

"Okay, okay," James stood with a sigh, held up a hand. "I was just thinking of all the … never mind."

"Right," Sylvie said. "Let's go."

"One more thing," Malcolm said. "We need a couple of guns."

"*Excuse me?*" Sylvie squeaked. James's eyes widened.

"We need a way to protect ourselves in case they find us and come for us."

"This is Canada, *chéri*," Sylvie said. "We can't just go out and buy you firearms."

"They've killed one person, tried to kill another. They've threatened to kill our families. You want us to wait like sitting ducks?"

"Take it easy," James said. "Guns are not our department. To say the least. But I think I can probably find you a couple of weapons –"

"You categorically cannot!" Sylvie jumped on him.

"Decent weapons –" Malcolm interjected. "Something someone with no experience with a gun can shoot." He looked at Geraldine and Claire, who nodded. "A couple of revolvers."

"I'll do my best," James said. Sylvie was looking at him as though he'd just dropped in from outer space. "Hush," he told her. "We're against war, not self-defense."

"James," Claire said. "Call Paulo Soares in Portugal too – on a secure line, of course. Ask him again about that zinclolinium spill, three or so years ago. Just on the off chance."

"Yeah, sure," James said wearily. "I think it's a waste of time, but okay."

Tiffany's rubber-soled shoes made soft sucking sounds as she walked down the hall, spiffy in a white uniform, carrying a syringe on a tray. What she'd had to do that morning to get its contents had been long and complicated, so she was pleased to see that, as promised, no one was standing guard outside the room, in fact no one was anywhere in sight. She didn't relish this little operation, but whatever it took to save Marco's ass. She nudged the door open, glimpsed Richardson lying as still as a corpse. She grasped the syringe in her gloved hand, and strode in.

"What's *that* for?" It was a menacing male voice. Tiffany jumped so high she nearly dropped the equipment. She turned and saw a man in late middle age, sitting in one chair and using another to prop up his long legs, a laptop computer on his knee. There were papers and magazines on a small table beside him, and several coffee cups. The bulge of his shoulder holster was apparent.

"Who are you?" she inquired, attempting a voice of authority.

Jack Lenoir looked directly at her. She was tall, blonde, and had a body like he'd never, ever seen on a nurse, even in buff, bodybuilding California. It was hard and coiled like a cobra. "I think the real question is, who are *you*?"

"Shawna Andrews," she said with a toss of her head, "IV nurse. I've got a special injection for Ms Richardson."

"Well, I'm Detective Jack Lenoir. You bring the head nurse in here, and let her tell me all about that special injection." Where the fuck did this guy come from? Tiffany thought in a rage. "Otherwise," Lenoir said, hand on his holster, "you touch Ms Richardson there over your dead body."

Tiffany wondered if she could take him. He saw her look and pulled his gun. "Put that syringe down and put your hands against the wall."

"In your dreams," Tiffany spat, turned on her heel and walked out, betting he wouldn't shoot a woman in the back. Lenoir went after her.

"Halt!" he yelled, but she had broken into a swift run and disappeared around a turn of the corridor. Afraid to leave Gemma alone, Lenoir ran back into the room and frantically pushed the call button. Tiffany found the stairs, ran down multiple flights, through the main concourse and to the parking lot. People looked surprised to see a nurse running and cursing like a sailor.

When a real nurse finally arrived, Lenoir went ballistic. "If I hadn't been here," he yelled, then quickly lowered his voice in deference to Gemma, who couldn't hear him anyway, "your patient would be dead now! Some broad with a humongous syringe just waltzed in here and nearly injected her."

"O my God, I'm sorry, sir!" the plump young nurse said. "I really am. But we don't operate a security service."

"Yeah, yeah, you're overworked and understaffed. I know all about it. But do me a couple of favors, will ya?" Lenoir said, softening. "Go down to the cafeteria and get me an egg-salad sandwich, and another coffee, black? And get the head nurse in here. Maybe if she calls downtown, we can get some real protection."

As Lenoir picked up the telephone to call Chief Willet again, his computer beeped. He turned to see what was coming in.

34

"IT says here that Charles Emerson died yesterday morning!" Governor Putnam was waving a copy of the *Burlington Free Press* and shouting at Paula McIntyre. "That his house burned down! What the tarnation is going –"

"I just heard about it myself, Governor," Paula said shortly. "He was murdered."

"I *beg* your pardon?"

"According to my friend, Mr Emerson was killed because he spent time with a journalist talking about that water pipeline. They tried to kill her too. She's comatose, in intensive care."

Putnam's face conveyed equally astonishment and horror. "What the hell are you saying, Paula? What kind of friends do you have?"

"The journalist is Gemma Richardson. The well-known environmental writer. She was attacked in her own home in Los Angeles a few hours before the fire in Emerson's house. All her computer files and back-up tapes were destroyed. And the people who originally found out about the project and who have opposed it – including my friend – have had serious threats issued against them, threats to kill their families, if they continue." She gasped for breath.

"What are you *saying*? This is unbelievable!"

"Well, I didn't make it up."

Governor Putnam's features froze in shock. Paula waited for the explosion, and it came. "I told you," he yelled, "I *told* you, there was nothing I could do about it! I gave you what help I could, and now … well, now …"

"He's dead," she said. "And I'm terribly sorry. But Governor, *my* friends aren't the ones who killed Emerson. You can get angry at me, but let's get real here. It's this consortium that deserves your anger!" She was shouting when she finished, and they glared at each other for a long, miserable moment.

At last, the Governor's shoulders slumped. "Jesus Lord," he said. "You think I should launch an investigation? See if we can prove it was murder? But I'm sure they didn't leave a calling card. And what if they go after you?"

"I don't know. Cla – my friend – wrote in her e-mail that she and her colleagues were looking for some information, some lever, that would be damaging to the main principals in the consortium. She asked me to ask if you would be willing to be a messenger, *if* they can find the right message to send. She says they desperately need someone whose very presence would imply the possibility of exposure and opposition. I have to tell you, John, I'm frightened beyond words. But I'm passing on her request because I truly don't know what else to do. And yes," she added, rubbing her forehead. "I do think you should send a state homicide squad to Emerson's place."

"All right," he said brokenly. "I'll do it right away. Tomorrow I'm going fishing. I promised my brother a day on Memphremagog, and I plan to keep my promise. If you hear more from your friend, and she has something she wants me to do that makes sense, I'll consider it. But I'm very tired, and mightily aggravated. So don't call me unless you've got something real!"

"Yes, Governor," Paula replied. She suspected that behind the raging and storming, his soul was in great turmoil. Her instincts were confirmed as he stood up gravely, came around the desk and gave her a tight, desperate hug.

"You want some police protection yourself?" he asked.

"No, it's okay." She said it because she thought it was somehow expected of her, but really, it wasn't in the least okay. "Well, on second thought, yeah. I do."

"I'll arrange it. You take care of yourself, young lady," said the Governor. She smiled at the "young lady". "Keep your head down and stay in touch."

Marco Mostyn, plugged up with Imodium and dosed with antibiotics, was somewhat restored by a day of deadened sleep in an airport hotel. He called Jorge Echevarria in Washington from Dorval Airport in Montreal.

"I have a cellphone number for Denis Lamontagne, the man I'm following for Mr Boyle, but not a location. Can you help me?"

"We'll try," Echevarria said. "I can get SAT surveillance on the cell happening. But he's got to use the cell before we can jump on him. Sit tight."

Mostyn went to the airport bookstore, got a map of Quebec. He wondered whether there was something else he could do. He was considering calling Lamontagne himself, when his phone rang. It was Echevarria. "We got 'im. He's traveling in a car east on the north shore of the St Lawrence, about an hour out of Quebec City."

"Stay on him. I'll be airborne in half an hour."

Mostyn found a helicopter rental service, and with one thousand dollars in cash and a credit card payment for another five, dismissed the pilot and took the controls. Echevarria relayed satellite coordinates as Lamontagne made a couple of telephone calls. Mostyn checked in with Doug Boyle, who was running operations for the time being from Mr Greele's house in Indian Hill. The cold in Boyle's voice when he reported the news of another failed attempt on Gemma Richardson's life could have frozen alcohol. With the coordinates Mostyn gave him, they decided Lamontagne's car must be heading toward Chicoutimi. Echevarria called to say he'd checked Quebec transport records, and Lamontagne drove a blue Jetta.

It occurred to Helder Pereira, working-class son of the Villeray district in Montreal, that all his parents' attempts to keep him from getting drawn into a lifetime of crime had not, in the end, prevented him from being drawn into the crime of a lifetime; a huge, criminal sleight of hand being performed in a world in which he was as a babe in sharkland. These gloomy thoughts seized him as he sat in the back seat of Denis Lamontagne's nifty German car. It was a glorious day, but Madame Lalonde, in the front seat, was in a mood even blacker than his own. Lamontagne, on the other hand, with his black-rimmed glasses, his slicked-back brown hair and his aromatic Gauloises, was babbling on at her as they drove east along the north shore of the St Lawrence.

They'd left St Anne de Beaupré behind, then Baie St Paul. Soon they would turn northeast toward Lac St-Jean and beyond, where Helder was going to show Lamontagne the sites on which the water project had begun work, and planned to exploit. Lamontagne found Pereira's eyes in the rear-view mirror and said, "*Alors*, Helder. Please give me the details of the extraction sites and transportation routes, so I know the whole picture before we hit Chicoutimi."

Nicole gazed out the window. She was subdued and sick at heart. She knew that by now, Serge was suffering the agonies of the damned. By deciding to bring Lamontagne and Pereira together, she was consigning him to an even colder circle of hell. But Helder, scared witless, had made her participation a condition of this trip. Doing this to Serge, in spite of everything, felt like plunging a wooden sword into her own entrails.

"Reassure me, please, Denis," Nicole spoke at last. "What if Roch Vezina calls your publisher and tells him he can't run your story, and your publisher agrees."

"*Tabernac*, you're paranoid, Nicole," Denis said in disbelief. "There's been no pressure whatsoever on me on any of these stories. How about we cross that bridge if we come to it." He gave Nicole an amiable look. But she shouted at him, "We'll deal with it now!" and, taken aback, he swore on his mother's grave he would keep her confidence and send the story to *Le Monde Diplomatique*.

Nicole said nothing more. She wanted to call Sylvie but she'd promised Serge there'd be no telephone contact for the moment. She had such a bad feeling about everything.

Serge sat at his desk at home with the French doors open. It was only noon but he was smoking and drinking and quietly going out of his mind. He'd left his office after a huge blowup with Corbeil. The Minister was apoplectic because Greele called and told them that as far as he was concerned, the enabling legislation for the water project had to be passed by October 7, and that they were not accepting 90 per cent of the proposed modifications. Serge had never seen Corbeil so angry. The Minister told Greele there was no way he could force Quebec to act as he wished, Greele could take them in front of any tribunals he wanted. "Screw the tribunals," Greele had said. "Do as I say. I'll speak to you tomorrow."

Serge left one message, then another on Nicole's cellphone. Hour by

hour he grew more frazzled, wandering blearily in the mazes of "what-if" –
what if he'd never agreed to the stupid idea in the first place, what if he'd
passed it on to the other hot young deputies who wanted to get ahead, what
if he'd listened to Nicole, what if he'd said no at ten, twenty different points
along the way? He smoked and wondered long into the sweltering
afternoon, listening to the birds in the garden, sweating copiously enough
to start a bottling plant of his own.

Washing the tears off her face with cold water at the small auberge in
Laurentian Provincial Park, Nicole ached for Serge – a physical pain like
a wound she could not staunch. She wanted more than anything to turn
back, to reverse everything she had done. What good are values, she
lamented, if all they do is make you lose the one you love, the one you want
more than any other in the world? Let someone else fight. She wanted to
be back in their big bed on Rue des Braves, to hold Serge and laugh with
him again. She would tell them she wanted to go home.

But when she stepped back into the restaurant, she found Denis and Helder
waiting expectantly, and knew she had to forge ahead. They all piled back
into the car.

She was so engrossed in the effort of will it took to keep going that she
made nothing of the strange noise outside the car. Denis was driving northeast with the joy of a *coureur du bois*, singing Québécois folk songs about
flying canoes and forest spirits. He could see the headlines in *Le Soleil*, the
story picked up by *Le Monde*, himself interviewed on every television news
show in the French-speaking world, specials with him as consultant on
networks across the continent.

An hour out, the tension was so terrible that she knew she couldn't go
on. "I've changed my mind," she announced. The men looked at her in
astonishment.

"What do you mean?" Denis said, his demeanor changed from sunny to
furious. "We're here because of you! Forget it. I'm not turning back!"

In the helicopter overhead, Marco watched the car make its way through
the shaded spruce forest, up hills, down valleys, around hairpin curves.
When the target had stopped for lunch, he'd been bitten by a mosquito
while wiring the Jetta with C-4. Mostyn realized that he was much more
frightened of microbes than humans, and broke out into a cold sweat. He
reassured himself that Quebec mosquitoes were not carriers of yellow or
dengue fever. For now, anyway. He had read about a woman in Toronto

catching malaria in her own suburban backyard a few summers ago, and West Nile virus was spreading like wildfire. The antibiotics and his own resident parasite were waging painful microbial war in his bloated gut, but he clenched down and followed his quarry.

The car climbed up a high mountain, turned at its peak, and began its extended descent, entering a long, sharp, steep curve at high speed. Inside, Denis and Nicole were shouting and swearing at each other, oblivious to his proximity. The curve presented the perfect configuration and Mostyn pushed the remote. The explosive blew out the brakes, and in one second the car had spun out of control over the dirt shoulder. It crashed almost vertically down the mountainside, rolling over and over through breaking trees, until it hit a boulder at the bottom of the gorge. Another remote impulse blew the second explosive and the car burst into a huge fireball.

Around eleven, Sarah Greele became aware of her husband's footsteps coming down the corridor. They stopped in front of her room. Move on, she prayed silently as she imagined a panther sniffing at her door, move on! But instead, his knock came, imperious, and he strode in. He was in pajamas and robe, his hair standing on end around his bald pate and inflamed red smudges on his cheeks, clutching a piece of paper.

"Well," he said peremptorily, "I see you're still up."

"You too," she said, as calmly as she could. Her heart was beating fast. "I had Neville track down your M. Dalgety." She could hear the sneer in his voice. He waved the fax in her face. She felt her hands go icy. "You stupid, stupid bitch. I just can't believe it."

"Bill ..." Sarah started, without knowing exactly what she would say.

"Don't 'Bill' me," he snarled. "There's nothing to be said. If you leave me, if you make *any* move to leave me, I'll have her killed. In a very painful fashion. I won't think twice about it. Do you understand?"

He left the room, and slammed the door.

35

SERGE was sitting in his underwear in the kitchen early in the morning, wired like a hot steel guitar. The previous night had been the worst of his life. He'd left messages on every one of Victor's communication devices. He needed to talk to someone, and Victor was the only one with whom he could be even partially honest. Call, *tabernac*! Serge silently willed. Call now! The phone rang. Serge nearly jumped out of his shorts. "Victor?" he shouted into the receiver.

"It's not Victor," Robert Corbeil's voice shouted back. "It's me. I'm at the office. Get over here *immediately*! Greele just called me, demanding I call him back on a secure line. I told him my line is perfectly secure. And he told me – Christ, I cannot *believe* it – he told me his people have killed Denis Lamontagne! Which, he explained, is their way of telling *us* what they think of our modification proposal."

Serge was stunned into near immobility by Corbeil's call. He had thought he could handle the big boys, play them as they played him. What had Nicole said, the day she left? "It's going to be bloody." *Mon Dieu*. In a kind of trance, he made his way upstairs. As he was dressing, the telephone rang again. "Victor!" he said desperately.

A slow, rural voice said, "Monsieur Lalonde? Have I reached Monsieur Serge Lalonde?"

"You have," Serge said, trying to recover. "And who is this?"

"This is Sergeant Plouffe of the Sûreté de Quebec, Monsieur Lalonde."

"I'm in a hurry, Sergeant," Serge responded though he was moving with the speed of a sleepwalker. "What can I do for you?"

"Sir, I don't know a good way to tell you this, but we're at the scene of a terrible accident north of St Urbain. It appears it happened sometime yesterday. A woman's purse has been found."

"Let's go to the cinema this afternoon, *maman*! Papa says we can go!" Sylvie's daughter looked at her with radiant anticipation.

Even before Sylvie opened her mouth to make her excuses, they recognized the expression on her face.

"No, *maman*, no!" Tears sprouted like little springs from Manon's eyes, flowing over her cheeks. "But Papa *said* we could go!"

"What's this, Sylvie?" Georges asked, not a hint of softness or forgiveness in his voice. "I didn't know you had a meeting. We made plans last weekend to spend today *tous ensemble*, after you canceled our weekend in Bolton."

"It's an emergency, Georges," Sylvie responded. "I mean a real one. We have some extremely serious, dangerous even, developments with the water business. If I hadn't been asleep last night when you got home, I would have told you."

Manon tugged on her arm until it ached. "Come *on!*"

"This is a *real* emergency, Sylvie?" Georges said caustically. "And all those *other* emergencies you've had for the last ten years, those were false?"

"Georges," she said imploringly, "believe me —"

"Sure, sure," Georges said through pinched lips, his eyes blazing. He dragged Manon out the door. "This is the last time, Sylvie," he shouted, and slammed the door behind him. For a few minutes she just sat in despair. Then she set about preparing for the meeting. The doorbell rang.

Calice, she said to herself, who can that be? I'm not expecting anyone for another hour. She continued clearing up. The doorbell rang again, twice, and then the caller must have leaned on the bell because it shrilled non-stop until finally she screamed "*J'arrive!* " and flung open the door.

So unexpected was the sight in front of her that at first she couldn't assimilate it. There stood that traitor Serge Lalonde, with an expression that suggested, somehow, that her troubles were small compared to his. He was accompanied by an apparition with spiked hair, pierced in more places than she cared to count, in black biking shorts and a faded Grateful Dead T-shirt. It had its right arm around Serge's shoulder and actually seemed to be holding him up. Sylvie blinked, twice, but the picture didn't change. The entire Eau NO Committee was due on her doorstep in an hour, and here was the man whose actions might well have put her marriage on the rocks, and had completely devastated her best friend.

"What in the name of the perverse deity that reigns in this ridiculous universe are you doing here, Serge?" She was being cruel to an old friend, but couldn't stop herself from lashing out. Then, glaring at Victor Paquette, she said "And *who* are *you?*"

She saw Serge stagger against the apparition. "I'm Victor Paquette," it said, in a surprisingly well-educated accent. "Can we come in off the street? Please?" She saw, as much as heard, a great wracking sob tear Serge apart.

"Something's happened to Nicole!" Sylvie cried to Serge, but he was weeping so violently he was unable to speak. Sylvie directed them to the living room. Victor led Serge gently to the couch.

Serge looked at her with those heartbreak eyes she knew had enchanted Nicole, and they contained an agony she'd never seen before. She waited in dread.

Serge looked straight at her, struggled to make his mouth work. "Nicole is dead."

"Oh my God!" Sylvie moaned. "No …"

"Yesterday, apparently. Between St Urbain and Chicoutimi. Car accident." His head shook. "With Denis Lamontagne and someone else – the Sûreté said the fire was so bad they couldn't identify the bodies … But they found Nicole's purse." Another sob wracked him.

"So how do you know she was with Denis?" Sylvie asked, an avalanche of guilt descending on her. "Did she tell you she was with him?"

He shook his head again. "Hasn't returned my calls. Corbeil told me."

"Corbeil? You're not making sense."

"*Alors*," Serge said, and made a heroic effort to collect himself. "Not twenty minutes before the Sûreté called me to say they had found Nicole's purse, Corbeil called. William Greele had just informed him that he had had Lamontagne killed because he was going to write about the water project. Yesterday Greele told us we had to pass the enabling legislation by October 7, 'or else'. We didn't know what he meant."

Sylvie was progressing into greater and greater shock. "Greele *told* Corbeil this, over the *telephone*? Just like that?"

"Just like that."

Serge and Sylvie sat in silent horror. Victor muttered under his breath, "Fucking bastards."

"But why Nicole?" Sylvie wailed, already suspecting, already feeling crushed by guilt.

"Madame Lalonde was in touch with Lamontagne, about the water project," Victor said.

"Victor here did the telephone taps," explained Serge. Sylvie looked at him with loathing. "He told me I was on the wrong side."

"But *merde*, he was right."

Victor continued. "We caught one of her calls to him, on his office phone. We didn't pass on the tape to the Americans, though. So they didn't know about that connection. I –" he looked at Serge with pity and defiance, "I left a message for Corbeil telling him that Madame Lalonde had been killed.

239

The *salop* needed to know. And someone else was in that car too. The Sûreté told Serge two men."

"So you haven't spoken with Corbeil yourself, Serge?" Sylvie asked. Tears were streaming down her face.

Victor said definitively, "Screw him."

Serge sat straighter and looked Sylvie in the eye, "I'm a dead man," he declared. "My career is finished, my self-respect is in the gutter, when they find out I'm married to the woman in Lamontagne's car they'll probably try to kill me too. And I've as good as murdered my own wife. For Nicole, I want to help you. Let's call a press conference. Now!"

"Serge, it's not up to you," Sylvie said. "I'll have to consult the committee."

Jack Lenoir was doing push-ups and back stretches on the floor of Gemma Richardson's hospital room, trying unsuccessfully to rid himself of the vicious kinks a couple of nights sleeping on chairs had put in his back, when two things happened. First, the "you've got mail" sound beeped on his computer. He saw that Aubin was still very much on the job. He had sent a list of holdings for the Hurst Bank, Skypoint Industries, PETROCO, and Cyberonics. These he would forward to the address in Malaysia he was using to communicate with the fugitives. How they collected their e-mail from there he didn't know, and didn't care. Then, as he was scrolling through the long lists to see if anything stood out, he heard a moan from the bed. He quickly looked up, thinking his ears had deceived him. No movement, but another moan. Oh sweet Jesus, he thought, looking at the halo of golden hair that lay spread on the pillow, surrounding Gemma's angelic face. "Ms Richardson," he said, urgently and gently, "Gemma! Are you there?" Her eyelids fluttered for a moment, and his heart leapt to his throat.

In the evening, Sylvie, absolutely shattered, visited the house on Rue St Antoine, and reported to Claire and the others that Robert Corbeil had called her while the committee was assembled. Unless they had some very compelling reason to slow the process, the government was going to begin to move enabling legislation for the sale and export of bulk water from Quebec to the US through the committee process on Monday, and was going to pass it with their majority in the National Assembly within the month. The government had decided they would on no account agree to a moratorium, they had their water management plan drafted, and felt it was important to move forward to a rapid resolution of the issue. Then Sylvie told them about Denis and Nicole.

"This is beyond terrifying," Claire said, shaking with shock. "She was one of the most important POPs experts in the world. My God, what a loss!"

"She was my dearest friend," Sylvie said desperately. "And, you may as well know now, our informant here in Quebec. I was the one who pressured her, very hard, to find something to take to Lamontagne. Oh God!"

"Oh, Sylvie," Geraldine said. There was a long moment of silence. Words seemed hopelessly inadequate.

"We've got to come up with something," Sylvie declared. "Corbeil demanded that we call him back by five o'clock to assure him that our protests over his decision would be, how did he put it, 'pro forma' only. And that's what we did. The committee will not go ahead with the big protests unless we can guarantee the consortium will stop killing people. They wouldn't even let Serge call a press conference, they're that frightened. With justification, I think."

"Has James reached Paulo yet?" Claire asked desperately.

"He's waiting to hear back."

36

EVEN in a world run amok with environmental malfeasance, crimes on the scale needed to counter-attack the consortium were not that numerous.

There were some truly sensational fires in tire dumps as vast as small cities – one outside Hamilton, Ontario, and one in Nairobi, Kenya – fires that had burned for months on end and sent poisonous plumes to the four winds, to dump their toxic loads far beyond national borders as well as on local backyards and farmer's fields. e-J toxics campaigners had projected remediation measures and damage to health costs that would easily approach the specified figure. But the governments involved had denied the drastic consequences predicted by the environmentalists; it was future damages and costs that would put these events into the billion-dollar category. And there was no direct link to the Amwatco consortium companies – at least not obviously.

Other forms of air pollution from huge installations presented much the same kinds of problems. No matter how poisonous the fumes from a factory, smelter, generating station, pulp and paper mill, or incineration plant; no matter how lifeless and lunar the surrounding landscape had become; no matter how elevated the statistics for lung and other cancers, emphysemas, chronic bronchial conditions, and asthmas, the costs of these injuries were diffused over time and space, often over borders and continents. And the crimes were as frequently the fault of governments as of corporations.

Out in the backyard, on tables and chairs and the postage-stamp lawn, they had pages of printouts from Jack Lenoir that had to be cross-checked meticulously with the tales of toxic events sent by eco-Justice staff. In terms of immediate, proven, up-front clean-up costs, oil spills headed the list – and they had two or three for every continent. Russ and Malcolm tried to tie them to Petroco, Wilbur Hayes's outfit. But none seemed to fit.

"Where are the chemical spills, the toxic disasters like Bhopal, for Christ's sake?" Claire shouted in exasperation. "They're everywhere, dammit! The planet is saturated with them!"

"What about the Superfund sites?" Geraldine asked. "Love Canal, Woburn, Massachusetts, whatever. They've received billions of dollars for clean-ups."

"The Superfunds are appalling beyond belief," Claire said. "And United Haulage has been named in at least two on the East Coast. There's also one in Montana, near William Greele's place, the site of a copper mine he used to own. The problem is that wherever they've been established, the situation has been legally resolved. That won't work for us. But my God, there's so much pesticide production taking place offshore now, especially in Asia. Isn't there *something* we can find without taking weeks to do it?" At midday the heat and humidity were so high they could barely breathe. "I guess James was right," Claire said bitterly, wiping her brow. Her stomach felt full of rocks, her shoulders ached. She was thinking, if I ever get out of this city alive, how, in good conscience, could I ever persuade another journalist to touch this story?

The doorbell started to ring insistently. Sylvie jumped. "I'll go," she said. Malcolm reached for one of the Rugers James had delivered. "And I'll be right behind you."

Every heart was beating with terror, every body pumped with adrenaline. But in a moment, they returned.

"Relax," Sylvie told them, though she herself was tense. "That was my assistant. He's working in the Oxfam office down the hall, so we don't give the listeners our information. This just came from Paulo. James obviously reached him."

The Americans eyed the paper in her hand. "And?" Malcolm prompted.

"Well," Sylvie said, beginning to skim, "it's about the zinclolinium thing you asked about. What is that stuff? I've never heard of it."

"It's an antifungal herbicide," Claire replied. "A known carcinogen and endocrine disrupter. In this case, an androgen blocker."

"*Ben*," Sylvie said, eyes skimming the first page. "So," and she began to read aloud:

"*Thirty-eight months ago a ship, the* Flying Esmeralda, *carrying a full cargo of zinclolinium was moored in Lisbon harbor for a week. Zinclolinium is an ingredient used in fungicides manufactured by William Greele's company Agrichem. Also the main ingredient in the same kind of fungicides made by Dupont and Monsanto."*

She looked up. "*Merde,*" she said. Her eyes returned to the page.

"*The ship limped into harbor with a hole in her side the size of the Rock of Gibraltar. It took the government eight days to plug it up. In that time, the toxic material poured out of her, and contaminated the entire port. The ship was registered to a Panamanian company and its chemicals originated in Uttar Pradesh — a place called Warangal. The government should have had every available crew in southern Europe flown in, and they should have patched the ship in twenty-four hours. But the authorities did not want to believe the environmental experts and did not get advice they were prepared to believe for four more days. Then they did not have enough people to do the job fast. They never made public the registration of the shipping company, and to this day the costs of the clean-up have remained classified information. Our organization protested it, and urged a number of community groups to begin immediately to monitor the water quality and wildlife in the harbor. A week after the spill, the concentration was 110 thousand parts per million, about 100 thousand times higher than levels considered safe."*

"Go on!" Geraldine said, when Sylvie paused to flip the page.

"Okay," said Sylvie, looking soberly at them, wiping sweat from her forehead and throat. Once again she read directly from the page.

"*Almost half of the frogs, fish, mollusks, mussels, and octopi we have taken from the harbor since the spill have something wrong with their reproductive tracts — most of them are hermaphroditic. We suspect that most of these were meant to be males. Most females, as well as the hermaphroditic animals, show gross disorders of the neurological systems, and there are very few normal, intact males. Their sperm count is down to almost nothing. To try to understand the effects of the diffusion of contaminants through evaporation in the immediate region — we cannot know where exactly wind plumes have taken the contaminants — we have been working with epidemiologists and community groups tracking problems in children who were born since the spill, or who were under five years of age at the time, and hence most vulnerable to developmental disruption.*

"*The three projects that have been monitoring local daycare centers report defects of the reproductive organs, defects of neurological development, and attention deficit disorders at 350 per cent higher than the rate in the usual population, and of much greater severity.*"

"Holy shit," said Russ.

"*It is possible that the real cost — classified — of the clean-up meets your specified threshold. Also, if what we suspect about the impacts on wildlife and humans is true, the future costs in dollars, in ecological disruption and human devastation may be completely beyond calculation.*"

"Wow," Geraldine, Russ and Malcolm said. Claire pursed her lips.

"Is there anything in this for us?" Malcolm asked.

"We've known this for a long time. If they haven't found out who's responsible, it's all old news," Claire said.

"How can they not know that?" Geraldine asked.

"The nub of the matter."

"Listen," said Sylvie, whose hungry eyes had skimmed ahead. "*The government has sealed the records. eco-Justice Iberia traced the registration of the Panamanian company that owned the* Flying Esmeralda, *but it was a numbered paper company that owned this one ship alone. We never discovered the individuals. The company went bankrupt after the spill, and has disappeared entirely. And the Warangal company that produced the zinclolinium is a local chemical company. It washed its hands of responsibility for the transportation problems.*"

"How could they do that?" Geraldine demanded.

Claire answered. "Who knows if their rejection of culpability would have held up in an international court? The producer is required to hire a carrier that can reasonably be expected to be legitimate and safe. But — it was a huge scandal – the Portuguese government never took the case to the international tribunals. Who knows why? Just the usual laziness and secrecy? Or a big bribe to someone important? We were never able to find out."

"Well, who was going to take delivery of the load?" Russ demanded. "Aren't they liable too?"

Sylvie looked at the letter. "Paulo says they don't know for sure. The shipment was bound for the US, but the Panamanian company took the liability hit, and the Portuguese authorities said it was not necessary to make the receiving company known, since it was in no way culpable."

"There's a satanical arrangement," Malcolm said. "The Portuguese get screwed, they pay for the screwing, and then their own government blesses it." Sylvie nodded agreement. "So how do we find out more about this – *now?*"

"Paulo says he will fax whatever else he has on their findings on the effects of the spill. But he really has no more information on the principals involved, the costs of the clean-up, and the human and ecological costs. His last point here, he says he can't believe that someone or some ones in the government don't have all this information. But, and I quote, '*our colleagues have tried over and over to get more, in Portugal and through the European Commission, and they've been refused every time. It's certainly a cover-up. But a very successful one.*"

Everyone considered this information.

"We need a spy," Malcolm said.

"We need a hacker," Russ qualified. "We're not going to go breaking into Portuguese government files in person in the next twenty-four hours."

"Can you do it?" Malcolm asked.

"I don't think so," Russ said. "We need someone *really* good, who knows his way around European government and European Commission security systems, *and* who can move rapidly and creatively when he gets there. Above all, we need someone who understands Portuguese, probably French as well as English. Not a unilingual amateur like me." Exhaustion and depression settled over them, deepened by the enervating heat.

Sylvie thought of Serge and Victor, holed up in her apartment. "Listen," she said. "Maybe, just maybe, we may have someone who can help. I don't know about the Portuguese part, but maybe the hacker, fluent in French and English. I'll be back in an hour. Can you get your LA guy to get through to Brussels for some information that would help someone here – tell him someone official, a deputy minister —" she sent up a silent prayer, "to get into the Portuguese government and the European Commission databases?"

"We can try," Malcolm replied. "Getting a list is one thing. Breaking in to government systems may be quite another."

"Well, tell them the details. Do it fast. I'll come back to report as soon as I can. Maybe we can find out more about Lisbon. *A très bientôt*, gang."

At six o'clock Sunday evening, Staff Sergeant Jean-Luc Perrinault gently prodded the three-inch-thick entrecôte on his barbecue on the back balcony. He'd bought the steak at his favorite Italian butcher, and marinated it in red wine and garlic. He'd sautéed shallots in butter, prepared a tarragon Béarnaise sauce, homemade *frites* and fresh green beans, and was looking forward with enormous relish to a long summer night, a good meal, a great beer, and some quiet reading. His girlfriend was in Italy visiting family for the month of August, and though he missed her, he was also looking forward to a sixteen-ounce steak without a lecture on cholesterol and bovine spongiform encephalopathy. He breathed a sigh of contentment and checked for the sizzle just as the doorbell rang shrilly down the hall. "*Maudit tabernac!*" he cursed out loud. If I'm lucky, maybe it'll just be a couple of Jehovah's Witnesses. I'll tell them I'm a Buddhist.

Standing on his wrought-iron front balcony was a most peculiar trio. The spiky hair pierced his Sunday evening reverie first. Victor Paquette, alias Radisson, stood at close quarters with, yes, Deputy Minister Serge Lalonde, though Lalonde looked like a ghost of his former self. Next to him stood a stranger, much older, with deeply lined features, calloused workman's hands, and eyes that looked as though they'd seen a holocaust. All three were regarding Perrinault intently, as though measuring him up for some important task.

"Monsieur Lalonde, Victor, *bonsoir*. What a surprise," Perrinault said politely. "Ah, nice to see you, gentlemen. To what do I owe this … very unusual visit?" Something wild was up. He didn't even know how they'd found his address.

"Staff Sergeant Perrinault," Serge began stiffly.

"Please Monsieur Lalonde, call me Jean-Luc," Perrinault said and gestured inside. "*Entrez*. Please tell me what I can do for you." He showed his visitors into the living room. The smoke that started to pour into the open kitchen door seemed to bring Lalonde out of his trance.

"Something horrible is burning," Lalonde observed dully.

Perrinault cursed and ran out the back door.

When he came back, Lalonde introduced Helder's father, Tony Pereira. "His son has been missing for a couple of days now, and we fear that he may be dead."

Now Perrinault's eyebrows shot up. "Why?"

"He swore his mother to secrecy about some assistance he was going to give my wife, and the timing of his disappearance corresponds to the time my wife disappeared. She was killed yesterday morning," he held up his hand to stave off interruptions, "along with *Le Soleil* journalist Denis Lamontagne –"

"*What are you talking about?* Since when is Denis Lamontagne dead?" The news hadn't made the papers because the Sûreté were instructed by Corbeil to wait as long as they could to break the story.

"I'll explain in a minute, but it's an absolute certainty, and so is the fact that it was murder. There was a third person with them, a young man, according to the coroner. I believe it's Helder, Monsieur Pereira's son. We're here against my better instincts, Jean-Luc. Victor urged me to come to see you. I assure you it's out of dire need, and I am begging you, Jean-Luc, with every fiber of my being, not to go to your superiors and report what I'm going to tell you – not yet, anyway. We need your help to stop the killers. We need your support, we need your skills and we need –" here Serge stopped and looked around for Victor, who had disappeared into an adjoining room.

"– your computer!" Victor Paquette finished Serge's sentence for him. Spread out over two large trestle tables in the dining room was a hacker's wetdream – a big, sleek desktop computer, flat black top and bottom, with purple neon radiating from its transparent plastic sides, almost as promising as the one the Montreal police had made Paquette dismantle, and a fitting instrument for the job they had in mind. Victor had started to vibrate with excitement.

Serge and Victor told the hair-raising story and tried to convince the policeman that they were *compos mentis*. A good, aggressive cop, Perrinault questioned every statement, and thus made the telling longer, more difficult, and more confusing. It was a very difficult hour and a half, but Perrinault's respect for Lalonde's position and Paquette's skills, and the materials they had brought to show him made it impossible for him to ignore what they were saying. He put in a call to a friend at the Sûreté in the Lac St-Jean region, and asked whether they had a report of the death of a Madame Nicole Verlaan-Lalonde in a car accident earlier that day. His friend said yes, in fact, but they were still working on the identity of the other two people; both men, one likely in his forties, the other in his twenties. They'd been asked by someone high up in Quebec City to keep the information confidential.

He saw the Deputy Minister, wretched in mind and body, holding his hand to his forehead. He watched Pereira's wide, shocked eyes. In the end, he was unable to gainsay the hideous loss that carved crevices into the old man's cheeks. If Lalonde said that three Québécois and an American had been murdered, and another attempted assassination performed on an American journalist, all to protect a secret deal that he, Lalonde, had initiated, he was probably telling the truth. So Perrinault chose the just action, rather than official procedures. Knowing about Lenoir in Los Angeles and Aubin in Brussels made it easier.

"*D'accord*," he said. "I'll help you. What do you want?"

Serge explained the Lisbon spill, their need for information and for an accomplished hacker-hunter to assist Victor. Mr Pereira was willing to translate.

"My assistance is superfluous, *sans doute*." A tiny smile tugged at one corner of his mouth.

"No, man," Victor said. "I bet you know Europe like the back of your hand." The little smile on Perrinault's face grew somewhat broader, though officially he could admit to nothing. Victor pulled some more paper from his backpack, and showed Perrinault access codes and procedures for Portuguese government departments and a variety of desks in the European Commission.

"Where the hell did you get those?" Perrinault was agog.

"Our friend in Brussels," Serge supplied. Aubin, living on strong coffee and various baked goods, was thoroughly hooked on the hunt; it had been a long time since he could give his more … well, criminal inclinations, a good run.

"*Oh la la!* A baby could gain entrance with these!" Perrinault felt a rush. Now that his decision was made, the big beefy cop was starting to get excited. "Go and get us something to eat, Monsieur Lalonde. Please. I'm starving. You can do your analysis once we have found something."

37

FOR the first time in weeks, the gentle sounds of the summer night were matched by a softer ambiance at the white mansion in Indian Hill. William Greele was appeased. Vittorio Massaro, Nick Kamenev, Doug Boyle, and Wilbur Hayes had departed around seven. It had been a long two days, but at the end they'd had several rounds of celebratory drinks and a final war council, relieved beyond measure by the successful conclusion of the Lamontagne affair, the wholesale surrender of Quebec's Finance Minister, and the restoration – *thank God* – of their leader's emotional equilibrium.

Corbeil had said he deeply regretted that they did not understand the wisdom of pursuing a route of co-option, rather than confrontation. He further declared he could not be held responsible for the potential consequence of a backbenchers' revolt with such quick passage. He repudiated the direction the consortium members were so murderously pursuing. But he agreed to carry through on their demands. He confirmed that the environmentalists had informed him they were "reconsidering their strategy" and "had their plans in abeyance".

"That's all very well and good, Robert," Greele had said. "I'm pleased. But on careful consideration, it isn't quite enough."

"What on earth do you mean?" Corbeil's astonishment clanged abrasively over the speakerphone.

"'Enabling legislation by October, well, given the difficulties we're experiencing, it's just not secure enough, Robert. I'm having my COO draft a letter of agreement between your government and Amwatco that will bind both parties irreversibly. You should have a fax of the document by late afternoon tomorrow, and I'll fly up to see you and sign on Tuesday."

The silence lasted so long that Greele had to demand whether Corbeil was still on the line.

"Yes I am, Bill," the Minister said. "You are out of your mind. Such a document is a terrible mistake. Further it cannot be prepared and approved in such a ridiculously short time."

"I'm sorry, Robert," Greele said smoothly. "I feel we have no choice. You have Cabinet approval, we know our bottom line, the principle has to be set in stone. We're speaking of billions of –"

"Don't lecture me!" Corbeil roared, finally succumbing to overwhelming anger. But he was, in effect, helpless. "All right," he spat.

Kamenev, listening with the others on the speakerphone, gave Greele two thumbs up. A lock-in that would stand up in the NAFTA tribunals.

Greele had expected Lalonde to be playing gadfly as usual. Coldly Corbeil informed him that Lalonde had been called away on an unrelated matter, and would be out of town for the better part of the following week, perhaps longer. Corbeil was desperate to track Lalonde down, but was certainly not going to share his thoughts with the sharks in Cincinnati. Lalonde's failure to appear at the Ministry as commanded, combined with the news, confirmed by the Sûreté, of Nicole's death, had set a series of terrifying scenarios dancing in the Minister's mind. What was Lalonde's wife doing in that car, what had she known, what had she told and to whom? Who was the third person, and what had that person known, said, and done? Was the whole edifice going to come crashing down like a house of cards? If so, no sense in prolonging the agony through a public consultation. Ram it through, *toute de suite*. Corbeil was grossly insulted by Greele's insistence on a binding letter of agreement. He tried to think how to stop a man whose ruthlessness far surpassed his own. With or without Serge, he was beaten.

Doug Boyle, sitting with the others in Greele's study, thought of his earlier suspicions and wondered at Lalonde's absence. But it did not fall to him to interrupt a conversation between titans. Afterwards, everyone was so euphoric that Boyle decided to maintain his silence. He didn't want to tarnish the polish that had so recently and so tenuously been restored to his and his operatives' reputations.

While the men drank whiskey in the air-conditioned greenhouse, congratulating themselves on a job well done, Greele went to his office and called Bunting Hurst, receiving warm congratulations and an apology for previous reservations. Greele kept his colleagues company another half-hour, until the helicopter came to fly them away.

Then he turned with pleasure and relief to piles of long-neglected business. At eleven o'clock, he retired to his bedroom, and slept the whole night, lulled by the sense of control he had finally regained, and the blessed silence in his own head where, for days, his father's voice had viciously excoriated him.

In the wee hours of the morning, the fugitives were gathered in the back garden in St Henri. The small apartment was like a baking oven, so the kitchen table had been exported to the patio. Long extension cables and power bars connected three laptops to assorted zip drives, external hard drives and a printer in the kitchen. There were sheets of paper on the patio stones, on the patch of grass, on every semi-flat surface. They were still attempting to correlate the list of environmental disasters with the list of holdings by consortium members. But if what Aubin said was true about offloading production – and Malcolm remembered what Jeff Brannigan had told him, which certainly seemed a confirmation – they knew their list of directly owned businesses was grossly inadequate.

They persisted because there was nothing else to do. They were unwilling to pin any substantial hope on Lisbon yet. They were too desperate to stop, and sleep was unthinkable. Geraldine had barely closed her eyes for an hour the two preceding nights, even with the help of sleeping pills from Sylvie, and the circles under her eyes were almost black. She looked pale and ill. Claire's nightmares had been so terrifying that she was afraid to put her head on the pillow.

Malcolm watched Claire, dark curls falling over her strained face, back hunched and arms pulled tight around her torso, poring over the pages Russ kept printing out, and he felt an ache in his bones. He didn't know how it had happened, but he had come to love her deeply and desperately, to think of her as the soul mate he had long ago given up finding. Now he experienced her pain as his own, and his desire to protect her made him want to kill Greele and Kamenev and Boyle. He had to fight the images that involuntarily flooded his mind, so many bloody ways of putting them to death. And he thought of Michael and Molly and Don – how vulnerable they were, how much he wanted to speak with them, how impossible contact was. He had always dealt with emotional pain or danger by taking action. But this time, in this tiny, confined, hidden space, the actions available to him were almost nil. He felt as though molten metal had been poured into the veins in his legs.

Russ looked up and caught Malcolm's gaze. "I hate to admit it," he said. "But we're fucked, man. Royally fucked. We got nothing."

"Two days of looking at environmental crimes in every country, on every continent. And *nothing* we can use," Malcolm said. "What are we going to do?"

"We're going to keep looking till we've finished." Claire said. "And we're going to wait to see what Sylvie and her people turn up. Maybe these people can help us, maybe Lenoir can help us, maybe Gemma will wake up and tell her story and we can get some protection, some action."

Silence followed her words for a moment. But then Geraldine detonated. "Oh, what's the fucking point!" she shouted. Because she articulated a sentiment all of them had been trying desperately to keep at bay, the tentacles of her demoralization dragged them down.

"Gerry, baby." Geraldine turned her stricken face in Russ's direction. "You can't sleep anyway. It's only a few more hours. What have we got to lose?"

"My sanity!" Geraldine screamed back. "That's what! If I have to plow through the details of one more atrocity and how the villains got away with it and how all the ordinary people in the community got completely screwed, and how their children are going to be deformed and sick, and how the government covered up for the guilty, then made the innocent pay, and *then*, on top of that, the whole exercise turns out to be totally useless, I'll go completely nuts!"

Russ reached for her, put his arms around her.

"Why don't both of you go take a cool shower," Malcolm suggested. "Take a break."

A knock came as Malcolm spoke. He and Russ answered the door together, armed, despite the prearranged tattoo. They put the guns aside when they saw Sylvie, and she introduced them to Serge Lalonde. They trooped out to the garden. Sylvie, too upset to sleep after the events of the last two days, had been catching up on some recent international jurisprudence when Serge had come to her door at two a.m.

Claire knew Serge Lalonde had been responsible for setting the project up in Quebec; she also knew he must be suffering terribly. "I'm very sorry for your loss, Monsieur Lalonde," she said quietly. "I knew your wife as a brilliant researcher and activist. We've all lost someone very special and precious."

Serge swallowed hard, and he nodded in acknowledgment. As he regarded the group he could see that they too were ragged with fear and exhaustion. He said, "We have found new information on the Lisbon spill."

"Any of our guys involved?" Malcolm was instantly energized.

"We don't know. That's not at all clear. But maybe."

"God," Claire said in exasperation. "What does that mean?"

Serge pulled out the printouts from his briefcase. "I'll summarize. You can all look over the whole dossier after, if you like."

"Cut to the chase, man," Russ commanded. He was ready to burst with frustration.

"We have material, from Portugal and from Brussels, showing that the Portuguese government knows exactly how much poison was dumped into the harbor – forty thousand tons, enough to kill any fungal life form on fifty million acres of farmland, an amount they had to keep hidden to stop the populace rampaging in the streets. If we didn't have to worry about inadmissibility of evidence due to theft, we'd have enough to indict half the Portuguese Cabinet and senior bureaucracy."

"That's good," Claire said. "But the question remains: who the hell was responsible? That's the key."

"Ah," Serge said. "I have here the registration number for the bankrupt Panamanian company that owned the *Flying Esmeralda* –"

"We had that," Claire said.

"– *and* the name of the man who was its owner."

Her eyes lit up. "Who is it?"

"A person called Jaime Gonsalvez, of Panama City," Serge replied. "Does this mean anything to anyone here?"

Heads shook and shoulders shrugged – no.

"We also have the name of the company in Uttar Pradesh that made the stuff. *And* all the names of its board of directors. Some of their names were never made public, as I understand. This too is new. And intriguing, no?"

"True, yes," Claire affirmed, but without much enthusiasm. The entire European anti-POPs community had worked hard to hang joint responsibility for the spill on that company, with no success. She wasn't sure that having the names of its corporate directors would make much of a difference.

Serge continued. "And we have a numbered registration for the American company that was going to take delivery of the stuff in Norfolk." He paused.

"And?" Several voices chimed in unison.

"Well, Jean-Luc and Victor spent about half an hour trying to find out who these three companies are connected to. But they're all private, so they're not listed on any stock exchanges. By the time I'd left, they had *rien*." Five belligerent faces looked at him, but he wouldn't be rushed.

"Now, Sylvie says that you are in possession of a, ah … rather special list from Interpol," Serge said, "of all the companies and subsidiaries that belong to the individuals and companies in the consortium. Instead of my associates spending the rest of the night hacking their way through security systems in those companies – which, in any case, may yield absolutely nothing – perhaps you could take these names and numbers and determine if there are any match-ups with your Interpol lists." Serge extended one piece of paper with three paragraphs in large bold print out to the

Americans. Russ grabbed it.

"Yeah," he said with heavy sarcasm. "Maybe we could." He turned his back on Serge, said to his companions, "Pull out the lists. Let's get going."

The beep of his computer brought Jack Lenoir out of a shallow sleep. They'd brought in a cot for him, and now a series of sympathetic nurses ran errands for him down to the cafeteria. The pain in his lower back was something awful. Detective (not for long if he didn't go back to work) Lenoir spent his days doing every stretch he knew just to be able to walk around his little hospital room without looking like a crab. His eyes were bleary and red. He hadn't trimmed his nose or ear hairs in days. His body couldn't take it much longer, though he knew this was a function of age, and he was ashamed.

Lenoir didn't know how long he could keep up his vigil. He needed fresh air worse than a drowning man, and he felt like an idiot going to the toilet with the door open all the time. But the e-mails had been coming in consistently, and he was playing middleman between the fugitives and Aubin. It occurred to him that Malcolm Macpherson, Claire Davidowicz, and their friends were on the wildest of goose chases and would soon lose the race, possibly in the most serious terms.

Their last communiqué had informed him that a cop in Montreal was in the game too. Maybe two reasonably senior police officers putting their cases together across the border could force the authorities to take notice and some sort of action. He'd spent a lot of time thinking about who in the press he could take the story to in case it came to that – maybe someone at Pacifica Radio. But then he'd look at ghostly, beautiful Gemma in her tomb-like bed. He had heard her stir several times, and was hoping against hope that she would wake up.

He struggled out of the cot, nearly upending the flimsy contraption in the process, cursed, and checked his e-mail. Kuala Lumpur again. DOUBLE URGENT: "Ask Brussels: what do they have on Sociedad JGG, calle de la Revolución, Mexico City? Our information: a company partly owned by Petroco (Wilbur Hayes). Initials may – stress *may* – be same as those of the owner of the bankrupt company that owned the *Flying Esmeralda*: Jaime Gonsalvez, middle name unspecified, of Panama City owned Panamanian Company 3472-93-36. Different address, but could it be same guy?" Lenoir forwarded the message, and prayed Aubin would be back in his office in Brussels, reading *The Economist* and drinking his coffee.

38

SERGE Lalonde heard himself being called from a far, far distance, fell back into the oblivion of sleep. "Wake up, for God's sake!" He didn't recognize the voice, wondered where Nicole was, and suddenly he was painfully, acutely awake, and looking into the eyes of Malcolm Macpherson. He was half strangled by the sheet, his nostrils itching from the dust on the carpet underneath the foam mattress. He sat up, pushed his dark hair back off his forehead. "Yes." His mouth felt like dirty cotton. "I am awake. What time is it?"

"Seven twenty. We need your team. Can you take us to them?"

"Ah," Serge managed. He was finding it hard to be alive. But the possibility of inflicting pain on the very people who had ruined his peace of mind forever animated him. "What is it?" he asked, standing and straightening his clothes.

"We may have something. But we need help. Do any of them speak Spanish?"

"*Si*," Serge said. "I do."

"We tried to link the information Serge here brought us to the holdings of every company and individual in the consortium," Claire explained in Jean-Luc Perrinault's apartment. "It's a spaghetti bowl of Möbius strips. The two most likely connections would be Wilbur Hayes and William Greele. Petroco owns a company called Yellow Rose Shipping, which owns a lot of tankers. We also tried to find some connections between Greele and the Uttar Pradesh chemical company and the numbered company that was going to take delivery in Norfolk. So far, we haven't gotten anywhere. We don't have the capacity."

She put the grimy pages they had printed a couple of days ago for Wilbur Hayes's holdings on the coffee table, and everyone bent to look at them. "According to you guys, a Jaime Gonsalvez was the owner of the company that owned the *Flying Esmeralda*, now defunct and bankrupt. According to the Panama Telephone Company, there are five people, all with a different middle name, named Jaime Gonsalvez listed in Panama City. The company Gonsalvez owned bore the Panamanian registration number of 3472-93-36. We need to look into the corporate registration records in Panama and see what other information we can get, if any, on this defunct company. We need some Spanish for this.

"Petroco also has significant interests in a number of other companies, a couple registered in the US, and several in other countries. They own part of a Mexican company called Sociedad JGG, head office in Mexico City. As it turns out, one of the five Jaime Gonsalvezes listed in Panama is a Jaime Geraldo Gonsalvez – JGG. We didn't know what to do with this, even if it meant anything, so we asked our guy in Brussels what he could find."

"And?" asked Perrinault, who continued to reassure himself that he was but one of a team of police officials working on the project.

Claire produced a newer sheet of printout. "JGG Enterprises owns several ships which ply the Latin American sea lanes with a variety of cargo, three oil tankers, some container vessels. None of them is the *Flying Esmeralda.*"

"*Tabernac,*" Victor Paquette said.

"But they also own shares in several other companies that also own ships. They have part ownership of a Paraguayan company, they have part ownership of a Guyanese company – regulation is not at its highest in these places – and, yes, Virginia – they had part ownership of a bankrupt Panamanian company which they list in their records as 000/34-72/3600. Now, being swifter of perception than we were at five o'clock in the morning, you will recognize among all those extra zeroes, slashes and dashes, the key numbers of Jaime Gonsalvez' company – 3472-93-36 – the proprietary company of the *Flying Esmeralda.*" She spoke the last sentence with the flourish of a magician producing doves from a top hat.

"So," Perrinault asked, hardly missing a beat. "What will we do with this?"

"First, we need to see if there are records – in Panama, in Mexico, in Texas, among any and all of the companies – that show us more about the links between these companies and individuals."

"No problem," Jean-Luc said, rubbing his hands. Victor had begun twirling in his chair.

Malcolm said, "While you guys are looking, Claire and I are going to stretch our legs."

"You want to leave *now?*" Jean-Luc asked.

"Desperate for some fresh air, yes," Claire said.

Doug Boyle paced his office like a caged panther. Every time he checked in with Echevarria, his fear of the whistle-blowers still on the loose got ramped up another notch. None of the four Americans had left any trail. None had called any of the friends, colleagues, and relatives whose phones and homes Boyle had paid security firms a small fortune to monitor.

He put in a call to Chicoutimi, where Marco Mostyn was still with Gabor Mezulis.

Mezulis's voice was muffled by the coffee and muffin he was wolfing down. "Hey, Doug. I was just about to call your boss. I've got some information."

"Good timing, then. Anything important I should know?"

"Yeah. Coupla things. The environmentalists and ecotourism entrepreneurs have organized opposition all over the region since the Morin concert," Mezulis answered, sounding remarkably cavalier. "They were getting some real momentum going. Looked like it was going to be a problem. Lots of stuff on the radio stations."

"That's just great," Boyle said tightly.

"Relax. Friday night, the construction unions finally had their big rally at the hockey arena. Banners, speakers, a band, free beer. The beer is incredible up here." As if I care, thought Boyle. "Anyway, my advisor, guy by the name of Gilles Dion, working very closely with all Vezina's people, attended as the special guest of the president of the construction workers' local. He's told them there's huge stuff coming. The union president and his guys were sending a very explicit message: they were welcoming big projects to the region with open arms. But also an implicit message: 'We're gonna break the knees of anyone who stands in our way.' Their prez said, and I quote, 'We're capable of direct action too.'"

"*Nice*," Boyle said appreciatively.

"The subsidies for ecotourism were severely cut this summer, and the word on the street this last week is they're not gonna be renewed. Corbeil and Lalonde have made sure the environmentalists have no carrots to offer here. As long as the Montreal Committee doesn't come in and raise hell, we're golden. One strange thing, though. Reason I was going to call Nick. A contact in the Sûreté de Quebec told Dion that the only identifiable body in the car that went over the mountainside was actually Serge Lalonde's wife." Mezulis dropped this piece of news matter-of-factly. "You still there?"

"I'm here," Boyle said, pulse racing. Carefully he weighed the possible significance of this information. Was this somehow connected to the bizarre behavior of Lalonde and his flunky? To the disappearance of the tapes?

Jesus. Corbeil hadn't said a thing yesterday. If it was true, surely he must have known. "That's very bad," he pronounced grimly.

"I'm not saying it's the gospel truth, Doug. I'm in no position to call up the local branch of the provincial police and start making inquiries. There's nothing in the news this morning, and I'd expect that to be headline material. Still, even if it is true, I wouldn't be too concerned. Crazy things *always* happen on projects like this. Bottom line, if there are no big waves of opposition rolling in from Montreal to galvanize dissent, and the local opposition has no economic incentives to offer, the people fighting the project here are gonna fizzle and die. End of story. And Bill tells me there's gonna be a binding letter of agreement this week. So whatever hanky-panky is going on, I'd say we're in pretty good shape. We're putting the roads in fast. Soon it'll all be academic."

Boyle wanted to take comfort from Mezulis's sanguine interpretation of events. But there were some scary little live wires dangling around. He thanked Mezulis for his information and asked him to put Mostyn on the line. "Okay, Marco," he said. "All rested up? Get your ass back here and we'll figure out how to finish up what you and Tiffany buggered up. But I'm telling you now. You screw the pooch one more time and you're both completely finished."

Boyle hung up, then punched in the number for the Quebeckers' traitorous little telephone tapper.

"*Ouais*," a heavy voice like a throttled duck responded.

"Hello?" Boyle barked. "Who's that?"

"Dis is Sergeant Godbout, Sûreté de Québec." The man Corbeil had chosen to replace Victor Paquette spoke English slowly and painfully, as though someone had made him eat something repulsive. "My call display unit tell me you are calling from Seattle. Please to give me your name."

"Where's Paquette?" Boyle demanded.

"Nut 'ere. 'Oo is dis?" Godbout was beginning to sound belligerent.

"I need to speak to Paquette immediately," Boyle said.

"Too bad. 'E is not 'ere. I say *nutting* until you tell me 'oo are you."

"This is Doug Boyle, for Christ's sake. I'm –"

"Ah. I know 'oo are you. Why you nut say –"

"When will Paquette be back?"

"I do nut know. Like I sayed."

Boyle tried to soften his tone. "Do you know how I can reach Mr Lalonde?"

"Monsieur Lalonde? *Non*."

What the fuck, over? thought Boyle. "Tell me, Sergeant Gawdboo. Have you folks identified the two other people who were in the car with that journalist, Dennis Lamontagne. The one who –"

"*Non*." The answer was so fast, so brusque. It didn't feel true.

"No leads at all?"

"Nut yet."

"*Nothing?*" Boyle put all his skepticism into the word, all the menace he intended if Godbout was holding out.

"*Rien du tout*. Nutting."

"And I don't suppose, Sergeant Gawdboo, that you've seen any trace of the four Americans we asked you – Paquette that is – to look out for?"

"Nutting."

"I want you to get a message to Paquette for me."

"*Ben*. I will try."

"Tell him I need to speak to him, and tell him I need the Lamontagne tapes today. Got that? *Today*."

"I will to pass dat on," Godbout said.

Boyle had the feeling that this was exactly what he would do – pass it on, into the nearest broom closet. In frustration he said acidly, "I'd appreciate that. And do another thing for me." Boyle just couldn't bring himself to say please. "Put immediate surveillance on all the offices and homes of eco-Justice Canada staff in Montreal and Toronto, and put live taps on all those lines. Paquette should have done that days ago."

"We 'ave de taps on all de lines," Godbout said. "Dey talk to each odder. Dat's all."

"Well, get your people off their butts and see who's going in and out of their offices and homes, for Christ's sake!" Boyle yelled.

"We do nut have peoples in *Toronto*," Godbout said, highly offended. "Dis is de Sûreté de *Québec*."

"Haven't you ever heard of liaising with other police forces?" Boyle had completely lost his cool and was fulminating into the phone. On the other end, Sergeant Godbout smiled a slow smile. "Get on it!" Boyle finished, and hung up. He picked up the phone and put in a call to the Colonel, to get permission to go straight to the Finance Minister. Fuck this shit.

THE opportunity to stretch their cramped legs was a sweet blessing. At a convenience store on the corner of Parc and Bernard Avenues, Malcolm changed a twenty-dollar bill into one and two dollar coins. They continued walking west, past fashionable furniture shops, beauty salons, food boutiques, and found a Romanian café with a couple of telephone booths tucked away at the back. The chatter of chic Montrealers drinking their morning *café au lait* and catching up on the weekend's gossip provided the perfect backdrop.

In the men's room, Malcolm sat down in the stall, took off his right shoe and, with his penknife, removed a piece of the heel that he'd cut out in another toilet stall on the flight from Seattle to Los Angeles just a few days ago. Though he'd committed it to memory, he didn't trust himself to remember the number he'd written on a scrap of paper, then glued to the piece of leather. He opened the washroom door. "You want to speak to him, or should I?"

"Maybe you should," Claire said. "If I talk to him, he's going to start lecturing me. Let's not let the personal stuff get in the way."

"Right." Malcolm punched in the number. He heard the connections being made, a telephone start to ring. It was a satellite phone, and he knew it would probably take a long time for anyone to answer. Even so, on the twentieth ring, he was getting seriously antsy. Some speaker somewhere is picking it up, he told himself. Answer, dammit.

On the thirty-first ring, a muffled voice said, "Yeah."

"I'd like to speak with Jeff. This is Malcolm." He had no idea if any of it made any difference at this point, but he thought he'd try to give as little information as he could. A long moment's silence ensued. "Hello?" Malcolm said, damping down panic. "Anybody there?"

He got a question for an answer. "Claire's friend?"

"Yes. Claire's friend. Is that you Jeff?"

"Where are you calling from? I hear a lot of noise."

"A telephone booth back of a café, no one else can hear a thing. I chose the place at random. Won't name the city for the time being."

"You think the phone's secure?" The voice was clearer now.

"Well, short of a complete Big Brother scenario – you know, a TV and a live tap on every phone in existence – it's as secure as I can make it right now. But let's be mindful of using trip words for that hard-working system-that-cannot-be-named-without-alerting-it."

"Right."

"Jeff," Malcolm took a deep breath. "We need your help."

"What's happening?"

With Brannigan there was no "that can't be true", "you're out of your mind", and "I don't believe it". He took it all in without a word. He didn't even say "I told you so" when Malcolm said he feared for their lives. Malcolm concluded with a description of their desperate attempts to find some way to blackmail the consortium into pulling back. Brannigan asked for some more information about the potential connections between Wilbur Hayes and the *Flying Esmeralda*.

"I've given you all we have," Malcolm said. "They're working on it as we speak."

Brannigan said dourly, "Hayes owns more dirty ships than anyone can count. In the eighties he had more tanker accidents than any other ship own-er in the world, and he got *real* tired of paying the fines. As pathetic as they were. So in the nineties he 'divested' and 'diversified' – meaning, in fact, that he hid his liability – through buying up controlling interest in a bunch of offshore companies, setting them up as fronts. I don't keep records for him, but you keep looking, buddy. If anyone besides that Gonsalvez guy is behind the Lisbon ship, there is no reason to think it couldn't be Hayes."

"Well, that's encouraging." Malcolm said though he didn't need a cheerleader. He needed some facts.

"Don't stop looking for the connection. It may very well be there."

"I hear you, Jeff. Thanks. Now I've got another –"

"You want me to take your Uttar Pradesh info, and the registration number of the company that was going to take delivery in Norfolk and see if I can find anything that links them to Greele. Do I have that right?"

"Yeah. Exactly. If anyone is likely to be connected to those companies, Greele is the obvious one – he's the agricultural chemicals guy."

There was a thoughtful silence for a moment. Then Jeff said, "Greele has big interests in Hyderabad – in Uttar Pradesh. Agrichem owns a chemical plant there, yes. But he's been contracting out more and more of his business. My information is he's looking to decommission his own plant soon, do all the manufacturing through independent contractors. Doesn't want a Bhopal on his hands, doesn't want to pay for decent safeguards. I've been keeping tabs."

Malcolm felt like someone had just given him a shot of amphetamines. "Do you really think —"

"Don't know for sure, and for God's sake don't assume anything," Jeff cautioned him. "I can tell you're gonna crash harder than a falling boulder if this doesn't pan out. But it's not as long a shot as you might think."

"I'm an atheist, Jeff, but I'll pray. Fervently."

Jeff gave a dry laugh. "It'll take me a little time. I've got to get to my computer, do some cross-checking, get back here. 'Bout an hour and a half, round trip, I'd say. Can you call me back?"

"You bet."

"And do me a favor. Call me from a different phone. Someplace far away from where you are now."

"No problem." He was conscious of how sore and tired his eyes were and how profoundly he wanted to sleep. Claire, watching his every expression, looked as tired as he felt.

Jeff could hear Malcolm's flagging spirit. He put a lot of energy into his voice, as though urging on a dying man. "Just call me back in ninety minutes, okay? We'll see. And Mal." Malcolm thought he heard Jeff's voice thicken a little. "Give my regards to Claire." The phone went dead.

The minute they opened the door to Perrinault's apartment, Malcolm felt the electricity in the air. "What?" Claire demanded. "What have you found?"

Russ led them into the living room where everyone was talking and drinking coffee and eating donuts. "Wilbur Hayes," Russ said triumphantly, "via Yellow Rose, owns Jaime Geraldo Gonsalvez and, by connection and extension, Sociedad JGG and the *Flying Esmeralda*!"

With Serge Lalonde's Spanish, they had visited — well, broken into — several informative sites, beginning again with the Mexican government, proceeding to the Panamanian Business Registry and Finance Ministry, moving from there to the financial database at Yellow Rose Shipping — by far the biggest challenge — and returning to the Panamanian Business Registry. Now they had a big, big stick to hold over Hayes. "The threat of announcing that an entrepreneur responsible for the worst fungicide spill in history — *and* for covering it up — is in charge of building a water pipeline should be sufficiently threatening to wrest some demands from this devil's spawn," Russ said. "Maybe it'll even stop the project."

But Serge wasn't celebrating yet. "The government is fundamentally committed," he said pessimistically. "I wouldn't put it past Corbeil to declare that Hayes was one member of an otherwise impeccable group. Ask the consortium to drop Hayes and proceed with the project." Everyone came to a standstill. "In fact," Serge concluded, "with only the Hayes connection we might simply blow your cover without stopping the project."

The elation that had refreshed the apartment like a sea spray evaporated. Soon, it was time for Claire and Malcolm to step out again.

"What's with the all the walks?" Perrinault demanded querulously.

"Don't ask," Malcolm said, grabbing the handle of the door.

As they looked for another telephone, both of them tasted the coppery flavor of adrenaline. At a little store in the easternmost reaches of the plateau, they bought some chocolate they didn't want, got a big handful of coins, then they stepped into several ethnic eateries and cafés but couldn't find a telephone. It was ninety-five degrees, and the sweat poured off their faces and down their backs. Finally, on St Hubert, they found a pizza place with a sheltered telephone in the rear. They ordered a slice of whatever was up on the platter, a bottle of San Pellegrino. There were people eating and the sound of their conversations was loud enough to cover any exchange.

"Want me to call again?" Malcolm said. Claire nodded. With his heart hammering, Malcolm punched in the number.

Jeff picked up on the first ring. "Yeah," he said.

"Jeff?"

"Hey Mal. What did you find out about Hayes?"

"*Stee-rike*. Through a number of different interlocks, Yellow Rose owns Sociedad JGG. If our information is correct, Hayes has legal liability for the Lisbon spill."

"Great balls of fire!" Jeff was gleeful. "Oh, to nail those bastards! Amazing how fast you guys put it together."

"Yeah. It only took five hackers and police moles on two continents, speaking three languages, working night and day and breaking every law of confidentiality on the planet. No sweat."

"*Great* work." Jeff was thrilled and sincerely admiring.

"And we've got a lot of information on money laundering *and* unsavory toxic dumping by United Construction's haulage divisions, incidentally."

"Excellent."

"But it's still not enough to stop them. That's the opinion of our senior politico."

"He's probably right."

"You got anything?" Malcolm had an ache in his throat and chest. Claire's jaw had been clenched since they'd left the apartment. Now tension was visible in every tendon in her neck. They were all teetering on the edge of a precipice, and if Jeff came up empty-handed, the fall would break their collective necks.

"Sit down, buddy." Jeff sounded suitably grave.

"I can't. No seat."

"Hold on to your hat then."

"I'm holding."

"Get *this*. My information shows that our boy Greele as good as owns that plant where the stuff originated. I thought that might be the case — there's a guy in eco-Justice India who has been sending me information. Warangal sounded very familiar when you mentioned it. But I didn't want to get your hopes up too high, because I wasn't sure. Anyway, Anil Bandiopadi — the major stockholder of the company that made the stuff sitting in Lisbon harbor, according to the info you got from the Portuguese government — Bandiopadi is *entirely* financed by a combination of William Greele, personally, and AgrichemCorp. And the information from my informant at Greele Life corroborates this. His record for accuracy is flawless. I can't fucking believe it! I mean, I *can* fucking believe it, but holy shit, no wonder they kept the ownership of that company locked up tighter than a virgin's tw ... well, tight. You still there?"

"Yeah." Malcolm felt light-headed. "Having trouble breathing, is all."

"Okay. Part two. The numbered company that was supposed to take delivery in Norfolk, that's Greele too. It's very well hidden. But it's his."

"You're kidding." Had Malcolm been sitting on a chair, he would have fallen off it.

"Not kidding. I thought it might be his, because, well, of this recent windfall of information on Greele holdings I've gotten from high up. But again, didn't want to get your hopes going, in case I was wrong."

"But why hide ownership?" Malcolm asked. "I mean he's in the chemicals business, for Chrissake, what's wrong with taking delivery of an essential ingredient?"

"Liability, buddy, *li-a-bil-ity*. Transport has become a *huge* headache. Your carrier springs a leak on the high seas or in port or your tanker trucks crash near Hometown USA or your train derails in a pristine state park or some godforsaken suburb, you are looking at astronomical fiscal liability. Plus you get a huge corporate black eye, the loss of confidence of the

American people, hence loss of future market share. You're a big company transporting a gargantuan load of poison, every podunk town along your route gets alerted by the POPs network, you can't even get permission to bypass on the interstates. So you develop a bunch of numbered companies, just like Hayes did for his ships. If there's an accident the companies aren't capitalized to be able to cover the costs of remediation even if some government has the temerity to slap them on. They go bankrupt and you're home free. Let the public purse take the hit."

"Is that really legal?"

"Not really, *if* you have an enforcement apparatus capable of tracking down the false fronts and enforcing liability laws. But we don't, here or internationally. As long as the ownership stays private, and the companies are broken up enough, and hidden in twenty other ways, well, they don't have to worry. It's one of the most important reasons I started keeping my database ten years ago. Be aware. Globalization and corporate downloading have gone hand-in-hand. Monopolization has never been so high, liability has never been so low."

"Some irony."

"Business as usual. Anyway, buddy. Listen carefully. Very carefully. *You've got Greele.* No one has ever gotten him before. You've pulled it all together. You can threaten to blow him and a couple of his buddies to kingdom come."

"You think this'll do it then?"

"If you made this information public he'd have to assume liability. More – he and his good buddy Hayes would be seen as the darkest forces since Darth Vader. With Vittorio Massaro as their evil minion. Which would lose Greele the power he has spent his life amassing. I do believe Greele will do anything to avoid that. Right now you've got Greele by the balls. When you deliver the message, he's going to howl. It will be the greatest pleasure to Fed-Ex, fax and/or e-mail my information to you. The results should be atomic. But watch out for that lethal fallout."

Malcolm's hands were shaking. At last, he thought. The tables turn.

"Listen, Mal," Jeff said. "Let me give you some advice. *Don't* deliver this information yourself. Do *not* show yourself physically, do not let Greele know where you are. You are in tremendous danger. If you possibly can, send the message through someone he can't just kill. You got someone like that?"

"Maybe," Malcolm said. "Maybe Governor John Putnam of Vermont.

Greele had one of his land use planning officers killed. The guy I told you about."

"Putnam's an excellent choice."

"He's not ours yet."

40

"I THINK I'm going to lose my breakfast, Ramona." Paula McIntyre was sitting in her blue and white kitchen. From her window she could see the Vermont state trooper's car parked at the bottom of their drive. "This article on water," she waved her copy of *This Country Today*, "I don't know what makes me more angry. What they say or what they leave out."

"Hey, *carita*, take a deep breath." Ramona put a sympathetic hand on Paula's shoulder.

"Check out the presentation." She held up the paper. "FUTURE WATER NEEDS DEMAND ACTION TODAY," said the main headline, below which was a handsome color photograph of Energy Secretary Jason Stamper. "A sorrier piece of speculation, manipulation, obfuscation and —"

"Paula, can you drop the editorializing and tell me what it says!"

"Yeah, okay. Listen." She read. "*Politicians and businessmen need to jump in and get their hands dirty, grappling with the crucial question of water for the United States in the coming years.*' Can you believe that, 'get their hands dirty'? Anyway, here's all the stuff about growing needs, the Ogallala aquifer, blah, blah, blah. Now get this: '*Canada is the natural place for us to turn, as that country has two-thirds of this continent's fresh water. The North American Free Trade agreement provides the perfect framework for America to work out ways to bring Canadian water to where it's needed most. Now that a Free Trade agreement with Latin America is in the works, this vision is even more important.*'"

She looked up at Ramona. "I mean, not a word about polluted rivers, not a word about conservation, desalination, changes in water usage - nothing! Just, Canada's got water, let's get it! Then they do a whole bunch of stuff on that snake, Jason Stamper, like he walks on water, sorry no pun intended, oh, and on how important it is to secure strategic resources. Listen: '*With the Secretary's great vision and initiative, a group of good old-fashioned American entrepreneurs are already on the job and bravely going where none has gone before, exploring the possibilities in sharing Canada's fresh water….*' Hello?" Paula said. "Which 'good old-fashioned entrepreneurs' would those be? And *sharing* Canadian water? That's just —" Her eyes caught familiar words toward the end of the article and she groaned.

"What?" Ramona said.

"'*Canada has squandered its vast water resources, and treated its rivers and lakes with reckless abandon,*'" Paula read. "I said something like that to Claire just a couple of weeks ago. And listen, Ramona. '*We are persuaded that the positive pressures of trade will force a more prudent water policy.*'" Ramona made sympathetic noises. In mincing tones, Paula read, "'*This is the first of several background pieces in an occasional series on America's water needs. Several state governors are in discussions with Secretary Stamper, working hand in hand with him and American business to address US water needs in the very near future. Our series will cover their progress.*' Ramona, sometimes I'm ashamed to be an American."

William Greele allowed himself a luxuriant extra hour in bed. When he woke up and did his usual body check, he realized that the horrible pounding sensation in his carotids, that had been with him for weeks, had finally disappeared. He was returning to normal. He yawned, padded over to the mirror in his striped pajamas, saw that those telltale red spots on his cheeks had receded to little more than an attractive blush. The voice inside his head that had belittled him for more than two weeks remained blissfully silent. He called Greta, back from vacation, on the intercom, ordered her to prepare him a lavish breakfast of waffles, pork sausage, and Vermont maple syrup. Then he went for a long, slow swim in the pool.

As he read his copy of *This Country Today* over breakfast, Greele's contentment expanded into a sense of supreme delight. Franklin had hit just the right tone with the story on water. Before the sun made a walk unbearable, he headed out to the parkland of exotic grasses and walked through the long, waving swathes. The tips were beginning to turn color, and he looked forward with enthusiasm to his annual fall hunting trip. He was going to bag himself one big buck.

Settled down for a good day's work, he read Gabe Mezulis's positive assessment of the quality of the pipeline Wilbur Hayes had ordered, and of the progress on the roads being laid in Quebec. He put in a call to Bernie Vogel and brought him up to date on the good news. Vogel was ecstatic. Life was good.

"No point getting your shorts in a knot, Doug." Colonel Kamenev, crisply turned out and sitting ramrod straight in his chair, said to Boyle across his enormous desk. Boyle looked angry. "Corbeil claims Lalonde is out of town on government business. Why would he say so if it's not true?"

Boyle could think of one or two reasons, but clearly Kamenev was far from finished.

"We can force the issue of Lalonde if we want," Kamenev rolled on. "Insist on speaking to him, flush him out. But why push it now? Gabe is right. If the local opposition splutters down to nothing, and the Montreal opposition is too scared to go any further, and Corbeil signs this letter tomorrow and pushes the thing through the legislature – why upset the apple cart?" Kamenev paused. "And Bill won't like it," he added as though it were an afterthought.

That's the real reason, Boyle thought with disgust. He opened his mouth to protest. The Colonel overrode him. "Yeah, yeah. We have to make sure that the Richardson woman doesn't do any damage, make sure those fuckers Macpherson, and whatsisname, Stiller's guy, and the eco-Justice woman stay down. But it doesn't sound like Richardson's ever going to have much to say. And even if she wakes up with all her faculties intact, what's she gonna do? Say 'some guy followed me from Vermont and tried to kill me and trashed all my files'? Big deal. What guy? Where is he? The LAPD won't touch it. The press won't touch it. The NSA, the Trade Representative, the White House – they're all committed to the hilt. Richardson can scream that the guy she met in Vermont was killed around the same time she was shot. But that immediately lets her so-called assassin off the hook. Can't be in two places at once, can he? And you told me yourself Massaro's guy swears he left nothing behind to show it was arson. Take a Valium, relax."

You stupid, complacent fuckhead, Boyle thought. Forgotten everything you ever learned in combat. He'd noticed that being very rich didn't make people less aggressive or less mean or less greedy if they were already inclined that way. It just made them feel omnipotent. Thought they could buy their way out of anything. Made really dumb mistakes.

"Look," Kamenev said. "I know I pay you to be vigilant. I appreciate your tenacity here. We *will* take care of business. No way Macpherson is going to live a long happy life after fucking us over the way he did. But we're gonna have a letter of agreement in a matter of days. Legislation in a month. Let the Quebeckers take care of their own. If Lalonde is AWOL, you can bet your bazooka Corbeil's got his people out looking for him."

Boyle said nothing as his mind turned over. The Colonel is pissed, he'll shaft me if I push him any harder. But the pride he took in his job and the feeling in his gut just wouldn't let him quit. "Colonel, please. Promise me one thing. Call Mr Greele and tell him the rumor about Lalonde's wife. Rumors like that don't drop out of the sky. And if it's true, we may have big trouble on our hands. If Lalonde goes to the press, or, I don't know, talks to some oppositional politician, it could —"

"I'll *speak* to him, Doug. We have a conversation scheduled for this evening. You do understand that if the rumor isn't true, we risk getting him all crazy again, and that may be as big a risk to the project as anything we could possibly face from Quebec?"

"I understand, sir, but I still think you should do it. Now."

"I'll do it *tonight*," Kamenev said angrily, eyes flashing dangerously. "We just finished bringing Bill down off the ceiling. I'm not going to launch him up there again this afternoon. Dismissed!"

Around six o'clock in the evening, Greele poured himself a scotch, and sat back. His mind ran to water, trillions of gallons, pouring in a great man-made river from the Quebec north to the American Mid- and Southwest. The water swelled the dried fields, the water swelled his bank accounts, it made him kingmaker and king in Washington. He looked forward to spending a great deal more time at his Georgetown residence, considered ordering Sarah to have it redecorated. Or perhaps it was time to buy a larger estate? He had another scotch and congratulated himself on having had the intestinal fortitude to achieve his vision. Left to some of his faint-hearted associates, the project would have died. He was delighted with Nick and Vittorio, with their determination and resources. Some opportunities had been missed, yes. Some hideous, dangerous moments had transpired. But it had come out excellently in the end because he had had the nerve to stay the course, never blink. At six fifty-five the telephone rang. Must be Nick, Greele thought. But it was Neville Poindexter, his COO in Minneapolis.

"Governor Putnam's on the other line, Mr Greele," he said deferentially. "Insists on speaking with you immediately."

"Well, I suppose you can give him the number. What's the rush?"

"He wouldn't say, sir."

"Well ... tell him I'll be here waiting." He hung up, sat back. His telephone rang again. "William Greele here," he said assertively.

"Good evening, Mr Greele. It's Governor John Putnam calling from Montpelier."

"Yes, Governor," Greele responded with muted affability. Just get it over with. "What can I do for you today?"

"Well, Mr Greele, I suppose you could call off your goons, and withdraw from the water export project."

Silence.

"Mr Greele? Are you there?"

Greele shook himself. He was puzzled. "Excuse me, Governor. Could you repeat what you just said? I don't believe I heard you right."

"You heard me right, Mr Greele." The edge to the Governor's voice could have cut glass. "You heard me just right."

The request was so bizarre, so ... weird and inappropriate, that Greele was still astonished. "I know you weren't a big fan of the project, Governor. You made that clear when we had our talk earlier this sum —"

"I wasn't a big fan of all the secrecy," Putnam rudely interrupted. "That's what I told you then. What I know now —"

"And I told *you*," Greele interrupted in return, his voice like an unsheathed sword, "that *you* had no choice in the matter. I told *you* that the project carried the approval of the White House and the Secretary of Energy. I told you Jason Stamper would slap a federal override on you if you stood in the way. I told you the project had the active support of five governors, as many senior senators, and the Trade Representative. I told you any citizen opposition to it would be classified an issue of national security and taken up by the NSA. I told you it was a done deal. Is that not correct?" Greele had gone from zero to a hundred in ten seconds. His cheeks were on fire.

"Yes, Mr Greele. All correct. And completely odious to my mind."

Greele couldn't have cared less what was odious or not to Putnam's mind. "So what's all this nonsense you're handing me now, Governor?"

"Well, Mr Greele. I have some people sitting in my office with me now." Putnam let that sink in for a moment. "I don't know just how good your intelligence in Quebec is, notwithstanding the support of the Trade

Representative and his spies. But in an incident on the road from Quebec City to Chicoutimi that took the life of a Montreal journalist Saturday morning, two other people died." Putnam paused for the pro forma denial. None came. Greele was too stunned. "Now we believe that one of those other people happened to be an advisor to Mr Serge Lalonde. Name of Helder Pereira."

"Never heard of him," Greele said.

"And the other person, Mr Greele, we know was Mr Lalonde's wife."

Everything went black for a moment. All Greele could feel was a rushing sensation.

"Mr Greele? Mr Greele? Are you there, Mr Greele?" Governor Putnam's voice came from far away, and gradually grew louder.

Control yourself! His father's voice barked inside his head. Assert yourself! "Of course I'm here. I don't know what you're talking about."

"A bit late for that, Mr Greele."

"My good man," Greele said in as withering a tone as he could muster. "You're speaking in riddles. I'm sorry for Mr Lalonde's loss, of course. I had no idea —"

"That's what my visitors figure, Mr Greele." Now Putnam interrupted. "They say you were out to kill the journalist before he blew the whole story on the pipeline. They doubt you had any idea who the other people in the car were."

"But that's preposterous!" Greele responded, regaining strength with rage. "I never authorized any such —"

"Apparently you told the Quebec Finance Minister himself you authorized that killing. That it was your little message to the Quebec opposition."

"Who's there?" Greele shouted. "You be careful what kind of slanderous —"

"Upon hearing the news of his wife's death, Mr Lalonde drove to Montreal and met with the — what's it called? - the Eau NO Committee." Now the rushing sensation and the breathlessness returned with a vengeance. Greele had to grip the side of his desk. "Furthermore, Mr Greele," and this part Governor Putnam delivered very slowly, "my visitors say that you also authorized an attempt to kill an American journalist, one Gemma Richardson; she's just been moved from intensive care at Century City Hospital in Los Angeles, and there is a detective there who has some interesting knowledge of the case. And they tell me that your security people actually executed one of my very own land-use planning officers, a very valuable fellow by the name of Charles Emerson."

Greele was fighting a deadly interior battle as well as an exterior one. He began to feel increasing vertigo. "Governor Putnam," he croaked, "all these are baseless accusations for which there is not a shred of proof."

"Not baseless, I'm persuaded," the Governor rejoined. "Though you may be right about difficult to prove. I had the Vermont homicide squad pore over Emerson's incinerated property over the weekend, and whoever did the job did it well."

Greele found his breath again, though it was ragged and labored.

"But the matter hardly ends there, Mr Greele. It seems my visitors have remarkable talent with computers. And what I'm calling about, Mr Greele, in addition to informing you that you have gained Mr Lalonde's undying enmity, and my personal refusal to collaborate another instant with this project, are three things unearthed by my visitors. One – they have been able to download a good deal of your e-mail correspondence –"

"That's a criminal offense," said Greele belligerently, thinking, could Stiller's and Kamenev's guys be in that office? "It's private and privileged communication, and whatever they found is inadmissible in court."

"Not in the court of public opinion, Mr Greele. An important court, I'm sure you would agree. Two – it seems there's a good deal of information that shows your associate Vittorio Massaro to be implicated in serious infractions of toxics disposal laws in a number of Northeastern states –"

"What's your point?" For the moment he was holding on to his father's philosophy in life – never give an inch – like a drowning man to a raft.

"Lots of people would think that's outrageous, Mr Greele. They don't want someone with that kind of record involved in the future of water on this continent. You can drop him from your consortium if you like. But it won't address the third matter. And that is the liability for a very big, *very* toxic spill of the chemical zinclolinium, a powerful endocrine disrupter and key component of your leading fungicide, in Lisbon harbor in 1996."

Governor Putnam heard a sharp intake of breath, a thundering silence on the other end. Got you, you arrogant bastard, thought Putnam. "And the information that my visitors placed on my desk but a few moments ago, well, it seems that this liability is shared more or less equally by you and your consortium associate, Mr Wilbur Hayes."

Red flooded William Greele's eyes and eyelids, blood pounded in his ears. I will not have a stroke, he commanded his body, I will not. But his heart revved like a Formula One racer with no place to go.

"Mr Greele? Are you there? Apparently files from the Portuguese government and the European Commission – I have copies of those files on my desk right now – these files estimate the costs of remediation for the damage done to the harbor at well over ten billion dollars. And the environment and health departments of the Portuguese government have studies that show that most of the aquatic life in the harbor and a whole generation of young Portuguese children living within a certain radius of the site have been grievously harmed. The costs of this damage are practically incalculable.

"I am advising you, Mr Greele, that before I made this call to you, I took the liberty of calling governors Caccia, Pulaski, MacFarland and Arlington and I gave them all this information. And, Mr Greele, I have also called your associate Mr Bunting Hurst. I filled him in on what I know and what I am prepared to do. As I think you know, Mr Greele, I'm acquainted with Mr Hurst. His bank is working with us to finance a new cheese cooperative north of Burlington. He will be calling you momentarily. But let me tell you that he is intending to drop this project faster than a burning poker, rather than face the shame an association with a criminal like you would bring him in his community. And I have asked him to call your other associates and tell them that if any more harm comes to the people who have opposed you, I will personally go to the media with the material they are holding. He agreed and told me he would do the –"

Dreadful sounds from the other end of the telephone greeted Governor Putnam, then what sounded like a clattering of a telephone receiver on the surface of a desk. "Mr Greele," Putnam said, then louder, "Mr Greele? Are you still with me?"

Sarah Huntington Greele was watching the seven o'clock news. She was a prisoner in her bedroom suite and she held on tightly to her fourth gin and tonic. A heavily made-up anchorwoman was reading stiffly from the teleprompter, enumerating various fires, droughts, hurricanes and floods.

"The UN is warning that the number of environmental refugees this will create will put an enormous stress on national and international systems. Our UN reporter, Barry Fitzgerald, has the story in New York."

"Oh God," Sarah groaned. Matty had opened her eyes to a lot, including the catastrophic state of the environment, and now it seemed that every time she turned on the TV or the radio, some new horror was being reported. She focused again, as best she could, on the set.

"Meanwhile, after a summer of huge international demonstrations, heavy lobbying and conflict in Congress, and a tally of forest-fire losses exceeding those of the past five years combined, the President of the United States has confirmed his earlier decision that the US will not be bound by its previous commitment to meet the standards for greenhouse gas emissions set by the Kyoto Accords, signed in 1997." The President, resplendent in a light summer suit and crisp white shirt, appeared on-screen.

"You want to know what I say to GO KYOTO?" he asked in his singsong way. "I say, go *away*, Kyoto. Go *away*. Nothin' wrong with the United States producing 25 per cent of the world's carbon dioxide. And anyone who says so, well, it's just negatism and fearmongering." The national press corps, sweating like pigs in the sweltering sun, squinted at him respectfully, and made notes. He carried on. "We're an *optimistic* administration. Nothin' wrong with burning oil and coal. Fact is, we got an energy *crisis* on our hands. California needs more of it, for one example, and there's no reason on God's green earth why we can't give it to them."

Sarah seriously questioned her sanity as she listened to the President. She thought of Matty, her inability to pay her electricity bills, Bill's enthusiastic endorsement of utility deregulation. She reached for the remote, when a frantic knocking at her door made her jump. "Mrs Greele! Mrs Greele!" It was Greta, shouting and desperate. "Something terrible has happened!"

PART FOUR

41

THE fall days were clear; under cerulean skies, light in shades from pale butter to marigold yellow flooded city streets and country fields. Sharp overnight frosts paired with warm languid days turned the leaves into shimmering jewels of canary, tangerine and scarlet. Yellow sunflowers dozed in the warmth, and like Quebeckers, soaked it all up in preparation for the long winter ahead.

Outside Montreal's downtown conference center on Rue Viger, hundreds of demonstrators waved bilingual placards with slogans in green and blue – "Water is a human right," "Clean water – public ownership," "green policies equal blue water" – at passersby and the endless stream of traffic. Inside, people spilled out of one huge meeting room. The sign outside the door announced hearings on "Quebec's geographical, political, financial, social, and environmental needs with respect to water in the continental and hemispherical context". Up on the dais, behind a long table draped in red cloth, ten solemn commissioners presided over the opening day of the public consultation on Quebec's water.

During the morning, several politicians spoke of the need for Quebec to assert sovereignty and deal independently with the United States, clearly the largest consumer-to-be of Quebec's waters. The Minister of Finance, Robert Corbeil, finished off the morning session with a passionate oration. His suit was rumpled and streaked with cigar ash, his voice blurred by phlegm. Yet his determination registered clear and strong.

"This afternoon," he said, nearing the end of his presentation, "you will hear all the details of a framework for the future use of Québec's 'blue gold', one that has been developed very carefully by an inter-Ministry team over the last six months. This will form the basis of the government's proposal. It features a partnership agreement between several ministries in the Québec government, Quebec's most powerful entrepreneurs, and several American companies, the latter to be finalized pending approval of the framework."

Commissioners Sylvie Lacroix and René Dubois, representing the Eau NO Committee up on the dais, gasped in astonishment. "Why the American component?" Corbeil asked rhetorically. "Because we must, at all costs, achieve 'buy-in' from American interests if we want cooperation for our approach."

"*Salop!*" Dubois muttered under his breath.

"*Cochon!*" Sylvie added.

Corbeil sailed on. "I hope and trust that the commissioners will see the wisdom of this framework and build their recommendations around it. I look forward to the soonest lifting of the moratorium so Québec can get back to business!"

Scattered shouts of "Sell-out!" greeted this statement. Corbeil didn't falter for a minute. "Some months ago," he said, "the Québec government pursued the possibilities of a partnership with one particular group of American companies. However, in light of investigations by my office, some members of that group turned out to be less than ideal for the envisioned collaboration. New partners will be found after a plan is approved. Québec must make its own alliances, in its own name!" The majority of people gathered on the floor of the ballroom knew nothing of the history of the issue, and cheered at Corbeil's last words. Lunch was announced.

After lunch, Deputy Minister Pierre Gosselin took the intervenor's microphone and delivered three hours of mind-numbing bureaubabble. No mention was made of a public authority for water – a central demand of the environmentalist lobby, and one that Corbeil had promised to include in the government presentation. Much rhetoric was expended on the importance of environmental standards, but none on the mechanisms of their enforcement. By the end, no one could remember what had been included or omitted, and everyone wanted a coffee break so badly they didn't care.

René and Sylvie were horrified at the promises betrayed and at the circus tent of diversionary tactics. Each demanded permission to question Gosselin. The chair, a sleek Laval University engineering professor named Gaetan Lavelin, yawned, put his reading glasses in their case, and said the proceedings were over for the day.

During September Russ and Geraldine had been painting, building shelves, ordering inventory and advertising for the computer store they were planning to open soon in New Paltz. The small town in upstate New York, nestled in the lovely Catskills and home to a small branch of the State University of New York, had welcomed Russ back as the most popular adjunct professor of computer studies they'd ever had. Russ's parents were thrilled beyond words at the return of their prodigal son. Geraldine Morrow's sunny ways won them over in no time, and they spent many happy evenings on the wide verandah of Russ and Geraldine's newly purchased wood-frame house, getting to know their son again.

On one of those evenings, when Geraldine was in the kitchen making potato salad, Russ told his parents that he had left Cyberonics because he had caught his boss and some other corporate players out in a gross breach of ethics, and had blown the whistle on them to certain authorities. He would not elaborate, saying they were better off not knowing the details. But he did say that Andrew Stiller was bound to hold a grudge, and that if anything untoward happened to him, they should contact his friend Malcolm Macpherson, who had been involved too.

He'd used up all of his savings, but he was glad to be alive, to be with Geraldine, to be out of the corporate fast lane. He could watch birds off his verandah, and be in near-wilderness in ten minutes from home. If he needed to, he'd do some freelance programming to make ends meet.

Sitting in the loveseat on the first evening of the Montreal hearings, listening to the wind in the autumn leaves, Geraldine turned to Russ. "Honey, I still wake up in the middle of the night terrified that they'll come after us."

Russ put his arms around her. "Governor Putnam told us, Gerry. Between him, Malcolm and Claire and the everlasting fury and power of that banker, Bunting Hurst, he's sure it won't happen."

She was silent for a moment. "I'm so happy here, Russ. I count my blessings every day. Hope things go well in Montreal."

"It's for you, Sylvie," Georges called down the hall to the study where Sylvie was having an emergency strategy session with René Dubois and several other committee members. She picked up the telephone.

"Sylvie, *comment vas-tu?* It's Serge."

"Serge, how are you?" It had been many weeks since she had spoken to Lalonde, and the sound of his voice evoked very complicated feelings. The committee members heard his name and pulled disapproving faces.

"I've decided I'm not coming back, Sylvie. Nothing for me in Quebec just now." His voice faltered, and she understood the freight those words carried.

"Of course, *mon ami*," she said hastily. "Have you seen Nicole's family?"

"No. I don't know what to say to them."

"I understand. Perhaps one day. What are your plans?"

"I'm going to do some consulting, I think. Economic development, cross-fertilization of enterprises. Paris is a good place to do it from, and it's amazing how good my contacts still are." Sylvie sensed a forced optimism.

"That's good, Serge," she said. "Just don't start with all that genetic engineering and toxic pesticides stuff again. Now that you're your own boss, you don't have to, you know."

"No. I won't." The voice was chastened. "How are things there?"

"Not good, as it happens. We've just finished the first day of the water commission hearings. The government went back on all its promises to us."

"What?" Serge asked.

"I was so angry at the end, I nearly resigned. It was a charade!"

"Sylvie! You should know better! *Do not resign!* That's exactly what they want you to do."

"Maybe so, Serge. But we're caught. If we stay on we'll make a bankrupt process look legitimate –"

"Yes, yes. But be careful, you could put yourself right out of the game."

"Oh shut up, Serge! I don't need your advice. We wouldn't be in this mess if you hadn't –"

"I know. Please. I'm just saying, don't let them rout you."

Sylvie calmed down. "*D'accord*. The problem is, Serge, unless you're prepared to come back and testify about what you know, we have nothing more to fight with."

The silence on the other end of the line was long and painful.

"I want to, Sylvie. But I feel that I'll go to pieces if I come back now. Even as it is, there are some days I'm not sure I can get through ..."

"Well," Sylvie said after a lengthy pause. "I have to get back to my meeting."

"Wait. I have some news you need to know, you should pass on to your committee. I was in Brussels this week, and I looked up the fellow who helped us – Jean-Marie Aubin, that Interpol officer. I was really curious to meet him, homesick in a way too, and it felt like a connection somehow. A very nice fellow, as it turns out."

"I should think so. And?" Her colleagues were getting restless.

"Well, he said that he'd kept track of how the Lisbon spill was being handled, once the eco-Justice people had leaked the information to the European anti-POPs groups. Says he wants to start an environmental crimes unit at Interpol. He's going to use this case as an illustration of the need."

"That's very good. And very much overdue."

"But he says that some strange things have been happening. You know the European POPs Monitoring Network held a big press conference in early September."

"Of course. I've been expecting to hear about an ensuing tempest."

"But you haven't, have you? According to Aubin, the American Secretary for Energy, Jason Stamper, made a visit to the Portuguese Prime Minister just two weeks ago. Offered him ten billion dollars in foreign aid, to clean up the harbor. On one condition."

"Which would be ...?"

"Silence. Total informational blackout. Make the story disappear."

"How –"

"Portugal is a poor country."

"But you can't silence a continent-wide movement!"

"Maybe not. But the Portuguese persuaded the European Commission *and* media that silence plus remediation was better than continuing toxicity and no money to clean it up."

"I see." Sylvie felt despair flooding in. "No reprisals, then?"

"No reprisals. Once again, power has all the prerogatives. Justice is a bad joke."

"A very bad joke, Serge." He could hear her suppressed anger. "It's a rotten joke. Now I have to say goodbye."

"All right, Sylvie, all right," Serge said.

"All right what?"

"Tell the Commission you'll blow the whistle, and that I'll come back and testify against Corbeil."

Tuesday was the day dedicated to the environmental groups. The mayors of Jonquière, Chicoutimi and Tadoussac led off, speaking strongly against the government's hidden agenda for pure commercial exploitation and environmental disaster, explaining how ecotourism industries had been starved and undermined to build support for jobs in water exportation.

Somehow most of the written submissions from the other environmental groups had gone astray somewhere between the Commission's offices and the conference center. The silver-haired head commissioner, impeccably tailored, peering magisterially over his reading glasses down to the floor, chided the administrative staff for this "shocking failure". His staff ran around like chickens with their heads cut off in search of the missing material, stepping in front of speakers, tripping on microphone wires, interrupting oral submissions to ask him questions. A ten-minute limit was imposed on each "special interest" group, even when the audience protested loudly. All of which made the submissions seem incoherent.

Sylvie and René stepped out at noon and conferred with the marshals supervising the demonstrators. The marshals agreed to escort a couple of hundred people into the hall if they got the signal, an act sure to cause pandemonium, even if they were arrested by the cordon of police standing at the ready. Then Sylvie went inside, sat at her place and wrote a press release describing the complicity of Finance Minister Robert Corbeil in the cover-up of the murder of Denis Lamontagne. She found Lavelin, handed it to him, and told him that if the environmentalists' documents were not "found" and if presentations were again interrupted, and if the Commission did not find that a moratorium on water exportation was the only way to go, the hall would be flooded with protestors and the press release would go to the media. She suggested he consult Robert Corbeil on the matter.

The battered Saab pulled up in front of the peeling stucco house on the beach. Jack Lenoir pulled a folding wheelchair from the trunk, picked Gemma up from the front seat and deposited her in the chair. The October wind whipped at her blonde hair, and brought the roses back to her cheeks. Lenoir's light jacket made a soft flapping sound as he pushed her up the ramp that now covered the front steps and out to the deck. For some long moments both gazed out over the sea. He looked down at her and noticed her tears. He didn't press her with questions. She looked up, caught his gaze, smiled bravely. "It's okay, darling," she said, sniffing. "I'm alive. I've got my brains —"

"Such as they are —" Jack said. He found she responded best to gentle mockery and a little distance, rather than pity and too much intimacy.

"Such as they are," Gemma agreed. "And I've got this unbelievable day. And I've got ..." she swallowed, finding the words of love immensely difficult to articulate, "well, I've got Claire and Malcolm and, well, I've got you, really, darling, haven't I?"

"You do, baby."

"And Bonafabrica's withdrawn their fucking lawsuit. Hah!" It was a triumphant laugh, reminiscent of the old Gemma, whom he'd never known, but recognized anyway. "Fucking cowards! Still, can't go tromping through the fields in chase of the mutant berry anymore, can I?"

"No. But the people who can, can come and talk to you. And you can think about new stories now."

"Right."

"Hey, baby, you're gonna do fine," he said. And was rewarded with a dazzling smile.

As the Tuesday afternoon session of the Montreal hearings was called to order, the missing documents miraculously appeared in the mezzanine, and were handed out to the members of the media. Ovide Obansawon kicked off the afternoon, explaining how the government water framework rode roughshod over the rights of Quebec First Nations, and, ultimately, represented their ruin in the affected areas. Lorraine Beckman, on behalf of a group of national and provincial public-sector unions, argued that private ownership of water would have disastrous consequences for Quebec and the continent. Michel Herriveault, well known and respected, spoke with brilliant authority about the long-term ecological consequences. Olaf Gunderson finished off the powerful sequence with an alternative framework, based on public ownership and management, on conservation and renewal.

By five o'clock, when all the reporters had left to file their stories, the government framework was in tatters. It was clear that the demand for a moratorium would be recognized as the first recommendation of the Commission.

"Not," as Sylvie caustically observed to René as they left the hall, "that this will mean anything in the long run. Watch Corbeil wait a year, then try it all over again."

42

A WEEK after the Montreal hearings, while dew still sparkled in the meadows and a hawk hunted for field mice, Claire and Malcolm sipped their morning coffee at the picnic table outside Claire's little house. They still had moments when they felt dazed and shaken, full of fear or rage. But Claire had taken a three-month leave of absence for some badly needed holiday time, and to work as a consultant to a commission of inquiry in Vermont, beginning its public hearings this week. Malcolm had never returned to Skypoint. His vet had put Bonnie and Clyde on a flight to Montreal and they'd taken to the farmhouse with animal joy. This morning, as usual, Malcolm sent up a prayer of thanks to a god he didn't believe in that he, Claire, Russ and Geraldine had been delivered from certain death or the need to flee to some obscure corner of the earth. He looked at Claire, dressed up and ready to go, and found her intelligent, beautiful face and warm, bountiful body so exquisite it brought tears to his eyes. As she regarded him, similar thoughts ran through her mind, and her prayer was offered to a goddess she had lost but thought she might just regain.

"I bet you can hardly wait to see Ewen and Jim," she said, smiling.

She'd met the Coanda plane's eccentric inventors and liked their folksy, down-to-earth manner immensely. When they'd encountered Malcolm for the first time since things went bad at Skypoint, they'd all stood there for a moment, awkwardly shuffling their feet. Then Jim had said, "Aw, what the hell, Mal!" and put his big arms around Malcolm. They decided that Malcolm should take the plans to Bombardier in Montreal. Bombardier was not part of the military network of aeronautics producers, had proven itself creative and flexible and prescient on many occasions in the past, and needed something big and splashy to recover from the collapse of the civilian air industry. Claire wished Malcolm good luck, and he her. Then they got in their respective vehicles, he to go to the half-hour to the big country estate on the shores of Lake Brome where Bombardier's CEO had arranged the day-long meeting, she south to Montpelier.

The Vermont State Commission of Inquiry on Bilateral Water Usage began its hearings in the southern wing of the State House. The room held only half the number of people that had attended the Quebec hearings, but Governor Putnam was very glad that the person he had chosen to head and select his commission – Dr Paula McIntyre – could be counted on to listen to, and think about, the real issues. Claire was at the main microphone. He sat at the back of the room, and gave her his undivided attention.

"Dr McIntyre, Honorable commissioners, Governor Putnam, citizens of Vermont," she said in her strong, lovely voice, "let me begin by saying how thrilled I am that you have chosen to take on a national leadership role and initiate a commission of inquiry and planning into long-term water usage for this country and this continent. This is a proud and fitting role for the citizens of Vermont: strong, intelligent, freethinking and responsible citizens." She looked at Paula, who gave her a deadpan wink. She smiled at the visible straightening of backs, the nods of appreciation.

As she had two months ago at the Bear Pond bookstore, she reviewed the reasons for the crisis of water, globally, continentally, regionally. But this time she used these issues to motivate Vermonters to stand up and lead in the debate on private appropriation of water versus its public ownership.

"Some of you may find my insistence on the need for public ownership, planning and management of water difficult to reconcile with the traditions of American business," she declaimed, looking around the large room so that every person there felt addressed directly. "If so, let me remind you that Vermont has *always* understood that there is a precious *commonweal*, which, if damaged, damages the all-important individual. Vermont has always recognized that community depends on sharing, cooperation, planning to make a context for individuals.

"This approach to water is shared by North America's most thoughtful and important environmental organizations, and it's a fundamental tenet of the United Nations. In the spring of 2002, the United Nations Environment Program – or UNEP – released their third Global Environmental Outlook – or GEO-3 – report. What they said then holds even more true today.

"'The world is at an environmental crossroads'," Claire read the words from a binder on her podium, "'where the choice between greed and humanity will decide the fate of millions of people for decades to come.'" Claire looked up. "That's right, ladies and gentlemen. 'The choices made today are critical for the forests, oceans, rivers, mountains, wildlife and other life support systems upon which current and future generations depend.'

"Now, this report drew several possible future scenarios ranging from what it called the 'greed-driven, markets-first' future to the 'caring and sharing, sustainability-first approach'.

"Under the markets-first approach, the UN predicted that by 2032, more than half the population would be living with drought and serious water shortages, 70 per cent of the remaining land and animals would be under threat and sixteen billion tonnes of carbon dioxide would be belched into the air each year from fossil fuels." The people of the green state of Vermont sat silently, horrified.

"Under the 'caring and sharing' scenario, by contrast, let me quote, 'cities and highways would eat up less land, drought would be kept at bay by better water management, the pressure on land and animals would stabilize, and global carbon dioxide emissions also stabilize at just half' of what UNEP dubs the 'greed policy route'.

"Now so far, ladies and gentlemen," Claire spoke soberly to her audience, "we are well and truly launched on the 'greed policy', the 'markets-first', route. GEO-3 tells us that in the decade since the first world Earth Summit in Rio de Janeiro, fifty-eight species of fish, one mammal and one bird species have become extinct; a remaining quarter of the world's mammals and one-eighth of its birds have been put on the critical list. Life-giving forests are being ripped apart, fertile land is disappearing under concrete or into the sea, and waterways are drying up or dying of pollution. The world's seas, already under attack from litter and poisons, are being plundered to the extent that the world's great fisheries are on the verge of collapse."

Claire's eyes lifted to her audience. "Every time I read one of these reports – and I'm sad to say that I read reports like this many times every year – I feel despair overtake me. But the UNEP spokesman for the GEO-3 report, a former German environment minister, stressed that while the picture was bleak it was not beyond redemption. And it is this that must both guide and sustain us.

"'Decisive action can achieve positive results,' he said. He urged global decision makers and local citizens to face the relationship between stark economic disparities and environmental catastrophe and to 'set clear, achievable and effective targets to tackle poverty and deprivation without destroying the environment. We need a concrete action plan, concrete projects,' he said, 'and above all a clear political declaration.'" And now Claire's speech slowed and her enunciation grew even more crisp than usual. This was the point of it all. "Words we have had in nauseating abundance. What we need is political will. That means real plans, real organizations, real enforcement policies and powers, a major system of economic incentives and disincentives, subsidies, penalties – *tools* to achieve goals. Without these, it's all hot air, and we've had far, far too much of that already."

Stunning in deep amethyst silk, Sarah Huntingdon Greele headed down to what had been Bill's grand gymnasium.

"He seems low today," a nurse in a starched white uniform greeted her.

"Isn't that too bad," said Sarah without a trace of sincerity. "Not feeling well today, dear?" she inquired brightly, walking toward her husband where he sat in his wheelchair, limp, twisted and paralyzed. The only body parts he was capable of moving were his bloodshot eyes, and with these he cast a gaze full of hatred at Sarah. William Ericsson Greele did not attempt speech. His dignity prevented him from uttering sounds that made him sound like a wounded pig.

The door opened again. "Good morning, Neville," Sarah turned and extended her hand to the thin, pale, middle-aged man in a dark gray pinstripe suit. He had the look of a person who doesn't get enough sunshine or vegetables. His nervous eyes looked to Sarah with pleasure. "And good morning, Piers," she said, turning to the tall blond giant who headed the army of attorneys employed by Greele Life Industries. Piers Magnusson shook her hand. The new boss, he thought. And he didn't know if she was a saint or an idiot.

"Sit down, gentlemen," she said. "I thought we'd do the formalities here, so Bill could enjoy this as much as me." Magnusson and Poindexter took seats across from Sarah. Magnusson drew a sheaf of papers from his briefcase, and spread the pages on the table. Page upon page showed little red stickers to indicate where Sarah's signature should go. Poindexter presented her with his fountain pen. "Thank you, Neville, for this wonderful idea, as well as your exceptional support during these last two months."

"You're welcome, Mrs Greele," he said to her. You have no idea how welcome, he said to himself. And he thanked God, for easily the thousandth time, that his brown envelopes had found their place and purpose and that he had been spared, rather than discovered and beheaded. Had Mr Greele found out about Poindexter's betrayal while still healthy, Neville had little doubt that he would now be at the bottom of the Mississippi, decomposing in the run-offs of pesticides and herbicides manufactured by Greele Life Industries.

"And thank you, Piers," Sarah continued as she signed and initialed steadily, "for getting this all done in time."

Sarah affixed her final signature. "Let's go." All three rose as the nurse stood behind William Greele. "Goodbye, darling," Sarah said. "Oh," she turned to the opening door. "Matty. You look divine."

Mattina Dalgety, long of limb, broad of shoulder, with corn-silk hair and limpid blue eyes, in apricot leather slacks and a cream angora sweater, put her arm through Sarah's and said, "I'm ready." Behind the women's backs, Piers Magnusson swallowed hard and Neville Poindexter smirked.

The Bentley was waiting at the front door. They all got in and Sarah drove, down Indian Hill Road, west into town along Madison, then Martin Luther King Drive, until they reached the Faculty of Engineering on the campus of the University of Cincinnati. They made their way into the main lecture hall and Sarah climbed to the stage. She greeted a portly, balding man wearing heavy glasses and a good suit – the Chancellor of the University. Then she extended her hand to a very tall, very thin man with craggy features, dancing eyes and formidable brows. He looks like a stork, she thought. "You must be Governor Putnam," she said warmly.

"And you must be Mrs Greele," he said. "Such a pleasure to meet you in person at last."

"Please, call me Sarah." She took her seat next to his. "I feel I know you already." They'd been having daily telephone conversations for weeks now.

"Ladies and gentlemen," the Chancellor boomed from the podium. "Would you kindly take your seats. It is a great honor to preside over this occasion, made possible by the astounding generosity of Mrs Sarah Huntingdon Greele. I know you have come to hear her, so without further ado, may I present this most extraordinary benefactress."

Sarah quickly took her place at the podium. "Thank you for coming to help us celebrate this occasion, everyone. As some of you may have heard, late in August my husband had a tragic stroke. As these things do, it shocked me out of my complacency." Liberated me from a fate worse than prison, in fact, she thought with infinite relief. "It made me reexamine my priorities and think about the future. Serendipitously, our trusted COO in Minneapolis, Mr Neville Poindexter, approached me and explained to me things I had never understood about the crisis of water, in this country, on this continent. Nev, please stand up and take a bow." This Poindexter did, rather stiffly, thoroughly nonplussed by this public acknowledgment. "And Mr Poindexter put me in touch with Governor John Putnam, next to me here today, who has recently begun a crusade to raise American awareness of this issue.

"In short, ladies and gentlemen," Sarah said, wasting no time, "I have decided to assist in this process, and I am here today to announce a new foundation, with Governor Putnam as its honorary chair. The CEO of this foundation will be Mr Poindexter, and one of its first grants will be an endowment of a new chair in hydrology at the Faculty of Engineering right here at this University. The endowment for the larger foundation, which we have decided to call Water for Life – is one billion dollars ..."

Near Thompson Falls and the Lolo National Forest, at the foot of the giant Bitterroot Range northwest of Missoula, Montana, the leaves were gone from the cottonwoods, and the dark, bare branches stood out bleakly in the sere valleys. The thousands of acres of sparse pine forest that made up a good part of the Bar G Ranch revealed nothing but endless brown dirt and gray rock beneath. Though desolate and joyless, the forest made for long sightlines and easy pickings for wolves and human hunters alike. And both were out in force this season, competing for the same deer. In the melancholy gray light, the orange vests of hunters stood out like radioactive neon. As Jeff Brannigan left his house and drove down the dirt road to the highway, he caught flashes of orange through the trees. He spat out the window.

Wearing his old buckskin jacket, a faded flannel shirt and jeans, Jeff pulled up to the doors of the small building at Johnson Bell Field in his beat-up Ford Bronco. Malcolm Macpherson stepped out. He regarded Jeff's mud-covered vehicle with concern. "Jesus, Jeff, will this thing get us where we're going?"

"Just get in." Malcolm did as he was told. Brannigan turned on the ignition and produced a deep, full-throated roar. Mal raised an eyebrow. "My apologies."

"Don't sweat it."

"I'm not sweating it. It's frigging freezing in here." He rubbed his arms up and down.

"Heater's broken. Got to fix it before winter."

"I thought this was winter." They headed out to the I-90, traveling northwest.

"How'd you settle up here, anyway?" Mal asked as they rode.

"Used to be a smoke jumper, long time ago," Jeff replied. "Used to fly out of Johnson Bell Field. Missoula *International* Airport now. That's a good one. Got to know the land around here. Suits me fine."

"Greele know you?"

"You're joking, right? Man like that, I'm smaller than a bug he can squash. No. His ranch manager did though. Out of a job now. My informant at Greele Life tells me the ranch has been sold. Wonder which billionaire snapped it up. Other big changes coming too, in Minneapolis. That escapade up in Quebec apparently ate a couple of billion out of the family fortune."

"A drop in the bucket, I gather."

"You gather correctly."

They rode in silence for a long time. As they approached the dirt road that led to Jeff's house, he said, "Got two places here. One for public consumption not far from the road. Everyone knows I live there. The other one … well, it's dug deep into a hillside and no one in town's ever seen it or even heard about it. Get to keep my … well, supplies I guess. I don't have to go far if I have to lie low for a while."

When they had parked beside the log house, made a fire in the wood stove and brewed some hot coffee, Malcolm said, "Jeff, I don't know how to thank you enough for your help."

"It's nothing," the big man said, attempting a scowl, but highly pleased. "Disaster averted."

A moment of silence. "Or at least postponed," Malcolm said.

"Yeah," Jeff replied. "You may be right. Be a fucking miracle if the enviros keep all those provincial governments from selling water to the highest bidder."

"And if Kamenev and Stiller and Hayes don't come gunning for us, one of these days," Malcolm said. "Despite the promises that Putnam and Hurst extracted from the rest of the consortium. You know, Jeff, Putnam had that banker, Bunting Hurst, on speakerphone. You should have heard him blow. It was thermonuclear."

"Would have given anything to be there. You got all those printouts stashed safely?"

"Uh-huh. From the consortium, and from Portugal."

"Well, maybe that'll keep people under control."

"Maybe. Plus Putnam's and Hurst's threats to go public if anything bad ever happens to us." But Malcolm was thinking of Nick Kamenev and Doug Boyle, their egos, their machismo and their military mindsets. "Maybe not."

"Uh-huh. So let's work out those contingency plans you wanted, buddy," Jeff said. "Just in case we have to use them."

"Okay." Malcolm smiled. "That would help me sleep at night."

"Let me show you my other place, why don't you?" Jeff said. And they got their jackets and headed out to catch the final hour of daylight.

END

ACKNOWLEDGEMENTS

Louise Vandelac first drew my attention to the urgency of the crisis in water in 1996, and inspired me to take action, then to write about it. The people with whom I've worked over the years in and around Greenpeace have also inspired me – it is they and people like them that give me hope when confronting the environmental crises of the globe: Peter Blyer, Larry Brown, John Doherty, Jo Dufay, John Foster, Henri Jacob, Rebecca Moerschel, Jeanne Moffat, Steve Shallhorn, Peter Tabuns, John Willis, Karen Wristen, and many, many more – heroes all.

I was very lucky to have the following people read the manuscript at various stages and give me critical feedback: John Willis, Eric Wiener, Richard Wecshler, Ruth Shuster, Michael Kimmel, Michael Kaufman, Lin Grist, Deirdre Gallagher, Ron East, Dan Burston and Tariq Ali. I am very grateful to Stan Alluisi who so generously shared his knowledge of computers and weaponry with me. In addition, three people went far beyond the call of friendship to help me. Lynn King, dear friend and a brilliant aficionado of political and crime fiction, read the manuscript and supported me all the way along. Hugh Ballem read the manuscript and provided encouragement, but also drove me to Chicoutimi in a blizzard in the dead of winter so I could see for myself the locations I wanted to write about. Andrea Knight, a gifted editor, read and worked on the manuscript with me, and provided the encouragement without which, I do believe, I would not have had the confidence to proceed. Vern Sparks gave me feedback on the first draft, and, along with Barb Mitchell, copy-edited it.

Jennifer Barclay, editor, advisor and book doctor extraordinaire, gave me detailed feedback on the first draft and edited the second. In addition, she provided invaluable assistance on various matters literary, and I am deeply indebted to her. Emma Smith did a wonderful job of copy-editing the text. My thanks to Tim Clark and Jane Hindle at Verso for their kindness and patience, and to Mark Martin for his careful proofing of the manuscript.

I was hit with some challenging health problems during the writing of this book, and want to thank Drs Anita Shack, Sharon Mintz, Ciler Ataner and Alexander Haskell for the many ways they helped me get through. Love and gratitude go to my parents and brothers who encouraged me to take on a new way of writing. And topping the love and gratitude list is my co-conspirator in life's adventure, the ever wonderful David Fenton, who provided support of every conceivable variety, from research to encouragement to the humor – albeit black at times – I found so sustaining.

June 30, 2003
Bolton Ouest, Quebec